PRAISE FOR THE NOVELS OF WENDY WAX

"[A] sparkling, deeply satisfying tale."
—*New York Times* bestselling author Karen White

"Wax offers her trademark form of fiction, the beach read with substance." —*Booklist*

"Wax really knows how to make a cast of characters come alive. . . . [She] infuses each chapter with enough drama, laughter, family angst, and friendship to keep readers greedily turning pages until the end." —RT Book Reviews

"This season's perfect beach read!" —Single Titles

"A tribute to the transformative power of female friendship. . . . Reading Wendy Wax is like discovering a witty, wise, and wonderful new friend."
—Claire Cook, *New York Times* bestselling author of *Must Love Dogs* and *Time Flies*

"If you're a sucker for plucky women who rise to the occasion, this is for you." —*USA Today*

"Just the right amount of suspense and drama for a beach read."
—*Publishers Weekly*

"A loving tribute to friendship and the power of the female spirit."
—*Las Vegas Review-Journal*

"Beautifully written and constructed by an author who evidently knows what she is doing. . . . One fantastic read." —Book Binge

"A lovely story that recognizes the power of the female spirit, while being fun, emotional, and a little romantic."
—Fresh Fiction

"Funny, heartbreaking, romantic, and so much more. . . . Just delightful!" —The Best Reviews

"Wax's Florida titles . . . are terrific for lovers of women's fiction and family drama, especially if you enjoy a touch of suspense and romance." —*Library Journal Express*

My Ex-Best Friend's Wedding

Wendy Wax

BERKLEY
NEW YORK

BERKLEY
An imprint of Penguin Random House LLC
1745 Broadway, New York, NY 10019

Copyright © 2019 by Wendy Wax
"Readers Guide" copyright © 2019 by Penguin Random House LLC
Penguin Random House supports copyright. Copyright fuels creativity, encourages diverse
voices, promotes free speech, and creates a vibrant culture. Thank you for buying an authorized
edition of this book and for complying with copyright laws by not reproducing, scanning, or
distributing any part of it in any form without permission. You are supporting writers
and allowing Penguin Random House to continue to publish books for every reader.

BERKLEY and the BERKLEY & B colophon are registered trademarks of
Penguin Random House LLC.

Library of Congress Cataloging-in-Publication Data

Names: Wax, Wendy, author.
Title: My ex–best friend's wedding / Wendy Wax.
Description: First Edition. | New York: Berkley, 2019.
Identifiers: LCCN 2018059573 | ISBN 9780440001430 (paperback) |
ISBN 9780440001447 (ebook)
Subjects: LCSH: Female friendship—Fiction. | BISAC: FICTION / Contemporary
Women. | FICTION / Romance / Contemporary. | FICTION / Humorous.
Classification: LCC PS3623.A893 M9 2019 | DDC 813/.6—dc23
LC record available at https://lccn.loc.gov/2018059573

First Edition: May 2019

Printed in the United States of America
1 3 5 7 9 10 8 6 4 2

Cover art by Focus and Blur / Shutterstock
Book design by Elke Sigal

This is a work of fiction. Names, characters, places, and incidents either are the product of
the author's imagination or are used fictitiously, and any resemblance to actual persons,
living or dead, business establishments, events, or locales is entirely coincidental.

This book is dedicated to my aunt Lois, who went to Richmond for a wedding and ended up engaged herself. Her sense of humor was legendary and so was her warmth. I've enjoyed and treasured my time with her. (With the possible exception of the day I was engrossed in the novel *Heidi* and she asked me if a certain character had "died yet.")

This portrait of her, in the wedding dress worn by generations of family brides, hung over my grandmother's bed my entire childhood and inspired this story.

Prologue

⚬

Kendra

What can I say about the wedding dress? I can tell you it's been in my family for generations. That after all these years it's still beautiful. And what happened the day I wore it wasn't the dress's fault.

It was designed and created for my great-grandmother's cousin Lindy's wedding. She was the only one of my grandmother's female relatives whose family came through the Crash with most of their money still intact. At the time it was made, THE DRESS, which is how we refer to it, cost more than your average house, a flagrant extravagance at a time when so many had no homes, or jobs, or even food to eat.

It's one of a kind. Ivory satin with a scooped neck, flange collar, and a cleverly fitted bodice. Long fitted sleeves narrow down to a gentle point just beyond the wrist. A creamy waterfall of satin cascades toward the floor and swirls around the ankles, rounds into a train. It's clean lined and elegant. No cutouts. No jewels. Its stark simplicity takes the breath away. With its Chantilly lace mantilla it's the kind of dress meant for a showy, yet tasteful, fairy-tale wedding to a handsome prince. And while happily ever after is never guaranteed, it's implied.

After Lindy, my grandmother and her other cousins wore it. So did their daughters and those of us who followed. Somehow it flatters any figure. A satin version of *The Sisterhood of the*

Traveling Pants long before it was written. In fact, I bet if you subtracted the alterations that were sometimes required and divided its cost by the number of family brides who've worn it, THE DRESS was probably a bargain.

Every single Jameson bride looked beautiful in it. I know because I studied the family wedding albums a million times when I was a girl in Richmond and imagined myself wearing it.

The portrait of my mother in the gown hung above my parents' bed until the day she died. It was part of the room. A touchstone. A reminder that even plain women are beautiful on their wedding day. When reality is suspended and everything, especially happiness, seems possible. When no one is thinking about what it will feel like to deal with sickness rather than health. Or anticipating the till-death-do-us-part part.

The dress fit me perfectly. A fact I interpreted as confirmation that my marriage was meant to be. That Jake was my destiny.

Try as I might to forget I still remember every detail of my wedding day. Sipping from a flute of champagne with my bridesmaids at our house on Monument Avenue while we had our hair and makeup done. The way my hands shook when I was helped into THE DRESS. How fast my heart beat on the way to the church. The way my pulse skittered while the 150 guests were escorted to their seats as the string ensemble played.

I walked down the aisle barely feeling my father's arm under my hand or the floor beneath my kitten heels. All eyes were on me. In the most beautiful dress ever.

I smiled at Jake. Saw the love in his warm brown eyes. Let him take my hand. He squeezed it as we turned to face the minister.

And then, although I've been replaying it in my mind for more than forty years now, I don't really understand what happened. It was as if everything I'd thought, everything I'd felt, flew out of my head. When Reverend Frailey cleared his voice and said, *"Dearly beloved,"* I was struck with a thunderbolt of clarity, or perhaps it was a thunderbolt of panic, that felt as if it had been delivered directly from above. (And I don't mean the choir loft.)

Suddenly I realized that I might be making a mistake. That I'd only just turned twenty-one. That it was 1978 and I was woman, but I had not yet even attempted to roar. That I might not actually be ready to start the family Jake wanted so badly or even commit the rest of my life to another person. Not even Jake.

Like I said, it wasn't THE DRESS's fault. And it definitely wasn't Jake's.

Three months later when the presents had all finally been returned and I discovered that I was pregnant with his child, his family wasn't speaking to mine and I'd already done far too much damage to tell him. Until then I hadn't realized that God was into irony. I mean what kind of deity would smite you with a fear of commitment at the worst possible moment and *then* make you a single mother, arguably the largest commitment ever?

So there it is. A slight wrinkle in THE DRESS's mostly unblemished history.

I'm hoping my daughter will have a happier ending in THE DRESS. If, in fact, she ever wears it.

One

⚭

Lauren

Three days to forty

New York City

"Oh my God. You're . . . you're Lauren James." The woman looks down at the book on her lap then back up at me. "I'm reading *Rip Tide* right now. I've read everything you've ever written. Every single word." She looks so genuinely excited. As if it's Christmas morning and she found me under the tree and can't wait to unwrap me. If her feet weren't currently soaking in warm soapy water she would be moving toward me, holding out the hardcover of my latest novel for my signature. "I just love your books. I buy them in print and digital. I listen to them on audio while I work out."

As other women look up, I thank my lucky stars that I put on makeup and washed my hair today. Writing is not the glamorous profession people think it is. In fact, authors spend long periods of time alone, unwashed, and on deadline. Grooming and hygiene can take a distant second to word count.

"Ah, so you're the one keeping me in print." My smile is real and so is my gratitude. No matter how many times you hear that someone loves what you've written, it feels good. It's like being told that your children are talented *and* beautiful. Or at least I assume that's what it feels like since I've never given birth. The thing is, if you don't have enough readers who love what you do no one will pay you to do it anymore.

She laughs at the very idea of being my only fan, because I've been successfully published for more than a decade and hit the *New York Times* bestseller list on a satisfyingly consistent basis. In fact, I've been dubbed the "Queen of Beach Reads." Which means I write the kind of books that those who want to appear literary like to sneer at, but that sell hundreds of thousands of copies. And allow me to own an apartment in a really great building on Central Park West.

"Thank you. I'm so glad you enjoy my books." I shoot the woman a last smile then turn my attention to my manicurist, Hanh. After a few words of greeting and a couple of polite questions about her children, which is about all we manage given my lack of Vietnamese and her gaps in English, I settle back into the big leather seat. I close my eyes and try to focus on the warm water swirling around my feet, but I'm careful to keep a pleasant smile on my lips so that none of the women who are currently Googling me can interpret my silence as diva-ish or carry tales about how rude and unappreciative I am.

My breathing evens out as Hanh's small, competent hands massage my feet. I attempt to visualize a bright-blue sky with puffy white clouds floating through it. Like the ones that used to form over the Atlantic Ocean in the Outer Banks, where I grew up.

I'm not very good at meditation, and although it's not supposed to be possible, I failed yoga. My brain refuses to slow down or follow instructions, and no matter how hard I try to shut down, I'm inevitably thinking about all the things I'm thinking about but shouldn't be. Then I think about not thinking.

At the moment, all I can think about is that I'm going to be forty in two days, twenty-two hours, and thirty-five minutes whether I'm ready or not. Then I think about how old that is.

How not like my body my body has become. Hanh lifts one foot out of the water and I think about how unattractive my toes are.

I take a conscious breath, counting slowly to seven then holding it before I exhale to a count of ten. This is supposed to clear your mind and help you turn your thoughts in a more pleasant, affirmative direction. I'm not any better at this than I am at not thinking, but I finally manage to pull up an image of Spencer, the man I've been dating for almost a year now, three months longer than I've dated anyone since I came to New York. He's a successful playwright and songwriter with a string of hit Broadway musicals to his credit. He understands what being on deadline means and he's every bit as driven as I am, only way better at disguising it.

I let myself try to imagine the surprise birthday dinner he's planning. I inhale again, even more slowly this time. I've spent more than a few birthdays alone since I arrived here just after my twenty-first and am beyond glad to have someone to face down forty with.

I was supposed to come to New York with Brianna, my best friend in the world; a friend who felt more like a sister from the day we met in kindergarten and discovered we were born on the same day. (We were both wearing paper crowns at the time.)

We practically lived in each other's houses while we were growing up. When we were in high school her grandmother died and her archaeologist parents went on yet another dig on yet another continent and never really came back and she moved in with us.

Bree and I inhaled books and dreamed of being writers. We wrote our first illustrated fairy tale together in second grade and turned it into a graphic romance novel when we were fourteen. We brainstormed and wrote part of a work of historical fiction while we were in high school and plotted out a contemporary novel set on our favorite beach in the Outer Banks in college. We planned to move to New York right after we graduated from college and find an apartment to share, and we were both going to get jobs to support us while we wrote the novel we'd plotted.

Two days before we were supposed to take the bus to New York, Bree pulled out without warning *or* any real explanation. It was a betrayal of everything we'd dreamed and planned our entire lives and all she said was, *"Sorry, I changed my mind."* Like she'd decided to order iced tea instead of Coke or thought she'd pass on dessert. I didn't know a soul in New York. I climbed onto the bus with wobbly knees, scared to death.

New York City is intimidating in its own right. Alone and without money it can be hard, cold, and inhospitable. A place to be survived through sheer force of will.

I was barely hanging on by my fingertips three months later, when I heard that Bree was dating Clay Williams, my boyfriend all through high school and most of college.

Six months later they were engaged. Even though we were barely speaking I tried to warn her that Clay was nowhere near ready to settle down; something I did out of the remnants of friendship and that she interpreted as jealousy. Then, although she's not a blood relative, she wore THE DRESS that's been in my family forever. And my mother forced me to be her maid of honor, because of some stupid promise and a pinky swear we made each other in kindergarten.

If that's not a novel, I don't know what is.

Bree

Two days to forty

Manteo, North Carolina

"Mary? Are you there?" The voice sounds tinny as if it's coming from a great distance, which it pretty much always is.

The voice belongs to the woman who gave birth to me. She and my father are somewhere in the Middle East. Or possibly in sub-Saharan Africa. Or maybe the Galápagos on some archaeological dig or another.

I was named after Mary Leakey, the famous fossil hunter, whom I've always hated because my parents clearly loved fossils and hunting for them more than they ever loved me.

I was five when I stopped answering to Mary and insisted on being called Brianna, which is my middle name. That was when my parents, who'd been dragging me from one archaeological dig to another, brought me to live with my grandmother Brianna in her house in Manteo on Roanoke Island so that they could continue to wander. My grandmother died just after my sixteenth birthday, forcing my parents to come back to bury her. They stayed long enough to decide that I was old enough to live on my own in the house she'd left me while they finished the dig they'd been in the middle of. After that they took turns coming back on occasion though I never sensed any method or thought to their comings and goings. If it hadn't been for Kendra and Lauren Jameson marching over and packing up my things and insisting I move in with them, I'm not sure what sort of pathetic hermit I might have turned into.

"I'm calling to wish you a happy birthday. Your father's out of cell phone range but I didn't want to miss this opportunity."

"Oh, right. Thanks." There's no way of knowing whether she realizes my birthday's not for two days yet. Or if the time difference where she is somehow makes up the gap. Or maybe she had the chance to call and realized it was close enough to my birthday to count. I really don't know and every year it matters less. My birth story is a little murky. I've heard that she was on an island off the coast of California searching for signs of Late Pleistocene Paleocoastal peoples when she went into labor and simply had me there in the sand before going back to work like Russian peasant women used to do back in the day. But instead of tying me in a sling to her bosom she handed me over to an assistant.

"Do you have special plans?"

"Oh, you know, the usual." This is a gibe because I can't remember more than a handful of birthdays my biological parents were around for. Which is undoubtedly why I've made a big fuss and party for each and every one of my children's birthdays, including Lily's sweet sixteen last year.

"What's wrong?" she asks, as if we've *ever* had a comfortable conversation since I became aware that I was never even a contender in the competition between my parents' love of their work and their love of me.

"Nothing. It's just that I'm at the store. And I can't really talk right now." This is a lie, but I can't bring myself to come out and tell her that her occasional awkward attempts to communicate just make me feel worse.

"Oh, that's nice." They've seen my bookstore, Title Waves, a handful of times. The same for their grandchildren.

"Thanks for the call."

I'd pace if the store weren't so crowded with bookshelves and display tables. I settle for breathing deeply and telling myself that an unsatisfying phone call is better than no call at all. Then I tell myself that turning forty isn't that big a deal. Ultimately, I do what I always do when I'm unhappy. Or nervous. Or angry. I pull my laptop out of my bag, boot it up, and open the manuscript file. I empty my mind and let go of my hurt and irritation as I read the scene I wrote last night when the house was finally quiet and I could sit down in the attic room I've claimed for my office. It's not as bad as it felt while I was writing it. I read the scene again. Then I begin to cut and paste, which is when I realize what's missing. I lean forward and begin to type. Everything else disappears as a picture of my characters forms in my mind. Heath would never take Whitney for granted or forget to bring home the paper towels like he promised.

"No, don't go. I can't bear for you to go." His smile was wry, his tone self-deprecating. His blue eyes gleamed with . . .

The bell on the front door jangles. My fingers freeze on the keyboard. It takes a few long seconds to blink myself back to the present.

"Good day, Brianna." Margaret McKinnon is a lovely woman of about eighty-five, an avid reader who loves books almost as much as I do and cannot bring herself to read in any format that doesn't involve paper. She's been a regular since I started working in this very bookstore as a teenager. She's one of my best customers and will come in to help out or even take a shift when I need to take time off or the student who works part time has a conflict. I make it a point to keep her favorite authors, and any that resemble them, stocked. Which means lots and lots of historical fiction and the occasional erotic novel disguised as a romance. Recently she's begun to wade into fantasy.

Since her husband died five months ago she's been coming in more frequently and staying longer. Some people drown their sorrows and losses in drugs and alcohol. Mrs. McKinnon drowns hers in the written word, which is an escape I can relate to.

"It's lovely out, isn't it?" she asks with forced enthusiasm. "March can be so unpredictable."

"That's for sure, Miz McKinnon," I say with a smile. Sometimes March brings record snowfalls but it's hard to argue with today's pale-blue skies, thin white clouds, and mild breeze. Not to mention a high in the low sixties. We'll have things mostly to ourselves until the season kicks off on Memorial Day weekend, something I will appreciate as a store owner and complain about as a full-time resident.

She returns the smile even though her eyes are red and swollen, and I imagine her forcing herself out of her cottage and into the stores simply to keep herself from crying.

"How's the book coming?" She aims a friendly nod toward my laptop. We live in a very small town on a narrow barrier island and it's no secret that I've been working on a novel for a decade and a half and have never let anyone read a word of it.

"It's coming." I started this book even before my former best friend stole the idea we'd plotted out together and launched her publishing career with it.

I smile again and am careful not to let it turn into a sigh. You'd think I'd be over Lauren's theft of "our" novel by now, but it's not easy to see someone you once loved not only living your dream, but succeeding at it on a level you never imagined. Sometimes I practically reek of jealousy. I mean, I wouldn't trade Rafe and Lily or my family life for anything—at least not on a good day. But I've had plenty of years to wonder if it really had to be either/or.

"I have a hankering for something exotic," Mrs. McKinnon says. "What have you got for me today?"

We spend a lovely hour together browsing through the shelves. She chooses a Mary Balogh, Deborah Harkness's *A Discovery of Witches*, and the fifth in Jim Butcher's The Dresden Files. Like I said, she's an equal-opportunity reader.

We talk about the next book club meeting at the store and then she stays to chitchat until I lock up. It's clear she doesn't want to go home, and I feel terrible when I finally have to usher her out onto the sidewalk. I've got to hit the grocery store and pick up Clay's shirts at the dry cleaner. Lily's dress is ready at Myrna's Alterations. And then maybe I'll run over to the Sandcastle and visit with Kendra for a bit.

Sometimes I don't want to go home, either.

Two

Lauren

T-minus 24 hours to forty

New York City

My agent, Chris Wolfe, takes me to The Palm Court at The Plaza for the champagne tea the day before my birthday. Somewhere between forty and fifty, she's small and stocky with a strong chin, a no-nonsense manner, and no patience whatsoever for anyone who doesn't bring their A game, which is fine with me. She was a huge step up from my first agent, who was the only one willing to take me on when I was a struggling waitress/ blogger/occasional ghost writer/aspiring novelist. In traditional publishing it's all about trading up—in the beginning you take virtually any deal you can get at a major publishing house and then do everything humanly possible to convince them to get behind you. The more books you sell, the more valuable you become and the more options you have. The same is true with agents, the gatekeeper's gatekeeper.

The trellis-patterned carpet is plush beneath our feet as we're led to our table. There are no windows, but the restored stained glass ceiling and strategically placed palm trees give the elegant space a bright airiness. It's a bit kitschy, but we toasted my first six-figure deal here and have been toasting milestones and occasions here ever since. Today we're celebrating my birthday, but even before she air-kisses my cheek I know that she has news to impart and that news is not good. As if turning forty tomorrow doesn't suck enough.

Normally, Chris's poker face is world-class. I've seen her stare down titans of publishing and threaten to walk when we had nowhere to go, but I've been with her long enough to know her tells. She's smiling when our glasses of champagne arrive, but her eyes are too focused and there's a tiny crease between her brows that I've seen only a handful of times.

"So, how are things?" she asks.

"Good," I say automatically because I'm determined to be positive about my looming date with old age—at least in public. But I watch her face carefully as I say it because all writers, regardless of their level of success, are appallingly insecure. "They are good, right?"

Chris blinks. Which in anyone else would be a shriek of panic.

"Oh God. What is it?" My jaw tightens to hold back the whimper that threatens. "I knew I shouldn't have agreed to do that anthology."

A little voice in my head shouts, *Mayday! Mayday! We're going down!!* Without bothering to toast we both finish our champagne.

"No, it isn't that. Well, not exactly." She hesitates again. "But they were relying on your name to sell that book. And the numbers weren't even close to what was anticipated."

I'm getting older by the minute and it's possible that new gray hair is sprouting. I'm in no mood to pry news I don't want to hear out of her. "And?"

"And neither is *Rip Tide*. In fact, there's been a decided dip in sales over the last two reporting periods. A cooling, if you will."

Our eyes meet. Without discussion her hand goes up. The waitress hurries over and refills our champagne glasses. I remain silent as I wait for Chris to finish. It's not as if I don't watch my numbers—all writers do. Given online sales rankings and the author portals set up by publishers that supply sales figures on an almost daily basis, it's almost impossible not to have a decent idea of how things are going. But I'm always on deadline, and I've discovered the hard way that nothing shuts down my imagination faster than fear. So I try not to check too often, and I've developed an aptitude for denial. I continue my silence and add a raised eyebrow when the waitress departs.

"There's been a general falloff in women's fiction over the last eighteen months. You're not the only one who's lost readers."

Lost them? Where did they go? Siberia? And am I really supposed to feel good about not being the only loser?

"What is Trove planning to do about it?" This is, after all, supposed to be my publisher's issue. I'm supposed to write the books, they're supposed to market and sell them. Hitting the big lists is something of a self-fulfilling prophecy. Once you've done it a time or two in a big-enough way it can become almost automatic. The thrill gives way to expectation. Everyone forgets that it can stop at any time. There are plenty of once-huge names that aren't anymore. And I'm not anywhere near ready to go quietly into that good night.

"Well," she says with a sigh. "They don't think it's marketing. They think you may have lost some of your focus. That you may be just kind of going through the motions." She swallows and manages not to drop her eyes.

"So I just have to write a better book and everything will be fine?" I can hear the anger and panic in my voice. When I was first starting out publishers would put almost nothing behind a debut and then blame a lack of sales on the author. I've seen what they can accomplish for an author when they want to and I've been fortunate enough to be on the receiving end of their largesse for almost long enough to have forgotten what being overlooked feels like. My readership has been growing for so long I've let myself forget that anything that can get bigger can also shrink.

I'm not hungry, but I reach for the tea sandwiches anyway. Tears threaten but I refuse to shed them. Not here in The Plaza. And not in front of this woman who has helped make me what I am.

"Don't worry. Your *core* fan base is incredibly devoted. True diehards. They'd read the phone book if your name was on the spine."

Is it just me or does this imply that my books don't have to be that good because my readers—or at least those who haven't gotten lost—will read them anyway? I want to put my face in my hands and cry. Actually I'd like to put my head down on the table and *close* my eyes. But only if I could wake up tomorrow younger, firmer, and with sales numbers that don't make it so hard to swallow.

"So what are you doing for your fortieth?" she asks brightly.

"I'm sleeping in tomorrow and I don't plan to write a single word." Though under the circumstances maybe I should. "Spencer is taking me out to dinner."

"Oh, where?"

"I don't know," I say, matching her smile even though my brain is running around in circles shrieking in distress. "He said it was a surprise."

"He's a keeper, that one," she says with another smile.

There've been quite a few men over the last two decades. I mean, I'm not exactly a femme fatale, but I'm not chopped liver yet, either. Though I guess I might be after tomorrow. Happily, Spencer Harrison is smart and funny and he understands the rigors of succeeding in a creative field. Relationship-wise we're in the perfect place—monogamous and committed without any of the angst that comes from wanting to take things to another level. I mean, it's not as if either of us is looking to get married. I've pretty much stopped thinking about my biological clock and have accepted that I may never be a mother.

Chris raises her glass. "To you, Lauren. To your fortieth. And to your talent and to future success. I know this next book will be your best yet!"

We clink and drink then decimate most of the desserts even though every bite is difficult to swallow and sits in my churning stomach like a lead weight. We talk about the weather and plays and movies we've seen. We don't speak any further about my sagging sales. But then we don't need to.

Bree

D-day

Manteo

Someone is in the room. I realize this at the same time I notice that my cheek is pressed against a hard surface and my neck is stiff, as if I've been in this position too long.

A hand grasps my shoulder, shakes gently.

"Wha?" My mouth is dry and cottony. My eyes are caked shut.

"Happy birthday." The voice belongs to my husband, Clay. I can feel him leaning over me.

I yawn and blink my eyes open. I discover that the hard surface underneath my cheek is my desk. I apparently fell asleep with my arms spread across it in supplication. The fingers of my right hand are locked around my computer mouse. The pages I printed out yesterday are damp with drool. I manage to raise my head, swipe at the corner of my mouth, and focus on Clay's face.

He's six-two, almost six-three, and I have to crane my aching neck to meet his eyes, which are a bright, changeable blue. His blond hair has darkened. He's still broad and solid, but not the football star heartthrob he once was. He's holding a chocolate cupcake with one lit candle in it. Our sixteen-year-old daughter, Lily, stands next to him bearing a mug of coffee. She sings "Happy Birthday to You" quickly, on key, and with a minimum of emotion.

"Did you finish?" she asks, and I remember that I told them both I was going to type *The End* before this morning or die in the attempt. That I refused to turn forty until I'd finally finished what I started all those years ago. I know from experience that it's not a good sign about the material when you fall asleep *while* you're writing it. In my heart I know that if I'd finished *Heart of Gold* I wouldn't have still been up here. I would have been downstairs celebrating. Or at least asleep in my own bed. Still, I unclench my hand and rouse the screen and make myself look. "Nope."

"Here." She sets the mug on the desk. "You're close. And it's not like you have a real deadline or anything." It's hard to tell if this is the dig it feels like. If I had a real deadline, as in a contract with a publisher like my former best friend does, it would have been done a decade ago.

Clay sets the cupcake in front of me. It's a tradition my grandmother started when my parents first left me with her—birthday cake for breakfast—that used to make the day feel extra special. Now it's just something that he knows I expect and remembers to do. They both look at me expectantly, so I lean over and blow out the candle. "We're going to have your birthday dinner at Kendra's, right?" Lily says.

"Yes." This is another tradition, the joint celebration of Lauren's and my birthday, that Kendra started when she took me in and made me the third member of their family. I can still remember how she'd cook all day to make Lauren's and my favorite dishes, the homemade birthday cake with both our names written across the top in interlocking letters, how we'd make our wishes then blow out the candles together.

"Six thirty." My voice wobbles with memory.

"Okay." She hugs me then returns downstairs.

"I'm going to head out, too." Clay doesn't quite meet my eyes. "Are you all right with, um, celebrating later?"

"Sure. No problem." I smile and try to mean it then watch him turn and leave.

I eye the cupcake but can't quite bring myself to eat it. In the first few years we were married, birthday cake was a prelude to spending the morning in bed. And even then I would sometimes wonder if he wished I were Lauren. Because they'd gone steady for so long. It was only after I stayed home instead of going to New York with her that our friendship turned into something more. By the time we got married I'd convinced myself that we were better suited than he and Lauren ever would have been; that we wanted the same things. In my experience you can talk yourself into almost anything, and even believe it for a time.

Now we rarely do anything in bed together but sleep. When we do I worry that he wishes I were someone else. While I wish he were more like Heath, the hero in my novel. Loving and physically affectionate. And completely faithful.

Still, he's given me Rafe and Lily, my two greatest accomplishments. Both of us love them more than anything. But it's gotten harder for me to pretend Clay doesn't have "fidelity issues." Manteo is way too small for secrets.

The phone rings and I know it will be Kendra calling to wish me a happy birthday. Just like I know she'll serve all of my favorite foods for dinner tonight and that she'll lead the singing when she brings out the cake she will have baked from scratch. Even though it will have only one name on it.

Kendra Jameson is the mother we all wish for, but rarely get. Some people are born that way. Others are born to hunt for fossils and dig up civilizations. I would never have known how to be a mother if I hadn't learned by watching my grandmother and Kendra, who never let her widowhood or lack of family stop her from always putting her daughter first.

I love Rafe and Lily. It's been a joy and a privilege to be their mother. It's the one thing I've excelled at. I would slit my wrists before I let them down. Or disrupted our family. Or took their father away from them.

Three

∾

Lauren

D-day

Being forty sucks even more than I thought it would. And it turns out I am just the woman to embrace its suckiness. I drank too much at The Plaza then passed out fully clothed on my bed only to wake at two A.M. and every hour after that, my sense of apocalyptic dread growing with each bathroom run.

As I lie in bed hungover, my makeup caked all over my face, my bedding a testament to the tossing and turning I've done, it occurs to me that the dip in my career increased the suckiness of today's milestone. (Yes, *suckiness* is a word, a noun in fact, and is defined in multiple dictionaries as "the state or condition of being sucky." Feel free to use it in your next Scrabble game or Words with Friends.)

The phone rings and I pick it up reluctantly. My mother's cheerful voice on the other end hurts almost as much as the sunshine slanting through the blinds. "Happy birthday!" she says with what I know is a huge smile. "I feel like it was only yesterday that I held you in my arms for the first time. Just wanted to wish you a great day and tell you how much I love you and how proud of you I am."

"Thanks." Her words don't exactly make me glad to be forty, but my mother's love and praise have always helped slay the dragons of doubt and insecurity. When I was little I used to beg for details of the day I was born and of my father who died while she was pregnant with me, and about how she left her aunt Velda's, who was her only living relative, and brought me to the Outer Banks when I wasn't even a week old. All she ever really told me was what a wonderful man my father was, how much he would have loved me. Then she'd sniff back tears and get this funny look on her face and I would know that the topic was painful and that I needed to drop it. The picture of her in THE DRESS standing next to him in church on their wedding day is still my most prized possession. Along with the photos of the grandparents I never met. My mother's cheerful perseverance in the face of adversity was my greatest inspiration. At least after I began to get over the fact that I seemed to be the only child I knew who had only one parent. It wasn't until I became best friends with Bree that I understood that having one mother who loved you more than anything in the world was better than having two parents who did not.

"So what are you doing tonight to celebrate?" my mother asks.

"Spencer's taking me out to dinner. He refuses to tell me where we're going, but I have my suspicions."

"That's so sweet," she says, and I hear a slight tremor in her voice. My mother has dated some over the years, but nothing that ever really lasted. "You have to give a man points for understanding the importance of a dramatic gesture."

"Mom, he *is* in the theater. Dramatic gestures are part of his DNA." But I smile when I say it. My first of the day.

"Point taken. But even if he comes by it naturally you still need to enjoy and appreciate it." There's a beat of silence as if she's considering her next words, but she says only, "Bring him down here soon. I'd like to meet him."

I try to envision Spencer in a place where the sidewalks roll up at nine or don't even exist at all. Where you can't get food delivered at any hour of the day or night. Can't wander into an all-night deli or restaurant. Can't get a good bagel. A place where the only live theater is the longest running *The Lost Colony* on Roanoke Island and there are only two movie theaters within the hundred-plus-mile stretch of barrier islands.

"You could come up here to meet him, you know. We could see some shows, do a little shopping. I have tons of frequent-flier miles you can use." I don't add that I won't have to see Bree that way. And I definitely don't ask what Mom's doing tonight, because I know she's already cooking for what used to be our joint birthday dinner like she does every year. As if Bree were actually her daughter. And Bree's children her grandchildren.

"We'll see," my mother hedges. "But it's been way too long since you've been down. I don't want you to forget your roots. Or shake off all that sand in your shoes."

I don't say no but I don't say yes, either. This is not the day to argue.

"Well, enjoy the day and your birthday dinner, sweetheart. We'll be thinking of you and sending love." My mother makes the exaggerated kissing sound that ends all of our phone calls. "And when you blow out your candles don't forget to make a wish."

⌒⌒

Later that day, way before there are candles, I wish I hadn't wasted so much of my birthday nursing a hangover and trying not to worry about my career. It took a lot of the fun out of the bouquet of flowers and balloons Spencer sent, and made me eat more of the tower of chocolates that came with them than I meant to. I heard from a few friends and saw the thousands of happy birthdays posted by readers on my author Facebook page. Presumably from those who haven't yet disappeared or defected.

Despite the beautiful March day going on outside my window I don't leave the apartment. In fact, I barely leave my bed until it's time to shower. The makeup artist I use for special appearances and occasions arrives at seven—now that I'm forty I'm going to need a lot more help not looking it. Barry, my long-time hairdresser/stylist/friend arrives at eight to fuss and cluck over me.

He twists my shoulder-length hair into a messy knot at the base of my neck and pulls out tendrils to arrange around my face, giving me a casual-yet-elegant look that I have never achieved on my own. Then he helps me into a very simple black sheath that turns my lanky body into something far more feminine. Diamond studs, Christian Louboutin heels, and an evening clutch are my only accessories. It's Barry who taught me that less is more, that designer fashions are designed for bodies like mine, and who finally convinced me that being tall is an advantage not a liability.

"Not bad," he says as he brushes a small piece of lint from the three-quarter sleeve and straightens the dress's boat neck slightly. From him this is high praise.

"Turn." He motions with one finger and rewards me with an approving smile. "You are now fit to be seen and photographed."

I face myself in the mirror and am relieved to see he's right. Like most authors I'm an introvert at heart. I spend long periods of time alone in front of a computer, but I've learned how to handle myself in public, speak to book clubs, give keynotes, get interviewed, deliver sound bites. I can switch into bestselling-author mode when I need to but being *on* isn't my default setting. I have no desire to be the center of attention.

Barry escorts me downstairs and leads me to the black car Spencer has sent. "Nice touch. A modern version of the fairy-tale coach. Let's hope it doesn't turn into a pumpkin pulled by field mice at midnight," Barry teases as a liveried driver opens the passenger door.

"I guess this will just have to do." I sigh theatrically as Barry wraps me in a hug then watches the driver help me into the backseat. Barry leans in before the door closes and whispers, "I expect to hear details. Not from the bedroom necessarily. Though some of us do like to live vicariously. That man of yours is quite hot."

"I'll be sure to tell him you said so," I tease back. Then I draw the spring evening into my lungs and remind myself how fortunate I am. An entire day of wallowing is more than enough.

It turns out the ride is a brief one straight through Central Park. It ends less than fifteen minutes later in front of The Surrey hotel, where Spencer is waiting to help me out of the car and sweep me into his arms. "Happy birthday!" He looks delighted to see me and his voice is almost a purr when he presses a kiss to my neck and adds, "Ummm, you smell and look divine."

So does he, of course. He's even taller than I am, with a lean runner's body, dark hair, and features that are somewhat ordinary on their own but somehow manage to pull together into something quite arresting. I couldn't tell you exactly what he's wearing. I only know it's disconcerting to date someone whose style actually is effortless when you require professionals. But then Spencer grew up here on the Upper East Side while I grew up in a place where the wind off the Atlantic wreaks havoc with hair, shoes are often optional, and evening wear is likely to be a sweatshirt over your bathing suit.

"I know it's kind of cheesy, but I thought we'd come back and relive our first date at Café Boulud," he says as he walks me to the restaurant entrance.

"It's perfect," I say, meaning it. A nice, quiet dinner suits me just fine. Who needs fanfare at forty?

Spencer's latest Broadway musical, *The Music in Me*, has been running for two years now and he and Daniel Boulud are friends, so we're shown to a discreet yet prime table that we've come to think of as "ours."

Champagne arrives the moment we're seated and we raise

our glasses and stare into each other's eyes. His are a beautiful green and are framed by long dark lashes. They're filled with intelligence that's almost always accompanied by a glint of humor. His mouth is wide and mobile, his hands long and beautiful. Whenever I look at them I think he should have been a concert pianist or sculptor. Or maybe even a surgeon.

"Happy birthday." He smiles over his champagne flute, flashing the dimple that creases one cheek. "May we always have such happy occasions to toast together."

I smile my thanks and clink my glass to his. The champagne is light and bubbly on my tongue, and I remind myself to enjoy the evening and not dwell on the reason for it. I'm hardly the first woman to turn forty and I won't be the last. As they say, one must consider the alternative.

Moments later warm bread arrives. Menus don't.

"I hope you don't mind, but I went ahead and ordered the same meal we had the first time we came here."

"How lovely," I say, but I can't help wondering how he could possibly remember what we ate a year ago. We've consumed countless meals together since then, many of them memorable. Meals are to Spencer what game plays are to sports fanatics, but still. One meal a year ago?

"I see the doubt," he says easily. "But I've never forgotten that evening. I knew then just how remarkable you are. Even if we'd never seen each other again I would have remembered every bite and every detail of your face."

I'm afraid he's going to tell me what I wore that night and in fact he does. Which speaks to Barry's styling abilities. I would go everywhere in stretch pants or sweats, which is what I work in, if I could get away with it. And frankly I don't pay that much attention to food. Most of the time I couldn't tell you what I ate on any given day or what color sweatpants I was wearing when I ate it.

Our appetizers of Escargot en Vol-au-Vent and a Chestnut Veloute arrive and are happily consumed. They are followed in perfectly timed succession by an endive salad and entrées of Striped Bass "en Prupetti" and Duck Breast in Magnolia Leaf, which don't look remotely familiar. They're paired with what I'm sure are the perfect wines.

"Wow. Did we really eat this much on our first date?" I feel a rosy glow from the alcohol and the spectacular food and the way Spencer is looking at me.

"Well, I think we may have drunk more than we ate that first time. But I was so entranced with you that the meal is indelibly stamped in my brain."

It's beautifully said but I catch myself wondering if he keeps some kind of food diary like some men keep a little black book. Or maybe he simply knows that I'm never going to call him on his food recall. Ever. I can recite a bad review back to you word for word years after it's been written, but a meal? It's never going to happen.

"I remember the meal because I shared it with you," he says softly, staring into my eyes. And I catch myself thinking how much Bree would appreciate this scene. I mean, I would never write a line of dialogue like that. She was always the one wanting to turn everyone into a hero—on the page and in real life. She inhaled romance novels like an alcoholic consumes booze and insisted on believing in happily ever afters.

"You are a flatterer, sir," I reply, as if I'm a heroine in a historical romance.

"No. I'm a man in love." His wink takes some of the schmaltz out of our exchange. He leans across the table to kiss me.

Before I can wonder at this display of affection in such a public place our dessert arrives, a Molten Chocolate Cake with vanilla ice cream and a single candle on top. Forty candles would turn it and our table into flambé.

"Happy birthday, darling." He takes both of my hands in his. His smile grows larger and his eyes gleam with what I recognize as anticipation. Out of the corner of one eye I sense movement. A small group of people materialize beside the table. Before I can turn, the group begins to sing "Happy Birthday." These are not a ragtag group of friends belting out the song. These are professionals. As I turn I see part of the cast from *The Music in Me*. They're wearing their costumes and beaming at me.

The rest of the room falls silent. Just as the song ends the cast members step back, lock arms around one another's backs, and begin to sway and do some kind of doo-wop background thing. Still holding on to one of my hands, Spencer stands and moves around the table, where he drops to one knee. At first I think something's happened to him. That one of his legs has given out. But then Merry, Kai, Jen, and Robert break into these big grins. Their doo-wop volume gets softer.

Spencer looks up at me expectantly. Suddenly there's a velvet ring box in his hand.

I'm having a hard time taking it all in. My first thought is *This is so sudden*, but it isn't exactly. He told me he loved me a month to the day after our first meal here. A month after that I said the same. But saying you love someone doesn't mean you intend to marry them, does it?

As Spencer tells me all the reasons he loves me my heart is pounding so hard that I can hardly hear or think. My life flashes before my eyes like they say it does when you're about to die, which seems like a bad sign.

Then he flips open the box and the diamond sparkles in the light. It's huge and pear shaped with baguettes of diamonds on either side. Without meaning to I compare it to the ring Clay gave Bree, which might have come out of a Cracker Jack box. This pretty much screams Tiffany.

"I love you," Spencer concludes emphatically. "Will you do me the honor of becoming my wife?"

I swallow as I try to corral my random thoughts. I love him. But everyone's staring. I feel a flash of anger that he's done this so publicly and without warning. I'm happy with things the way they are. I thought we both were. But how can I say no in front of all these people? And if I do what are the chances we're going to simply go back to how things were? No. He'll be humiliated and I'll never see him again. I'll be forty and alone with a declining career and . . . No, those are not the reasons to get married. I shove them out of my head and try to think logically. But I can't seem to think at all.

I want to shout at the cast to stop singing. To go away and leave us alone. I wish I could turn back time to just before dessert arrived. That I'd had some warning this was coming.

I see a shadow of worry steal into his eyes, turning them a mossy, less brilliant green. It has obviously not occurred to him until now that I might say no.

"Lauren?" He swallows and I see just how vulnerable he feels. "Will you marry me?"

And then I'm smiling and crying, though not necessarily for the reasons I should be.

"Of course I will. How can I possibly say no to all this?" These are the truest words I can come up with.

The cast swings into a well-rehearsed version of "Chapel of Love."

Those close enough to have heard my answer stand up and applaud. It's the cast that takes the bows.

Four

⊙

Kendra

The Sandcastle, Nags Head

Have you ever done something without thinking it through? I did on occasion when I was a small child, before I understood what my mother's "rest" vacations really were or that a crayon masterpiece drawn on the formal dining room wall would not entice her to leave her darkened bedroom to play with me. Or that the attention I'd get from my father for that kind of transgression was not worth seeking.

I did it on my wedding day when I choked at the altar and again just after I gave birth. That was forty years ago and ever since I've been excruciatingly careful not to leap without looking.

At the moment I'm unloading the dishwasher and eliminating the remnants of last night's birthday dinner and remembering the months leading up to Lauren's birth. Even after all this time most of the memories are painful.

My mother started crying the moment I halted the extravagant wedding that she'd planned. She cried harder when I told them I was pregnant, and never really stopped. This precipitated another of her "rest cures," which were no longer referred to as vacations. My father's first words were *How could you do this to us?* As if it were all some elaborate plan to make them look bad.

As if my mother's nervous breakdowns hadn't already sparked unwelcome speculation. He barely looked at me after that.

His plan was to send me to a home for unwed mothers where I would give birth, hand over my child for adoption, and come home to Richmond as if nothing had ever happened. I knew a lot of girls who did exactly that. Because on the one hand the '70s was a time of streaking and free love, but getting pregnant and giving birth without the benefit of matrimony was heavily frowned upon. In Richmond, in my parents' circle, it was a mortification not to be borne. (Yes, bad pun intended.)

In the end he took me to Charlotte to my mother's older sister, Velda, before the truth became undisguisable. It was a better and kinder option than being sent to some group home, but the end result was supposed to be the same. Give the baby up then come home and get on with my life. As if she'd never happened. I was way too numb to argue or come up with a plan of my own. I vaguely remember sleeping those months away. But giving birth wakes you up in ways you never imagine. Once I held her in my arms and felt her tiny fingers clinging to mine, there was no way on earth I could ever hand her over to anyone else. Not even to wealthy, loving, potentially great parents. I didn't really think. I just took her and ran, scared to death but determined to be the mother mine didn't have the emotional wherewithal to be.

I pour myself a cup of coffee and carry it to the kitchen table, still unable to believe how little thought I gave to the most important decisions of my life. How much I underestimated how hard it would all be. How little I considered the potential fallout. It had never occurred to me that my father would be angry and embarrassed enough to cut his daughter and granddaughter out of his life and force my mother to do the same. Or that they would die before either side could forgive or make amends.

And, of course, I never imagined that when my brain cleared and the panic subsided and I realized that Jake was the man I actually would love "till death do us part" he would already be engaged to someone else.

And then my aunt Velda—the only member of our family who wanted to have a relationship with me—and who never lost touch with her girlhood friends in Richmond, started sending me tidbits about him and the woman he married. Things I really wish I'd never heard. Because the more I heard the more I knew that I could never tell him about our daughter.

Lauren

New York City

"Oh my God. Let me see that ring."

We're with friends at a crowded table in Bar Centrale, a small unmarked place built into what was once an apartment above Joe Allen's restaurant on 46th in the middle of Restaurant Row.

I hold out my hand somewhat dutifully and let the stone speak for itself. It's been doing a lot of talking lately and so has Spencer. I now know all the smallest details about his shopping expedition to Tiffany, the other stones that were considered and rejected, the planning of the proposal, and the logistics required to orchestrate it.

"Were you totally surprised?"

"Yes," I answer truthfully. Everyone seems so satisfied by the absolute theatricality of it all that there's no way I can say that I'm still stunned and trying to absorb the fact that I'm engaged to be married or that a more private proposal might have left me a little less off-kilter.

These people live and breathe drama. They are delighted by spectacle. They create it for a living. They are thrilled that Spencer has pulled this off.

I can see how sincerely happy Spencer seems. How glad he is not only that he pulled the proposal production off so seamlessly, but that he is genuinely happy to be engaged to marry me. I know I should treasure this enthusiasm, given that so many men have to be lassoed and hauled to the altar. I love him and I have no real doubts about marrying him. But at the moment I'm wishing that at least one of these normally loose-lipped people had tipped me off.

"Have you set a date?"

"Where are you going to hold the wedding?"

"Ohh, a museum would be cool. I went to a wedding at the Guggenheim that was absolutely gorgeous."

"Or what about the Park Avenue Armory or The Frick? They're both so elegant."

I can't really keep track of who says what. All of Spencer's friends are talented and driven and most of them have made it to the higher rungs of a ladder that's ridiculously hard to climb. I like and respect them. Usually I enjoy them. But they're still more his friends than mine.

I have a handful of longtime writer friends, but our friendship is a quieter thing and typically plays out online via group e-mails or texts or in an occasional phone call. We get together when one of us needs human contact. And to celebrate when something good happens or to support one another when news is bad. But losing Bree was so painful (kind of like having an arm ripped off) that I've been careful not to let myself get that close—or be that vulnerable—again.

So far tonight I haven't had to say much, which suits me just fine. I really don't have it in me to start contemplating logistics. It's all I can do to beat down my discomfort at how important a topic our wedding plans have already become.

"Will the wedding be in New York?" A lighting director named Martin asks.

A shocked silence follows this question.

"Well, don't people typically get married wherever the bride is from?" Denise often handles casting for the touring companies of Spencer's plays.

"Where are you from again?" This comes from Spencer's favored choreographer, Brett.

Puzzled looks follow. Despite the fact that Spencer is the only person at this table who was actually born and raised in Manhattan, those who have chosen to live here and in many cases fought hard to be able to afford to stay here, like to pretend their lives began only after they arrived.

"Lauren's from the Outer Banks," Spencer says. "Nags Head." He pronounces the name of my hometown with relish.

"What a great name."

"How cute! I love the sound of it."

I try not to cringe as I tell them that some claim the name comes from locals tying lanterns to horses to try to lure ships onto the rocky shoals in order to scavenge the resulting shipwreck. The Outer Banks is composed of a long string of barrier islands that are bounded by the Atlantic Ocean on the east and the sounds that separate it from the North Carolina coast on the west. Its beauty is even more dramatic than the people assembled here. It's majestic. Breathtaking. Its easternmost coast is referred to as the Graveyard of the Atlantic, for God's sake. And while some parts of it have become a bit built up and bulge with tourists during high season, *cute* is not a word I would ever apply to it. Nor would any Banker.

"You never told me what your mother said when you called her." Spencer smiles comfortably. He's planned and pulled off the proposal. All is right in his world.

I give myself a moment to finish my wine. Then I pat my lips dry with a napkin. Only then do I meet his eyes. Which look first horrified and then hurt. "Was she upset that I didn't ask for her permission?"

The concern on his face is really kind of sweet. But I'm a

forty-year-old woman who's been on her own in New York for close to two decades. I can't imagine why he'd ask my mother.

"No, of course not. She wouldn't be expecting that. I mean, you two haven't even met yet."

He gets an odd look on his face and I hurry to rephrase. "In fact, when she called the other morning to wish me a happy birthday she told me I needed to bring you down to meet her."

He goes very still and I realize my mistake. That call took place before his proposal.

"You mean you haven't told her?"

"Well . . . no, not exactly."

"Really? You got engaged to be married and you didn't think that merited a phone call?" His tone turns cool but I can see the shocked surprise in his eyes. I know that Broadway Spencer has a thick skin—almost reptilian—you don't make it in the entertainment fields if you're too soft. And he tends to lead with his cocky, successful, privileged-yet-talented persona, but I have seen inside him to his very real flesh-and-blood self with complex thoughts and hurtable feelings. It's clear I've hurt them now.

"It's not that I haven't wanted to tell her." I'm scrambling now. "I've left her several messages, but I didn't want to leave great news like this in a voice mail." This is a lie but I put everything I have into selling it. "Maybe we can try and reach her together tonight when we get back to my place." I offer a hopeful, half-pleading smile.

"Sure." His eyes are plumbing mine. "That's a good idea." Then he matches my smile and puts his arm around my shoulders. But I can see that the damage has been done.

Five

༄

Bree

The Sandcastle

I can tell as soon as Kendra picks up the phone that Lauren's on the other end of the line. There's something in Kendra's voice that's there only when she speaks to her daughter. It's not that she gushes or overemphasizes or anything but there's a subtle something extra there, a connection, an instinct, like that thing that lets an infant know to cling to or fall quiet for its mother. I get a special tone, too, but it's slightly different in timbre. I'm aware of the widely differing vocal cues from long years of comparison. I hear what steals into my voice when I speak to Rafe and Lily; it's there even when I'm frustrated or angry with them. My own mother has no tonal variation that I've ever been able to discern; she has one tone whether she's speaking to me or a class or a group of possible sponsors.

Kendra doesn't leave the kitchen where we've been drinking hot cocoa or make any attempt to exclude me—she hates the distance between Lauren and me and has made it clear to both of us that she'd like nothing more than to see us "kiss and make up." So I not only hear the happiness in her voice and see it on her face, I also see the slight tension that settles on her shoulders as she listens. Something has taken her by surprise.

"Oh my goodness! Really?" She holds the phone tighter to

her ear. "Why . . . how . . . oh my gosh! Right there in the restaurant? How wonderful!" She listens again intently. Then she
covers the mouthpiece and whispers, "Lauren's engaged!"

Shock and surprise take my breath away. Waves of conflicting emotion wash over me. There is excitement, even delight.
Lauren and I dreamed of this when we were little girls. Whis-
pered about it for hours on end. Imagined our weddings and
each other's roles in them repeatedly, sometimes even scripting
them out.

Those initial happy emotions give way to darker ones. Dis-
may. Regret. A yawning loss. Because I'm hearing this second-
hand where once I would have heard it even before Kendra.
Would have known it might happen. The stab of jealousy comes
last, and I latch on to it because it's the sharpest and most familiar, the one I've been nursing the longest. And it doesn't hurt as
much.

I watch Kendra's face for more clues. It must be the playwright that I Googled not long after they started dating. A high
achiever even by Lauren's standards. Good-looking and from a
wealthy, philanthropic family. Lauren has never done anything
by halves so I guess I shouldn't be so surprised. Since there's no
longer any need to pretend I'm not listening, I move in closer to
mine Kendra's voice and body language for more clues.

"He wants to talk to me?" Kendra asks, clearly pleased. "Of
course. Put him on."

There's a long pause as she presumably listens to the man
who's about to become her son-in-law use his gift with words
on her.

"Of course I forgive you for not asking me first," she says,
like the Richmond debutante I know she once was. "I promise
I've been asking her to bring you down." She laughs. "Yes, she
can be a little stubborn." And then because Kendra would never
willingly hurt anyone's feelings, especially her daughter's (how
else could she walk the minefield between us all these years

without being blown up?) she adds, "But I believe she comes by that naturally."

Apparently there's more because she chuckles, nods, smiles. "Yes. Lauren and I can talk about the details later. But I'm so excited for you both and I look forward to meeting you."

She laughs at whatever he says next and then adds, "I know just how discriminating my daughter is, so you are clearly a paragon of all things." She laughs again. "Besides, how could I not approve of someone who loves my daughter?"

I busy myself rinsing out our mugs and puttering about until the good-byes are finished.

I spend a little of that time secretly hoping that Lauren will ask to speak to me, that she'll want to use this pivotal moment to apologize for appropriating the book we plotted together and using it to become the Queen of Beach Reads. (At which point I might attempt to point out that my not getting on that bus to New York was not about her. That she is not in fact the center of everyone else's universe.)

This doesn't happen, of course, and so I focus on smashing my jealously back down into the dark hole where it lives so that Kendra won't see it. I owe this woman virtually everything and will not intrude on her right to be happy for her daughter. I'll have to settle for being happy for Kendra.

When she hangs up she's crying what are clearly happy tears. "I'm so happy for them both. And so incredibly grateful that she'll have someone to love and to share her life with. Like you do. It's not even too late for children." She whispers this last part as if Lauren might overhear her.

I just nod and smile in a brainless bobbleheaded way while Kendra continues to both grin and cry; a contradictory response that reminds me of "a monkey's wedding," a phrase my parents once told me South Africans use to describe a sun-shower.

It's odd how huge this announcement feels to me when in truth it has nothing to do with me at all. Kendra envelops me in a hug and I wish that Lauren and I were still five-year-olds who believed we were sisters and that a pinky swear could actually last forever.

Neither of us mentions that there's been no talk at all of THE DRESS. And whether Lauren plans to wear it.

Kendra

I guess I shouldn't be surprised when I dream about weddings all night. It's all vague, barely formed images. Bits and pieces of everything from Princess Di and Charles's "wedding of the century," to Prince Harry and Meghan Markle's more recent joining. Liz and Chris on *30 Rock* appear. Bree and Clay's wedding flits by and includes shots of Lauren's unhappy face. Of course, no disturbing dream sequence would be complete without a highlight reel from my own botched ceremony. Me being helped into THE DRESS. Me walking down the aisle on my father's arm. The expression on Jake's face as he watches me draw near.

I wake groggy and distressed and with an odd sense of foreboding that no amount of splashing cold water on my face dispels. I pull on my bathrobe and walk into the kitchen to brew my first cup of coffee, telling myself that it's silly to react this way to such good news. That Lauren is a grown woman who knows her own mind and not the panicked twenty-one-year-old I was. I pull my wool shawl from its hook near the back door and wrap it around me then carry the coffee outside to the back deck, where I lean over the railing and stare out across the dunes and the narrow strip of beach that separates them from the ocean.

Even as I sip coffee in my favorite spot on earth, my mind is still filled with images of my wedding day, the horrible way it ended, and all that followed.

I had no idea where I was headed when I tiptoed out of my

aunt Velda's house, more to keep my aunt from being an accessory than because I thought she'd bar my way, buckled my swaddled newborn daughter into the bucket seat next to me, and fired up the engine of the blue 1970 Dodge Challenger convertible my father had given me on my sixteenth birthday. I just got on Highway 64 and headed east until I reached the coast of North Carolina, then drove over two long, wind-battered bridges that seemed to go on forever and left no question that you'd left the mainland behind.

I stopped for gas and snacks on Roanoke Island, where the Outer Banks begin, then took yet another bridge that spanned Roanoke Sound to NC 12, a winding, narrow two-lane strip of asphalt that connects most of the islands together and that locals still refer to as the Beach Road.

From my deck I can see the vague outline of Jennette's Pier jutting out into the ocean a couple miles down the beach. That's where I ended up that first day and where I carried Lauren all the way out to the tip of the fishing pier where I stood right out over the ocean.

I still remember those first heady breaths of air. How blue and clear the sky was. The rush of wind in my ears. It was wild and untamed. I felt freedom and possibility all the way down to my toes.

At the time there was nothing much around but a few restaurants and businesses and a couple mom-and-pop hotels and cottage courts. Weathered houses on stilts backed up to the beach. There was scrub everywhere and small cottages here and there.

Even now when I catch myself complaining about the traffic and the noise and the outlet malls, I remember the emptiness that stretched between small outposts of civilization. How few structures stood in the way of the near-constant wind. The sand it tossed and blew around, building mountainous dunes that became part of the scenery. The sea oats bent double beneath its onslaught. The sound of waves crashing or sometimes swishing on- and offshore.

It was so bold and so intensely beautiful I thought my heart might stop. And despite having been raised in the carefully manicured city of Richmond, it felt right. A place you would run to, not from. And of all the mistakes I made then and in the years that followed, it was the one thing I was right about.

As the sky lightens and separates from the Atlantic I settle into an Adirondack chair and try to picture my daughter and her fiancé together. I've seen Spencer's picture but never a photo of the two of them. Lauren's told me all about his plays and his talent and how much she admires his work, but only small scraps about his background and his family. I wonder what their relationship is like and how marriage will change it. Who will move in with whom? Or if they'll start fresh in a place that they can think of as *theirs*?

The sun continues its rise and even after all these years I don't take the sight for granted. I breathe in the salt-tinged breeze, my face turned up to the warming sun. Finally, I make my way back into the kitchen to pull ingredients for the blue-berry muffins I'm due to deliver today to two B and Bs. My triple-chocolate and Italian wedding cakes are delivered fresh several times a week. On select mornings I cook a full breakfast on-site for the guests.

I began learning how to cook out of desperation not long after we arrived here. My mother had always had "help," and I didn't really pay much attention to how food got on the table. In college at Washington and Lee I lived in a sorority house where food also miraculously appeared when I was hungry.

I was surprised to discover I had a knack for cooking and especially for baking. That it was relaxing in its way, and that it could help supplement the odd jobs I ended up working to keep a roof over our heads, food in our bellies, and clothes on our backs. I'm still not Julia Child or even Mrs. Fields, but cooking has been an important addition to my skill set.

While I pull out the mixing bowls and preheat the oven, I'm still thinking about Lauren. When I start letting myself imagine her wedding day, I realize that I have no idea if they already have a date in mind or whether they might consider having it here. There was something in her voice last night that told me to tread lightly and not to ask too many questions. Like why she's never even hinted that a proposal might be imminent.

I know that Lauren can more than take care of herself, so there'd be no reason other than love for her to get married. I'm not one of those mothers who's stewed and fretted that her daughter was still single, but now that it's happening, I realize just how glad I am that she'll have someone to share her life with. Isn't that what every mother wants for her child?

I close my eyes and stop stirring the batter. I have always chosen to believe that my mother loved me. But she never could stand up to my father even when I knew she wanted to. She could hardly stand up to life at all. Her abdication, her inability to cope, made me stronger. It made me vow to always be there to protect my child. No matter what the threat. To give my love and approval without rules and strings and hoops that had to be jumped through to receive it.

I manage to pull my thoughts back just before they plummet into the abyss of anger and regret that always accompanies memories of my parents and the ridiculously impulsive acts that set me on a path I never saw coming.

I'm debating whether to have a third cup of coffee or get dressed when I hear a car pull into the drive. Bree was just here last night and my friends know I spend most mornings baking and delivering, so I peek out the front window to see if it's a lost tourist or maybe the new baking pans I ordered from Amazon.

The car is low and sporty and too expensive for an Amazon

delivery. The man who unfolds from the driver's seat is tall and overdressed. No doubt some tourist who hasn't figured out which way the mileposts run. Or thinks the Sandcastle is one of the Unpainted Aristocracy built by early-summer families that front the dunes a little farther south. Though the Sandcastle is newer than those, it's obviously not one of the brightly colored and oversized beach rentals that now fill every inch of what were once long stretches of sand and scrub. Maybe given the way he's eyeing my house, he's a Realtor looking to snap up yet another original beach box house from someone who can't afford to hang on to it.

I begin to turn away with the intention of ignoring him if he knocks when I notice something familiar about the set of his shoulders, the way he moves. He glances at the steep wooden staircase that leads up to the front porch and I see his face. My stomach drops. My heart pounds painfully, and I wonder for one of those heartbeats if it's possible to summon someone simply by dreaming or thinking about them. But if that were true he would have been here years ago.

I step back from the window so I can't be seen, but I can't stop looking at him. His dark hair is threaded with silver and there's not as much of it as there used to be. But he's still tall. And he's still absurdly handsome. His taste in clothes has definitely improved.

The last time I saw him he was wearing an ill-chosen powder-blue tuxedo. And I was wearing THE DRESS.

Six

I'm frozen in place, my feet glued to the wood floor, as he walks up the steps to the front porch. The windows are open so I hear the echo of each footfall. He hesitates before he raps on the front door and I squeeze back against the curtain, unsure what to do. Run very quietly for the bedroom and simply wait until he gives up and goes away? Or open the door and brazen it out? I do neither.

I've imagined seeing Jake a million times in the last four decades, but in each imagining I was completely prepared. And I was definitely never wearing a stained chenille bathrobe. Or cowering behind curtains.

My mind is a hamster on a wheel, round and round, getting nowhere. I'm a teenager again. I can practically feel pimples popping out all over my face. I wouldn't be surprised if I touched my mouth and discovered I was wearing braces.

He's the first man I ever loved. The first man I slept with. The man I meant to and should have married. And, let us not forget, the father of my child.

I decide to go into my bedroom and put on clothes. And maybe a little makeup. If he's still here when I get back I'll open the door.

I turn to tiptoe from the window and the floorboard squeaks. Afraid to move, I hear him walk from the door over to the front window. I will myself to disappear. Or shrink. Or anything besides what I'm doing, which is quivering like a trapped animal in plain view.

"Kendra?" He speaks quietly but the sound of his voice slices through me. In that instant I remember how it sounded when he first told me that he loved me. How it quivered when he asked me to marry him. The wry little observations that he'd whisper in my ear when we were in a group of people.

I tell myself I can still go straight to the bedroom, close the door behind me, and pretend I didn't hear him. That I can hide as long as I need to. What's another couple minutes after all this time? It's not like he's going to break the door down or anything. If he'd ever really wanted to find me he could have done it a long time ago.

He raps on the window. "Kendra? Is that you?"

I consider the distance to my bedroom. It's not far but he'll be watching me run away. Which is no doubt how he remembers me. Only last time I was dragging a train behind me. A train that kept getting caught on the pews.

I straighten, set my shoulders, and raise my chin. Grateful that there's no mirror in the living room, I turn. And see him step from the window and move back to the front door.

There's no help for it. The time I've both wished for and dreaded has finally come. I tell myself it's a relief. But I'm too nervous to believe it. I feel like a clown who's been juggling balls for so long that he has no idea what to do when they fall on the floor and go skittering across it.

I move to the door. Run my sweaty palms down the sides of my robe and wish I didn't have to do this in my pajamas. Armor would be good. Or at least a little emotional Kevlar. I take a last deep breath, open the door, and stick my head out. Do I have toothpaste on my chin? Is my hair standing straight up? I honestly can't remember.

"It *is* you." It's a statement and a question.

I nod. It's all I can manage. I have no words. I just keep looking into his eyes, studying his face, mapping every line—the small web of them around his eyes. The brackets on either side of his mouth. I note that his chin is still square and his jaw is firm. His cheeks are slightly ruddy. And his eyes—they're still a whiskey-colored brown. But the warmth and twinkle of good humor that I remember is absent. He may be strong and sure on the outside, but his eyes tell a different story.

"May I come in?"

I step back in answer though I'm still debating whether to turn and run. He steps inside and glances around the room with its faded woven Native American rug, the sparse garage-sale furnishings, the wall of bookcases bulging with books and seashells and decades of found objects that share shelf space with framed photos of sunrises over the ocean and sunsets over the sound. Scenes I keep shooting in hopes of one day doing them justice.

He's zeroing in on baby photos of Lauren and his eyebrows knit. I honestly can't think what to say or do next. The oven timer goes off and I motion him toward the kitchen, where I pick up the oven mitts, pull the muffin trays out of the oven, and set them on the racks to cool.

"You bake." Once again a statement and a question.

"Yes. I'm actually kind of good at it. Believe me, no one's more surprised than me." I wince as I realize I'm babbling. "Would you like some coffee?"

He nods and I wave him toward the table then busy myself pouring him a cup, carrying the cream and sugar over. Anything to keep moving, to put off whatever's coming. I overfill my own cup and watch it slosh over the rim as I bring it to the table.

Then I sit across from him, which is as far away as I can get while still being able to look at him as much as I want. His hands are clenched tightly on the table as I study him studying me.

I still can't believe he's here. Emotions I can barely identify swamp me and I know that he can see everything I'm feeling. I don't play poker because I don't have the face for it. His gives away little. Or perhaps I've just forgotten how to read him.

I'm trying to think of an opening line. Something mild and nonconfrontational that will allow me to prepare myself, put up my shields. If I can just keep the conversation civil then maybe . . .

"Is Lauren James my daughter?"

Any hope of chitchat and working up to the hard stuff is blown out of the water.

Still I hesitate. Despite all the years I've had to prepare I'm not prepared at all.

His eyes are pinned to my face. I nod numbly.

"How could you not tell me?" He doesn't raise his voice, but his anger is sharp and clear now. So is his pain.

"I wanted to. When I first found out I was pregnant I was too ashamed of what I'd done to you—leaving you at the altar like that—to say anything. And then my parents sent me to my aunt Velda's to have her. They wanted me to put her up for adoption. Only I couldn't . . . couldn't do it."

"And it never occurred to you that I would want to know her? Be a part of her life?" He runs a hand through his hair. His voice breaks.

"Of course it did." This is an understatement. There were days, sometimes weeks, that I was desperate for him, for his love, which I'd destroyed, for his help, for any contact with him at all. "But I'd made such a mess of everything. And by the time I'd worked up the nerve, I heard you were marrying someone else and I . . . I knew I didn't have the right to disrupt that, too."

The bleak look on his face brings me to a halt. I swipe at the tears that are slipping down my cheeks and try to understand why this is happening now. "How did you find out?"

He takes a newspaper clipping from his pocket and lays it on the kitchen table. It's a brief piece about a book signing in Charlotte. It includes Lauren's author photo and a caption that reads *Author Lauren James to speak at Park Road Books as part of a tour of the Southeast to promote her latest novel.*

"My wife saw the resemblance to my mother. And of course she knew about what happened at our wedding and that my former fiancée's mother's maiden name was Jameson. She turned out to be quite the amateur sleuth. She figured it out."

"But that photo, that tour was almost fifteen years ago." I put the clipping down, trying to understand what had changed, why this was happening.

"Yes. She put together a file on Lauren James, who grew up Lauren Jameson in the Outer Banks. Only she never mentioned it to me."

"Why not?"

"Because no matter what I did to try to reassure her, she was convinced I was still in love with you. She lived in terror that you would show up one day and try to take me away from her and our children, break up our family." He scrubs at his face. "I never once looked at another woman or said or did anything that might make her believe that. But she could never let go of the idea. She fed on it. She was . . . unstable." He looks up at me. "Like . . ."

"My mother." I say it quietly, but I can't bring myself to tell him how much Aunt Velda told me about his marriage and his wife. About her unpredictable behavior. The institutions she'd been in and out of. That it was Jake who had been mother and father to their two sons. Staying quiet and keeping out of the way seemed the only choice, the only way to protect both Lauren and her father.

"What made her decide to tell you now?" I ask, still trying to sort it out. When Aunt Velda died ten years ago so did news of Jake. At the time I told myself it was better not to be privy to the details of his troubled marriage or his family life. That I had to let go completely. I was careful never to Google or search for any sign of him. "What made her change her mind?"

"She didn't." His smile is a horrible twisted thing. "She died six months ago. She'd apparently been hoarding her sleeping pills until she had enough to go to sleep and not wake up. She used to call that a coward's death, but I guess it became too attractive to resist."

He falls silent and the regret and guilt are written all over his face. "I only found the clipping when I was cleaning out her things last week. It took about fifteen minutes to do the math and track you down. After all those years of being so careful not to, for fear of tipping her over the edge."

I have the oddest feeling that both of us are going to cry. If I had any right at all I'd put my arms around him and offer comfort.

"It's ironic, isn't it?" he says. "Both of the women I chose to marry decided I didn't deserve to know that I had a daughter." Anger seethes under the sadness.

I take the jab. I deserve it and more. "I am sorry, Jake. I really am. I . . . I had to do what I thought was best for Lauren. I couldn't put her in the middle of what was going on in your marriage and your life." Nor did I want to add to his burden after the blow I'd already dealt him.

His smile breaks my heart. "You know what hurts the most?"

I wait in silence for his answer, because from the tone of his voice it sounds like everything hurts.

"That all this time Lauren's assumed I didn't give a rat's ass about her. My child who is now an adult has spent her entire life believing I abandoned her."

"Oh no. That's not what she thought." I sit up, eager now to tell him the good news. "She never thought that. I'd never let that happen."

"No?" His tone says he doesn't believe me. And so do his eyes. And who can blame him?

"No, of course not because . . ." I stop when I come to my senses and realize that what I did tell her was in many ways worse than the truth.

"Because what?" His eyes narrow.

I swallow and it takes everything I have not to drop my eyes or leap up from the table so that I can run and hide. "Because . . ." I swallow again. "She doesn't think you abandoned her. She thinks you're dead."

Seven

Bree

I'd like to pretend that turning forty hasn't thrown me. That I've successfully treated it like any other birthday. That I'm not upset that Lauren is getting married or jealous that she's not only having the career I once dreamed of but is now venturing into the territory I staked out for myself.

I've been snippy and out of sorts since the big four-oh! and the engagement news has only made it worse. Not that anyone seems to have noticed. Clay and Lily are busy with their own lives and don't really notice what I'm up to unless I force them to. Rafe, who's in his junior year at Carolina, communicates primarily by text and most of his communication revolves around asking for extra spending money or complaining about a professor, or his part-time job, or whatever else is on his mind in that moment. I am the recipient of his thoughts and emotions; something I treasure as a mother even as I've come to believe that no news really is good news. And, of course, it rarely occurs to him to ask about me in any way. To my children I'm simply She Who Is Always There. And given how *not* "there" my parents were, I'm proud of the fact that my children never had reason to doubt their parents' love or affection.

But the truth is I could be out burgling houses or doing some other shocking thing that no one would ever expect of me, and no one would believe it even if they stumbled across me wearing a stocking over my head and climbing into someone's window.

I walk to the front of Title Waves and prop open the door to let in the fresh air and sunshine, bothered by the fact that they're right. I never do anything unexpected. Or wicked. Or unacceptable. I am a people-pleaser. Knowing that you're this way because your parents virtually abandoned you doesn't help you stop bending over backward to satisfy others. Or encourage you to go on a local crime spree. (Not that you could get away with anything here, where the population is still shy of 1,500 and everyone would recognize you during your B and E despite a mask, a hood, or any other disguise you might come up with.)

When the members of the Classics Book Club arrive at noon sharp, we settle at the round table in the front window and spread our Regency era–themed potluck meal across its scarred maple top. We kicked off our reading of Jane Austen's classics five months ago with a special screening of *The Jane Austen Book Club* at the Pioneer, which has the distinction of being the longest-running family-owned movie theater in the country.

Today we're discussing *Persuasion*, the last novel Austen completed before she died. In my opinion it's the most beautiful of her works even though it's not the witty drawing room comedy of manners she was known for. A number of the club members have followed recipes from *Cooking with Jane Austen* and *Dinner with Mr. Darcy*, cookbooks that I ordered to complement the reading.

Mrs. McKinnon has brought a "pigeon" pie, the center of the crust decorated with slash marks meant to look like pigeons' feet. We also have cold meats and cheeses as well as biscuits and jam, which we wash down with a modern version of elder wine as we talk. For dessert we enjoy the same plum cake that was served at Mrs. Weston's wedding in *Emma*, and a lemon cake, because it was Mr. Darcy's favorite.

The food is delicious and the discussion lively. We linger until the members with young children have to head out for after-school activities. Mrs. McKinnon, who also belongs to the three other book clubs I host at the store, including the some-what rowdier B's, short for "books, broads, and booze," stays to help me clean up.

"Did you finish?" Mrs. McKinnon isn't the first person who's asked whether I'd typed *The End* before my fortieth, and I give her the same answer I've given everyone. "Almost. But I decided that after all the time it's taken me, I don't want to rush the ending."

"Of course, dear. I understand completely." Her smile is kind, but I can see that she doesn't understand at all. Even I am not sure how it's taken me a decade and a half to write this book.

"I imagine it will be difficult to let go of it once it's done."

This observation strikes home like an arrow to the heart. Am I afraid of finishing? Is it that and not my family, or my business, or the other demands on my time that have stretched it out all these years? Do I have a fear of failure? Or is it a fear of success? Or am I just afraid of competing with Lauren? If no one ever sees *Heart of Gold*, I can tell myself it's the best thing ever written. Once someone else reads it I may have to accept that it's not.

"It will be odd, that's for sure." I hug her good-bye and am still thinking about her question and my lack of a definitive answer as I settle at the front desk and open my laptop. I've written the "black moment" when everything falls apart and it seems as if there's no hope, and rewritten it more times than I can count. All I have to do now is craft a satisfying resolution for my characters that demonstrates how much they've grown and changed. In my experience characters that stay the same are never really interesting. Neither are people.

I skim through the last chapter I finished, trying not to think about how little I've changed over the years. How much my life stays the same. It takes a few minutes before I manage to shake these thoughts off and sink into the story. I feel welcomed by old familiar friends—friends I've tortured and forced into situations they were ill equipped for—and whom I now have to bring out the other side.

Just when I'm about to give up, I see the way I can bring the threads together. I feel a small thrill of anticipation as I lower my fingers to the keyboard, and I barely breathe as they begin to move of their own accord. I'm typing dialogue without conscious thought as if my characters are living the scene and I'm just trying to capture it. I am sucked into the story. I occupy their heads. After all these years I know them in ways I may never know myself.

My shoulders unclench and so does my jaw. Everything, including the store, disappears. Although I'm following their lead, I feel powerful. I have control over everything. Who lives and who dies. Who is beautiful and who is loved and cherished. Who discovers they're so much more than they realized. Who discovers they're less.

Whitney is direct and sassy and asking for what she wants. Making it clear that she doesn't *need* Heath even though she loves him. Demanding that Heath live up to his promises.

As the scene plays out, I lose myself in the culmination of their journeys. But then, after two full pages of witty, yet heartfelt, dialogue my fingers falter. If I finish their story Heath and Whitney won't need me anymore. And I'll have nowhere to disappear to. My eyes close as I try to push myself to continue.

Which is when I hear footsteps and a clearly masculine clearing of the throat. "Excuse me."

I look up and see a nice-looking stranger somewhere in his early to mid sixties.

His eyes are brown. There's something in the way he holds his body and cocks his head that seems familiar, but he's definitely not a local. "Do you have any books by Lauren James?"

I do sell Lauren's books. In fact, I sell a ton of them since she's a native and occasionally uses the Outer Banks for her settings. I always smile when someone asks about her, though most people who've been here long enough know not to ask.

I have, of course, read all of them, including *Sandcastle Sunrise*, the book we plotted and were planning to write together. That was possibly the most painful thing I've ever done. And I've been through natural childbirth.

The entire time I was reading it I kept imagining how *I* would have written it and how different, maybe even better, the book would have been if I'd coauthored it. Not that any of the reviewers, even those who didn't love it, seemed to think there was anything missing.

"I understand she grew up around here. My wife has always been a big fan of hers and I thought I'd stop and see if you had any signed copies."

I put on "the smile." I do, in fact, have signed copies. Lauren's publisher sends me a certain number of each new release, which delights my customers and which I'm very careful not to point out is probably Lauren simply trying to rub her success in my face.

We chitchat a little as he selects then buys signed copies of every one of Lauren's books that I have on hand, and I think what a nice gesture it is for a man to make toward his wife. I doubt Clay knows my reading taste well enough to choose a book for me. But I do know he'd know not to bring me one of Lauren's.

"I've always believed that you can tell a lot about an author by their characters. Would you agree?"

"I think it varies," I say honestly. "Especially if an author is prolific."

"Do you know Lauren James?"

"Mm-hmmm." My lips purse as if I've sucked on a lemon. And I'm nodding for some unknown reason. "We went through school together. We were friends before she moved to New York and all." I attempt to unpurse my lips, but they're stuck so I just keep nodding.

"Well, thank you very much." He takes his box of books and turns.

"Thank you. I hope your wife enjoys them."

His shoulders flinch slightly but he keeps walking. After he's gone I manage to get my lips unstuck. The temperature has started dropping, so I close the front door, move back to the counter, and return to the manuscript.

I feel my brow furrow as I try to count up the scenes I still need to write. Maybe five or six. Maybe one final chapter and an epilogue could do it. I won't really know until I get the words on the page, but still I feel a rush of excitement.

If I bear down and push myself, I could be finished in a matter of days. I imagine the exhilaration of finally typing *The End*. The euphoria that will follow. I've never done it as an adult, and I'm desperate to prove I can.

But this tiny voice that I recognize as my most insecure self pipes up with, *Not so fast. Once you type* The End, *then what?*

Lauren

New York City

The best part by far of writing a book is getting to type *The End*. Of course it doesn't really mean you're finished. *The End* is just the prelude to revisions, which can be anything from a few small tweaks to a gut job. Then come the copyedits, which require you to address any query the copy editor assigned to review the manuscript has noted. (This can be anything from the incorrect day of the week based on their assessment of the timeline that they have taken the time to lay out on an actual calendar, to the questioning of the accent you've given your character even though you're the one who grew up with this accent and they've never left Manhattan.) They used to work with red pens, now they make their comments electronically on the manuscript in a little balloon off to the side. After that you'll proof the galleys, which requires another complete read-through while you look for small typos and mistakes. And don't even get me started on the regret you sometimes feel over a word choice or a missed opportunity that you can't go in and fix.

This is why by the time all of these passes are over a lot of authors can't bear to even look at their creation again. Afterward, when readers start e-mailing about the typos they've noticed, I'm always surprised. All I can tell you is it's not due to laziness or a lack of concern. It's just that people are not perfect and shit happens.

With a groan I reach for what I'm pretty sure is my fourth cup of coffee, though I know from years of experience that while caffeine can help you stay awake it doesn't make you more talented or creative any more than alcohol makes you wittier and more entertaining.

My engagement ring sparkles on my finger as I lift the cup to my lips, and I catch myself wondering if it has somehow sucked all my creative energy into it. As if I could blame a beautiful piece of jewelry when it's clearly what the ring represents that's thrown me. Between the surprise proposal and my declining sales figures, I've barely written a usable paragraph.

Part of the problem is that it's been three days since we

called my mother to tell her about the engagement, and I know she's waiting to hear from me. Only I have a hard time lying to her and given that I'm still processing things, I'm not sure I'll be able to sound as happy and excited as I *should* be.

I write one more sentence then waste another hour waffling. Finally I slap a grin on my face—I've read that pretending to be happy can actually produce endorphins that make it so—and pick up the phone.

"Lauren?"

"Hi, Mom!" I say cheerily.

"Hi, darling!" she exclaims back, and I know I need to dial it back a notch. "I can't stop thinking about your good news."

"Yeah, it's really great, isn't it?" I'm still grinning like a crazy person.

"Yes, it is." I know that she's smiling and I suddenly wish we were in the same room. "How are you feeling? Has the excitement simmered down to a dull roar?"

"Yes. No. I don't know. I was just so taken by surprise I'm having a hard time sorting it all out."

"So you'd discussed marriage, but you had no idea he was going to propose that night?"

"Not exactly. We had discussed living together, but not in any really serious way."

"I can't believe he did it in front of an audience and with backup singers."

"Yeah, well, you know that question about if a tree falls in the forest and no one's there to hear it, did it make a sound? With Spencer if there's no audience then it probably didn't happen."

There's a silence on the other end. She knows just how much I hate being the center of attention and I have no doubt that she's already seen through the grinning. But she's a bit off her game, too. Normally she'd already be all over the positives of the situation.

"But you are glad? I mean, you do want to marry him, don't you?" she asks more tentatively.

"Who wouldn't want to marry Spencer?" I say even though we both know this is not actually an answer. "Of course I want to marry him!" I add the exclamation point because it's true and because my grin is slipping. "I just wasn't expecting it. And you know me, I don't really like surprises. Plus, the cast was singing and everyone in the restaurant was watching."

"It does sound like a very significant romantic gesture." There's the positivity I'm used to.

"Yes," I reply, my grin slipping further. "But I guess I would have preferred some warning. And maybe a little more privacy for such a private moment."

"Aww, honey."

Her understanding makes me want to cry. "Well, I suppose one person's romantic moment can be someone else's uncomfortable one." My attempt at humor falls flat. And there's another silence on the other end.

"You do realize that you're allowed to change your mind and your answer. Until you walk down the aisle. And even sometimes after you do." She pauses and something I can't identify steals into her voice. "There are people who suddenly change their minds even at the altar. I read a statistic somewhere that five percent of marriages get called off *on* the day of the wedding."

I snort. "Where in the world did you read that? I mean, who keeps those kinds of statistics and who besides a crackpot would show up and then change their mind?"

There's another silence on the other end. I gather that I'm missing something, but I can't imagine what.

"Have you talked about where you'll get married?" she asks.

"No, not yet." I've given up on the smiling and am now going for matter-of-fact.

"Well, you know I can't wait to meet Spencer. When could you bring him for a visit?"

"I agree it's definitely time for you and Spencer to meet. But why don't you fly up here?" I try not to beg, but the very last thing I want to do right now is come down and parade Spencer around. And how will I explain the ex-best friend I've barely mentioned and the former boyfriend she's married to? "You could meet his family and we could discuss possibilities. There's plenty of time to work out wedding details. It's not like we've set a date yet or anything."

"I'd really prefer that you come here, Lauren. It's been far too long and I'm sure Spencer would like to see where you grew up."

It's unlike my mother to insist. She's the last one to push or prod and she's generally been willing to come to New York or meet me somewhere before. We've had "girls'" trips to Charleston and New Orleans. Once we spent a week in the Keys.

"Is everything okay?" Suddenly I'm imagining all kinds of worst-case scenarios. "Are you all right? You're not . . . sick or anything, are you?" I can't handle even the idea of my mother being ill. I swallow. (A turbocharged imagination is a much bigger asset when you're writing fiction than it is in real life.) Within ten seconds I go from illness to incurable. She is my entire family. We are all the other has. Is forty too old to be an orphan? Clearly all that grinning has turned me into a crazy person.

"Of course I'm not ill," she says. "I'd just really love for you two to come down so that Spencer and I can get acquainted and we can show him around. Maybe we can even look at venues. And, of course, that way you can try on THE DRESS."

She has just dangled the ultimate carrot in front of me. And given how rarely my mother ever asks for anything, it's not as if I'm going to refuse. "All right. I'll check Spencer's schedule and see how soon he can get away."

Eight

————————

᳁

Lauren

Spencer's parents, Gene and Nancy Harrison, are very lovely people who sometimes seem to forget that New York City is part of a larger country. In their early seventies, they look and act younger—which is easier when you are wealthy, of course— and get on remarkably well for people who met in grammar school and started dating when Nancy was only fifteen. They have a wide circle of friends, enjoy good food, see every show and performance worth seeing, are almost fanatic supporters of the arts, and serve on numerous boards and committees. They live in an incredible brownstone on East 65th between Fifth and Madison, just a block from Central Park, that's been in the Harrison family for a couple generations. While they have traveled extensively in Europe and Asia and parts of the Middle East, if they had a family motto it would be "If you can't do it or get it in New York it is most likely not worth doing or having."

All in all they've been very welcoming and I've grown increasingly comfortable in their home, but I don't see myself sprawling on the Louis XIV sofa anytime soon.

Tonight we're celebrating Spencer and my engagement with a family dinner that includes Gene and Nancy, Gene's mother, Grace, who is in her early nineties and has a private suite of rooms that take up half of one floor of the five-story home, and Spencer's younger sister, Molly, her husband, Mac, and their two-year-old twins, Matthew and Mariah. (Who could totally appear on *Sesame Street* the next time the letter *M* is presented.) Spencer's older sister, Anna, along with her second husband and his children from a former marriage, lives in San Francisco. A city these dyed-in-the-wool New Yorkers visit on occasion, but about which they seem ambivalent.

Although this was billed as a casual family meal, it takes place in the formal dining room, and we're served by two maids in uniform.

"I know how nervous Spencer was," Grace says after we're seated. "Were you surprised?" This is my first clue that everyone in his family knew he was going to propose before I did.

"Definitely. In fact, it took me a little while to understand what was happening," I admit.

"I wish you guys could have been there," Spencer says. "But at least we have video." He reaches for his iPhone. "I had Peter film it for posterity." Peter is Spencer's publicist/social media person. This explains how a statement, select clips of the performance, and the proposal appeared online and across all social media platforms within minutes of my acceptance.

He hits play and holds his iPhone up so we can view the screen and I'm relieved to see that it was shot over my shoulder so that the focus is on the cast performance and Spencer dropping down on one knee. I wonder briefly whether the angle was chosen to give me privacy or as a protective measure in case something went wrong or my answer wasn't what he was expecting, but then I realize the reasons don't really matter. What matters is his eagerness to make the proposal special and that he loves me enough to want to share the future with me. It's not as if I'm unaware of his flair and larger-than-life personality—it's that openness and enthusiasm that first attracted me. I'm not the first woman to choose a man who is in many ways her opposite.

They applaud when the video ends and Spencer stands and

takes an exaggerated bow, which is something that has clearly played out within this family many times before.

"Well done, big brother!" Molly says as the first course is served. "This is so exciting. Which venues are you considering?"

Their eyes turn to me. "Oh well, we haven't really talked about that yet," I stammer.

"We could have it at the Harvard Club," Nancy suggests as if it's just occurred to her. "The facilities are so beautiful."

"Or how about The Plaza?" Grace asks. "It's a classic. I spent my wedding night at The Plaza."

I try not to wince as I think about my recent tea there with Chris.

"Ooh, I know. What about the New York Public Library?" Molly asks. "We looked at it for our wedding. And Carrie Bradshaw chose it in *Sex and the City*. She was a writer, too."

"Yes, but she didn't actually get married there," I point out. "Remember when Big just drove right by?" I don't add that Carrie Bradshaw is a fictional character. Or that when Bree and I used to imagine our weddings, mine was always small and intimate.

"Oh, right." She puts a forkful of salad in her mouth.

"By that line of reasoning we could have it at the Music Box." This is the Broadway theater where *The Music in Me* is playing. "I could write a new song and have Brett choreograph it. Maybe the wedding party could perform it as we take the stage for the ceremony." Spencer's tone is teasing, but the reality is that while Spencer actually could appear in one of his musicals, I could not. "I don't think I'm up for dancing up the aisle in a long white gown and heels." Nor could I bear to have a crowd of people watch me try.

There's no shortage of ideas, each one larger and splashier than the last. I'm grateful when the main course is served. As his rack of lamb is placed in front of him Spencer says, "As soon as I can clear my schedule we're going down to the Outer Banks for a week, so that I can meet Lauren's mother and see where she grew up. And Kendra's already brought up the idea of having the wedding down there."

"Oh, but that's so . . ." Nancy stops herself just before her nose wrinkles. "I've certainly heard lovely things about the Outer Banks. I understand there are some very large, beautiful beach homes that can hold multiple families. But I don't know how many of our friends or even family would be willing to travel down there. I guess it would depend on . . ." She cocks her head in my direction. "What date have you chosen, dear?"

The piece of lamb I've just put in my mouth doubles in size and threatens to choke me.

"We haven't really discussed that yet," Spencer says, and if my mouth weren't still unpleasantly full of meat, I'd kiss him for not mentioning that he's already tried to have this conversation. "There's no need to pick a date right now, although as far as I'm concerned, the sooner, the better." He takes my hand and gives it a squeeze and I think back to the discussion we did have about how to find a place to live that will work for both of us given that I prefer the Upper West Side and Spencer loves the West Village and that I need absolute quiet to work while Spencer's work is often collaborative and noisy.

"Oh, of course. There's no need to rush," Nancy says. "There isn't, is there?"

It takes me a moment to understand what she's asking. When I do, I actually blush. Spencer rolls his eyes. "No, Mother. This is not a shotgun wedding. Though I wouldn't be averse to a couple of rug rats of our own one day."

I put down my fork. I just turned forty and while I've imagined menopause in the not-too-distant future, this is the first time I've let myself imagine having a child. Something I'd once dreamed of but more recently assumed was off the table. We eat for a few minutes in silence if you don't count the stream of chatter from Matthew and Mariah or the number of times their utensils clatter to the floor.

"Do you have a dress style in mind?" Molly finally asks. "Vera Wang and Carolina Herrera have salons right here on Madison. God, I loved trying on wedding gowns. There is a certain exhaustion that sets in, but I was almost sorry when I fell in love with one and the search ended."

"Yes, what a shame," Mac teased. "But not nearly as big a shame as what they cost, given that you're only going to wear it once."

I sit up and realize this is a subject I can definitely weigh in on. "Actually, there's a wedding dress in my family that's been worn by three generations of Jameson women."

"Really? How quaint."

Spencer laughs at his mother. I love his laugh and the fact that he has no problem letting it loose even on his parents. "It's not quaint. It's brilliant. Is that the dress your mother's wearing in the photo in your apartment?"

I nod as I think about the wedding picture of my mother and the father I never had a chance to know, which sits on my nightstand. Brianna looked beautiful in THE DRESS, too, only I was too hurt and angry to say so.

"But how can so many people wear the same dress?" Grace asks.

"Well, it gets altered slightly for each bride and the amazing thing is, it's always looked perfect on whoever was wearing it," I say. "It was originally designed for my great-grandmother's cousin Lindy. Then my grandmother wore it. And so did her sister, my great-aunt Velda. Then my mother and some of her cousins." I can feel the smile on my lips. "I used to dream of wearing it when I was a little girl. But until Spencer dropped to his knee the other night, I never really thought I would." I meet Spencer's eyes and feel a shimmer of exhilaration as I picture wearing it on our wedding day. My imagination tacks on a tremor of concern about my mother's health that it refuses to let go of then adds another, more recurring worry. Maybe she's having financial difficulty. She has refused to let me contribute financially even though I know that sometimes she only just gets by. The only things she's never refused are the trips I've planned for us or an outright gift. I tend to buy her extravagant things that she would never buy for herself, so that she can either enjoy their frivolity or return them for a refund. "I'll be trying it on while we're down there."

"Send pictures," Molly says, enthused. "A vintage gown could be very cool."

I don't really listen to the rest of the conversation. Every day my shock at the surprise proposal lessens and my excitement at sharing the future with Spencer grows, but I haven't been home in more than a year. Now I'm going to have to go back and navigate the mess I've spent all these years trying to forget—with a fiancé in tow.

Dessert arrives. I consume the chocolate mousse without really tasting it while the conversation flows around me. I'm thinking about the trip back to Nags Head and wishing that I could rewrite the past and edit out all the mistakes I've made, like you can on a manuscript. And then there's my mother's request that we come as soon as we can, which probably means absolutely nothing, but has sent my imagination into overdrive.

As they say in my line of work, "the plot thickens."

Bree

The Sandcastle

"Are you sure you're all right?" Kendra asks.

We're at her kitchen table with mugs of coffee and a plate of fresh muffins between us and I know that the all-nighters I've been pulling for the past week in an attempt to finally finish *Heart of Gold* are showing.

"I'm fine. Just a few too many late nights." I shrug in an attempt to appear casual, but Kendra's known me since I was five.

"You know you have nothing to prove to anyone." She looks me in the eye and it's all I can do not to respond, "Of course I do." I have everything to prove to everyone, especially myself. Finishing before Lauren arrives is a nonnegotiable point of honor. I'd rather die than face her without a completed book to my name. "When do they arrive?"

"They're flying into Norfolk Friday, April fifth. I expect them to be here mid to late afternoon."

"Oh. Great." Mostly because that means I have just over a week to force my characters to stop resisting my attempts to wrap up their story lines. I swallow back a semi-hysterical laugh, no doubt born of exhaustion, at the idea that the fault lies with anyone but me.

Kendra peels the paper off a chocolate chip muffin and pulls it apart. "I'm hoping you two can meet each other halfway and at least try to make peace."

I want to say yes. I'd do almost anything for Kendra, but Lauren has never even come close to apologizing for appropriating *Sandcastle Sunrise*. She's built a career off that book and she's flaunted her success every chance she's gotten. Now she's coming down with her famous fiancé on some sort of victory tour. "I will if she will."

Kendra sighs and sets the muffin down. "I know a little bit about the consequences of not repairing important relationships. And I can promise you it only leads to heartache and regret." She's looking right at me, but I'm not sure she's talking about Lauren and me anymore. "Someone has to take the first step."

I nod but I don't promise. I've learned to accept who my parents are, but I will never be able to forget or forgive their total abdication and rejection. I once seriously considered Lauren my sister and assumed that relationship came with unconditional love, but I was wrong. There's been way too much water under our emotional bridge for us to suddenly kiss and make up. Which is what we used to do when we were five.

"I'll try to stay open," I hedge, then get up and pour us each another cup of coffee. When I carry them back to the table I remember the customer who came in the store. "Speaking of Lauren, it was the weirdest thing." I take a sip of coffee. "This man came in the other day and bought an entire set of Lauren's books."

"Hmmm." An odd look steals into Kendra's eyes. "Did he say why?"

"He just said that his wife had always been a fan." I try to remember what it was about the man that had seemed familiar, but you can't sit up night after night for days on end and expect your brain to fire on all cylinders. "He did seem curious about her. He asked if she ever came back to visit."

"Oh." Kendra's tone is casual, but she's started shredding the muffin into tiny pieces that lie scattered on her plate. "When was this?"

"It was right after book club ended, so that would have been last Wednesday. Just a couple of days after Lauren called to say she was engaged."

"Is that right?" Her voice is so soft it's almost as if she's speaking to herself.

"Umm-hmmm. I didn't think to ask where he was staying or if he was just passing through. I don't even know if he walked over or drove." Title Waves is just a block from the Manteo waterfront so lots of visitors simply wander in. I drain the remainder of my coffee in a few long swallows then stand and carry my mug to the sink. I need to get to the store, but the only place I'd really like to go is to my bed.

Kendra dumps the shredded muffin in the garbage and covers the ones we didn't touch.

"Well, I guess you can't really complain about a man doing something nice for his wife," she says with a shrug. But when she puts her arms around me and pulls me into a hug, there's an odd sort of tension in her arms.

"No," I say as I head toward the kitchen door. There are a lot worse things a man can do than buy a gift for his wife. "No, you can't."

Nine

∽

Bree

"Mom!" Lily's voice shouted up the stairs the next afternoon is loud and strident. "Nothing's happening in the kitchen. What time is dinner?"

I look up from the computer screen and the accusing blinking cursor. It, too, has been shouting at me. *Write something! Don't just sit there! Stop staring at me and put some words on the page!*

I'm used to "attitude" from Lily. After all, she's sixteen and hormonal and certain the world revolves around her. My computer has never spoken to me like this before. It has always welcomed me, crooked a finger in my direction, and offered me an escape. But that was before I gave myself an actual deadline and began counting down words and pages that have to be completed in the time I have left.

I massage my temples in a futile attempt to make the pounding in my head go away. Then I run my fingers through hair that I haven't looked at or thought about for days. I offer up a silent moment of gratitude that there's no mirror up here.

"Dad's out!" I yell back, and I'm careful not to think about where he's been spending his evenings while I've been locked away up here. "Try the leftovers!"

"They're gone! Finished them yesterday." She gives up yelling and texts, *We're out of everything. The cupboard is bare!*

There's a stab of guilt. For a moment I consider getting up, getting dressed, and running to the grocery store. I've gone to great lengths to make sure my family, and especially my children, feel loved and cared for. In fact, it's been my number one mission to be everything my parents weren't. Which means being loving and most of all "present"—not just emotionally but physically.

Except Lily's not a baby bird or a helpless child any longer and I have not abandoned her. She's sixteen and has a driver's license. She can take my car and drive to Food-a-Rama for groceries or stop for a sandwich at Subway or drive through McDonald's. Or she can order a pizza. In fact, it occurs to me that she's now capable of doing anything that I can do. And that I was not actually born with a cooking, cleaning, or laundry gene that no one else in this family possesses.

Busy here. Please pick up some groceries and something for dinner, I text back.

I picture the shock on her face and half expect to hear her pounding up the stairs to try to guilt or con me into coming down to solve her food emergency. But a few seconds later the front door slams. Feeling victorious I turn my thoughts back to the screen. Where Whitney, who has wanted nothing but Heath's love since I created her, suddenly doesn't seem so sure that she wants to marry him and move to Montana to help support his dream of becoming a park ranger. In fact, as I flip back and skim the stack of manuscript pages that I've printed out, I notice that although she's still twenty-one she doesn't really sound that young anymore. Somehow she's evolved into someone who wants more than love, marriage, and children. And who may not want to walk away from her own dreams in order to help Heath fulfill his.

Shit.

I have no doubt other writers' characters march across the page to the beat of their creator's drum, becoming exactly who and what they're expected to be. For about five seconds I wish I had someone who could tell me how to keep them in line and how I can counter this rebellion.

My head recommences its pounding as I berate myself for letting this happen. For having wasted fifteen years on one book that I can't seem to finish and that will most likely never be published or read by anyone but me.

What is the point? Why do I even care anymore? My eyes blur with tears while I seriously consider quitting once and for all. Walking away and getting on with my real life. Only the idea of quitting is even more demoralizing than this manuscript that I've lost control of.

As usual I straddle the middle ground between quitting right now and forging ahead right now. I tell myself that I'm not really deflating like a balloon even though I can feel the air seeping out of my lungs and my body shrinking and folding in on itself. I tell myself I'm just tired. That if I lie down for a brief nap things will be clearer and more positive when I wake up.

I stumble over to the daybed, shove the books and papers off it, and curl up on my side in a distinctly fetal position. It's a wonder I don't stick my thumb in my mouth.

My last semiconscious thought is that I do know a writer who deals with these issues on a daily basis and that she could give me pointers on how to handle Whitney and tell me how to make myself finish this bloody manuscript.

That writer will be here soon. Only I'd cut out my tongue before I'd let her know that I needed her.

Kendra

The Sandcastle

It's still dark, the sun not yet up, when my phone rings that Saturday morning. It takes me a while to find and answer it.

"Kendra?" The voice belongs to Deanna Sanborne, a long-ago roommate and a best friend practically since the day I arrived in the Outer Banks. During the week I deliver muffins and cakes to her Dogwood Inn, a six-bedroom B and B in a beautifully restored Arts and Crafts home near the Manteo waterfront. I cook and serve breakfast there at least one Saturday a month, but I don't typically arrive until seven thirty to begin serving at eight thirty. According to my bedside clock it's only six A.M.

"Is everything all right?"

"Yes. Sorry to bother you so early. I'm calling to ask if you could put a little extra pizzazz into this morning's breakfast."

"How much pizzazzier are we talking?" I'm sitting up now and swinging my legs over the side of the bed and trying to kick-start my brain so that I can remember what I have on hand.

"Pizzazzy enough to impress a hotel industry VIP whose management company puts out the definitive guide to upscale B and Bs and who's started buying strategically placed properties up and down the Eastern Seaboard. I only found out late last night who he is."

"Ummm, sure." I don't bother asking her if she hopes to sell or anything else, because as I get out of bed and head for the kitchen with the phone tucked under my chin I'm considering and rejecting menu ideas. "What do you have on hand?"

I hear the sound of her refrigerator opening as I reach the kitchen and open my own. "Two dozen eggs, orange juice and milk, some cheddar and spinach. Oh, and a bunch of red grapes." There's more background noise. "And I've got a couple of bottles of champagne here so I thought we might offer mimosas as well."

"Sounds good. How many for breakfast? Or are we just sending something fabulous up on a tray?"

"I've got seven here besides him and I don't want to be too obvious, so I'd like to serve everyone in the dining room like we normally do."

"No problem. I've got sausage and fresh fruit and I can stop for potatoes and onions and any other basics I'll need." I set things on the counter then locate my recipe box. "I've gotta have at least a couple dozen assorted muffins and breakfast breads in the freezer that I keep for emergencies. What time are we aiming for?"

"We'll stick with eight thirty. I just wanted to give you a heads-up."

"No worries." I stumble toward the bathroom. "As long as there's coffee waiting and you're willing to assist, we're good."

"Great. Thanks so much." The relief in her voice tells me just how important this is to her.

"All right. Be there as fast I can."

I splash water on my face, brush my teeth, and twist my hair into a knot at my neck. Then I pull on the jeans lying on my bedroom chair, slip my arms through a long-sleeved T-shirt that's soft and roomy enough to cook in and has the grease splatters to prove it, then shove my bare feet into a pair of mules.

In the kitchen I thumb through my favorite recipes and finally pull one for eggs Florentine—the dish itself is simple but can be presented elegantly. I pull everything in my refrigerator and freezer that might come in handy and stuff them into the go bag that I always keep at the ready. Then I make a quick list of the things I'll need to stop for.

It's early and the season hasn't started yet so both the Beach Road and Highway 158 that parallels it are quiet. So is the Washington Baum Bridge that takes me to Roanoke Island. Even with my stop at the grocery store I'm at the Dogwood by seven fifteen. I pull into the grassy area between the Dogwood and Deanna's house as quietly as I can then almost tiptoe up the porch steps and in through the kitchen door.

"Bless you." Dee hands me a cup of freshly brewed coffee and takes my bag from me. "I'm going to finish setting the tables. Let me know what else I can do."

"Aye, aye." Halfway through the cup of coffee, I've got the spinach sautéing in the pan and am cracking eggs into a big bowl. The frozen muffins are thawing on the counter next to a melon, a pineapple, several bananas, and a bunch of grapes. Confident that everything is in place I pop in my earbuds and tuck my iPhone into my pocket. I like to cook to music because it enhances my focus and helps me get in a rhythm. Sometimes it's Joni Mitchell, other days it's Bette Midler, or maybe even Bob Marley. Today I go with Lynyrd Skynyrd because I'm still trying to wake all the way up. Deanna walks in and out of the kitchen while I chop, mix, and sauté to "Sweet Home Alabama."

At exactly 8:29 A.M. everything's ready. The eggs Florentine, breakfast sausage, and roasted potatoes sit on a warming tray beside a cut glass bowl of fresh fruit ready to be plated. I place pitchers of juice, an open bottle of champagne, and champagne flutes on the sideboard in the dining room then carry a basket of warm muffins and flower-shaped pats of butter to both tables and smile at the guests who are making their way to their seats. I'm about to head back to the kitchen when Jake, wearing a pair of dress jeans and a white oxford button-down with the sleeves rolled up, walks into the dining room.

He hesitates briefly when he sees me, but he doesn't look anywhere near as surprised to see me as I am to see him. I take a step back toward the kitchen as he takes a seat, but his eyes follow me as I back out of the room and past the butler's pantry and half bath. I peek out from behind the kitchen doorframe and wish there were somewhere to hide. There are no doors between the living room/dining area and the galley kitchen.

"Dishy, isn't he?" Dee asks from behind me.

"Who?" I try to sound nonchalant, but my heart is sprinting in alarm.

"Tall, dark, and good-looking," she says. "His name's Jake Warner. He's the one I told you about. He owns Warner

Holdings." She goes out to pour and pass mimosas while I garnish and prepare plates then carry them out to the guests, careful not to look Jake in the eye. It takes everything I have not to turn and race back to my car.

I knew that he hadn't left town right after he came to see me when Bree told me about the man who'd bought Lauren's books, but I had assumed he was long gone by now. I promised him that I'd tell Lauren the truth and make the introduction and I will, but I think we were both too shaken at the time to negotiate an exact time frame. And I sure as hell haven't thought out the details. All I know is that I need a chance to try to explain everything to her before they meet. I know I'll have to do it while she and Spencer are here. But I'm so afraid. She's had trouble dealing with an unexpected proposal. There's no way I can introduce her to her up-till-now deceased father without sufficient warning. Somehow I'm going to have to make her understand that I kept him from her only for her own good. And, I tell myself yet again, for his.

Dee flits in and out while I try to look busy even though I'm cowering at the farthest end of the kitchen. I'm so shaken by Jake's presence that I don't even ask Dee whether she's serious about selling. I prepare a fresh pot of coffee then make a round of the tables, refilling coffee cups then muffin baskets, smiling somewhat inanely without making eye contact. When people finally begin to leave the dining room, I do washup at double speed and begin shoving things in my bag like a burglar making a quick getaway.

"I heard Lauren is engaged to her playwright," Deanna says on her way in with the empty champagne bottles. "You must be so excited."

I don't ask who told her. The Outer Banks may stretch for hundreds of miles but the number of full-time residents is small and people are connected in surprising ways. News travels fast. "Yes." I hear Jake's voice in conversation with someone out in the dining room, but I lower my voice anyway. "He surprised her by proposing on her birthday."

"Wow. Are they going to get married here?" She's known Lauren since she was a baby and is genuinely excited about the news.

At the moment all I want is to get out of here. "I don't know. They're planning a visit down. I'm hoping we'll look at places while they're here." I grab my things and turn, intending to tiptoe out the kitchen door. But when I glance over my shoulder I see Jake standing inside the kitchen. I can tell from his face that he's overheard at least part of our conversation.

"Jake Warner," Dee says, stepping toward him with a smile. "I'd like to introduce you to the person who cooked your breakfast. This is my good friend . . ."

"Kendra Jameson."

"Why, yes." She looks to me and I see the question in her eyes. It's Jake who answers. "Kendra and I go way back."

"You do?" Puzzled, she glances between us trying to figure out why neither of us seems surprised to see the other. And why I hadn't already mentioned knowing him.

"Yes." I swallow and search for something that will resemble a smile. "We knew each other growing up in Richmond."

Dee is watching my face closely. She's a good friend, but I've never even hinted at the truth about Lauren's father. I hope like hell that Jake's not going to blurt anything out.

"Our families were good friends." He's staring at me and although his tone is matter-of-fact, I can see the question—make that the suspicion—in his eyes. Although I promised him that I'd tell Lauren the truth, I wasn't necessarily planning to do it immediately. And I certainly didn't expect him to hang around waiting to meet her. "I didn't mean to eavesdrop, but did I hear you say that your daughter's coming to town?"

"Yes," I bite out, though I'm pretty sure I'm still smiling. "I didn't realize you were still in town."

We stare at each other. One dark eyebrow sketches upward. He's seized the upper hand and he knows it.

"How long do you plan to be here?"

Dee is watching us, her eyes moving back and forth, as if we're a match at Wimbledon.

"I have to be in South Carolina and Georgia most of the week, but I've decided to keep my room here to use as a base. Ms. Sanborne does a great job. The Dogwood's a fine property."

"Oh, please call me Dee." She smiles with pleasure.

I'm having trouble holding on to my smile. And my thoughts. I need time and space to figure out how to explain things to Lauren. And then I need to sit down with her while she and Spencer are here. Once she and I have hashed this out then the three of us could get together and . . . This is where the scenario falls apart. On the one hand I want . . . I have to believe that Lauren will understand that I was trying to protect her. On the other . . . I force myself to meet his eyes. Is a good outcome for all three of us even possible?

"I'll be back Sunday," Jake continues.

"Oh well. I . . ." I glance down at the bag I'm clutching to my chest as if it were a shield.

Although he's already given me his cell number, Jake steps forward and hands me a business card. "This has all my contact information. I look forward to meeting her." His voice is polite but steely. Then he nods and turns to go back to the dining room, and I realize that he's issued a command not a request.

Ten

⚭

Lauren

New York City

The closer our trip home gets, the more nervous I become and the crazier I get. I just can't seem to focus on anything, including the book I'm writing. Which is not good because every day I don't meet my page count I feel that much more out of whack. Writing a novel isn't like cramming for a final exam—you can't just sit down the night before it's due and bang out a hundred thousand–plus words, though I do know a few writers who've tried.

For me, writing a minimum number of pages every day is critical. It's like exercising a muscle. As anyone who's joined a gym in January only to stop going in February knows, the more days you don't exercise the harder it is to start again.

Addressing the page on a daily basis also helps you burrow all the way into your characters' heads, which is key. A book that can't be put down doesn't come from a mind that is leaping from thought to thought like a frog across lily pads. It comes from tunneling deep inside your characters' heads and staying there—or at least knowing how to find your way back in each day when you sit down to work.

Today is Monday, April first. We leave for North Carolina in four days and at the moment I'm leaping lily pads at the speed of sound. I've been sitting in front of my computer for almost an hour now without actually touching the keyboard when my phone rings. Normally my phone stays off until I've finished the day's pages, but there's nothing normal about me, or my life, right now. The number belongs to my editor, Melissa Sanchez, which gives me a semi-legitimate reason to pick up.

"I hope I didn't interrupt."

"No, not at all. I was just taking a break." A long one. I stand and move toward the window to stare down at the people striding up the sidewalk.

"I have some exciting news," she says, diving right in.

"Okay. Exciting's good." At least a certain percentage of the time.

"Sales and marketing have come up with the most wonderful idea." Melissa pauses. "We want to publish a fifteenth-anniversary edition of *Sandcastle Sunrise*!"

I have no idea what I was expecting but it wasn't this.

"Genius, right?" She sounds genuinely excited, but I can also hear how hard she's selling it. "We think this is the perfect time to remind everyone who you are and how beloved your books have been. And what better way than with the book that started it all?"

I try not to notice that she's using the past tense, but as bad as losing part of my audience seemed, the idea that another part of that audience has "forgotten" who I am feels even worse.

"And we thought we'd release it immediately before your wedding. Your engagement's been all over the entertainment news and your sales have had a serious uptick. Even the anthology's moving. It will give your fans something special and introduce your first big book to a whole new batch of readers."

It doesn't happen often, but I am actually speechless at the impact of our engagement on my book sales.

"Publicity is already fielding requests for you and Spencer to appear together on the morning shows. *People* magazine is talking about giving you two the cover." She takes a breath, possibly the first one since I picked up the phone. "When *is* the wedding?"

"We haven't picked a date yet."

"Well, we'll need time to redo the cover, design the new edition, and do serious marketing and publicity outreach. June of next year would be perfect."

I remain silent. I'm relieved my numbers are improving, but I hate the idea of using our wedding, which should be a personal and intimate life event, as a sales and marketing tool, and I'm not sure whether I'm more afraid Spencer will feel the same way I do or that he won't. It's not as if we've ever talked about what kind of wedding we'd have. Or have some date that's so special to us we'd want to get married on it.

Clearly we're going to have to start figuring out the details. But right now all I care about is making sure Spencer and my mother hit it off and surviving any encounters with Bree. I also need to find out why my mother was so adamant that we come there. So far I've imagined worst-case scenarios that include bankruptcy and a brain tumor—and I've made it through only the first two letters of the alphabet.

"Obviously you'll need to talk to Chris Wolfe about the anniversary edition," I finally say, turning my back on the window. "Spencer and I are going to visit my mother, and I'm sure we'll reach some decisions about the wedding while we're there."

"Of course." Melissa's tone turns apologetic. "I'm sorry. I know I'm a little ahead of myself. It's just that everyone's thrilled about your engagement—congratulations again! When do you head down?"

"Friday morning."

"Perfect. Danielle asked if you could stop by that cute little bookstore while you're there," she says, referring to my publicity person at Trove. "Wasn't the owner a friend of yours?"

"Yes." This time her use of the past tense allows me to answer in the affirmative. Brianna *was* my best friend in the world. Once.

"She asked if you could get some photos of you in the store and also on the real beach where most of *Sandcastle Sunrise* is set."

"Um-hmmm." I drop down on the office sofa and try to slow the thoughts spinning in my head.

"She wanted me to find out if you know any photographers down there or if we should send someone. That way we'd have all the photos we need and someone who could send things back daily for posting to social media."

"I'm sure we can take the photos," I say as I debate whether I need to put my head between my knees to stop the room from whirling. "But I need to go now. I want to get my pages done for the day and then I'm going to meet Spencer for an early dinner before we go to the theater."

"Oh, that's great. Be sure to ask him what he thinks of . . ." Her voice fades until it's no more than an indistinct buzzing in my brain.

I hang up. Then I just sit there staring at the wall as I picture Bree's face when I show up in her store with news about the anniversary edition of the book she thinks I stole from her. Today may be April Fools' Day but this is no joke.

Bree

Manteo

This morning I wake up on the daybed in my office to the patter of rain on the roof and the smell of bacon and hash browns frying. The gurgle of coffee brewing is accompanied by its lovely scent and faint whiffs of cinnamon and bacon.

Clay has been known to fry up fresh-caught fish or throw the occasional burger or steak on the grill, and Lily did, in fact, bring home groceries the other day, but putting meals on the table has always been my job. So when I follow these heavenly smells down to the kitchen I'm not surprised to find Kendra pulling a fresh batch of apple cinnamon muffins out of the oven while Clay wolfs down the massive breakfast she's just served them and Lily nibbles on a piece of bacon.

"Wow, Mom." Lily looks me up and down. "It might be time for a shower and a pajama change."

Clay's lips tilt up but he's smart enough not to laugh or agree. It's Kendra who says, "That's unkind, Lily. I happen to have it on good authority that that's what a writer on deadline is supposed to look like."

I flinch slightly at her allusion to Lauren, though maybe she's just trying to desensitize me before I have to face her in person. I lean forward to peer at the stainless steel refrigerator door and see my murky reflection topped by a head of hair standing up in so many directions I might have stuck my finger in an electric socket.

"I think these two could have managed breakfast," I say as I hug Kendra and pinch a still-warm muffin from the basket she's put them in.

"I was up early anyway and thought I'd pop by. There's a hamburger casserole in the refrigerator for dinner. Gina stopped by with a pan of lasagna and an apple pie." Gina is Clay's mother and a far better cook than I am. She's a one-woman force of nature and practically runs the vacation rental arm of the family real estate business singlehandedly while Clay and his father buy and sell properties and handle repairs. One of my favorite things Clay brought with him to our marriage is his large, extended, rowdy family that's been on the Outer Banks for generations.

The rain outside makes the kitchen feel even warmer and cheerier. Surrounded by the easy chatter of three of the people I love most in the world, I'm not prepared when their faces blur and memory yanks me back into the empty silence of this very kitchen in the weeks after my grandmother died. It got even quieter after my parents, having decided that sixteen was old enough to live alone in the house my grandmother left me, departed to once again dig up an ancient civilization in some far corner of the world.

Technically I *could* take care of myself, just as Lily could if she had to. But sixteen-year-old girls are not designed to live alone, connected to no one. I shudder slightly and feel my hands wrap around the heat of the coffee cup even as the remembered chill of loneliness seeps inside me. I remember the brutal ache of isolation. The time I spent weeping, and struggling to understand how the house that had once overflowed with her warmth and love could be so still and cold.

I went to school each day, where I pretended that I was like everyone else. And then came home each night to the chilly quiet and the unavoidable knowledge that I wasn't. That my parents didn't care about me enough to come back for any real length of time, or send for me, or alter their life in any way. That the only person who had ever really loved me was gone.

Lauren had spent plenty of after-school afternoons with me at my grandmother's while we were in elementary and middle school; afternoons we spent eating homemade treats while we made up stories then acted them out.

In the days and weeks after Gran's funeral, it was Lauren who helped fill the silence. She filled it with friendship and a VHS of *Pretty Woman* that she found buried in the bottom of an old trunk.

We loved everything about that modern-day Cinderella story. But our favorite scene was the music montage of Vivian trying on clothes on Rodeo Drive. We replayed that scene over and over, ultimately deciding that we liked it even more than the makeover scene in *Clueless*.

We watched *Pretty Woman* (with popcorn) as a regular pre-homework treat. We watched it so many times that we could (and did) recite scene after scene of dialogue along with Vivian and Edward. Sometimes we lowered the volume and delivered the lines ourselves.

It was our favorite movie and Roy Orbison's "Pretty Woman" became "our song." We hummed it and sang it. When it came on the radio, wherever we were, we belted out the words and bobbed along. One rainy afternoon we choreographed a dance number to it, which we performed for our own personal entertainment whenever the opportunity arose. Even now the first drum licks of that song set my head bobbing and my body moving. I'm sixteen again and my best friend is at my side.

"Bree?"

"Hmmm?" I jerk my head up and see all three of them staring at me.

"Are you okay, Mom?" Lily has her schoolbooks, and Clay's got the car keys. They've both pulled on raincoats.

"Absolutely, sweetheart," I say in my heartiest mom voice. "I'm just a little lost in the chapter I'm working on." As my lips brush across their cheeks it's a reminder of how lucky I am to have them. When I married Clay and we decided to live here I vowed to turn it back into the kind of home my grandmother's presence had made it. And mostly I've succeeded.

"Go ahead and get back to work while it's fresh in your mind." Kendra's eyes are filled with concern as she hands me a plate to take up with me. "I'll clean up and let myself out."

"Thanks." I feel a swell of love and gratitude. In those months after my grandmother died I spent almost every weekend at the Sandcastle. The day Lauren admitted to Kendra that I had been left on my own was the day they came to pack me up and take me home with them—no longer just a best friend but a member of their family.

Where would I be without her?

Back at my desk I gobble down a piece of bacon, a couple bites of scrambled egg, and most of a muffin. While I look at the notes I've scrawled all over the manuscript in my race toward the finish line, I sip my coffee and go back through all of Whitney's scenes one last time.

It's only now, with food in my stomach and the comforting soundtrack of Kendra puttering in the kitchen downstairs, that I'm ready to finally accept the truth about the characters I've come to love and thought I knew so well.

Somehow, and I'm really not sure how, Whitney has grown and evolved in ways I never planned or noticed. In fact, I wish I were half as fleshed out as she is. That my dreams and goals seemed as clear and obtainable as hers.

Of course, there's still tweaking to be done, but Whitney is surprisingly strong and resilient. Frankly, if Heath doesn't get his shit together he's going to be left behind.

I shake my head in wonder. Then I smile and finish off the muffin, considering. I've only ever wanted a traditional happily ever after for this woman I created. But now when I see what she's become I can't help wondering if she'd be happier going it alone.

Kendra's handled being single with aplomb. And from what I've heard and observed, Lauren has never needed a man to make her happy or "take care of her." I have to admit I'm curious to see what kind of man it took to win her.

Neither Kendra nor Lauren feared being alone like I did, like I still do. But then they've always had each other.

I eat another piece of bacon. As I lick the grease from my fingers, my eyes are drawn to the paragraphs I wrote late last night. I sense Whitney's presence and hear her begin to speak. After all these years her voice is as familiar as my own. I cock my head and listen, surprised again at what she has to say. And then I'm typing rapidly, trying to catch every word, as if I'm simply taking dictation.

Her decisions, which she lays out quite clearly, shock me. She's made the kind of hard choices I've been afraid to even consider.

Eleven

Kendra

The Sandcastle

The sky is a steel gray. The heavy clouds that hang low over the ocean are a shade darker. Surf pounds onto shore. The wind howls, pelting the walls and windows with sand. It's been raining for three days. Which means the freezer is now stuffed with enough home-baked chocolate macadamia nut cookies, salty caramel brownies, and snickerdoodles to last a lifetime. The refrigerator contains all of Lauren's favorite foods. As if the perfect meal might somehow soften her outrage when I tell her that her father is not dead, but alive. Or consuming enough chocolate could stimulate forgiveness.

Between the weather and my nerves, I've worn a groove in the wood floors from pacing. My hands are cramped from wringing. At the moment my knees are shrieking in protest as I duckwalk the living room cleaning the baseboards, something I haven't done in years and don't need to do now since it's doubtful that Lauren will notice or that my future son-in-law has packed a pair of white gloves with which to test the baseboards.

I know my way around cleaning products. I cleaned houses and motel rooms in the first years after we arrived because we needed the money and because I could bring a baby with me while I did it. But even while I was acquiring the skills I'd never learned growing up in a home with full-time help, I wasn't particularly interested in achieving household perfection or stamping out every last dust mite—that was always more my mother's goal than mine. It went hand in hand with her need to please and appease my father.

As always the thought of my parents is a one-two punch to the gut. First comes the burst of anger that still burns far too brightly—that my father expected obedience in all things and that his love was completely conditional on compliance. That my mother was too weak to stand up to him, too timid and too dependent to insist on a relationship with me and Lauren after I disobeyed his edicts and refused to give up my child. Too fragile to be the woman I always wanted her to be.

The anger is followed by the quieter sting of remorse that my mother and Lauren never knew each other and that I never found a way to mend the breach before my parents died.

I like to think that my mother would have loved this box of a house as much as I do even though it's small and utilitarian without a single grand element or statement piece. An aging woman who is not embarrassed by her wrinkles.

Everything here is designed to stand up to salt, sea air, and sand. The cedar shake exterior has darkened over time and the wooden steps and railings that lead to front and back porches are weathered. The interior is splashed with color and consists of sturdy rattan with brightly patterned cushions that hide the spills and stains that have accumulated over the years. The run of east-and-west-facing windows lets the sunshine in and turns the space bright and airy, which is what I care about most. Give me plenty of natural light and I'm happy. Darkness has never been my friend. On days like this the windows frame the wild and turbulent beauty that first drew me and that I've never grown tired of.

Still antsy, I scrub every inch of the bathroom starting with the claw-foot tub and finishing, once again on my hands and knees, with the original black-and-white tile floor. I take pleasure in prevailing over the grout and breathe a little easier when everything begins to sparkle, but that lasts only until I let myself remember that I'm not just preparing for a meet-the-fiancé weekend, but a revelation that will change history as Lauren has known it. My pool of dread keeps deepening.

In Lauren's bedroom the twin beds that she and Bree slept in sag slightly in the middle. Even now I can't understand how Bree's parents could abandon her like they did. Only one of them made it back for her wedding, and I don't think they've visited more than a handful of times between them since then. Lauren was the center of my universe for so long, my reason for being and especially for being here. Why have children if you don't intend to make time for them?

I vacuum the turquoise rug that Lauren chose when she was nine and dust the dresser and nightstand. It's on this nightstand that Lauren kept the photo of me and Jake standing at the altar just moments before I turned and ran. The photo that I let her believe was of her parents getting married. I even made her a small photo album of Jake and me during our dating years.

My eyes water and I sniff to hold back tears. In my attempt to protect Lauren and Jake, I saw no way to make her known to his parents and so I let them "die" in the fictitious accident that claimed my parents.

What was that Hemingway quote? "The coward dies a thousand deaths, the brave but one"? Ha! I've been fearing this for so long that by all rights I should be relieved to have the truth come out. But I know how shocked Lauren is going to be, how confused and upset she'll feel. In a matter of days she'll realize how many mistakes I've made. How many lies I've told.

I lift the nightstand out of the way. When I push the beds together their sagging centers look even less appealing. Unless I figure out a way to anchor them together, whoever ends up in the middle is going to be sleeping on the crack or possibly the floor.

At the moment that seems like such a small thing in comparison with what lies ahead. I can only hope that when Lauren meets her father she'll . . . what? Not be angry that she's finding out only because I've been forced to tell her? Tell me she doesn't begrudge the last forty years?

No matter how many times I remind myself that I altered the truth for the best of reasons, even I haven't found a way to forgive me.

Lauren

New York City

We fly home tomorrow. My bag is packed and sitting on the ottoman in Spencer's bedroom. The black-and-electric-blue Trina Turk pants outfit with its wide, elastic-waist pants and flowing top is carefully folded over the back of the matching club chair. A pair of black Jimmy Choo flats that I can wear with everything in my suitcase sits on the floor waiting to be stepped into.

Spencer is sound asleep beside me and when I asked him why he wasn't packing earlier he told me that he'd have plenty of time in the morning. Even though we're leaving for the airport at nine A.M. sharp.

Of course he fell asleep in seconds, because to him flying is like taking a bus or a train—just another form of transportation.

To me it's a potential brush with death at thirty thousand feet. Which is why despite the two Tylenol PM I took an hour ago, I'm still staring up into the ceiling trying not to think about midair collisions, engines exploding, or plummeting to the ground in a ball of fire.

I do have a system for managing my fear. Typically I knock

myself out the night before—come on, Tylenol! Then I take a Xanax an hour before takeoff so that I can make myself get on the plane. Once on board I have exactly one drink as soon as possible. (I discovered the hard way on a cross-country trip that two drinks is one too many.) This drink prevents me from blubbering in fear and begging to be let off the plane. (Which I suspect would not play well on social media.)

As I wait for the Tylenol to kick in, I remind myself that the flight to Norfolk is relatively short and that, since it's not yet tourist season, the drive down to Nags Head should be an easy one. There's no reason there should be any real issues once we get home, either. My mother, who is the least judgmental person I know, is bound to love Spencer and I can't imagine him not loving her back. And it's not like he's going to have to deal with some big family looking him over. Now that Great-aunt Velda is gone, I have only a couple of cousins and none of them lives in the Outer Banks.

I turn on my side and pull my pillow under my head. There's Bree and Clay, of course, and their daughter, Lily. It might be a good idea to share a little more of our "backstory" with Spencer before we get there. But while I wish I didn't have to go to Title Waves or even tell Bree about the anniversary edition, it's not as if there's anything she can do about it.

I draw in a deep breath and feel my eyelids growing heavy as I tell myself that there's no point in worrying. A week hanging with my mom, showing Spencer around, and maybe looking at a few possible venues for the small, intimate wedding I'm hoping for should be fun. The Outer Banks are beautiful and the beach and the water surrounding it are guaranteed stress busters. After all, it's not as if we have any big issues to resolve.

Bree

Manteo

It's one in the morning when I suddenly realize that it's over. *Heart of Gold* is finished. Afraid I might be hallucinating, I go back and reread the last pages of the manuscript. It's possible that my lips move as I read—that's how exhausted I am. But it seems I've tied things up satisfactorily. Everything makes sense. Whitney is satisfied, Heath not so much. There's nothing else to say.

With trembling fingers I type the magic words *The End* a few lines below the final paragraph. I stare at those words on the page in the pool of light that spills from the desk lamp. A smile spreads across my face. It's so large I can actually feel my skin stretching.

I retype the words again. This time all in caps. *THE END.* Then I go back and add an exclamation point because the occasion demands it.

"Oh my God!" I get up then sit back down. I scrub at my eyes. I am so exhausted I could crumple to the floor at any moment. Or I could go outside and run through the streets.

Hysterical laughter bubbles up as I imagine what the sight of me racing around in the rain in my ancient pajamas and ratty robe whooping and hollering might do to any neighbor who happened to be up. They might call the sheriff's office. I could end up in jail for being dangerously and deliriously happy.

I don't go anywhere. I just sit there grinning and laughing. Then I notice that I'm crying. I feel an odd sort of reverence almost like I did when Rafe and Lily were first placed in my arms. I wonder if the agony of the fifteen years I've spent on this manuscript will fade the way the remembered pain of childbirth did?

Next I whoop and circle-pump my arm because I've finally

done it. When Lauren gets here tomorrow—make that this afternoon—I will no longer be the loser still struggling to finish a single manuscript after a decade and a half. Whatever does or doesn't happen next I have made it to the end. *The End. THE END!*

I whip open my office door. The house is dark and silent but there's no way I'm going to be able to keep this to myself for six more hours. Maybe I should sneak into the bedrooms and adjust the alarms so that Clay and Lily wake up simultaneously and I can tell them.

I practically float down the stairs. As I pass Lily's room I reject the idea of waking her. Lily doesn't come back to consciousness easily or happily. When she was a baby I used to go to great lengths to keep her from falling asleep while we were running errands in the car—and what kind of mother would wake her child at one A.M.?

The need to share and celebrate this moment pushes me down the hallway past the Jack and Jill bathroom and Rafe's empty bedroom. More than anyone else, Clay knows how long and how hard I've worked on this book. He knows how much it means to me. And why.

Whatever we've been through, whatever vows he's stretched or broken, he's still my husband. On our wedding day we promised to love and honor each other. To be there for each other in sickness and in health. We've made it through his infidelities, which I've tried to file away out of sight under the label BAD TIMES. But that vow included the good times, too. And for me this moment is as good as it gets.

When I reach the master suite I tiptoe directly to the bathroom, where I wash my face and brush my teeth. The whole time all I can think is how glad I am that I continued writing. That I persevered long after any sane person would have given up. It's over. I've done it. I throw the ragged pajamas and robe I've been living in into the hamper and pull on a fresh nightgown. I spritz on the perfume Clay bought me for my birthday and imagine him rousing and pulling me into bed beside him. I'm beyond grateful that I have him to celebrate this momentous occasion with.

The bedroom is dark and the blinds have been drawn. I don't want to turn on a light so I feel my way to my side of the bed and slip under the covers. I'm so eager to reach him that I barely breathe as I slide gently across the mattress.

I'm already imagining how I'll break the news when I realize that the mound I saw outlined in the dark is just the crumpled sheets and covers of an unmade bed. Clay's pillow is cold. His side of the bed is empty and clearly un–slept in.

With the angry, pain-filled yelp of a dog that's been unexpectedly kicked by its master, I throw off the covers. My feet hit the floor. I get out of bed and stalk to the window, telling myself that he could just be downstairs asleep on the couch in the TV room. Or in the kitchen getting a late-night snack. But my stomach is already queasy with knowledge as I open the blinds and look down onto the driveway.

If I were that dog I'd be howling. My Jeep Cherokee sits alone in the darkness. Clay's truck isn't here. If my husband is in bed right now, that bed belongs to someone else.

Twelve

Bree

If finishing my manuscript last night was the crest of a wave, this morning is the trough. With all the adrenaline rushing through me and lying in wait for Clay with accusations flitting through my head, I barely slept. Or so I think until I wake up to the sound of clanging pots and pans in the kitchen. I yank on my robe and go downstairs to find him making breakfast, which is something he's only ever done as an unspoken act of atonement. Lily sits at the kitchen table, clutching a mug of cream that includes a dash of coffee. She's still glassy eyed with sleep, and I'm glad I didn't wake her last night.

"Good morning." My husband says this as if it's just any other day, and I realize that maybe to him it is. With the number of all-nighters I've been pulling, not to mention the nights I simply fell asleep at my desk, it's very possible that last night was not the first time he stayed out so late but only the first night I noticed. (Not that you have to stay out past midnight to do things you shouldn't.)

"How's the book coming?" he asks more to make conversation than because he thinks I'm ever actually going to finish.

"It's done." I look him right in the eye. "I typed *The End* last night."

"You're kidding."

"No, I'm not. I finished right around one." I watch his face and for a long moment I let him see the hurt and anger in mine. I want him to know that he's sucked far too much of the pleasure out of finishing, even if I don't want to have that conversation in front of Lily. I'd give a lot not to have to have that conversation at all.

"That's so cool, Mom!" Lily's genuine enthusiasm flows over me. "You should have woken me up to tell me."

"I considered it. But it was the middle of the night and I knew you had a math test this morning."

Clay's eyes widen, and I know he's trying to decide whether to continue pretending he wasn't out much past one or make up something that will justify why he was. But even if he claims he was just out drinking with friends will that be better than what I suspect he was doing?

He dishes up plates for Lily and me. All the things I want to say but won't are stuck in my throat, so there's no way I'm eating. Even if I could eat, I wouldn't. But as furious as I am and as much as I'd like to see him squirm, I know that I'm not going to throw his behavior in his face like I'd like to and not just because Lily's here. But because I don't know what it would accomplish. Or even if it would make me feel better.

I look down at the eggs and back up at him, so tired of this dance we do. We've been at this a long time and I know his tactics. He'll either pick a fight—because the best defense is a strong offense—or he'll come up with a conversational diversion that will give him more time to put an alibi together.

"It's so fabulous that you finished the book," he says. "I knew you could do it. We'll have to go out tonight and celebrate. I bet Lauren will be shocked."

Bingo.

He smiles at me then adds, "It'll be interesting to meet Lauren's fiancé, don't you think?

Well, there you go.

"I mean, this is the first guy she's brought home." He doesn't sound particularly concerned. While Lauren and I have had issues since she left for New York and I didn't, Clay didn't wait all that long after they broke up before he started dating again. When she's here he treats her like everyone else he's known since childhood. I'm the one who can never forget that he was the person she gave her virginity to or how when she came home and told me all about it I caught myself wishing it had been me in the backseat of the Mustang he's kept all these years.

"When are we going to see them?" Lily asks. She has no interest in her parents' lives before she existed and is only vaguely aware that Lauren and I aren't as close as we used to be. She does, however, know that Lauren is a pretty big deal in the book world and is not averse to using the connection to impress others.

"We're invited to Kendra's for brunch tomorrow at eleven." I'm actually relieved that we're not joining them for dinner tonight. I think Kendra's right to keep the evening for just the three of them. Plus, I'm in no hurry to do that thing Lauren and I do for her mother's sake—where we smile and attempt to talk politely without really saying anything.

Saying nothing isn't as easy as it should be. There are times I wish we could just shriek it out, maybe even throw a few punches, and finally get everything out in the open so that we'd at least have a chance at getting whatever this impasse is over with somehow.

Every once in a while I let myself wonder what her grievances actually are. I mean, I'm not the one who stole a manuscript and used it to build a career and I don't see why she'd still be angry that I didn't go to New York with her when she clearly succeeded in every possible way without me. And it's not like she could be jealous of me and Clay when they'd already broken up before he asked me out. Unless it's pure selfishness—not wanting me to have something even though she didn't want it herself.

I close my eyes and wish I could eject all the old arguments and justifications circling in my head. When we see each other tomorrow we'll be bringing all the old baggage with us.

Even having finished *Heart of Gold*, I wish I didn't have to see her. That I didn't have to make polite conversation with the person I used to share my deepest secrets and aspirations with. Back then it was as if something hadn't taken place until we'd had a chance to tell the other about it.

I look up and realize that Lily's saying good-bye and that she and Clay are leaving.

"You decide where you'd like to go for dinner tonight," he says as I notice the dirty pans and dishes he's left piled in the sink. After the kitchen door closes behind my husband, I try to imagine *wanting* to go anywhere with him let alone to celebrate such an important milestone, but my imagination isn't up to the job. It is, however, up to picturing all kinds of nasty fates for him. Including him being so tired from his nocturnal activities that right after he's left Lily off at school, he falls asleep at the wheel and has some sort of horrible and possibly disfiguring though not fatal accident.

I'm still standing at the kitchen door staring out through the screen long after they leave. Of course, the sun would finally come out today. Of course, the weather's perfect. No doubt because Lauren's gracing us with her presence and not because I managed to finally type *THE END!*

Lauren

En route to LaGuardia Airport

Just as he predicted, it took Spencer all of fifteen minutes to pack this morning, which is beyond annoying. He whistled while he was doing it then ran out to our favorite bodega for egg, cheese, and bacon sandwiches. Normally this would have made me happy, but I don't eat before I fly. Ever. At least nothing that might come up when the plane goes into its final death spiral.

He wolfed his down while I was doing deep-breathing exercises and trying to visualize an outcome that didn't include falling out of the sky. Then he ate mine so it wouldn't go to waste.

We take a black car to the airport and shortly after we pull out into traffic he puts his arm around my shoulders. "You okay?"

I nod mutely. I'm not, but I've learned that admitting my fear out loud somehow makes it worse. But while I don't want to talk about my fear, I do appreciate his concern. He's driven and highly competitive, but everything is not all about him. He never forgets about the people around him. It's one of his best qualities.

I stare out the window as the city whizzes by, each building filled with countless stories and personal dramas that I normally like to imagine but am too nervous to contemplate. At the airport we wait in Delta's Sky Club, where Spencer happily drinks coffee and reads the papers while sending and receiving texts. I continue to breathe deeply and try not to think about dying.

I linger in the restroom on my final bathroom run. I'd still rather spend the rest of the day here in this stall than get on a plane. Fortunately the Xanax has done its job by the time we need to leave for our gate and I'm numb enough not to barricade myself inside.

Spencer flies only first class so we board quickly. I sink into my window seat, a necessity because I feel slightly less claustrophobic when I can see out, even if it's dark and even though I'm still trapped with no control over what's about to happen. I'm careful not to meet the eye of anyone who has to walk by us to get to coach. It feels inherently wrong to make those passengers witness others being treated better than they are. But not wrong enough to refuse the preflight drink I'm offered.

"You okay?" Spencer whispers in my ear and because we're

still on the ground and I've got a nice little buzz going I'm able to smile. "Yes, thanks."

"Good." He drops a kiss on the top of my head then checks messages and sends a few more texts while I continue to try not to think about dying. Which of course makes me imagine it in gory detail. What can I say? My imagination didn't come with an on/off switch.

The flight attendant makes an announcement urging everyone to get seated, so that we can leave on time. I'm in no hurry to take off. Sometimes I even pray for delays. But today everything moves like clockwork. When the pilot instructs the flight attendants to take their seats, I breathe more deeply. It's all I can do not to whimper as I stare out the window and watch the terminal recede.

As we taxi Spencer's hand finds mine. Our fingers interlace. I try not to hold on too tightly as we thunder down the runway then rocket into the air. I swallow back the panic and stare unflinching out the window as the city falls away. Beneath us the buildings blur together, the East River grows smaller and less distinct like a blue vein beneath the skin of a hand. The boats are tiny flecks of white.

I'm still squeezing Spencer's hand when the engines cut back and we begin to level out. He squeezes back, and I dip my head briefly onto his shoulder in what I hope he knows is gratitude. Don't get me wrong, I'm not about to relax completely or lower my vigilance. There's still a small part of me that believes that keeping up my guard somehow keeps the plane in the air. I turn down a second drink and am probably the only person in first class who's glad they don't serve meals on flights this short because lowering the tray table makes me feel even more trapped, and I know from experience that setting food and drink on it causes turbulence.

I do accept a bottled water so that I won't die of thirst should I manage to survive a crash, but mostly I just hold on to

Spencer's hand and stare out the window, fiercely glad that I'm flying with a man who understands me well enough not to tell me it's silly to be afraid, or that flying is a thousand times safer than driving, or yammers on thinking that this will somehow distract me and make me feel better.

I steal a glance at my watch. Then I breathe deeply and fix my gaze on the blue sky and the carpet of clouds below us. I wish we were already back on the ground. I wish instantaneous teleporting from one spot to another didn't exist only in science fiction novels. I wish that this fear would go away and never come back.

Then Spencer gently squeezes my hand again and I know that even though none of these wishes are going to be granted, there's a hell of a lot to be said for facing down your demons with someone who knows how and when to hold your hand.

Thirteen

⟲

Lauren

I'm still slightly numb from the Xanax when we arrive at the car rental counter at the Norfolk Airport, aka ORF, but I'll be driving to the Outer Banks for one simple reason. As a lifelong resident of Manhattan, Spencer has never felt the need to get a driver's license.

I haven't driven since the last time I came home, so I take my time adjusting my seat and all the mirrors in the "medium"-size car that I'm pretty sure was a compact last year, before backing carefully out of the parking space and following the signs that lead out of the airport to the highway.

"Do you need me to navigate?" Spencer asks.

"You can pull the address up on my phone, but we're just going to take 64 to 168 to 158. It's pretty straightforward."

You don't really notice how compressed a big city is until you're no longer in it. It's especially true of Manhattan, which feels immense until you see one of those aerial establishing shots in a movie or TV show that reveals just how much stuff is crammed onto that tiny island surrounded by water.

As we drive, the distance between buildings increases. Residence Inns and chain hotels give way to industrial parks that ultimately give way to farmland. There's space, room to breathe. Here, trees and bushes aren't confined to parks or rooftops. They're not lone survivors jutting out of a sidewalk. As we leave town they grow with abandon, their leafy limbs climbing up into a vast blue sky that is not pierced by skyscrapers. The greener it gets the more deeply and easily I breathe.

We drive through Chesapeake then over the Intracoastal Waterway. The first sight of water does what no amount of Xanax can. There are still things to worry about, but they've dipped below the surface.

We watch the scenery in silence for a while. Passing into North Carolina we wind our way through Moyock, Harbinger, and Grandy. A succession of isolated farmhouses, mobile homes, and old wooden homesteads with family graveyards flash by, broken up by stands of trees and patches of green. Miles of railroad track curve in and out of sight. I point out a few longtime barbecue joints, farmer's markets that have been there as long as I can remember. Near Powells Point I breathe in the dark earthy scent of the marsh. Then we hit Point Harbor and before I think to introduce it we're on the Wright Memorial Bridge crossing over Currituck Sound.

The afternoon sun shines bright over the brownish water of the sound. The seabirds soaring through the cloudless sky caw what sounds like a welcome. My heart kicks up a notch. *Home.*

"I've never seen that peaceful look on your face before."

I turn to meet his assessing gaze for a moment before turning my attention to the bridge.

"Yet you don't come back very often."

"I would have come back for the holidays if we hadn't gone to Bermuda with your family. But, as much as I love this place and my mom, coming home can be kind of . . . complicated."

"By?"

The time has come to share my backstory, the past without which no character, or human being, is complete. "Well, you're going to meet my former best friend, Brianna. She'll be at my mom's with her husband, Clay, who I dated through high school and most of college. I'm pretty sure their daughter, Lily, will be with them."

"So your ex-best friend married your ex-boyfriend? We're talking soap opera material."

"Theoretically, yes. But Clay is really not the issue."

His look is skeptical.

"No, really. I mean, it's a little weird but he and I were already finished. Bree and I had a pretty significant falling-out. We had always planned to go to New York together after college. We'd been saving money for the bus tickets practically our whole lives. We were both going to become successful novelists."

"Which you accomplished."

"Two days before we were supposed to leave she told me she wasn't coming with me. Ultimately she married Clay and bought the bookstore she'd worked at all through school."

"Ahh, right. The place where you're supposed to take those publicity photos."

"Yes." I hear the dread in my voice and see that Spencer does, too.

"I assume she's jealous of your success."

"She's been working on a manuscript for a long time now. I think it's safe to say that we have quite a few unresolved issues." I shrug, but it's not the casual thing I intend it to be. "The fact that my mother still treats her like a daughter hasn't really helped."

"So, the jealousy cuts both ways." He's watching my face for reaction and I realize I shouldn't be surprised at his quick assessment. Spencer creates characters and their motivations, too. "But surely she'll be glad to have the publicity for the store. And given that *Sandcastle Sunrise* is set here and written by a local, the anniversary edition will be a big seller for her."

I wince. "I'd appreciate it if you wouldn't bring that up. I'll need to find the right time to tell her." I say this as if there could possibly be a "right" time for this.

"Why is that?" He's still watching my face.

"It's a long story," I mutter as we come off the bridge. And since it's a story I have no desire to share at the moment I officially welcome him to the Outer Banks, point out Milepost 1, and give a quick sketch of where we are (Kitty Hawk) and why we're going to skip the more commercial areas along 158 (aka the North Croatan Highway) in order to drive down NC 12, that locals still call the Beach Road, because, well, it is.

I breathe in the familiar smells and sights of my childhood as we drive south, parallel to the Atlantic, passing through the eastern edge of Kitty Hawk and Kill Devil Hills, where both sides of the narrow two-lane road are lined with stilt houses and cottages.

Spencer rubbernecks. "I had friends whose families used to drive down from New York every summer, but I really had no idea how beautiful it was."

We pass hotels, stores, and restaurants. As I point out the places that were a part of my childhood, we get occasional glimpses of sea oats bobbing on dunes that frame the vibrant green ocean. At the moment it's swishing rather genteelly onto shore.

"Wow." Spencer sits up straighter. "That's just . . . wow."

I smile. Even writers have a hard time coming up with adjectives that do this place justice.

"There've been a lot of changes since the Outer Banks got 'discovered.' It's way more developed. A lot of the mom-and-pop hotels and small businesses are gone, and there are so many huge rental homes up and down the beach now that it's hard for regular people to afford to live here. And, of course, between Memorial Day and Labor Day the population quadruples. For locals it's definitely a love/hate thing. Can't live with the tourists, can't live without them.

"Now we're in Nags Head. That's Gallery Row." I point to the collection of shops just south of Milepost 10. "And that"—I gesture to a slightly sagging white clapboard building on the corner of East Bonnett Street just south of the space-themed putter golf that's been there as long as I can remember. "That's where my mother first rented a room when we got here. It used to be called Snug Harbor."

My heart is actually racing as we pass the Nags Head Fishing Pier. I take a deep breath as I slow to turn onto the sand-strewn driveway that leads back toward the beach. "And this is the Sandcastle, where I grew up."

I'm not even at a complete stop when the front door opens and my mother is outside, smiling and waving from the front porch.

Kendra

The Sandcastle

Lauren's at the wheel of some sort of small silver compact and I'm already clattering down the stairs before she pulls to a complete stop. My heart pounds as they open the car doors and climb out. I feel Lauren's arms go around me and we sway and hug. In that moment I finally let go of the dread and anxiety that have colored my anticipation. In that moment I feel only love and excitement. There isn't room for anything else.

And then she's stepping back. "Mom, this is Spencer Harrison. Spencer, my mom, Kendra Jameson."

Spencer is every bit as good-looking as he is in photos, maybe better, and he has a truly blinding smile. I'm prepared for a bit of snobbery or big-city superiority, but his smile is wide and genuine and I see no judgment in his emerald-green eyes. Rather than putting out his hand he wraps me in a friendly hug. "It's a pleasure to finally meet you."

"Ditto." It's the only word that comes to mind, but I mean it.

I feel a small bit of hope that he will help deflect some of the turbulence that Lauren will feel when I tell her about Jake. And I'm beyond relieved that she won't be alone when she learns that her father is alive and has been for the last forty years.

I tell myself to stay in the moment and not waste it worrying about what lies ahead, but all I can think about is what that revelation will do to our relationship. The line "So, Mrs. Lincoln, other than that how did you like the play?" runs through my head. I realize that both Spencer and Lauren are looking at me. "I'm sorry, what did you say?"

"I said I can certainly see where Lauren gets her good looks," he says again.

I am not averse to flattery though in fact I've always known that the person Lauren resembles most is Jake's mother. Just as Jake's wife deduced. Anxiety flutters back up to the surface at this thought. Once again I tamp it down.

"Thank you." I turn to Lauren. "He had the good sense to ask you to marry him *and* he's flattering his future mother-in-law." I tap a finger to my forehead. "Smart man."

"That he is." My daughter stares at me then turns and presses the key so that the trunk pops open.

"What can I carry?" I ask as Lauren slings an overnight bag over one shoulder.

"Nothing, thanks." Spencer pulls out two midsize bags, closes the trunk, then follows us upstairs and across the porch.

I see him take in the living room, but there's nothing but pleasant interest on his face.

"You can put those in here," I say, showing him to Lauren's room. "Now that you're engaged I guess it's okay if you sleep together."

Lauren shoots me a look and I know she's wondering where all this nervous chatter is coming from. But the truth is no matter how many times I tell myself I don't have to address the Jake issue immediately, I'm unable to push it far enough away to relax. Sometime before Sunday I'm going to have to explain the unexplainable. I feel a little like a condemned man contemplating his last meal. How on earth could he possibly enjoy it given what's going to happen after dessert?

In the kitchen I pour cold drinks, set out a plate of snickerdoodles, and wonder, as we settle around the table, if there's some way to ease into the subject that might somehow soften the blow. But even as they munch on the cookies and chat comfortably with me and with each other, I know that no matter how I frame the news, or when I introduce it, there's going to be an explosion. I just hope there'll be survivors.

I refill glasses and pass the plate of cookies around again. Soon we're down to crumbs. "Would you like to take a walk on the beach and then maybe go somewhere sunset-worthy for dinner?" I ask, deciding it's okay to just enjoy tonight and figure out the best way to bring up the topic tomorrow.

"Yes and yes!" Lauren answers for both of them. "Come on." She reaches for Spencer's hand. "I want to grab a pair of flip-flops. Be right back, Mom."

I busy myself putting the cookie tin away. Then I wipe the counters and the kitchen table. As I do, I imagine some unseen hand tossing a grenade in through the open window. I hear it roll across the floor and finally come to a stop near my feet. But I will not bend over and pick it up. And I'm most definitely not going to pull the pin.

Fourteen

ᕫ

Lauren

I don't believe shoes should be allowed on the beach so I walk barefoot—flip-flops dangling from my fingers "just in case"—letting my toes curl in the soft, cool sand. If feet could talk I'm pretty sure they'd be sighing with pleasure.

My mother doesn't bother with flip-flops, either. Spencer is wearing his sneakers but I have no doubt he'll see the light once enough of the beach finds its way inside them.

"My folks have a place in the Hamptons but these dunes are a little different than I'm used to." Spencer nods to the rounded mounds of sand that edge the beach, formed by wind and waves and time.

My mother smiles.

"You ain't seen nothin' yet," I brag. "Wait till I show you Jockey's Ridge, which just happens to be the tallest active sand dune system in the eastern United States, and the Wright Brothers National Memorial. The monument sits on top of a ninety-foot hill that began life as a sand dune."

Spencer laughs but also manages to look suitably impressed.

Although the signs of heavy rain are still apparent, Mother Nature is gifting us with blue skies, pulled taffy clouds, and calm seas. The ocean washes in and out with a friendly, non-threatening whoosh that nonetheless whittles away at the ground we walk on. Over time it reshapes these islands and spits of land.

It makes some larger and others smaller. Sometimes it swallows them completely along with whatever was built on top of them. As any Banker will tell you, it's best not to forget that even the gentlest nibbling can become a gobble. That the breeze can become a gale that sends the ocean pounding in like an agitated sumo wrestler. More than a thousand ships have gone down along this shoreline. There's a reason lifesaving stations were so important here, even before they came under the rule of the Coast Guard.

We walk at a leisurely pace that I'm pretty sure is illegal in Manhattan. For a while I just soak in the sun and enjoy the breeze tossing my hair. I listen with half an ear to my mother and Spencer go about the business of getting acquainted. It's clear they don't need me to interpret or facilitate.

Always interested in people's stories, Spencer asks her how we settled on the Outer Banks, and I hear my mother's account of how shortly after I was born she just got on the road and drove east until she reached the ocean and couldn't go any farther, an impulsive decision she blames on postpregnancy hormones and lack of sleep. There's no mention of her grief at becoming a widow so young while she was pregnant with me. Or the horror of losing her parents to a car accident not long after, which is why there are no pictures of them with me. She has always presented her arrival here as the beginning of a great, if unplanned, adventure. (Which is odd given how planned out and organized she's been since I've been aware enough to notice.) But I think, not for the first time, how very alone we were and how frightened she must have been.

I left for New York at the same age she came here and in much more dire straits than I would have faced if Bree hadn't wussed out on me, but I always knew I could come home if I had to. Plus I had a mother who was my biggest cheerleader just a phone call away.

I tune back in as she explains how her aunt Velda in Charlotte became a mother and grandmother to us. She looks off across the ocean and I admire her all over again for all she lost and all she survived. "She was the keeper of THE DRESS. When she died it came to me." My mother's voice breaks and I take Spencer's hand and give it a warning squeeze. I learned as a child not to ask too many questions about the series of events that brought us here.

"Ahh," Spencer says. "THE DRESS. Lauren showed me a picture of you in it. It's beautiful, and I love that it's been in your family for so long."

My mother nods but her smile is a careful one.

"From what I've seen, Jameson women are not only beautiful and talented but fearless. You picked up and went somewhere completely new with a newborn. Lauren climbed on that bus to New York by herself. I'm not sure I would have had the nerve to do either of those things at twenty-one. I could barely make myself try a different deli or bagel place at that age."

"Well, New Yorkers are loyal to their favorite restaurants and sports teams to the bitter end and against all logic," I point out, grateful that he's introduced a lighter tone. I've never told my mother or Spencer how traumatic that first year in New York was and I'm not planning to unburden myself now.

"Too true," he concedes. "But you both demonstrated a lot of chutzpah. I admire that."

My mother looks around and draws what looks like a steadying breath. "I still love it here more than any place I've ever been, but I wish you could have seen it the way it was when I first arrived. There was a fraction of a fraction of the houses that are here now. And when you became a full-time resident it was like you'd become a member of a club—only it had no rules or membership dues. There was no mold you had to 'fit into' unless it was the lack of a mold." She smiles and something in her loosens. "Things could get a little wild and crazy. But at the same time you could live alone in a house with no neighbors for miles and miles and feel completely safe. The electricity went out at the drop of a hat or the approach of an incoming storm. The roads that were here would get buried in sand or end up under-water. You had to have a pioneer spirit and a willingness to live without a lot of the comforts of 'civilization.' It helped you bond with the people around you—and we were there for each other. Kind of like settlers circling the wagons."

"God, Mom, how *did* you manage?" I've always admired her stamina and positive attitude, but like any child I simply took her strength for granted. So many of the women I met growing up here were also strong and fiercely independent. I just assumed that was a female trait.

"Well, when you have a baby to feed you do whatever you have to," she says with a shrug. "I waitressed and cleaned houses and hotel rooms. I peeled shrimp. Sold bait. There was almost always work if you were willing to do it. And it was so blissfully casual here—when I couldn't bring Lauren with me I left her with other mothers I knew. And I kept their kids in turn. But it was my job at the Galleon Esplanade that became the closest to full-time and kept me going."

We're getting close to Jennette's Pier now and I can see the gulls swooping down, no doubt eyeing the fishermen who've dropped their lines.

"There were a lot of people around my age on the beach when I got here. Many of them came to surf or work at a hotel or restaurant for the summer. A lot of them never left. It's a place that can speak to you if you're listening."

She's smiling full out now and her long dark hair with its threads of gray streams out behind her.

"Now, that's a pier." Spencer takes in the local landmark and whistles admiringly.

"It's been rebuilt three times," she tells him. "The first two times it was made of wood. This one's concrete and way longer.

If you walk all the way to the end you're a thousand feet out in the Atlantic."

After that we turn back toward the house and walk in silence for a time until the sun begins to lose some of its intensity.

"What do you think?" my mother asks. "Are you hungry? I thought we could grab dinner at Miller's. It's a great place to eat and watch the sunset."

"I'm game," I reply. "Except I'm still stuffed from all the snickerdoodles. Maybe we can just do drinks and appetizers?"

"Absolutely," Mom says.

"Sounds good. Do we need to change or anything?" Spencer asks as we near the house.

Mom and I laugh. When we arrive at Miller's the downstairs is hopping but there's no wait because it's comfortably preseason. Heads turn as we make our way through the main dining room toward the back deck. We return smiles and waves the whole way, but don't stop until we're outside and on the dock that sticks out into Roanoke Sound.

"Wow. What a view." Spencer takes it all in, his eyes roaming over the marsh grass, across the slightly choppy water, and up to the great red ball of sun as we make our way out toward the end of the dock. Shards of reflected light shimmer and dance across the surface. "Did you actually know every person in the restaurant or did it just seem that way?"

"Most of them." My mom smiles. "That won't be true in season but right now there are a lot of locals."

As if in confirmation a couple I've seen but never met looks up from their table in the cupola as we approach. They get up to hug my mom and congratulate us on our engagement before she makes the introductions.

I see Spencer's questioning look as we reach the end of the dock and lean out over the railing. "Think of them as theater folk in New York only with flip-flops and an affinity for fishing.

I'm guessing word went out by smoke signal five minutes after we called to break the news."

"There are no secrets here," my mother says automatically, then adds, "Or at least not many."

The sun slips a little farther and the brine-scented breeze stiffens. The sea grass sways at the edge of the marsh. We simply stand and breathe it all in for a while. Spencer is beaming and I realize I'm smiling, too. My shoulders are looser, my body more fluid. As if it understands it's in a place that doesn't require the same level of readiness.

"The wind's picking up and the temperature will drop as soon as the sun sets. Let's go upstairs and grab a table in the bar. We can watch it set from there." Mom turns and leads us back the way we came, then up the outside staircase and through the doorway to the bar, where we settle at a high top positioned in front of a windowless opening with a stellar view and fresh air.

Before we're fully settled on our barstools a twentysomething-year-old with blond dreadlocks and a sunny smile comes out from behind the room-length bar. After hugs all around and congratulations on our engagement, he takes our drink orders.

Spencer grins.

"Holden is the son of a good friend of mine," Mom says by way of explanation. "And an excellent bartender."

Our margaritas arrive in minutes. We raise plastic glasses emblazoned with the words *Peace, Love, and Sunsets* and clink them in toast. They're tart and delicious. We're all smiling after the first few sips, our eyes pinned on the glowing sun.

"Gosh, I can't think when I've felt this relaxed and we've only been here a couple of hours," Spencer says after another sip of his margarita.

"This place can do that to you." My mother is clearly pleased. "Maybe it will inspire something. Wasn't Lin-Manuel Miranda on vacation on an island when he first read Alexander Hamilton's biography?"

"True," Spencer says. "Hawaii, as I recall."

"Well, just let us know if a song starts coming to you, and I'll ask for extra napkins," I tease, although he has in fact started more than one song in just this way.

He laughs but in truth this *is* the most relaxed I've ever seen him if you don't count the first minute or two after sex.

We look over our menus, and I worry slightly that Spencer is going to try to turn this into a foodie experience, but he says, "All the appetizers look great. I'm happy to try anything you put in front of me."

And so he does as we work our way through orders of tuna nachos, fish tacos, mussels, steamed crab legs, and everything else we can think of that he might like until the sun puddles into the water, sending up a last celestial glow. Full and content, I lean against Spencer while he charms and entertains my mother, who is always a first-rate audience.

It's close to nine by the time we head back to the house. Inside, both Spencer and I yawn.

"Must be all the fresh air. I have some reading I need to do and I wouldn't mind doing it horizontal. If you'll excuse me, I think I'll call it a night." He leans over and kisses my cheek then hugs my mother. "Thanks for dinner."

"My pleasure. Sleep well."

He nods pleasantly, but I know from experience that's the last check he'll let her pick up.

"I won't be too long behind you," I say before following my mom into the kitchen.

"So?" I drop down onto a dinette chair.

"So . . . what?" She sits across from me with an innocent look on her face.

I look back.

"Seriously? I can't believe you even have to ask. He's a great guy. I like him. And he's clearly crazy about you. Which in my book takes precedence over pretty much everything else." She hesitates. "But the only thing that matters is how you feel. And that you're certain."

My mother's always taken this approach. No pushing, no agenda. I don't know where she learned this given how young she was when she lost her parents or if she was just born that way, but at the moment I'm incredibly grateful that when fate spun the mother roulette wheel, I hit the jackpot.

"Yeah." I feel a warm glow at her praise. "He *is* great and I *do* love him. I want to marry him. It was just that there were some work things that took me by surprise. And then I turned forty and then there was the proposal. You know how badly I react to the unexpected. I just needed time to process."

An odd look of distress passes over her face, and I try to imagine why. My need to be prepared so that I'm not taken by surprise is, after all, no surprise to her.

"And we come from such different places and backgrounds. He has no idea what it's like to be without money or a family to lean on."

There's that look again and then she says, "You and I have always had each other and friends who *feel* like family. And I hope . . . well, I know it hasn't been easy, but I hope it's been enough. I . . ." She clasps her hands and presses them in her lap. Her face clears, but not without effort. "What I mean is you and Spencer wouldn't have lasted a year and Spencer wouldn't have asked you to marry him if you didn't have enough in common. You're both creative. You both love and feel at home in New York. Although I don't have much experience with marriage, my guess is you don't necessarily want to spend your life with someone who's exactly like you. Where would the fun be in that?"

Her words make sense but there's something off. She stands and begins to putter, getting coffee ready for the morning, double-checking ingredients for brunch tomorrow. This forces me to think of Bree and all the crap that's piled up between us. I retrieve a sponge and wipe off the table and the already clean countertops. I wonder if I can get away with skipping the store visit and just ask Spencer to snap a candid photo of me that can be Photoshopped in front of Title Waves.

As if she's reading my mind my mother looks up from the cabinet she's closing. "I hope you'll try to mend fences with Brianna." She swallows. "She could really use a friend right now."

My "hmmph" is barely audible. I don't even ask why she thinks Brianna needs a friend. It's not as if I didn't need Brianna when she bugged out on me and the plans we'd made. And then when I tried to warn her that Clay wasn't really ready to settle down yet she accused me of being jealous and petty and not wanting to see her happy. When I came back to be her maid of honor because of a promise we'd made in kindergarten and because my mother was planning it, she acted as if she'd been invited into some secret sisterhood that I couldn't possibly understand.

It only got worse when she started having children and I got published, which happened right around the same time. Ultimately, we had nothing left in common except a shared birthdate, a former friendship, and a mother who still treated us like sisters even when we so clearly weren't.

I pull silverware out of the drawer and start setting the table, mostly to have something to do with my hands. I nod so she knows I heard her, but I don't promise anything. I can't. Even if Bree and I both apologize for letting the other down—and that's a big *if*, I don't really see us suddenly being BFFs again as if nothing happened. I don't care what those glass-is-half-full people say. Positive thinking and good intention can take you only so far.

My mother carries juice glasses over to the table and begins to place them rather emphatically as if in punctuation. "You know, sometimes people make mistakes." Blam. "One bad choice can lead to another." Blam. "And then another." Blam. "Before you know it your life is upside down and you've hurt people you never meant to." Blam. "People you love."

This of course has nothing to do with what we've been talking about. Or if it does she hasn't explained what that connection is. Plus, her voice is kind of shaky and it's a miracle none of the glasses shattered.

"Mom?" She isn't looking at me. She's studying the table as if wondering how the glasses got there. I feel a prick of fear. "Are you all right?" I step closer and reach for her hand.

Her head jerks up. There's a haunted look in her eyes I've never seen before. But it's gone in seconds.

"Of course I'm all right. I'm just overexcited. All I need is a good night's sleep and I'll be raring to go." She yawns as if to illustrate, but once again something feels off. "I know you never sleep the night before you fly. I'm guessing you could use a good night's sleep, too."

I watch her closely as she brushes off my concern. My mother always urged us to share our worries and problems and I'm an adult now. Good God, I'm middle-aged. "You do know that I love you and that I'm here for you, whatever you need, just like you've always been for me."

Her face clears and her smile is warm, but I can tell the change required effort. "I know, sweetie, and it means a lot to me. But I think I need to get to bed now."

There's a reticence in her manner, a watchfulness. Something is bothering her and for some reason she's unwilling to share it.

"Okay," I say, finally blowing a hank of hair out of my eyes. "Until tomorrow, then." I lean over and kiss her cheek. "Sleep tight."

"Don't let the bedbugs bite." She completes our bedtime ritual automatically, and I turn reluctantly and leave her there.

As I walk to my old bedroom, I think of all that she's sacrificed and done for me. How we've always shared everything, how she's always given and demanded total honesty. At least with me. She's always treated Bree as if she's somehow too fragile for such things.

My imagination sits up and gets to work spewing out a stream of worst-and-even-worst-case scenarios. Potential illnesses fill my head. I attempt to beat them back but there are too many possibly awful diagnoses to demolish them completely. I tell myself that whatever it is we'll deal with it together. Sick is not a death sentence. I can handle sick. I have resources. And some of the best doctors in the world are in New York City. Terminal, however, is out of the question. I am not ready to even contemplate a world without my mother in it.

෬

I enter the bedroom where Spencer is sleeping peacefully in the center of the joined mattresses, clearly unconcerned with the crack. His arms are thrown out in abandon. I love that he sleeps with the same enthusiasm he does everything. I slide gently into bed, careful not to wake him. Then I curl up against his side and lay my head on his shoulder.

I'm watching his chest go up and down, cataloguing each breath, when I hear my mother moving around her bedroom. I used to fall asleep to that sound, soothed and comforted by the fact that she was just across the hall. The wind kicks up another notch and I hear the sand pelt the house. The Sandcastle begins to sway.

Now I send up a silent prayer to counter my out-of-control imaginings. *Please, God, don't let her die. I'll find a way to be okay with anything else but that.*

Fifteen

⟅⟆

Kendra

Given the confession I'm going to have to make tomorrow I expect to spend the night wide-eyed and awake, but I fall asleep almost as soon as my head hits the pillow.

When I wake early-morning light is creeping through the window. Telling myself this is a good omen, I wash my face, brush my teeth, and dress, then head into the kitchen to make coffee.

The warm dark smell wafts through the kitchen and wraps itself around the salt-tinged air, and I tell myself that everything will somehow work out. That I'll find a way to explain. That I'll keep talking until I make Lauren understand that I never set out to pass myself off as a widow but that when I saw the sign in front of Snug Harbor and went in to see about renting a room, I burst into tears and admitted Lauren and I were pretty much alone in the world. When I stopped crying long enough for Barbara, the landlady, to tell me that she knew how hard it was to lose a husband, I didn't correct her mistaken assumption.

When I realized that I was going to have to let go of Jake completely for his and Lauren's sake, I had no choice but to jettison his parents, too.

The story I made up about the tragic loss of my parents came not long after when Barbara inquired whether I didn't have any "people" at all. When they actually died in a car crash a year and a half later, I worried that my lie had tripped some "kill" switch or something in the universe. Between the fictional deaths and the real ones I felt like some sort of serial killer for whom forgiveness would always be just out of reach.

But it did allow me to show Lauren pictures of her father and both sets of grandparents without making her feel unloved or ignored by absent relatives. Looking at the small photo album that was one of the few things I'd left home with was one of her favorite pastimes. For me it was more like a penance.

I drink the last of my coffee to the soundtrack I love; the quiet chirping of birds, the rustle of wind in the trees, and the distant but ever-present sound of the surf advancing and retreating. The house settles companionably around me and for a time I manage to lose myself in the tasks at hand. There's a part of me that knows I should also be preparing for "the talk" we have to have today, but I'm not sure this is something that can be prepped for. I tell myself not to be afraid. That this is my daughter, the person I love most and am closest to in the world, and that somehow I'll not only recognize the right moment when it arrives but will also know exactly what to say. I believe this because I must. I simply can't consider the alternative.

When Lauren comes out I pour her a cup of coffee then continue my preparations as she settles at her old seat to drink her coffee. She is not a morning person, my daughter, and I know from long experience it's best to let her let you know when she's ready for conversation. My heart thumps too wildly while I wait.

"What can I do to help?" she finally asks mid-yawn.

"You can just keep me company for now."

The yawn ends on a nod. "What are we having?"

"I'm going to do a triple-cheese and asparagus scramble with buttermilk biscuits and crispy potatoes. Plus, stacks of my world-famous chocolate chip pancakes with homemade syrup." I realize I'm rushing my words and force myself to slow down. "Bree's bringing a blueberry crumble for 'dessert.'"

"Glad to see you're keeping it simple and low-cal." Her tone is light but her eyes on my face are not. "So you *are* feeling okay." It's a statement and a question.

"Yes." I take her empty cup and refill it. "Of course." I find a smile. I know it's selfish, but I need these last few hours to feel as normal as possible. "I was just thinking that you might want to try on THE DRESS later today."

I see her eyes spark with excitement and I tell myself that it's all right to allow myself the pleasure of seeing her in THE DRESS before I launch into any kind of explanation. I keep the conversation light as we catch up. But I hate having to watch every word and I breathe a shaky sigh of relief when Spencer arrives and places a kiss on the top of Lauren's head. "Okay—was it my imagination or was the Sandcastle actually swaying last night?"

Lauren snorts. I welcome the smile that tugs at my lips.

"Is that a yes or a no?" He drops into the chair next to hers.

"Yes, it was swaying," Lauren says. "But that's a good thing. Houses are built on stilts so that they can move and give in the wind rather than snapping or collapsing."

"Ah, so I didn't actually need to lie there with one eye open in case we had to escape the rubble or something."

"Nope." She's holding back another snort.

"That would have been good to know *before* I went to bed. You know, so that I wouldn't have spent most of the night worrying about dying."

"Sorry. That's exactly how I feel the whole time we're in the air." Lauren leans over and busses his cheek. "Here it's just part of 'home.' You looked so sound asleep when I came to bed I didn't think to wake you and warn you of what might happen if the wind picked up." Her amusement is clear.

"I'm sorry you had a rough night. I've always liked the feeling—it's kind of like sleeping on a boat." I like him, and I'm incredibly grateful that Lauren will have emotional backup if my confession goes badly. "How do you take your coffee?"

"Black, thanks. And lots of it. I'm going to need extra caffeine to make up for the hours I lost imagining the roof caving in."

"Poor baby," Lauren teases. "Around here warning someone not to be afraid of the wind is like telling a tourist in New York not to worry about all the people. It's just part of the package." She finishes off her second cup of coffee and gets up to serve as my assistant.

"Are you two planning to look at potential wedding venues while you're here?" I ask in an attempt to imagine some outcome of my talk with Lauren that will not end in her refusal to ever speak to me again.

"Absolutely," Spencer answers quickly. "I think we should look at all the possibilities then sit down and hash it out."

"That's very practical of you," I say. Have I mentioned how much I like him?

"Well, I'm only planning to get married once. We might as well take the time to make sure we know what we want."

"The Elizabethan Gardens are really beautiful," Lauren says. "We can take a look around when we go over to Roanoke Island."

"Roanoke Island?" Spencer looks up. "Isn't that where those early colonists disappeared from?"

"Yes, in fact the Beach Road out front is also called Virginia Dare Trail. She was the first English child born in the Americas and disappeared with the rest of the colony. Every summer *The Lost Colony* is put on in this cool waterside theater near the spot where the fort once stood."

"Interesting."

"Yeah. It's America's longest-running outdoor drama—it'll be eighty-two years this summer."

"Eighty-two years, huh?" Spencer smiles. "Kind of puts a good Broadway run in perspective, doesn't it?"

"I thought you'd appreciate that." She smiles impishly at him.

"You should definitely take Spencer back to Jennette's Pier and show him the event space upstairs," I add. "It's got high ceilings and tons of glass. The view is gorgeous and there's a covered outside deck."

Lauren laughs. "Do you remember when one of the grooms-men at a destination wedding slipped off the pier and went into the water in his rented tux?"

"Hey, I have a few friends who could use a good dunk now and then," Spencer says amiably.

I keep the discussion going, peppering them with questions and suggestions as I get out the brunch ingredients. Right now all I care about is hearing as much of my daughter's voice and laughter as possible.

Bree

I slept in my office last night and I'm still barely speaking to Clay on Saturday morning when it's time to head over to Kendra's. I'm not sure I can bear to be in the same car with him even for this short a ride. Not today of all days.

"I'm going to take the Jeep. I need to run back to the store afterward anyway and that'll save me a little time. See you there."

Clay shoots me a look, but I just grab my keys and head outside. Lily climbs in the passenger seat, her thumbs flying over her phone screen, unaware there was a choice to be made. "Dana says she thinks Spencer Harrison is hot. You know, for an old guy." She buckles her seat belt. "I've never met anybody who's a famous playwright and songwriter. That's pretty cool, right?"

"It is." I'm careful to keep the irritation and, yes, the jealousy out of my voice. If I'd gotten on that bus with Lauren I might have had the same success she has *and* I could have fallen in love with someone creative and worldly and *faithful*. And while I realize that plenty of people in Manhattan probably cheat on their spouses, I'm pretty sure *everyone* doesn't know it. Of course, if I'd gone I wouldn't have Rafe or Lily. Or the bookstore. Or Clay's family. Or the closest thing I've ever had to a mother, just around the corner.

My hands are tight—too tight—on the steering wheel. I manage to unclench them by reminding myself that I haven't failed at anything. I've got the home and family I dreamed of. And now I've finished my novel. It's not about how long it takes to write a book, but how good it is. Plus, no marriage or relationship is perfect. I'd like to forget all the nasty things I said to Lauren when she informed me that Clay wasn't ready for marriage, though I'm sure she never has. I'll need to be careful not to let my anger at and disappointment in Clay become too obvious. As far as I'm concerned I'm the wronged party in her and my personal mini-drama. And I'm not about to open myself up to an *I told you so.*

Normally, arriving at Kendra's is a mood brightener, but my stomach roils as I make the turn onto her driveway. Clay pulls in right after us, but I don't look back. I will not walk into the Sandcastle scowling and unhappily married. I intend to at least *appear* friendly and approachable just like Kendra asked. If Lauren chooses not to respond in kind, that will be on her.

Lauren's smiling when we walk through the door and already hugging Lily before she makes it all the way into the kitchen. "Oh my gosh! Look how grown-up you are!" Lauren exclaims in what looks like delight. I try not to stare at the perfect haircut that frames and flatters her face or the jeans and blouse that appear casual but are no doubt "designer." She's still tall and lean, which makes the extra six or seven pounds I can never seem to drop feel like twenty.

Lily dimples as Lauren introduces her to Spencer then expands the introduction to include Clay and me. Clay hugs her without the slightest hesitation then shakes hands with Spencer while Kendra throws her arms around Lily and Clay. Lauren and I don't turn our backs on each other, but we don't move any closer, either. "Congratulations on your engagement." My words sound hollow and stiff in my own ears even though I'm pretty sure I'm still smiling.

"I hear you did it up right," Clay says as he shakes Spencer's hand. "Down on one knee in some fancy restaurant with people doo-wopping."

"Yes," I say without stopping to think. "I can just imagine how Lauren felt being surprised that way." My comment goes right over Clay's and Spencer's heads, but Lauren's eyes meet mine for a split second. An acknowledgment of how well we once knew each other.

We linger in the kitchen that's filled with the warm and wonderful smells Kendra's cooking always produces and that I've filed away under the category heading of *home*. I watch Lauren surreptitiously. We used to know what the other would say before they did. And would have felt free to weigh in with anything that crossed our minds. But that's no longer true. What would have been a simple observation then, would be a criticism now. We've been avoiding each other for so long that the best course of action is probably not to see or say too much. For the first time I realize that this works both ways.

Kendra pours mimosas and hands them around. Even Lily gets a tiny bit of champagne in hers. Then Kendra raises her glass and says, "To Lauren and Spencer. I'm so thrilled that you've found each other. I know we all wish you a real-life happily ever after."

"To Lauren and Spencer!" We all clink glasses and drink. I'm careful not to look at Clay, who seems to see no irony in drinking to happily ever after, after trampling all over ours.

Lily laughs and downs what I assume is her first sip of champagne then lifts her phone to get a photo of the happy couple.

"Clay, can you refill the glasses?" Kendra asks as Lauren and

I automatically stand and begin to carry food to the table as we have so many times.

I glance at Lauren at the same moment she glances at me and I know we're both remembering the three of us sitting around this table together. Of all the meals we shared, it's the dinner that Kendra prepared the day I moved in that I remember best. Not because of what it tasted like but because of the thought that Kendra put into it. The lasagna was made from my grandmother's recipe. The crusty garlic bread was baked fresh that day, because Kendra knew how much I loved it. Dessert was Kendra's now-famous triple-chocolate cake that she was trying to perfect at the time and that she said was not yet good enough to serve to anyone outside the family.

I remember how grateful I was to be the third member of this tiny family. How I thought Lauren and I would always share everything. When she's in New York the loss and betrayal are muted, but when she's here . . . Her presence is a stark reminder that that was little more than wishful thinking.

"This looks great." Spencer appears genuinely pleased with the food that's coming his way. Conversation flows around me as we fill our plates. Clay, who's been making conversation with Spencer, throws back his head and laughs. Since I'm trying to ignore my husband I have no idea what was said, but I feel a fresh spike of anger that he seems to be having such a great time.

Then Kendra says, "Before we dig in, I'd like to toast one more happy event."

We all raise our glasses and Kendra says, "Brianna has finished her novel. I think that's something well worth toasting."

I feel the blush spread over my cheeks even as I note Lauren's surprise. Clearly, she never thought this would ever happen. That surprise stings and it's all I can do not to tell her where she can shove her Central Park West apartment and her multibook contracts. I can barely bring myself to take a sip after everyone clinks glasses.

"I always knew you'd do it," Kendra says. "Look at all you've created—your family, the store, and now a completed novel. You just put other things first."

"She put *everything* first," Lauren says.

I tell myself not to respond, that this is not the time or place, but the words nonetheless come rushing out. "Maybe that's because I didn't have someone else's outline and notes to work from."

Kendra winces. Clay takes a long pull on his mimosa. Spencer looks confused.

"I take it Lauren never mentioned that her first published novel was one we brainstormed and plotted together?" I grind out.

"That was fifteen years and twelve books ago," Lauren snaps. "I think our publishing records speak for themselves."

"That book jump-started your career," I shoot back, shocked at how easily the words I've swallowed all these years spew out.

"That and all the ad writing, and articles, and blogging and ghostwriting," Lauren responds. "Not to mention all the crummy jobs I had to work to stay afloat when I lost the roommate I was counting on. And FYI—notes and a rough outline are not a book—and certainly not a bestseller." She barely pauses. "And it wasn't like *you* were ever going to do anything with it."

I take the blow. There's some small part of me that acknowledges the truth in her statement. But that book belonged to both of us and today I can't seem to turn the other cheek. "Maybe not. But it was a huge hit and in all these years you've never once mentioned or acknowledged that you didn't come up with the idea yourself."

"Girls. Please." The distress in Kendra's voice is evident. We both know she wants us to do more than stop arguing. But I'm far too angry to apologize. Lauren stares straight ahead and chews as if her life depends on it.

We sit in an uncomfortable silence. Some of us pretend to eat. Clay doesn't look at me. Neither does Lily.

Finally Kendra scrapes back her chair. "I think it's time for dessert," she says, standing and picking up her plate. We all jump up to help clear the table, men included. "I'm pouring coffee. Will you please serve your blueberry crumble, Brianna?"

I do as Kendra requests, not bothering to ask who wants any before I thump plates of it around the table, wincing when I realize that I thumped Clay's hardest of all and that eagle-eye Lauren no doubt noticed. I feel especially small and petty for ruining the meal for Kendra, but I can't bring myself to apologize and I'm sure as hell not going to take it back. It's only the truth. I should have said it a long time ago. I've imagined telling Lauren off a million times. And in every imagining having my say made me feel infinitely better. But that's not how I feel now. In fact, although I wouldn't have thought it possible, I feel even worse than I did when I arrived.

Sixteen

∽

Lauren

Clay shovels the dessert into his mouth and keeps his head down. Lily excuses herself to go to the bathroom while Bree sits there with a kind of sick look on her face. Spencer picks up his fork and begins to eat the blueberry crumble. My mother glances back and forth between Bree and me. It's clear that all she wants is for us to "kiss and make up."

I'm way too furious to eat so much as a bite of Bree's dessert. The childish angry part of me would love to reach into the Pyrex dish, pick up a glob with my bare hand, and shove it into her face. But that can never happen.

Because although I saw Bree as a sister, my mother has always seen Bree as a victim of her parents' neglect and disinterest, vulnerable and in need of our protection. She treated her like a wounded bird that had been pushed out of the nest and I understood that I needed to do the same. That because I was stronger and had a mother who loved me, I had to be careful of Bree's feelings, that I should not be jealous of the attention my mother gave her, that lashing out at her like a real sister might was not an option. The way my mother has continued to treat her like a daughter even after our friendship fell apart . . . Well, it's as if the three bears decided to adopt Goldilocks and then took the little bear's chair away from him and gave it to Goldilocks because she "needed it" more.

But Bree's an adult now, a wife and mother, a business owner. She has even, as it turns out, finished a novel when no one including me ever thought she would. Am I still supposed to pull my punches?

Bree stands and turns to my mother. "I hate to run off but Mrs. McKinnon is at the store today and asked me to come by after brunch. She had some problem with the sales receipts. Clay's going to drop Lily off at her friend's house. But they can help you with the dishes before they go." She doesn't even look my way.

"Oh, but I assumed you'd be here while Lauren tries on THE DRESS. I hoped you would." My mother gives us both imploring looks. "Couldn't you come back after you finish at the store?"

"Oh, I'm sure you and Lauren don't need me in the middle of . . ." Bree says at the same time I say, "It makes no sense for Bree to get that close to home and come all the way back out to the beach again." As if it's some major journey and not a fifteen-minute drive across the Washington Baum Bridge and another couple minutes to the store.

"Actually, I have a few errands near Title Waves. Let me go grab my list. You could go with Bree and pick up the things I need while I supervise cleanup then get THE DRESS ready." She turns to Clay. "Perhaps you could take Spencer with you and show him around a bit after you drop off Lily."

She scampers off to her bedroom to retrieve—or, I suspect—concoct the list of errands before anyone can refuse. Spencer considers Bree and me. "You should go. It'll make your mother happy and you can take a few photos while you're there." He gets up and reaches for a remaining plate and glass to carry to the sink. "If Clay's busy I'll hang out on the back deck or take a walk on the beach. I don't think the groom should be here while the bride is trying on THE DRESS anyway."

"You're welcome to come along, man," Clay says. "I have to stop by one of our rental properties in Corolla—that's north of

Duck—but I can show you some of the sights up there and on our way back."

"Beach bars, more likely," Bree huffs then glances to see if I noticed.

"I have nothing against bars on beaches," Spencer says. "In fact, it occurs to me that being on vacation pretty much compels me to visit at least a couple."

My mother comes back with a list. She hands it to me with a determined if satisfied smile. "I'll have THE DRESS ready when you two get back."

"Right."

I look at Bree out of the corner of my eye as we leave the house and take the stairs down to the drive. She looks every bit as uncomfortable as I am at being thrown together. Neither of us speaks as we climb into her Jeep. I'm annoyed and oddly nervous. It's no accident that Bree and I haven't been alone since her wedding.

As she pulls onto the Beach Road my thoughts ping all over the place, ill-formed and at random, a mishmash of the past and the present. The day Bree and I strutted around with those cardboard birthday crowns on our heads. Our certainty that being born on the same day meant something important. The way we could talk for hours and hours without any effort at all and then call each other to talk some more. The years we spent sharing a bedroom and then a college dorm room. The countless meals we've eaten together. The problems we've hashed out.

I've avoided her as much as I could on my visits home not just because of my long-held anger at her, but because it hurts to have to weigh each word with someone with whom you once shared a private language that gushed out in a stream of consciousness.

It's easier to not think about her when I'm in New York. But she was such a part of who I was here that without my connection to her this place feels out of context, much less like *home*.

I try to tamp down my impatience. Surely my mother doesn't think that putting us in a car together and sending us out to do unnecessary errands is going to fix everything between Bree and me. But then I think that if my mother *does* have some sort of medical issue or illness—something my imagination refuses to let go of—then maybe that's what's driving her to get us back together. Maybe this is some sort of Hail Mary pass.

We're on the Washington Baum Bridge, Roanoke Sound flying by on either side—a drive we've made together countless times—when I surprise both of us by asking, "Have you noticed anything odd about my mother's behavior?"

I continue to stare out the window but I feel her eyes on me. "*Odd* meaning . . . 'out of character'?"

"Yes," I half snap because I'm already sorry I was first to speak. And because I'd forgotten Bree's habit of double-checking definitions. "I'm pretty sure that's what it means."

She turns her eyes back to the road. Just when I think she's not going to respond she says, "Well, she has seemed a little stressed out lately. Why?"

I'm not going to tell her what my imagination has been conjuring. How out of control it's been lately. "Nothing concrete. She just feels a bit off to me."

"Maybe you don't see her often enough to be able to tell the difference."

Before I can react to the dig she says, "Sorry. That was out of line. I'm just irritated with . . ." She cuts herself off as if there's any chance I don't know she's complaining about Clay.

"But I'm guessing you've already turned your mother's behavior into a fatal illness." She smiles almost reluctantly but her voice is no longer quite so irritated. "Remember when you had the flu that time, but you were convinced you were dying? It was right after we saw that revival of *Love Story* at the Pioneer."

Her words stir memory. I can still smell the acrid, burned metal smell of the projectors that almost drowned out the smell of popcorn. (Which was no mean feat given how much buttered popcorn had been popped in that place since it first opened in 1918.) "I may have overreacted a little."

"A little? As I recall you wrote out your last will and testament."

"Hey, you were going to get my prized copy of *Gone With the Wind*."

"Completely dog-eared." Without looking I know she's rolling her eyes.

"Well loved," I counter.

As we come off the bridge and turn east to Manteo, more memories knock on the door I thought I had nailed shut. This is the route my school bus took to Manteo Elementary School, where we first met, and which I know from my last visit bears no more resemblance to its old, original self than we do. I stop just short of asking if she knows what happened to Mr. Daniels, who was our favorite PE teacher. Open too many floodgates and a person can drown.

She takes a right on Sir Walter Raleigh, which is lined with nicely maintained clapboard homes with beautifully manicured lawns then passes Essex, where my mother's friend Deanna's Dogwood Inn sits on the far corner. The waterfront is a block away. I can see the tip of the re-created Roanoke Marshes Lighthouse at the edge of the boardwalk that lines the Shallowbag Bay Marina.

Bree turns into an alley and pulls into a reserved spot with a sign that says, I READ THEREFORE I PARK.

"Nice."

"Just one of the perks of being a titan of business." She reaches for the door handle. "Come on. Mrs. McKinnon is expecting me. Do you have the list?"

"Such as it is." I slam the car door and follow her into the tiny pharmacy that has somehow survived the onslaught of chains and superstores.

"Why, Lauren, how great to see you." Mrs. Endicott, a jovial woman who's had a cloud of white hair for as long as I can remember and merry blue eyes that sparkle with mischief, greets us from behind the counter and congratulates me on my engagement. Her husband, who died shortly after I moved to New York, had a white beard and a belly that jiggled when he laughed. When I was little I used to imagine that Mr. and Mrs. Endicott were Mr. and Mrs. Claus in disguise and that maybe he delivered gifts from here in the Outer Banks instead of the North Pole because it was closer even though I never saw a sign of an elf or a reindeer or even a sleigh.

"Thank you. It's nice to be back."

"You need to come home more often. Right, Brianna?"

"Um-hmmm," Bree says with a polite smile that is decidedly noncommittal. As I pay for the Aleve and hand sanitizer, both of which I saw this morning in my mother's medicine cabinet, I warn myself that however far I wander down memory lane it doesn't eliminate the distance between Bree and me.

At the dry cleaner's Mrs. Humphrey congratulates me on my engagement, gives Bree a hug, then hands over an ancient wool blanket that's been wrapped in plastic for storage until next winter. It's clear there was no hurry in retrieving it.

Back outside I wait while Bree puts the blanket and other unnecessary items in her car. I shift from foot to foot as I stare into the display window of the Attic Addict.

Some of my favorite clothes came from this consignment store. I played dress-up here as a child while my mother cleaned it. Adele Martin, a round, fleshy woman who had a big-city past she often alluded to but never really talked about, owned the store. She referred to herself as a "chocoholic" before the word existed and would slip me Snickers and Milky Way bars and set aside outfits she thought would look good on me as soon as they came in. I loved tottering around in high heels and making up stories to go along with the more exotic articles of clothing so much that it took me a long time to realize that my mother was trading her cleaning services for used clothing because we couldn't even afford the basics at Davis's Everything to Wear. Later Bree and I shopped here together for prom dresses and funky scarves and accessories. Adele claimed to know the history behind each article of clothing, but Bree and I entertained ourselves creating our own.

Bree steps up beside me and I see her reflection join mine in the store window—me tall and angular, her short and curvy. For a moment I see the two of us as we once were. Let myself remember how we could lie on our beds or on the living room floor reading for hours in total silence or talk nonstop for what felt like days at a time. How as teenagers we called each other *bitch* and it was a term of endearment.

"Do you remember the stories we used to make up about the clothes we tried on and who they used to belong to?" she asks.

"Are you kidding? I still have that trench coat that once belonged to Mata Hari. And the rhinestone necklace that we were certain had been designed by Paloma Picasso."

"Adele's funeral was so beautiful," she says quietly, staring straight ahead. "Mount Olivet Church was packed. Everyone wore bright colors and some piece of clothing or jewelry that she'd chosen for them. Afterward, at the reception, there were tables and tables of chocolate desserts—all of them made by hand. Kendra brought her beignets with chocolate pot de crème, and I ate so many I thought I'd get sick."

We both stare at our reflections and, I think, our past. The musky scent of Evening in Paris that clung to Adele and her clothes teases at my memory. I banish a dull ache of loss as we walk into Paramount Office Supply, where we pick up—I kid you not—an individual block of sticky notes. This is when I remind myself that I could have been out showing Spencer around or walking with him on the beach. Hell, I could already be trying on THE DRESS.

My grumble is automatic but I hear my mother's plea for us to mend fences, and I keep the grumble mostly under my breath as I follow Bree to the bookstore. A bell jangles as she pushes open the door to Title Waves.

For a brief second I take in the store, the tables that display bestsellers (including my own) along with local guidebooks and tomes on Outer Banks history. The floor-to-ceiling shelves. The whimsical artwork. I haven't been in for a while and either she's remodeled or I've forgotten (or possibly blocked) how warm and cozy it is. The store has flooded more than once—you can't be this close to the bay and not deal with the threat—but as far as I know this store is not going anywhere.

Then there are shouts of "Congratulations! You did it! Woo-hoo!!" And a group of women pop out from behind the walls that separate this side of the store from the side that houses the extensive children's section and register area.

I run into Bree's back with an "oof." When I detach myself and look over her shoulder, I see the women who are whistling and applauding. All of them rush forward. Digital flashes go off, and I close my mouth because I can feel it gaping. I take a step back from the onslaught and only then do I notice that it's Bree, not me, that they're rushing toward, Bree that each of them hugs.

Mrs. McKinnon steps from behind the desk and sails toward us. I was slightly in awe of her as a child and not only because she rapped my knuckles more than once when I grabbed more than my share of snack at Sunday school. As she puts her arms around Bree and crushes her to her breast, I vaguely remember my mother telling me that she'd recently lost her husband to whom she'd been married since God was a boy. It's clear that she's the one who organized the surprise celebration. I can't remember the last time anyone made a big deal about my finishing a novel—that's just part of what's expected—let alone threw a party.

"We are all so proud of you!" Mrs. McKinnon tells Bree.

"We knew you could do it and none of us can wait to read your novel once it's published."

I clamp my lips closed even more tightly as another flash goes off and only just manage to stop myself from snorting at their assumption that just because someone finishes a manuscript a publisher will want to buy it. I wonder uncharitably how anything written over such a long period of time can be at all cohesive. But then Bree glances over her shoulder at me, and I realize she knows what I'm thinking. Or at least knows very well that things don't work that way. As they shower her with obvious love and affection and—yes—admiration—I remind myself that I once greatly admired her and her writing talent, too. The only time Bree ever stuck her head in the sand was when it came to Clay.

I'm reintroduced to a woman named Leslie Parent, a tall, pixie-haired woman in her fifties who is the founding member of the B's, which is apparently short for "books, broads, and booze."

They all smile at me and offer congratulations on my engagement, but their real enthusiasm is showered on Brianna. It's obvious how much she means to them, how highly they think of her. I feel an unexpected tug of envy for the community she's built, the friends surrounding her. But this time instead of allowing the envy to reignite the flame of hurt and anger I've been stoking all these years, I feel a wave of longing for the friendship we once shared.

"May I get a photograph of the two of you?" Mrs. McKinnon asks. "And then one of the whole group right over there next to the sign? We could include it in the book club newsletter for those who couldn't be here today."

"Of course," Bree says as we're herded into position, though I sense she's more interested in pleasing Mrs. McKinnon and the assembled book club members than in having a picture that documents my presence.

Nonetheless I give my best smile for the camera and tilt my

head to its most flattering angle as Bree and I slip our arms gingerly around each other's backs, a move that once would have been instinctual and welcome. I keep smiling as everyone piles in around us and Leslie, who lays claim to the longest arms, attempts to include the entire group in her selfie.

As we're led to the celebratory punch and cookies, I try to shake off the sense of loss and regret swirling inside me. I know I need to replace it with something positive. Something concrete. Like the fact that I didn't even have to ask Leslie to send me a copy of the photo or tell Bree about the fifteenth-anniversary edition of *Sandcastle Sunrise*.

As I drink a glass of punch and answer questions about the "exciting" life of a bestselling author, I realize that although I'm not about to say so, I'm not entirely angry at my mother for sending Bree and me together on her made-up errands.

Seventeen

∽

Kendra

The Sandcastle

I'm not exactly hyperventilating, but I'm not anywhere near calm, either. In fact, I've been pacing the house since everyone left. At the moment, the pool of dread inside me feels as deep and unpredictable as the Atlantic. I haven't been this anxious since the morning I left Aunt Velda's with my four-day-old baby, afraid that if I lingered too long my father, who could be frighteningly persuasive, would show up and somehow convince me to give Lauren up.

I unwrap THE DRESS with clumsy fingers and lay it gently on my bed. It came to me shortly after Aunt Velda's death just as her will stipulated, accompanied by a handwritten note from her asking that I continue to make it available to any Jameson bride who wanted to wear it. I suspect it was her attempt to bring Lauren and me back into the family fold. It arrived along with things that had belonged to my mother. My baby book that she'd meticulously filled in, a silver brush and comb set engraved with my initials, and the portrait of my mother in THE DRESS that had always hung above my parents' bed. My father refused to forgive me or allow my mother to see me up until the moment he drove the two of them into a tree one wintery night after suffering a heart attack behind the wheel.

My hands shake as I arrange THE DRESS on a padded hanger and hook it carefully over the top of the open closet door. I take my time positioning the train in a perfect swirl on the floor and place a pair of satin high-heel pumps next to it. Half of me can't wait to see Lauren in it. The other half is afraid I won't be able to bear it, given the confession that will follow.

I stand next to the dress and stare into the dresser mirror on the opposite wall, taking in my ramrod-straight back, the careful way I'm holding myself, the look of terror on my face. If an artist were to paint me in this moment the work would have to be titled *Woman Awaiting Doom*. Or perhaps more succinctly, *Impending Doom*.

I turn my back on the mirror and look instead at THE DRESS . . . What can I say about the dress? Only that it's still beautiful. And that whatever happens next will not be its fault. Any more than it was to blame when I turned and ran. As far as I know I gave it its only black mark. Plenty of women have worn it all the way through their ceremonies. Many of them have lived happily ever after. Or at least happily enough.

Not for the first time I let myself wonder if my mother was ever happy.

Pictures of her as a girl show her with an uncertain, tentative smile. After she married my father her face looked increasingly serious, ever more careful. Pictures of her holding me as an infant show her pinch faced and anxious. The only time I remember her laughing out loud were those rare occasions when she was with her sister and my father was nowhere in sight.

Bree

Lauren doesn't say much as we get in the car for the drive back to Kendra's and neither do I. I'm too busy thinking about the celebration we just left and whether Kendra wanted

Lauren to witness it or was only bent on throwing Lauren and me together.

Of course, I might have been able to enjoy the celebration more if I hadn't been so aware of what Lauren must have been thinking of making such a big deal of such a small accomplishment compared to hers. And if I hadn't recognized the too-careful expression on her face.

That's the problem with knowing, or having known, someone so well. You're forced to recognize the truth whether you want to or not. It's easier not to think about Lauren or miss the friendship that once meant everything to me when she's not here as a reminder. I've spent a lot of years trying to let go of her, but while I've met, liked, befriended, and even admired lots of women, I've never gotten that close to any of them. I think that kind of effortless bone-deep connection comes along maybe once or twice in a lifetime if you're lucky.

I guess that's why what she thinks still matters to me. And why I cringe when I imagine how she must see me. How silly that "party" must have seemed to her. Lauren's actually accomplished the things I only dream about. And I'm not stupid. The chances of *Heart of Gold* ever getting published are probably about the same as Clay never looking at another woman.

I almost snort at the thought, but manage to stop myself in case Lauren is watching. In fact, I feel her gaze flicker over me. Am I just imagining that the silence feels different? Or is it the result of letting myself remember how much she used to mean to me? How much we meant to each other.

Uncomfortable with the silence I can't quite identify, I flick on the radio. There's a commercial for a new restaurant in Kill Devil Hills, a public service announcement for an upcoming 5K run, a sale at Miss Lizzie's boutique. And then out of nowhere, the opening drum licks of Ray Orbison's "Pretty Woman" fill the car.

Lauren and I turn to face each other. We don't speak or

comment or ask what the odds are of "our song" playing on this particular radio station at this exact moment. Our heads are already bobbing to the beat. We turn our eyes back to the road as the opening guitar riffs come in, but our heads continue to bob. Our chins get involved. Our chests. Our shoulders. We sway and bob from the waist up.

We hit the first line, "Pretty woman, walking down the street," right along with Roy and we stick with him word for word, phrase by phrase. We bob the whole time, doing double bobs and shoulder-drop sways in the exact spots we once choreographed them. The beat and the music and the memories swell inside me.

Lauren's eyes close. Her hands go up. Her bent arms move to the beat and I know she's seeing us dancing together in my grandmother's living room, filling its empty silence in the same way she and this song helped fill the emptiness inside me.

I keep my eyes mostly on the road but my brain reenacts each step, bob, bump, and sway. My lips stretch into a smile that mirrors Lauren's. Her fist goes up like a microphone and I automatically lean toward it. Our past slams into the present as we shout/purr "Mercy!" in unison. We do the same on Orbison's signature "rrowwwwllll." We do not miss a single word or nuance. We're at a stoplight when we shout the final words of the song together with identical emphasis, "Oh, ohhhhhh . . . pretty woman!"

We turn into Kendra's driveway moments later in shocked silence.

"Wow," Lauren finally says. "I don't guess there's any way my mother could have arranged that?"

"No, but she would have if she could have." I pull to a stop in front of the Sandcastle, where I stare out the windshield. "That was so . . ."

"Bizarre?"

"Yeah. Completely crazy."

The car's still running and we're both trying to come to terms with our musical blast from the past. I've decided I'm not going to be the one to suggest that the universe is trying to tell us something when Kendra comes out the front door and leans over the porch railing. "Come on, you two. I've got champagne. THE DRESS is waiting."

I turn to Lauren and summon the courage to be direct, which has never been my forte. "It's your call. I don't want to intrude if you'd rather share this moment with Ken . . . with your mother."

Our eyes lock. I brace for a pithy put-down or a nasty send-off, but for a second or two I see the Lauren I once knew better than anyone.

"I always pictured you standing beside me while I tried it on," she says so quietly I think I might be imagining it. I catch my breath in surprise. Her face tells me she's surprised, too.

Lauren wasn't here when I tried on THE DRESS, but she did come back for our wedding. She came back angry and bitchy. Acting as if my decision not to go to New York was a huge hardship and betrayal of our friendship. But she did serve as my maid of honor even if it was grudging. Still, I'm not about to take a chance that I've misunderstood. "Which means?"

She takes a deep breath then lets it out slowly. Her face still says she's as surprised by her invitation as I am. Then in a friendly tone I haven't heard in twenty years and thought I'd never hear again she says, "It means let's go inside and drink some champagne, so I can try on THE DRESS and make my mother happy."

Lauren

When we both get out of the car and join my mother on the porch, her face, which looked a little bit like a dog's expecting to get kicked, breaks into a smile. Although she's flashed

her teeth numerous times since Spencer and I got here yesterday, this is the first true smile I've seen.

Her ridiculous ploy has worked. Somehow—and I know I'm
not the only one of us who wonders how—made-up errands, a
short ride in a car, and a series of short, unexpected sprints down
memory lane have, at least for the moment, lessened the hostility between Bree and me. I have no intention of examining this
temporary cease-fire closely or counting on it too heavily, but in
this instant I feel lighter than I have in a long time. As if I put
down a heavy suitcase and only realized how much it weighed
after I no longer had to carry it.

When we enter the living room it's clear my mother has
been busy since she shooed us out of the house. She's spent that
time setting the scene for my "trying on of THE DRESS" and
for a minute I'm sorry Spencer isn't there to admire her stage-
craft. Classical music floats from the Amazon Alexa I gave her
for Christmas, each piece light and airy and romantic. Three
champagne flutes sit on a silver tray on the cocktail table. Bree
and I don't throw our arms around each other or anything. But
neither of us is scowling or trying to get farther away from the
other as my mother fills the glasses.

We clink rims and raise them to our lips. I've never been a
huge champagne fan but the bubbles tickle my nose like they're
meant to and there is something about champagne that elevates
whatever you do while you're drinking it.

We look at each other, unsure what to do next. We're out of
practice as a threesome. I think we're all afraid of making a
wrong move.

"THE DRESS is in my bedroom," my mother says almost
timidly. "Shall I help you put it on?"

"Hell, yes," I answer, hoping to see the smile again. It flickers briefly.

"I'll wait here with the champagne," Bree says. "I may even

pour us each another glass while I'm waiting for you to come out and model."

Bree's eyes search my face then my mother's. They turn back to the champagne bottle. Talking directly to each other without trying to inflict hurt is oddly strange and fascinating. It's like being in a foreign country you haven't visited for so long you're not sure you'll remember the language.

In the bedroom I shed my clothes and step carefully into the satin pumps. My mother bends down and holds the dress open for me, leaving a bull's-eye of carpet inside the circle of pearl-colored satin to aim for. I take a breath and place my hand on my mother's shoulder.

"I hope you know how very much I love you," she says so softly I have to strain to hear her. "How important you are to me. You are by far the best thing I've ever created."

I wobble slightly as I lift one foot. "I don't know, your beignets with chocolate pot de crème are pretty spectacular."

She laughs lightly as I balance my weight on her shoulder and step as carefully as I can into the circular opening.

Once I have both feet inside, I stand perfectly still while she pulls the dress up so that I can slide my arms into the sleeves. The satin is cool and slippery against my skin as I hold the bodice to my chest and wait for her to step behind me so that she can pull the sides together.

"Here we go."

I hold my breath as she slides up the side zipper in the skirt then begins to button the long line of satin-covered buttons. She works quickly and though I'm prepared to suck anything in that holds her up or slows her down, there's no hesitation and no snag or delay. The dress cups my body like a caress. Even before she's finished buttoning, before I steal a first peek in the mirror, I feel like a fairy-tale princess.

There's a gentle tug at my back as she arranges the train into a rounded arrow of Chantilly lace dense with flowers behind me. Next she retrieves the ivory headpiece from the bed and lifts it up so that she can place it on my head like a crown. Then she fusses with the floor-length floral lace veil so that it skims lightly over my shoulders and flows down my back to puddle with the train.

I've never felt so feminine or so elegant. For the first time I can see myself walking down an aisle to a waiting Spencer.

My mother kisses my cheek before stepping back to take me in. "It fits you perfectly. We won't even have to hem it." I flush slightly as I remember my delight at how many times the hem had to be doubled up when Bree wore it. A reminder that she wasn't a Jameson by birth or blood. Because real Jameson women are tall.

"Just like it fit you," I say, and am surprised when I see her grimace.

"Better." She says this forcefully as if saying it strongly enough will make it so. "Here, come look."

I follow her toward the full-length mirror but I move even more slowly than I need to, afraid that the way it looks can't possibly live up to the way it feels, but it does. The satin clings to my shoulders and shows a creamy expanse of chest without being at all revealing. My neck might belong to a swan. And the bodice drops and nips in giving me a 1940s pinup waist then falls to the ground in soft satiny folds. The lace mantilla is a sheer work of art in a fall of flowers that float over the satin. Every inch of it is beautiful. And in it so am I.

"Do you need a hand in there?" There are footsteps. "You shouldn't have left me out here with the bottle I think I'm getting . . . Oh!" Bree stands in the bedroom doorway blinking rapidly and I'm not sure whether she really has already had too much to drink or she's blinking back tears. "I'm very relieved that we're talking to each other again," she says with a slight slur that answers that question. "Otherwise I wouldn't be able to tell you how gorgeous you look."

"She does, doesn't she?" My mother's voice is thick. Her eyes shimmer with tears.

"Don't move. Be right back." Bree races out to the living room and comes back with her phone. Then she comes over and stands before us. "Stand over in front of the armoire so I can take some pictures of the two of you." She waves us in the right direction.

Usually my mother avoids cameras but she swipes at the tears and says, "I'd love that. Here, Bree can pick up the train, you hold up the hem, Lauren, and I'll keep the veil in place." We do as she directs, sidestepping toward the armoire with its burled wood and antique brass handles. Then Bree steps back. My mother moves up beside me and slips her arm around my waist. I feel the deep breath that she draws and turn to face her while Bree backs up farther and lifts the phone into position. "Are you all right?"

My mother nods. "I am. I just don't ever want to forget this moment." She hesitates. Her smile falters. "Whatever happens, no matter what it is or how it sounds, promise me that you'll remember how much I love you."

This does not make me feel better. "Mom . . ."

"Okay, you two. Smile!" Bree is already snapping photos and so I flash my best smile and tilt my head at its best angle. I tickle my mother's waist slightly in an attempt to make her laugh or at least smile.

"That's it!" Bree exclaims without a shred of detectable resentment or envy or anger or any of the other things that we've come to expect from each other. For a second I feel like myself in a way I haven't since I left for New York and Bree didn't. In this moment, I believe that Bree and I can find our way back to what we once had, that Spencer and I will live happily ever after, and that my mother is young and healthy enough that I can get my imagination to give it a rest. A few too-solemn words at a moment like this are to be expected.

"Can we take some photos in the living room? The light's better out there." My mother is smiling again. And I'm wearing the most beautiful dress in the world. It's crazy to look for trouble.

"Sure." I walk in bridal steps because, after all, I'm wearing a wedding dress and because it would feel sacrilegious to do anything remotely undignified. We sip another glass of champagne each and then Bree arranges my mom and me in a number of different poses. When my mother tells her to come join us for a selfie, I'm okay with it. In fact, since I possess the longest arms I snap the photos, careful to smile elegantly in the first three or four. I can't vouch for or be held responsible for the last few because I'm giddy from the dress, the champagne, and my mother's happiness at having Bree and me in the same room, talking and laughing together. I mean, neither of us are about to call the other a *bitch* for fear that the other won't remember it was an endearment, and I think we're both afraid this is only a temporary truce fueled by champagne and THE DRESS, but this feels like a legitimately happy moment.

Tires sound on the drive and we look at one another like little girls about to get caught playing dress-up. "Is Spencer allowed to see me in this? Isn't that supposed to be bad luck?"

I'm trying to turn to race back to the bedroom but there's a lot of train and dress that has to go with me. Bree goes to the front window and looks out as a car door slams. "Oh, it's okay," she says. "It's not the guys."

I'm still trying to get myself moving when footsteps sound on the deck. There's a knock on the front door.

"I'll get it," Bree says while my mother attempts to straighten me and the dress out.

I'm half turned when the door opens. A male voice says, "Oh."

"Oh," Bree says in surprise. "Hi."

My mother freezes. Not helping as I struggle to turn and face the door.

The man is tall and has dark hair peppered with gray. He looks familiar, like maybe I've met him before or seen him in a photo or on television or something. He stares at me without speaking for the longest time as if I'm some sort of apparition. I flush and take a step backward and my toe gets caught in the hem of the dress. I turn to ask my mother for help, but she's looking at the man and shaking her head and holding her hands to her mouth as if she's too stunned to speak.

The stranger steps closer. "You look even more beautiful in that dress than your mother did. And that's saying a lot."

Bree looks back and forth between the man and me.

"You were at my parents' wedding?" I can barely get the words out.

"Yes, I was." He looks directly at my mother even though I can practically feel her trying to hide behind me.

"I take it she didn't say anything to you about me." I hear hurt and disappointment along with a note of anger—none of which you expect from a total stranger. He's still looking at me in that too-intense way. Like I'm the most beautiful thing he's ever seen, but that I'm breaking his heart, too. Which makes no sense.

"Were you a friend of my father's?" I ask, still waiting for my mother to speak or explain.

She clasps my arm more tightly. When she speaks she's speaking to him, not me. "No, not now. Not yet. You weren't supposed to be back until tomorrow. You shouldn't have come without calling."

"I'm sorry," he says almost gently. But it doesn't really sound as if he is. "I did send you a text earlier, but frankly we've already lost forty years." He looks at my mother in a way I've never seen anyone look at her before. Like he knows her better than I do. Like he can see right through her. He's not violent or threatening, but it's clear he has no intention of leaving until he does whatever he came here to do. He's made my mother cry and I don't even know why.

Bree bristles as he comes closer. All three of us crick our necks to look up at him.

"Who are you?" I ask, forcing myself to meet his eyes. "What are you doing here? And how do you know my mother and father?"

He sighs. My mother's eyes flutter shut. I feel her sway beside me.

"Are you a relative of his? My mother said he was an only child."

"He was. In fact, he still is." His eyes look so familiar.

"I'm not related to your father," he says so quietly I think I might be imagining the whole thing. "I *am* your father."

Eighteen

∽

For a nanosecond I am Luke Skywalker hearing Darth Vader's claim to fatherhood. Like Luke, I assume that it's a lie. Only my mother doesn't deny it.

My arm falls from my mother's shoulder. I drop back a step then two. Numb with shock and disbelief I tremble where I stand as she and this man, whose name is Jake Warner, deliver their versions of the past. A past that bears no resemblance to the one I've lived.

I try to absorb the details of the story that unfolds, but it's hard to think when you can't catch your breath and your head is spinning. Revisions are one thing. The complete rewriting of your life, your world, and the people in it? That's something else entirely.

I stared at a picture of a younger version of this man all these years. I grieved his loss and the fact that I never had the chance to know him, when in fact I could have. The hair at his temples has grayed and lines radiate from the corners of his eyes and bracket his mouth, but it's him. The father I longed for and could never have. The father I learned to live without for no reason other than what? My mother's fear of revealing the mistakes she'd made? Her determination to prove she could go it alone? I don't even care what her reasons were though they're flowing out of her mouth now, urgent and unchecked, like a river flooding its banks.

"I was afraid my father would force me to put you up for

adoption. That's what he wanted me to do, that was his plan."
And then, "I didn't find out I was pregnant until months after I
ran from the church although I was already pregnant then and
didn't know it. Maybe there were just too many pregnancy hormones swirling around inside me to think clearly that day."

I fall back another step. "So you're going to blame all this on
hormones? On me?" Though I'm burning with rage my voice is
frigid. My heart is a hammer.

"No, of course not. I'm just trying to explain what I think
happened. Why I was so emotional and not thinking straight.
How I could panic and run from marrying someone I loved so
much and then could never see my way back." She drops her
eyes. "And when I wanted to reach out it was too late. He was
marrying someone else. Having children of his own. I . . . ."

Children who were more important than me. "How could it ever
be too late to tell my father that I existed? How could you lie to
me my entire life?"

In that former life, the one that has just been blown to
smithereens, the tortured expression on my mother's face, her
tears, her terror would have made me want to comfort her.

But at this moment it's all about me.

She puts her hand on my arm and I pull away.

"I'm sorry I've missed all these years," my father says. "Genuinely sorry."

I blink away my tears and look at him. At his strong, even
features, at the whiskey-colored eyes that I inherited from him
and have been staring at in the mirror all these years.

I have his nose, too, slightly too long and maybe a smidge
too thin. The same wave that's in his hair.

He pulls out a picture of his mother around the age I am
now and it's like looking at myself in the mirror. My mother is
tall and lean and dark haired so I always assumed, and was glad,
that I looked like her.

I feel like a kidnap victim who's been brainwashed to identify with their kidnapper, one of those people grabbed and locked up who comes to accept what is a travesty as normal and who is suddenly reunited with her real family and doesn't know how to behave.

"Lauren." My mother's voice breaks. Her face is red and mottled. Her eyes are twin pools of guilt and sorrow and I'm viciously glad that she's in pain. "His wife . . . she . . . she wasn't well."

"What does that have to do with me? With *telling* me?"

"Lauren." Bree's voice takes me by surprise. I've been so focused on the appearance of a father I never knew existed that I forgot she was here. "This is so . . . huge. Maybe you should all sit down together and, I don't know, figure out a way to talk through this and work it out."

"Work it out?" I turn on her. "Talk it out?" In this moment it's the very last thing I'd ever consider. "What planet are you living on?"

Every instinct I have clamors for me to get out of there and as far away as possible. *I need a cave. A place to lick my wounds and come to terms with my altered reality. I have a father!*

I turn to flee but my shoe gets caught in THE DRESS. "If you really want to help, get me out of here and out of this dress!" Even I can hear the panic in my voice as I shriek at Bree.

I half expect her to argue, in which case I'm going to kick and rip myself free and the hell with THE DRESS. The thought is viciously appealing. Because really, given all the untruths now coming to light maybe this dress isn't anything special at all. Maybe it's just a dress that my mother has made up stories about. My brain is already off and running when Bree takes my arm and helps me move off the fabric then steps around me to gather up the train. My mother is still frozen in place when I grab the train out of Bree's hands and prepare to make a break for the bedroom.

❧

"Lauren, please," my *father*—it almost hurts to even think the word—says. "I'm sorry everything spilled out this way. I truly regret taking you by surprise. I just couldn't wait any longer to know you. And I didn't realize a day would make that big a difference." Or maybe he was afraid my mother would find a way not to tell me at all. "Please. Stay, like your friend said, so that we can figure this out." He takes a step closer. "I know you're upset and rightfully so. But let's at least get acquainted. Start getting to know each other. We have a lot of lost years to make up for."

Blood whooshes in my ears. It's all I can hear. That and the frantic pounding of my heart. I swallow and prepare to turn. Before I can move, the front door opens. My head jerks up. Spencer and Clay walk in.

"Don't look!" The words are automatic. I cover myself as if I'm naked and not just wearing a wedding dress he's not supposed to see. In truth I might as well be naked given how torn apart and exposed I feel.

"What's going on?" Spencer strides to my side. "Are you okay?"

I look at my father, who doesn't seem to know what to do next, then at my mother, who's still standing there, mute. Even Bree is slack-jawed, unsure what's supposed to happen.

"No. I'm not okay. I need to get out of this dress. I don't care if I ever see it again. And I want to go home." I hear how childish the words sound and I don't care about that, either. I *feel* like a child, bereft and powerless. If I don't get out of here soon, I'm going to dissolve into tears. Or throw myself on the ground, kicking and screaming in the kind of tantrum I, as the only child of a struggling single mother, was too aware of the load she carried to throw.

"But what happened?" He looks around again as if searching for a weapon or some other threat.

"Bottom line? This man"—I point to Jake Warner—"is my father. The father my mother told me died before I was born, when in truth she jilted him at the altar and never told him that I existed." I wait for this soap opera plot that is my new reality to sink in before I continue. "The person I have loved and trusted my entire life—the person who taught me to never tell a lie—has been lying to me and everybody else for forty years."

His eyes are wide but he doesn't waste time asking for more detail. He takes my elbow and says, "Right, then. Let's get you out of that dress."

I could cry with gratitude. If I weren't already in love with him I would be now.

"Lauren, honey . . ." My mother steps toward us.

"No." I clutch Spencer's arm as I face her. "I'm taking off this dress and I'm leaving. I can't talk to you right now. I can't even look at you."

"Oh no. You can't mean that." My mother blinks back tears. My father looks as if he's watching a train wreck he doesn't know how to stop. "I know I was wrong not to tell you, but everything I did I did to protect you. And Jake."

My mother wrings her hands. My father moves closer to her.

"You may have told yourself that, but you had no right to keep my father from me." I sniff back what I tell myself are tears of anger. "And to think I've been worrying that you've got some horrible illness."

Brianna steps up on my other side. "I know this is a terrible shock. But you two are a unit. She's your mother. She's . . ."

"No." I turn my death stare on Brianna. "The fact that we managed to survive each other's company today doesn't give you the right to tell me what to do. Or how to feel. At least your parents were honest. They didn't act all selfless and noble when they were lying to your face."

"But, Lauren . . ." Bree's voice drops to a whisper that I tune out.

"Sweetheart . . ."

I cut my mother off with a look then glower at her and my ex–best friend. "You always wanted to pretend she was your mother. Well, be my guest. You can have her."

I turn my back on both of them and sail into the bedroom on a wave of righteous indignation. Spencer follows in my wake.

Five minutes later we're packed. I stalk back through the living room stopping only long enough to ask my father—my father!!—if there's a number where I can reach him. Because I'd like to spend some time with *him* and have a chance to know him. I watch my mother's face crumple as he hands me his card and tells me that he's staying at the Dogwood and in that moment I'm *glad* that she's suffering. I raise my chin, avert my eyes, and make my exit.

Kendra

I stand very still as the nuclear blast detonates in my heart and mushrooms outward annihilating everything. I may appear intact on the outside, but inside I am Hiroshima and Nagasaki.

I make no effort to stop Lauren or Spencer. He flashes me a look I don't know him well enough to understand and stops to say something to Jake before he carries the suitcases outside. All I know is that there's nothing I can say or do that will put things back the way they were. My face feels like Jake's looks— pummeled and bruised, stark with pain. The soundtrack in my mind is Bonnie Tyler's gritty rendition of "Total Eclipse of the Heart." I can practically feel the darkness obliterating the light.

I want to run outside and beg them to come back. Want to beg Lauren not to drive in the state she's in. But I know I'm the last person she'll listen to right now and so I do and say nothing even after the car peels out of the driveway.

The four of us who are left stand stupidly, not moving.

"Do you want us to stay?" Bree asks though even she looks at me differently. "Is there something I can do?"

I want to reassure her, tell her it will be okay, that we'll talk later, that nothing's really changed. But I just shake my head. There's nothing to be done right now. At least nothing that will alter or erase what has taken place. I would give everything to rewind, so that I had already confessed to Lauren before she ever put on the dress. There might have been less drama, but would that have ended any differently? I doubt she would have even tried it on.

"Okay. I'll check in with you later." Bree gives Clay a look and the two of them depart. I hear their cars start up and drive away.

Jake and I stand in silence. I wish I could blame this all on him, but I'm too raw to even pretend the blame belongs anywhere but with me. I had close to forty years to at least attempt to find a way to tell Lauren and Jake about each other. Surely I could have figured out how to do that without damaging Jake's marriage and his family further.

A stronger, smarter person could have done it. But I took the easy way out. I ran and hid and buried my head in the sand. I take a deep, shaky breath and exhale sharply.

I deserve what happened today. But Lauren doesn't. And neither does the man standing in front of me.

Finally I look Jake in the eye. "Not exactly what you were hoping for, was it?"

"No." He runs a hand through his hair in the way I still remember. His smile is small and wry. "Not even close."

I expel another breath of pent-up air. "It was exactly what I was afraid of." I feel the prickle of tears, but I'm too numb, too exhausted, to shed them. "All these years I told myself I was doing the right thing for both of you. But maybe I'm just a coward and the only person I was really trying to protect was myself."

His sigh is sad and heavy with disappointment. "I don't know, Kendra. Pretty much none of my life has gone as planned, starting with the day you ran from the church. But in my experience denial is no one's friend. We'll all just have to get through this the best we can. I've done without a lot of things. But I shouldn't have had to do without my daughter."

"I'm sorry." They're the only words that come to me. They're way too small and far too vague, but at the moment, they're all I've got.

As he walks out the door I sink into the nearest chair, too exhausted to stay on my feet a second longer. The sound of his car fades away and still I sit. If an artist were painting me now the finished piece would be titled *Woman Postatomic Blast*. Or *Woman After Hiroshima*. Or maybe even *Woman Viewing Total Eclipse with Eyes Wide Open*.

Nineteen

Lauren

Without actually planning, or possibly thinking, I drive to the Dogwood Inn, which makes it my second trip to Manteo today. I take Budleigh past the front of the inn, where its namesake is in full bloom, then turn onto Essex, where I pull the rental car up to the curb. Spencer follows me through the side yard and up the back steps. Wooden rocking chairs face the outdoor fireplace. Trellises that separate the back porch from the kitchen are threaded with wisteria and confederate jasmine. The latest in a long line of stray cats that all answer to the name "Cocoa" raises his head from his seat on one of the rocking chairs. His ears flick in casual interest as he blinks sleepily at us. Other houses are visible across the bright-green side yard but they're comfortably removed.

Spencer does a 360, taking it all in. "Very nice."

"Yeah. It's a 1919 Craftsman. Deanna spent almost two years renovating and finding period-appropriate details and furnishings."

When I pull open the back door that leads into the kitchen without knocking Spencer starts with surprise.

"I promise we're not breaking and entering. This door is always unlocked. Guests can come in late at night or from the garage apartments to get a snack or drink or to hang out in the living room."

"Okay," Spencer says. "So we're not in Kansas anymore. And we're definitely not in Manhattan."

As we step inside I wish more than anything that we were in New York. That I'd never been forced to discover that my mother lied to me my entire life. Though I guess that would also mean I still wouldn't know my father.

The galley kitchen to our right is empty. The office door is open on our left. Deanna gets up from her desk. One look at my face and she says, "What happened?"

"Did you know that Jake Warner was my father?"

She blinks, but in far more surprise than Cocoa the cat. "They ran into each other here last Saturday when Kendra came to cook breakfast. They said they both grew up in Richmond but . . . Holy shit."

"Yeah. They were engaged only she cut and ran. She left him at the altar. She never even told him about me."

I see the struggle on Deanna's face. She doesn't want to believe it. "I can tell you're serious. But I know your mother. She must have had good reasons."

"I thought I knew her, too." Once again I wish that this were some awful joke or misunderstanding. "She had reasons, all right. But that doesn't make them good ones."

I keep drawing breaths but I don't think any of the oxygen is reaching my brain. "I'm supposed to be the one who makes things up for a living, but she's been spewing fiction my entire life." I look Deanna in the eye. "You're her best friend. And she never told you?"

Deanna shakes her head, her confusion clear. I know the feeling. As angry and freaked out as I am I still can't quite take in the enormity of it all.

"We were both twenty-one and right out of college when we met. People came here to find themselves or to start fresh. I'd heard her husband had died. She never said otherwise." Dee exhales and shakes her head again. "Wow."

There's a beat of silence as she no doubt reflects on all the times she might have asked a question or my mother might have offered an explanation. Then she looks from me to Spencer and back. "I take it this is your fiancé."

"Oh yes. Sorry. Deanna, this is Spencer Harrison. Spencer, Deanna Sanborne."

She takes his hand and shakes it. "Nice to meet you."

"Ditto." Spencer gives her a smile.

"Quite an introduction you're getting to the Outer Banks."

His grin goes a little crooked. "Can't argue with that."

I watch them assess each other, but it's as if I'm floating somewhere up near the ceiling. A punctured balloon slowly leaking air, but with a bird's-eye view. Spencer keeps stealing looks at me and I know he's trying to figure out what I need from him. But how can he figure out what even I don't know?

"So, what can I do for you?" Deanna asks.

"Well, I needed to be somewhere besides the Sandcastle. And I'd like to get to know my . . ." I swallow. "My father." Thinking the word is surreal. Saying it is even stranger. I'm forty years old and this is the first time I've ever uttered those words as more than a prayer or a wish that I had one. "Do you have a room for us?"

I see the *no* on her face before she speaks. "I wish I did. But there's a wedding tomorrow afternoon at Mount Olivet. The bride and groom and their immediate families checked in yesterday. They're staying through Monday."

"Oh." I deflate further.

"I can make some calls to double-check, but it's a big wedding and I'm pretty sure the other B and Bs in Manteo are full." She thinks for a minute. "The closest hotels are the Surf Side and the Sea Spray but those are pretty bare bones and they're near your mom." She rejects this even before I shake my balloon head. "Or, you could head a bit north to Duck. The Sanderling's very nice. I could give the manager a call. Or I could check with Clay to see if any of their beach rentals are vacant."

The idea of staying in a strange place right now—when my past has been yanked out from under me—makes my stomach turn. This is not the moment I want to feel like a tourist.

Dee reaches out and wraps her arms around me. I feel her shaking her head again even as she pulls me tight. "I am well and truly gobsmacked. I can only imagine how you must be reeling."

Her sympathy brings tears to my eyes and I sniff in a fruitless attempt to hold them back. I've known Deanna virtually since birth. She was a tenant at Snug Harbor when we first came to Nags Head. We shared the Sandcastle with her in that first winter after it had been built when the owner was looking to put someone in it. She stayed on in later years because my mother couldn't afford it on her own. She was the first person besides my mother that I knew. The tension in her arms tells me she feels almost as shocked by my mother's secret past as I am.

"Listen, why don't you two have something cold to drink?" She throws open the mini-fridge that's always stocked so guests can help themselves—and pulls out two bottled waters and a Coke. "And maybe a snack." She motions toward the triple-chocolate cake under a glass dome on the counter that I recognize as one of my mother's, and my lips quiver. "Well, at least a cold drink." She puts a bottled water in each of our hands. "You're welcome to hang out in the living room. Or maybe you'd rather sit outside on the porch? It's a gorgeous day."

I nod numbly and she holds open the kitchen door for us.

"Give me a few minutes to make some calls and see what I can come up with," she says as Spencer and I drop into rockers across from each other.

I'm vaguely aware of the sunshine and the chirping of birds and the soft breeze that wafts through the porch, but I'm still slightly detached and floating above it all. Cocoa springs up into my lap, pads around my stomach, then curls into my arms. I stroke him absently as I rock and stare into the unlit fireplace. If I had a lap to curl up in I'd be in it.

"Are you all right?" Spencer asks.

"Not really."

Spencer runs a hand over his face, scrubs at his eyes.

"You don't look so good, either," I observe.

"Yeah, well. I've never felt quite this helpless. I hate how blindsided you were today. I keep flashing on how I'd feel if my parents suddenly told me I was adopted. Or, I don't know, that they stole me from a hospital nursery or something."

"You look exactly like your father."

"Yeah, well, you look a lot like yours, too."

I rock a bit faster as I try to come to grips with what's happened. How despite my hair-trigger imagination and all the things it has dredged up in my lifetime, it never even suspected anything remotely like this. "The thing I keep thinking is how could my mother have done this? And how could I not have known? I mean, she's the one person I've never doubted. If you had asked me, Who do you know who always does the right thing and puts others first, my answer would have been 'my mother.' I'm starting to doubt my instincts. Maybe I'm not the judge of character I've always thought."

"I hate that you're looking at me right now when you're saying that." His tone is gentle but nowhere near teasing. "But it seems she did do what she thought was the right thing."

"I don't see how keeping a child from knowing its father is the right thing—even if others could be hurt by it. And if I could be this wrong about my own mother how many other people have I been wrong about? For all I know you could be a serial killer. Or maybe the doorman at my building really is a spy."

He laughs. "I've met Tom and he's no spy. Unless they've started teaching that Long Island accent in spy school."

I smile and rock a little slower. I watch Spencer from inside the thin rubber sides of my deflating balloon wondering how after all the bad boys I was attracted to I ended up with some-one so sweet and well intentioned. If he weren't here right now I'd be . . . I can't even let myself think about how that would feel. I draw a deep breath. "I . . . I really can't believe this."

He nods and rocks and I love him even more for not arguing one side or the other.

"I honestly have no idea what I'm supposed to do next."

He rocks a time or two then says, "I don't think you're *sup-posed* to *do* anything. I think we just stay here for the rest of the week so that you can show me around and start getting to know your father." He's watching my face. "And then maybe we can go see your mother and sit down so that you can talk this out."

"No." I don't even let him finish. My refusal is a half bark that sends Cocoa vaulting off my lap. Even thinking about it makes my stomach roil. She made me feel as if I were her confi-dante, that we were a unit, in this life together. Only she didn't share the most important information of all. And then there's the fact that I can't stop thinking about what my life could have been with a father in it. Grandparents. I churn with what might have been, but wasn't. "I don't see what she could possibly say that could justify what she's done."

A car door slams out on the street then footsteps sound on the porch behind me. Cocoa looks up from his spot near my feet then returns to licking himself. Spencer smiles slightly, and I turn to see Brianna approaching. Her step falters as our eyes meet.

The kitchen door opens and Deanna walks out, but my eyes remain locked with Bree's.

"What are you doing here?" My tone is sharp and accusing. Whatever inroads we've made today are no match for the caul-dron of emotions bubbling inside me.

"I called her." Deanna steps up between the rockers.

"Why?" I try to back off the accusatory tone but I'm beyond

vocal control or, it seems, control of any kind. The walls of my protective balloon burst, leaving me singed and exposed.

"I told you this wasn't a good idea," Brianna says to Deanna. "Why don't we just forget about it and . . ."

"I called her because there are no available rooms in Manteo at the moment," Deanna says. "I did find something in Kill Devil Hills, but I know you'd like to be here in town so that you can get acquainted with your . . . um, with Jake."

I don't speak as I get to my feet. I can't.

"I'd be glad to have you stay in my cottage with me until the wedding party leaves," Dee continues, "but I've turned the second bedroom into an office. You'd be sleeping on a pull-out couch."

Bree steps closer. "Deanna only called to see if any of Clay's rental houses over near the sound might be open, but everything's booked up." She hesitates briefly. "Then I realized we have an extra bedroom. And I'd, we'd, be glad to have you."

I see the concern on Bree's face and I think of all the times we were there for each other. Then I think of all the times we weren't. This morning when we woke we were barely speaking to each other and while we may have mended a few fences, there are plenty of unresolved issues piled up between us.

I don't know whether I can handle staying at Bree's. I'm not sure I can handle anything at the moment, including the tears that are seeping out of the corners of my eyes.

Spencer steps over and puts an arm around my shoulders. "Thanks for checking around for us, Dee. And for calling Brianna." He turns his gaze on my ex-best friend. "I know I speak for both of us when I say how much we appreciate your invitation. We'd love to stay with you."

Twenty

Bree

With Lauren in the house it sheds twenty years. And in some ways so do I. I try to hold myself apart, or at least at arm's length, just to be on the safe side, but it's almost impossible not to think about all the hours Lauren and I spent together here playing and making up stories under my grandmother's watchful eye, the holiday meals we shared with Lauren and Kendra, and binge-watching *Pretty Woman* (before binge-watching was a thing) in the terrible months after my grandmother died.

When Clay and I got married we considered moving in to one of the rental houses his family owned up in Kill Devil Hills or Southern Shores, but this house my grandmother left me was the last bit of her I had. I couldn't bring myself to let go of it or rent it out to strangers.

"Where do you want me to put these?" Spencer holds up their suitcases and I lead him toward the stairs.

"It's the second room on your left. If you hit the one with the unmade bed that looks like a tornado swept through, you've stopped too soon."

Back in the kitchen Lauren is studying the space with genuine interest that seems to have elbowed her misery aside. "This looks like something off of *Extreme Makeover*. It's really beautiful, but still homey, too."

"Thanks. We tried to keep as much of the original Victorian farmhouse as we could. I didn't want to scare my grandmother and grandfather out of their graves." I gesture toward the cemetery across the street. "We started upstairs and worked our way down so it's been an ongoing project. I don't plan to live through construction ever again, but I'm really glad we did it."

"It's great. Your grandmother's table looks perfect at the center of the banquette and I always loved this sideboard. Especially when it was groaning under a holiday ham or turkey." Her voice breaks and she trails a shaky finger over the oak top of the cabinet that some long-ago ancestor brought over from England, then looks up at the arrangement of black-and-white photos on the wall above it. I see her zero in on the shot of her and Clay and me standing near the bleachers after a Friday-night football game. Clay's in his team jersey with Lauren and me bookended on either side of him. There's a more recent shot of Rafe wearing a Manteo High jersey with the same number 22 his father wore. Nearby is a current shot of Lily in her cheerleading uniform mid-cheer with pompoms raised.

As a child I hid inside books, wrapped in loneliness and self-doubt, wondering why my parents didn't love me enough to keep me. My greatest achievement is that my daughter is the opposite, and that she's secure enough to get snippy or show her anger; things I never felt secure enough to do with my parents. For a brief moment I wonder if Lauren regrets not having children.

Lauren turns and looks at me, really looks, for the first time. "You've changed."

"Over the last twenty years?" I snort. "Of course I have. We all change. If we're lucky we grow and get better. You just weren't around to notice."

Her eyes tear up and I feel like a jerk for chiding her, given everything that's just happened. I have no idea how she isn't sobbing hysterically. "Come sit down."

I wait while she slides onto the banquette that we built in beneath the bay window. Then I pull three wineglasses from the cupboard and retrieve a bottle of Chenin Blanc from the wine refrigerator.

Spencer comes back and sits beside her and I pour us each a glass then set the bottle and a bowl of mixed nuts in the center of the table. For a few moments we sip wine and look at one another. Spencer doesn't attempt to hide his concern over Lauren's emotional state and I'm impressed with his ability not to rush in and attempt to "fix" what's gone so horribly wrong.

I'm not doing so well with this, because while I still can't reconcile Kendra's behavior with the generous, caring woman I've always known, and I am beyond curious about Jake Warner and what he'll do next, I want more than anything to fix the damage that's been done. Or at least try to patch it. Because while I have managed to live without my best friend for the last twenty years, I know in my heart that Kendra will never be able to survive a life that doesn't include her daughter.

Lauren

"Are you sure you don't want me to come with you?" Spencer has asked me this at least five times since Jake—I'm just not ready to start throwing the word *father* around—called fifteen minutes ago to ask if I'd come over to the Dogwood to "talk."

I don't want to go alone but I don't want anyone to come with me, either. Not even Spencer. As I get up from the banquette, leaving him and Bree to finish the Chenin Blanc, there's a tiny part of me that imagines Bree coming and holding my hand—after all, she listened all those years while I tried to piece together a father from a photograph of a man in a powder-blue tuxedo.

I leave her house to walk the few blocks to the inn, my knees wobbly. I try my hardest not to even think about my mother and what she's done, but as I've learned while trying to clear my mind and to meditate, trying not to think about something *is* actually thinking about it. She might as well be walking right beside me.

As I near the Dogwood I see him sitting on the front porch swing. He's moving languidly, one long jean-clad leg bending and flexing as he swings back and forth. He appears deep in thought and as I watch him, it's clear some of those thoughts are troubling. I take in details I missed during our turbulent introduction earlier today. I notice that his nose is slightly hooked at the bridge. That his mouth is wide and expressive while his chin is square and determined. He's attractive in a subtle way, average until you really look at him. Or he really looks at you.

"Hi." His face lights up when he sees me. He halts the movement of the swing with his foot then motions to the empty space next to him. I take a seat, intensely aware of how momentous a moment this is. I feel shy and a little frightened. Yet I have an urgent need to know . . . everything.

"So."

He smiles. "So indeed."

"I don't know where to start or even what to ask. I mean, I've been imagining this in some shape or form virtually forever—having a father, I mean—but I never really imagined you . . ."

"Coming back from the dead?" His tone is wry but wrapped in a layer of hurt.

"I just don't understand how she could have done this to me . . . to us . . ." It takes everything I have not to cry.

"I know." He hesitates, as if searching for the right words or maybe he's trying not to cry, too. "When I first found out—it wasn't long after my wife died that I discovered she knew about you and had never told me—I was so angry I could hardly see straight. I was furious. With my wife, with your mother, with the world." There's a beat of silence and then I feel him dial it back a notch. "It's possible steam came out of my ears."

"Like Yosemite Sam?" I surprise myself by asking.

"Exactly like Yosemite Sam."

I turn and look up at him. He looks back. I still can't believe he's here. Real. In the flesh. Sitting right beside me. No longer the fresh-faced bridegroom in the powder-blue tuxedo who was stolen from me, but a grown man who's clearly weathered more than a few storms and known his share of heartache. "I can't quite . . . I don't know . . . I'm just so stunned. And I can't stop thinking if you hadn't shown up today she might never have told me about you."

He nods. "I understand. I've had a little longer than you to take it in, but I hope . . . For right now at least I'd like to try to set the anger aside so that we can start getting to know each other."

I don't answer at first, but as much as I don't want to ruin this time with him, I don't have the strength to pretend, and I definitely don't want to lie. There've been enough lies already. "I'm not sure I can do that," I say finally. "I mean, I want to know you more than almost anything. I'm happy to tell you about myself. But the anger? The hurt of betrayal? I don't see those going anywhere anytime soon."

He pushes off with one foot and the chains creak companionably. I tell myself this is really happening. I am not imagining it or making it up. This is real.

"Okay," he says. "You first. Tell me about yourself."

We swing in silence for a time as I try to think where to begin. How do you adequately summarize your hopes and dreams, your regrets, your favorite color, how you like your steak cooked, in one telling?

Because I actually want to know all of those things about this man whose DNA I carry and more. I need all those details, the kind I'd use to flesh out a character. Because those are the things that make us who we are, that set us apart, that make us real.

"I suck at synopses. I'd rather write a whole book than try to summarize it." I watch his face as I make this confession, but I see no judgment on it. He does not recoil in horror. "What if we just take turns asking questions?"

"I'm good with that," he says. "Ask away."

"Okay." I ask the first thing that pops into my head. "How long did it take you to get over being left at the altar?"

There's a long silence and it occurs to me that even after forty years he might still not be over it.

He's staring out at the Dogwood when he finally says, "Being left at the altar is a lot worse than it looks in the movies. I mean, there's the humiliation and all that, but when you truly love that person and know in your heart that you were meant to spend the rest of your life with them?" He shrugs. "It's pretty close to unbearable."

"But you married somebody else."

"I did." There's a world of emotion behind those two words. One of those emotions is regret.

For the briefest moment I imagine what it would feel like to marry someone who wasn't over the person who jilted them. "Was what my mother said about your wife true?"

"Yes." He looks me in the eye and his gaze doesn't waver. "There was a lot of . . . turbulence . . . in our marriage and in our family."

"So you did, I mean, you do have . . . other . . . children?"

"Yes. I have two sons." He pulls out a photo of two guys somewhere in their mid to late thirties standing in front of a colonial-style house. Both of them have his dark hair and a similar look about them.

I have brothers. I am not the only child of a man who died too soon as I've always believed, but one of three.

"This is Kevin." He points to the taller of the two. "And this

is Drew. The picture was taken in front of our house in Bethesda."
He tells me where his sons went to college, where they live now,
what they do for a living, but I don't really absorb much beyond
the obvious love and pride in his voice and the fact that I have
two brothers who may or may not have led the kind of family life
I dreamed about.

"I didn't want to do or say anything before I knew you were
okay with it, but I'd like you to know each other."

I feel a rush of excitement that's followed by another fire arrow of anger at all I've missed. I turned Bree into the sibling I
never had, missed her all these years as if she really were my
sister. Would we have been that close if I'd known I had flesh-
and-blood siblings in the world?

He takes out another photo. "These are your grandparents.
They lived in Richmond until they died two years ago. They
were married for sixty-five years and they died within hours of
each other."

Two years ago. I've been at Fountain Bookstore on book tour
numerous times and never even knew that Richmond was anything except the place where my mother was born. The rage
bubbles up briefly again. It's dampened only slightly by the regret that follows.

I look at the old photo of a white-haired man who looks like
an older version of Jake, standing with his arm around the same
rawboned woman Jake showed me earlier, only older and with
white hair. "She looks a lot like me. Or I guess I mean I look
like her."

He hesitates again. His smile is pained. "Yes. It was that
resemblance that my wife first noticed."

"Did they . . ." I swallow around the lump in my throat.
"Did your parents . . ." I can't quite bring myself to call them
my grandparents any more than I'm ready to call Jake my father.
"Did they know about me?"

"No. There's no way they could have known and not told

me," he says with certainty. "They were good friends with the Munroes right up until the day your mother stopped our wedding. Munroe is Kendra's last name. Jameson was her mother's maiden name. To my knowledge our parents never spoke after that day even though our mothers had known each other since childhood. If what Kendra says is true and her parents expected her to give you up, it makes sense that they wouldn't have told my parents. It could be why they severed ties with them."

We sit and swing, lost in thoughts of what was versus what might have been. Two half brothers and two sets of grandparents. How could my mother have deprived me of so much?

"Okay. My turn." His voice pulls me back from the path my thoughts have taken. "What was it like growing up here?" His voice softens. "Did you have the things you needed?"

I'm so angry with my mother that I want to tell him that it was horrible. That having no family ruined my life. But even now and despite my rage I know that's not true.

"She had to cobble together jobs to keep a roof over our heads and food on the table. I always knew that, but I don't really remember ever feeling any worse off than anyone else. Jobs were harder to get in the off-season but my mother always worked and she had lots of friends. People who lived on the beach here full-time—we all knew each other. And we were there for each other. We weren't original families like the Creefs and Daniels and Austins and Midgetts and such here in Manteo. Or even like the first families that owned the original beach houses the guidebooks call the Unpainted Aristocracy." Tears prick at my eyes again. "The only thing I didn't have that I really wanted was a father."

He draws a sharp breath, as if he's just taken a punch, but I'm not going to apologize for answering his question.

A few moments pass before he asks, "When did you start writing?"

I let a swing or two go by while I consider the question. "I almost can't remember a time when I didn't. Even when my mother was reading me fairy tales I was rewriting the endings in my head. Not too long after Bree and I learned to read we wrote our first story together." I actually smile when I remember us sitting at her grandmother's kitchen table with our fingers wrapped around No. 2 pencils, our tongues clenched between our teeth, trying to sound out the words we'd need to tell the story of a sea sprite that couldn't find its way back to the ocean.

He listens and nods. Then we skim along the surface for a while. I discover that his favorite color is blue while mine is red. That he likes his steak and burgers medium rare while I'm still feeling slightly guilty for eating meat at all. He has favorite football, baseball, and basketball teams while I haven't spent more than thirty seconds thinking about football since I graduated from college.

The sun slips in the sky and the breeze grows cooler. We're still tossing questions and answers at each other when the front door opens and Dee steps out.

"Sorry to interrupt." She hands us each a bottled water. "But I come bearing messages."

We screw off the caps and tilt the water to our lips and I notice how long and almost elegant Jake's hands are. The way his Adam's apple moves as he downs his first few gulps. Everything about him is new and fascinating.

I pat my pockets and remember that I left my cell phone at Brianna's because I didn't want to be interrupted and because I didn't want to know when or if my mother called. We wait for Dee to continue.

"Okay, first of all, Bree said she's making dinner and she's expecting you both by seven. It's six thirty right now."

"Thank you." I'm about to lob another question at Jake when I notice that Dee's still standing there.

"And your mother has called three times. She just wants a quick word with you."

My jaw tightens and I'm careful not to look at the father she kept from me. When I finally answer I keep my voice as neutral as I can because my *father* has asked me to let go of the anger. "I'm afraid she'll have to wait." It takes everything I have not to add the *until hell freezes over.*

Twenty-one

⁂

Kendra

I spend the rest of Saturday in my bathrobe, slumped in the old cane rocking chair on the back deck, staring out at the ocean. The wind is strong. Clouds scud across the low gray sky. Waves pound the sand in a relentless rhythm that drums itself into my head. I'm vaguely aware that I should go inside but I just sit there. Rocking.

When it gets too dark to distinguish sky from sea I go inside, but I don't even consider getting into bed. It's nightmarish enough replaying what happened in the daylight. I cannot risk reliving it alone in the dark.

The thing I've feared above all else for forty years has happened and I now know that anyone who says that the truth will set you free has never been forced to listen as someone else revealed it. If only I could have come up with a way to tell Jake and Lauren about each other without doing harm to either, none of us would be hurting right now.

The soundtrack of Lou Rawls's "If I Coulda, Woulda, Shoulda"—so sad and soulful and heavy with regret—plays in my head.

As I sit waiting and praying for Lauren to call me back, I tell myself that she's an intelligent forty-year-old woman who's about to get married and who might even have children of her own. Surely that will let her see this through the eyes of an adult rather than those of a hurt child.

I know that nothing I say or do is going to erase what's happened or eliminate the mistakes I've made. I'm going to have to live with the fact that our relationship may never be what it was. That she may never again look at me in the way she used to. But, oh God, please let her forgive me enough to be a part of each other's lives.

Just before sunrise Sunday morning I finally fall asleep on the living room couch, curled into a ball and clutching my cell phone. I blink awake to the sound of it ringing. Hope spikes through me. As I fumble the phone to my ear I tell myself that things are going to be okay. That Lauren just needed a day to cool off and absorb everything and that now she'll hear me out.

"Hello?" My heart pounds as I push out the word.

"You need to come right now and deliver a cake or something."

I slump back on the couch at the sound of Dee's voice. "I'm not scheduled to cook or deliver anything today." I scrub at my eyes and look out the window. The sun is already up. The sky is a clear, vibrant blue.

"I know. But Lauren's here having coffee with her . . . with her father." There's a brief pause as we both absorb the word. "I can find a way to keep her here until you get here, but you've got to hurry."

This time there's no spike or even glimmer of hope. "She hasn't answered her phone and she hasn't called back. What makes you think she's going to stand in the same room and talk to me?" The mental image of Lauren turning her back or brushing past me while I try to plead my case makes me curl back into a ball.

"Since when are you afraid to talk to your own daughter?"

The answer, of course, is since yesterday when she found out all the things I kept from her, but I can't even bring myself to say so. "I'm planning to give her a few more days to calm down. Maybe she'll be ready to listen then."

"That's an awful plan." Dee's voice drops to a whisper and I picture her hiding in her office off the kitchen because Lauren and Jake are communing nearby. "She could decide to go back to New York early. Or think you aren't taking her reaction seriously."

As if.

She lists other reasons why I'm making a mistake by not rushing over, but I can't listen to all the things that could make the situation even worse. Bottom line, I don't have the courage to try to force Lauren to accept my apology or listen to an explanation. I hit the salient points yesterday and she rejected them completely.

"Do you remember how long it took her to get over finding out Santa Claus wasn't real?" I ask. "I have just unloaded an emotional bombshell that would leave anyone reeling on someone who doesn't respond all that well to even a *good* surprise like a marriage proposal."

"But . . ."

"Really, Dee. I appreciate your concern. Your friendship means the world to me. But there's no point in trying to force her to listen to anything right now."

"But . . ."

"I'll talk to you later. Thanks for trying to help." I hang up before she can say anything else.

A moment later a text dings in from Dee, who has been known to like to have the last word. *You are making a big mistake.*

I try not to think about the fact that she could be right.

◡◠◡

I'm still lying on the couch hours later when someone knocks on the door. I burrow deeper into the cushions, cover my ears, and try to ignore it.

When it finally stops Jake strides into the living room and

over to the couch, where I'm curled up in a fetal position. "You're not dressed and your door wasn't locked."

"So?"

"So, I could have been an ax murderer."

"At the moment dying doesn't seem like such a horrible idea." I hate the pitiful whine in my voice. But I'm beyond pretense. I *am* both pitiful and whiny.

"You live here alone and you don't bother to lock your door."

I just look at him. Nags Head has gotten bigger and more crowded but most of us old-timers still don't bother locking our doors. At the moment I have much larger problems than someone wandering by and deciding to rob or dispatch me. I don't have the energy to point out that the inn where he's staying doesn't lock its doors, either.

"Fine." He runs a hand through his hair and leaves it standing up in that way that is still both attractive and endearing. Which reminds me that I haven't looked in a mirror once during the last twenty-four hours and am undoubtedly the opposite of attractive *and* endearing. "I understand that yesterday was a big shock for everyone. I am sorry the truth came out the way it did. But I'm not sorry it came out."

Tears gather and prick my eyelids. I attempt to blink them away, but I don't argue. I'm too tired. And as much as I wish he'd given me that extra day, I can't fool myself into thinking the outcome would have been any better. I mean, how do you start that conversation? "By the way, sweetheart, there's something I've been meaning to tell you about that father I told you was dead"?

No. As much as I wish I could lay the blame at Jake's feet, I'm the one who bungled everything so badly. In the end we're both getting what we deserve. I have been banished and he is finally getting to know his daughter.

"So." I straighten and swallow around a lump of pain and regret. "I hear you're spending time together."

His smile is a quick flash of white teeth. "She's lovely. And so smart and strong willed. And I like Spencer. I'm glad she's chosen someone who appreciates her." The smile fades. "But she's so hurt and angry. You need to talk to her and find a way to help her through this."

"I would think you'd be thrilled to have her to yourself."

"I probably would be if she weren't in so much pain." He shakes his head. "I was so furious when I decided to come here. I thought I'd sweep in, right some pretty big wrongs, and claim my daughter."

"And you've done that." I can barely get the words out.

"Yes." He runs his hand through his hair again. "Only she's miserable. She feels completely betrayed."

"Of course she does." I, who always sought to protect her, have done this to my child. "I'd give anything to make her feel better. But she's not answering my calls or returning them. She doesn't want to talk to me."

"So you're planning to just wallow on the couch and do nothing?"

I look at him through the blur of tears that I can't seem to hold back.

"The Kendra Munroe I knew was way too impulsive and made some really horrible choices, but at least she acted. She wasn't a coward."

"Yeah, well, that was a lifetime ago. Maybe two lifetimes." My voice cracks. Is that really how he sees me? As a coward? "And those horrible choices finally taught me that you can't just go charging into a situation without considering the consequences."

We look at each other. Me through the blur of those blasted tears. Him through the distorted lens of memory.

"You have to see her," he says. "This is not about us. Not now anyway. You have to at least try."

The floodgates open. Hot tears slide down my cheeks. I cry at the futility of trying to fix what I've broken. At his belief that this is even possible. I cry because I've been called a coward by some-one who once loved and respected me. And because he's right.

"I don't understand how you can just sit here and do *nothing*!"

My head jerks up at the accusation. He may think he still knows me, but I don't see how that's possible. I don't even rec-ognize me anymore.

"I'm not doing nothing, damn you! I'm grieving."

Lauren

Spencer and I spend a good part of Sunday afternoon wander-ing around downtown Manteo. We linger in front of the Tudor-style Pioneer Theatre, which has been owned by the Creef family since the '30s. "It's the longest-running family-owned movie theater in the country," I say proudly, as if I've had something to do with this other than growing up watch-ing movies here. "Bree and I used to come to the matinee every Saturday."

"What did you see?"

"Didn't matter. Then we'd go browse Davis's Everything to Wear or the Attic Addict and end up at Title Waves, where we'd read all the back-cover blurbs and opening paragraphs of the new releases and imagine our own novels on the shelves."

"It's not everyone who makes as many of their dreams come true as you have."

"No." I look into his eyes and a smile tugs at my lips. "We're lucky, aren't we?"

"Ummm-hmmm," he agrees. "What's that old saying? The harder you work . . ."

". . . the luckier you get. My mother . . ." I stumble on the word. "She used to say that to me."

"Lauren . . ."

"No." I can tell by his tone that he intends to use my mention of her as an opening, and I'm nowhere near ready for that. I turn and head for the waterfront and am relieved when he falls in at my side without argument. In silence, we stroll the boardwalk past boats bobbing in their slips at the marina then walk out the dock to the Roanoke Marshes Lighthouse. Sunlight dances on the water and marsh grass sways gently in the breeze on the opposite bank where the *Elizabeth II*, a reproduction of the ships that sailed from England to Roanoke Island in 1584 and 1587, is moored.

I keep the conversation casual. I tell him about how the waterfront was revitalized—turned from a working port into the idyllic setting it is now.

"This is really lovely."

Despite my efforts to keep things light, my head is still spinning with yesterday's revelations and the arrival of a father whom I'm thrilled to meet but who showed my mother to be so much less than I've always thought. "Sorry. What did you say?"

"I said, the waterfront is lovely."

"Oh. Yes . . ."

We watch a boat leave a nearby dock and head out into the sound. My brain keeps circling back to the one place I don't want it to go.

There are so many things I planned to show Spencer. A week is nowhere near enough time to do the Outer Banks justice. Or to look at even a portion of the possible places to hold a small, intimate beach wedding. Not that I have any desire to get married here now that my past has been so radically altered.

My mind stumbles on the word *altered* and I realize that it's not just the venues that have lost their allure. Now that I know my mother ran from my father and never actually got married in it, THE DRESS no longer feels like a harbinger of happily ever after.

Bottom line, if it weren't for Jake I would have driven us straight back to the airport yesterday. We'd already be home in New York.

"You really need to talk to your mother." Spencer says this quietly, but with determination.

"No, actually, I don't." I look at the boat, the water. Even the sky is preferable to meeting his eyes and engaging in this conversation.

"Okay, let me rephrase that. You really should talk to your mother. You need to hash this out. Both of you will feel better."

"She doesn't deserve to feel better."

"Lauren. Even really good people make mistakes."

I look up from the great blue heron that's perched on the distant shore and feel the anger wash over me again, an emotional tsunami. "A mistake is forgetting to pay a utility bill. Or accidentally calling someone by the wrong name." I take a breath, trying not to take my hurt and anger out on him. But it's not like I'm in control of my emotions. Between my lost mother and my found father I'm a mess. "Telling your daughter that her father is dead and letting her believe that she has no family, is not a *mistake*."

"It was wrong. But people often do the wrong things for the right reasons."

"You need to get your homilies straight. And the fact that she claims she was only thinking of me and Jake and his family doesn't make it true."

"But you can't know that unless you at least hear her out. Surely you don't want to go back to New York without talking to her. You owe her that, don't you?"

I'm on my feet now. "You don't know what you're saying or asking." My voice rises and so do the tears. "What if your mother had done this to you? Could you really go about your business as if she'd only made a silly mistake?"

"No, of course not. That's not what I'm saying. I just . . ." He reaches for me but I shrug him off. Something I've never done before.

"I don't want to talk about this right now. I can't." And I really don't want to cry in public, but it doesn't look like I'm going to be able to help it.

"Tell me what you want, Lauren. Tell me what I *can* do. Because I sure as hell don't seem to know what I am and am not allowed to say."

"Is that right?" I'm beyond anger now, and I can tell the tears are at most a couple of seconds away. For some reason my greatest concern is not the man in front of me—on whom I'm clearly taking out all my anger and hostility—but making my escape before I break down completely. "Tell you what. I'll give it some thought and get back to you."

And then I'm striding away from him as fast as I can with no idea at all where I'm going.

Twenty-two

~

Bree

Monday-morning breakfast is cereal and defrosted and reheated blueberry muffins that I'm hoping Lauren won't recognize as Kendra's. Clay devours two muffins and downs a cup of coffee while scrolling through his cell phone. Lily's still upstairs. Normally I'd be yelling for her to hurry—not that this ever works, it's just that you have to *do* something—but Rafe's bedroom door is still closed and Lauren and Spencer haven't shown themselves yet. It's possible they could still be sleeping.

I buzz around the kitchen like a bumblebee unable to find a flower, somehow needing to be in motion even if I'm not accomplishing anything. The whole world feels oddly upside down since Kendra's confession. Technically it has nothing to do with me. I'm not the injured party, but I can't quite come to grips with the fact that the woman I've revered and looked up to as a role model has apparently created a backstory that bears little resemblance to reality. Add to that the fact that my ex-best friend with whom I've communicated only on the most superficial level for the last two decades is sleeping in Rafe's bedroom with her fiancé. And, then there's the fact that the completion of my novel—something that has taken me more than a third of my life—feels almost insignificant in comparison to Kendra's bombshell and Lauren's reaction to it.

"Morning, sweetie." My smile for Lily when she finally enters the kitchen is automatic. The one that acknowledges having conceived, carried, and delivered this person into the world. Even when I'm truly angry at her behavior that smile—and the squeeze of my heart that accompanies it—is Pavlovian.

"Mmmph." Lily's blond hair falls across one eye and cascades over her shoulders in a way that looks natural but that I know took her a good thirty minutes. Her makeup is expertly applied and she's wearing her new jeans with the knees torn out and a sleeveless crop top that just barely reaches the top of her jeans. She has her father's height and slim build as well as his almost-aqua-blue eyes and the white-blond hair he had before it started to darken. She looks like she belongs on the cover of some teen fashion magazine. Which both amazes and frightens me because sometimes beauty opens so many doors there's no need to develop other attributes.

She reaches for a muffin as she plops down at her place, but I know she won't take more than a bite or two. I place a banana beside her plate and slide a glass of milk in front of it, because that's what mothers are supposed to do. Her eyes remain on her phone and the texts that are already dinging in. It takes every ounce of willpower I possess not to peel the banana for her or wave the muffin under her nose.

"You ready?" Clay wakes up bright eyed and bushy tailed no matter how late he goes to sleep and regardless of how hard he might have partied the night before; a trait I used to envy but now find extremely unfair and annoying. I mean, shouldn't a person pay some price for excessive behavior?

There's a creak of movement upstairs and Lily glances up from her phone. She's been following Lauren around like a puppy and peppering both her and Spencer with questions about New

York publishing and theater like some poor castaway on a deserted island who suddenly glimpses a rescue ship.

"If you're not going to eat, let's go." Clay's scraping back his chair and taking a last swig of coffee. "I need to get up to Corolla by nine."

Lily sighs the beleaguered sigh she normally aims at me.

"Or you can walk." He shrugs, making it clear he's not going to ask again.

Manteo High School is, in fact, an easy walk from our house, though not necessarily in the platform sandals Lily's wearing. She stands and gathers her books.

I peck each of them on the cheek and tell them to have a good day.

"Will you ask her for me?" Lily glances upward once more as if I might not know whom she's talking about. "Mrs. Parsons is really excited about having a *New York Times* bestselling writer come talk to our class."

I sigh. My daughter is even more excited about being the person who knows the *New York Times* bestselling author personally. "You should ask her yourself. But honestly this isn't the best time. There's a lot going on." Talk about your understatement. "And they're only here a few more days. Maybe on their next visit." I don't let myself wonder if there will be a next visit. Or if Lauren would actually leave without even speaking to Kendra.

"But it'll only take about thirty minutes of her time. Maybe Spencer could come, too, and talk about his Broadway show. It won two Tonys, you know." She tosses this out as if I might have somehow managed to miss this bit of information.

"You could maybe talk about the bookstore and, I don't know, maybe about your book now that it's finished."

"That would be a pretty jam-packed thirty minutes." I can hear just how dry my voice is but I'm pretty sure I manage to keep smiling.

"Will you just bring it up, Mom?" The smile she gives me is her most winning.

"I'll mention it if and when the opportunity presents itself, but you'll have to do the asking."

"Come on, Lily," Clay says. "I mean it."

With a final pleading look and a toss of her head she follows him out the door.

I'm on my third cup of coffee when Lauren and Spencer come downstairs. I can tell that they've been fighting. I've been in enough domestic skirmishes to recognize the signs.

They both say good morning to me but are careful not to look at each other.

"Coffee?"

They nod and I fill their cups. Lauren pretends not to watch Spencer take and butter a muffin, but her face reveals her displeasure at the reminder of her mother. She reaches over the plate of offending muffins to the fruit bowl to retrieve a banana then yanks off its peel, twists it apart, and pops the top into her mouth.

"So," I say into the vast silence. "What are your plans for today? Fort Raleigh Historic Site? The Waterside Theatre?" These are the closest and best-known tourist sites on Roanoke Island. "Too bad *The Lost Colony* doesn't start until Memorial Day weekend."

"Yeah. I'd really love to see it," Spencer says as we watch Lauren masticate the banana she's decapitated.

"Maybe you should leave those sites for later," I say, unable to watch Lauren's assault on the piece of fruit. "They're so close you can run over there anytime. The drive down to Hatteras is beautiful." Lauren's eyeing a bunch of grapes as if they, too, deserve a comeuppance. But then I guess I should be grateful she's taking her distress and hostility out on the fruit.

I pull open a drawer and retrieve an "Exploring Cape Hatteras" trifold to show Spencer the Cape Hatteras National Seashore. "It's a beautiful drive and there are lots of places to stop on the way down. The Bodie Island Lighthouse is well worth seeing though you won't be able to climb it right now. And you've also got the Pea Island National Wildlife Refuge and the historic Little Kinnakeet Lifesaving Station." I'm trying not to sell it too hard, but as a bookseller close to the historic waterfront I've done more than my share of directing and guiding tourists.

Lauren is still torturing the banana.

Spencer, who's been looking at the map, points to the shoreline. "Oh! There's Rodanthe." He pronounces it like the first-time visitor he is. "Isn't that where that Nicholas Sparks movie was set?"

Lauren and I turn as one.

"It's 'Ro-DAN-thee,'" she says icily. As if he should have known this.

"And you might not want to mention that movie while you're down there or anywhere on the Outer Banks, really," I add more gently.

His surprise is not surprising. "Seriously? I mean, I'm not a huge Sparks fan, either. He skews a little too close to melodrama for my tastes. But . . . why not?"

"Because the local population didn't appreciate being portrayed as country yokels," I say.

"And bluegrass and country music are not 'local,'" Lauren adds, clearly surprised that she's just taken up the mantle of a local while I'm relieved to see she's still got some civic pride and a native's perspective. I was afraid she'd checked them in when she took up residence in Manhattan. "As anyone who was on the beach in the '70s will tell you, a lot of big-name groups played here."

After that the double-team defense is automatic and rapid-fire.

"And because you will never see wild horses running on the beach in Rodanthe."

"Not ever."

"It was completely inaccurate."

"People around here don't appreciate outsiders who don't bother to get things right."

Lauren stops mid-rant and I can practically see her brain registering the fact that she and I have come down on the same side, instinctually filling in each other's blanks, anticipating the other's thoughts.

"Given that all of us at this table have a propensity for making things up, that seems a bit harsh," Spencer says, not particularly disturbed by the corrections and, if I'm not mistaken, as relieved as I am that Lauren has stopped mangling the fruit with criminal intent. "But I get it. 'Ro-DAN-thee.' And no movie references." He reaches for a second muffin. "Is there anything else Outer Banksters have a hate on about that I should be careful of?"

"Well, since you asked, the term is *Bankers*," I reply, still smiling.

"Lauren?" He draws her back in again. "Any other advice on fitting in?"

"Don't bring up the Weather Channel, either," Lauren replies almost begrudgingly.

"Why not?" Spencer asks before popping part of a muffin into his mouth.

"Because they show up here anytime there's even a one percent chance of a nor'easter or—God forbid—a hurricane. And they do stand-ups twenty-four hours a day making it sound like we're about to be blown off the face of the earth," Lauren explains.

"It's really bad for business," I agree, barely resisting the impulse to high-five her.

"Shocking as it may seem, tourists aren't eager to cross multiple bridges to get to a narrow barrier island when they've been led to believe a hurricane is barreling toward it."

"They blow everything out of proportion," Lauren adds. "Because if it's only a possibility of thundershowers and not a hurricane brewing, they don't have a story."

Spencer shakes his head. "Wow, you Bankers are a tough crowd."

"Now that you know how to avoid pissing off the resident population my work here is done," I tease, grateful that he's facilitated this conversation. "I believe it's safe for me to head to the store." I get up and pour the rest of my coffee into a to-go cup. "Make yourselves at home."

"Actually, I thought I'd give Dee a call before we head out to see what time our room will be available." Lauren tosses this out as if it's an afterthought—and just like that she negates whatever bond I might have imagined was forming. She can't wait to get out of here.

"Great." I'm not going to beg her to stay with me. Maybe Rafe's bed is too small. Or maybe she wants to stay in the same place with her father. Who knows? It's not as if a couple conversations are going to put our friendship back together anyway. I don't need more than basic communication if Lauren doesn't. But I know for a fact that Kendra does.

I exhale as I turn and walk outside to my car. The drive is just long enough to dither over whether to call Kendra now or wait until I get to the store. Or maybe I should swing by the Sandcastle after work. I have no idea how this whole mess is going to get resolved or what, if anything, I can, or even should, try to do about it. But I have to let Kendra know that I'm here for her if she needs me. She's always been there for me. I can't leave her to face this all alone.

∽

At the store I automatically begin to straighten shelves and dust the children's section, but Mrs. McKinnon, who filled in for a few hours yesterday afternoon, is a much better housekeeper than I am and everything's in perfect order. There's barely even a speck of dust. In fact, the whole store is extremely neat, maybe even *too* organized. Like a woman who's put on her Sunday best just to run to the market. There's really nothing that needs doing and if I were still working on *Heart of Gold*, I'd already be at the front desk booting up my laptop. Where I could lose myself in Whitney and Heath's relationship instead of examining my own. Or wondering if Kendra's okay. And what on earth I should do about it if she isn't. And whether I could forgive her if I were Lauren. Or Jake.

I pick up my cell phone and hit speed dial but Kendra doesn't answer. Finally it goes to voice mail and I leave a message. Over the next thirty minutes I try twice more with the same result. I beat off the stirring of unease and then the worst-case scenarios. Kendra's not exactly a techie or overly attached to her phone, but she's not someone who never answers, either. She's also not someone who's going to do herself harm or give up on attempting to make her daughter understand why she did what she did.

Too antsy to just sit there and actually wishing I still had a manuscript to throw myself into, I rearrange the new-releases table even though it clearly doesn't need it. Then, because I'm still worried about Kendra and feeling the unexpected blip of camaraderie from breakfast, I pull Lauren's books from the shelves and create a whole display of them in the front window. Then I decorate it with a neon-green bucket and shovel, a floppy sunhat, and an assortment of beach balls and sunglasses and drizzle it all with seashells.

I'm considering putting the BE BACK SOON sign on the front door so that I can go check on Kendra, when the front door opens with a jangle. Mrs. McKinnon and Leslie Parent walk in.

"Hello!" Leslie smiles cheerfully. Mrs. McKinnon looks around either to reassure herself that I haven't destroyed the order she had wrought or, perhaps, to reassure herself that I have.

"Hi." We meet halfway, which puts us right near the local cookbooks.

"It's funny to come in and not find you typing away on your laptop," Leslie says.

"It *is* funny. I was just thinking how odd it is to be done after all this time."

"When will you send it off to New York?" Mrs. McKinnon asks as if you just put *New York, New York* on the front of it and pop it in the mail.

"Well, I probably need to do another read-through. And it might need some revisions. Then I'll put together a list of agents who represent my kind of work. Then if I'm lucky enough to have an agent agree to represent me it would go out to editors that . . ."

"Has Lauren read it yet?" Leslie asks.

"Well, no." I'm very glad we're now on speaking terms, but I have no intention of asking her for help of any kind. And especially not a critique of my manuscript. I'm not sure I could survive that.

"She could probably just ask her agent to read it, couldn't she? And maybe her editor?" Mrs. McKinnon asks. "That way you could just leapfrog over all that rigmarole."

"Oh. Oh no. I would never ask her to do that." I'm practically stuttering. And wishing I had left for Kendra's before they arrived. "She's far too busy to . . ." I stop short.

"That girl has a lot on her mind now, doesn't she?" Mrs. McKinnon says not unkindly. "What with a long-lost father showing up and all."

"What, uh, what makes you say that?" I can barely get the words out.

Leslie rolls her eyes. "Plenty of people have seen them out on the porch at the Dogwood."

"Oh my. It's not supposed to be a secret, is it?" Mrs. McKinnon asks. "I mean, not anymore?"

"To think Kendra pretended to have been married all that time." Leslie shakes her head. "As if anyone here would have treated her any different."

"People might have," Mrs. McKinnon says. "Not everyone was so open-minded back then."

"Oh, I . . ." I close my mouth. It's not like I have anything to add to this conversation.

"I heard she left him at the church brokenhearted. And that's one fine-looking man." Mrs. McKinnon sighs. "But I suppose she must have had her reasons."

They both peer at me as if I'm going to tell them what those reasons were when I'm wondering that very thing myself. I have no idea what would have made the woman I thought I knew so well act so out of character. I take a step back.

"Lauren must be so upset," Leslie adds, but I can tell she's still hoping I'll weigh in. "Is she just furious at Kendra?" When I don't say anything she continues, "Clara over at the post office said she wouldn't be surprised if that girl never forgave her mama."

I take another step back. There's no room to retreat farther. I'm up against the shelves.

"Well, at least she's getting to know her father now. Better late than never, I always say." Leslie has clearly spent some time thinking this out. "Maybe he'll even give her away at her wedding." One eyebrow sketches upward. "Is he married?"

"Um, no. He's a widower." I'm relieved to have something to offer that isn't someone else's secret.

"Maybe he didn't just come to get to know his daughter," Mrs. McKinnon says with a wistful smile that reminds me of just how many romance novels she's purchased. "Maybe it isn't only about Lauren." She waggles her eyebrows in a way that reminds me that she's also been reading quite a bit of erotica. "Maybe he came back for Kendra, too."

Twenty-three

Lauren

"So tell me again why Ocracoke isn't pronounced 'Ockra-COKE-ee'?" Spencer is watching me from the passenger seat of the rental car as we head back toward Manteo from our drive down to Hatteras.

He's been asking this question since he spotted the signs for the Hatteras-Ocracoke Ferry and assumed the pronunciation of Ocracoke would be similar to Rodanthe.

I appreciate the fact that he's been trying to make up and jolly me into a better mood all day (not to mention applying his creative flair to capturing our outing for posterity and social media), but it also makes me feel worse. Because it's obvious that the only reasons we're fighting are my abject unhappiness and my inability to deal with what has happened.

I stare glumly out the window at some of the most gorgeous scenery on earth. It's been a bizarre point of honor not to respond to his teasing or even crack a smile. (Except in the over-the-top photos and videos he's staged and posted.) As if any sign of real levity or enjoyment might somehow absolve my mother of treachery. Or negate the horror of her keeping my father and me apart. Of making me mourn someone who was not only alive but living less than six hours away. Of depriving me of grandparents. Of family.

"I don't know," I say more gruffly than I mean to. "That's

just the way it's pronounced. Like how the letter *c* can be 'see' or 'kuh.'" I sound like a guest lecturer with a great big stick up her ass. "It's best not to question these things."

I set my jaw. Thank goodness I didn't take him to Ocracoke, which is still reachable only by ferry; a turn of events that has left them isolated to the point where some old-timers still speak Hoi Toider, a dialect heard only on remote islands in the Outer Banks. (A bit of trivia that sent Spencer to YouTube to hear the Ocracoke brogue for himself. After which he recorded and posted a video of us pretending to miss the ferry while singing a chorus of a hit song from *The Music in Me* in a mangled brogue.)

"Hey, I'm just trying to apply a little logic to the situation." He gives me the puppy-dog look and expectant smile he's used to coax me into performances and poses that are way outside my comfort zone. I've clung to my righteous indignation most of the day, but now, inexplicably, an answering smile threatens.

"Fahgeddaboutit," I say in my best Brooklyn accent. "I've been in all five boroughs and I don't think New Yorkers have a leg to stand on when it comes to accents and pronunciations."

"Point taken. I'll move on if you say Chicamacomico real fast one more time," he says, gleefully massacring the name of the historic lifesaving station we toured in Rodanthe. (After which he somehow talked me into crawling across the sand with a lifesaving ring around me and seaweed clinging to my clothes as if I'd just been rescued.)

I give him an eyebrow, still not completely ready to capitulate to his good humor. "And, FYI, you didn't have to say 'Ro-DAN-thee' quite so many times."

"Ah, but I did." His slightly sunburned face is wreathed in smiles. We both smell like a combination of salt air and sunscreen from the time we spent plopped down on the sand of an absolutely deserted stretch of beach. (Where he staged a shot of us discovering the actual remains of a shipwreck that had recently washed ashore.) "Not only that. Did you notice how many times I did NOT mention Nicholas Sparks or his movie or the Weather Channel?"

I give him a stern look that's no doubt ruined by the smile that tugs at my lips.

"I see you smiling and feeling superior, but come on. Who decided Bodie Lighthouse should be pronounced 'body'? That's just *wrong*."

I give a long, theatrical sigh, but I am in fact smiling, something I couldn't even imagine this morning when we left Bree's. I still feel like my head might explode every time I let myself think about the steady diet of lies my mother fed me, but while the anger continues to simmer inside me the tears aren't quite so near the surface. And while I have no intention of so much as being in the same room with my mother, I'm looking forward to continuing to get to know my father. Today has reconfirmed just how lucky I am that Spencer will be a part of everything that lies ahead. (Plus, I have no doubt his social media skills will thrill the publicity team at Trove.)

We're just coming off the Herbert C. Bonner Bridge when my cell phone rings. It's Deanna. I glance at my watch. It's just after four P.M., so I assume she's calling to see what time we're planning to check in.

"Lauren?"

"Hi, Dee."

There's a moment of hesitation. Then she says, "I'm afraid I've got some bad news."

And just like that I go from never wanting to see my mother again to a litany of worst-case imaginings. She's overdosed. Been in an accident. Dropped dead from a heart attack. "What is it? What's happened?"

Spencer sits up. His eyes are on me as he tries to pinpoint the source of the panic that has turned my voice shrill.

"I'm glad I caught you."

I hold my breath.

"There's been an accident."

"Oh my God." My head is spinning. There's not enough air in the car. "What, what's happened?" I swallow. "It's not fatal, is it?" My mind races through the plot points. Mother and daughter have a huge fight after which one of them dies, leaving the other forever bereft and guilty for not trying to repair the relationship in time. "Please tell me no one died. Should I go straight to the hospital? Do you want me to call a specialist?"

There's another pause. Then Dee says, "Only if that specialist is a plumber."

I notice the red light and barely mash on the brakes in time. "Did . . . did you say 'plumber'?"

"Yes. Not five minutes after the cleaning crew finished in the Sandpiper room we discovered that a pipe's been leaking in the wall. The wall is now ripped open and we're trying to get things cleaned up, but the room's not habitable and probably won't be for a couple days."

"But . . ."

"I'm sorry, Lauren. I know you were keen to move over today. I called around again but there's a family reunion coming in tonight for the rest of the week. When are you heading back to New York?"

"Friday morning."

"I'm sure your mother would be glad to have you both . . ."

"No."

There's another silence. I feel Spencer's eyes on my face.

I'm shaking now with nerves and anger. "And if this is some attempt to get me to go back to her place . . . or force Bree and me to spend more time with each other . . ."

"I've always been fascinated by how your mind works. But this is not some elaborate plot or even a stab at fiction," Dee says in a tired but wry tone. "It's just plumbing."

Heat rises to my cheeks as I end the call.

"Everybody okay?" Spencer asks as, with a shaky hand, I set the phone on the seat.

"It appears so." I feel like a car that went from zero to one hundred in less than sixty seconds, sprang out of control, then somehow didn't crash.

"So the plumbing will recover?"

I turn to meet his eyes. They're dancing.

"I'm glad you find this amusing. It looks like we're going to have to go back to Bree's." I snap the words out, but I'm beyond glad he's with me.

"Should we call first and make sure it's okay?"

I barely think about this, which, given everything that's taken place between Bree and me, is a pleasant surprise. I know without hesitation that Bree won't mind if we stay longer. "No, Bree'll be at the store until six anyway. And I think she mentioned that Lily has some after-school thing, so it's not like we'll be in the way."

"Do we need to stop and get a key from . . ." He stops midsentence. "Never mind. I forgot the come-on-in-and-take-anything-that-looks-interesting welcome mat is always out."

I take a right and then a left on Wingina. Clay's truck is parked in its usual spot, but the house looks quiet. We clomp across the front porch with our suitcases and carry them inside.

"I'll just run them up." Spencer hefts both suitcases and moves toward the stairs. Footsteps sound on the landing. It's Clay. His hair is still damp as if he's just out of the shower. He's looking down, buttoning his shirt as he takes the first step. The surprise on his face when he glances up and sees us is comical. Or would be if the blonde behind him, who also appears freshly showered and not quite dressed, was Brianna.

Clay's face goes white, but there's an unattractive smirk on the blonde's otherwise attractive face.

"Are you kidding?" Fury spikes through me. I'm about to give them both a piece of my mind when Spencer puts down the suitcases and takes my hand. A small shake of his head is meant to stop me from saying anything more. I stop talking, but only because I'm trying to come up with the most scathing indictment of Clay and this clichéd and offensive behavior possible. I mean, right here in Bree's own house? In the bedroom that once belonged to her grandmother?

"Oh. Hi." Clay is clearly at a loss. "I thought you were moving over to the Dogwood."

"Plumbing issue. Our room is uninhabitable," I reply. "We just found out a couple minutes ago. I didn't realize we needed to call and warn anyone."

I actually enjoy the sick look on Clay's face. At least he seems to care that he's been found out. I'm not so happy about the triumphant expression on the blonde's. She appears just bitchy enough to wish it were Bree who'd come in unexpectedly. In that moment all I want is to wipe that look off her face. Bree and I have had our issues, but no one deserves this. "Who's your *friend?*" I ask Clay.

Spencer nudges me.

"What?" I turn to him with the most innocent expression I can muster. "I *said* 'friend.' Not 'piece of ass' or even 'sleaze on the side,' like I wanted to."

Spencer sighs.

"Nobody you need to worry about." Clay says this quietly and I know him well enough to understand that's as close as he's going to come to asking me not to say anything to Bree. But I don't know what it means that he feels free to do this here in their home. Or whether Bree already knows.

I don't respond. Not even when the blonde, who doesn't look anywhere near as attractive close up and who really needs to do something about her roots, flounces past us.

"Did you really used to date that guy?" Spencer asks after the truck has started up and backs out of the drive.

"Yeah." Now that the encounter is over the adrenaline and

anger are seeping out of me. "But I was young and inexperienced. And my taste has obviously improved." I feel in need of a shower and somehow guilty just from knowing. "I did try to warn Bree that he was too immature to settle down. That was one of the things she's held against me. But I had no idea he was screwing around."

Spencer shakes his head. "Man, that sucks. I kind of liked the guy."

"I know. Me, too. He's got lots of good qualities, but . . ." I slump. It's all too much. My mother's lies. Clay's cheating. "In case you're wondering, that's not something I would ever put up with."

"Yeah. Me, either. As far as I'm concerned, that's the antithesis of what marriage is about." Spencer puts his arms around me and pulls me close until our foreheads touch. He's so real and solid.

"God, I wish we were back in New York."

"We can go if you really want to," he says gently. "But I thought you'd want more time to get to know Jake. And show me more unpronounceable yet very cool sights." He hesitates for a moment. "And, well, I still hope you can at least sit down and talk to your mother."

I don't bother to say no as I follow him up the stairs to Rafe's bedroom. But that's not going to happen. I also know that telling Bree what we just witnessed would be a big mistake. She's made it clear before that she doesn't want to hear anything bad about her husband. Only, I don't know how I can look her in the eye and *not* tell her what we just saw.

Kendra

It's Tuesday morning and I am still hiding inside like a frightened mouse. Look at me the wrong way and I will squeak in terror. Since I'm not really sleeping, I started baking at three A.M. and had everything that was promised for today ready by six thirty. I even got dressed; something I haven't done since Saturday. But at the last minute I couldn't take the first step off the front porch. When my neighbor Julie, who's delivered before in a pinch, came over to pick up the baked goods, I could barely meet her eye.

I am frozen in place, unable to break free. I can't bear being alone with my thoughts and mistakes and regrets, but the longer I hide here the harder it is to contemplate going out.

Virtually everyone I know has called, but I don't answer the phone. My voice mail is full and I can't bring myself to listen or delete. Mouse that I am, I have locked the front door and brought the key inside for the first time in memory. I cower behind the curtains at the first sound of a car turning into my driveway. Jake has been here twice in as many days and both times I could hardly think or hear for the pounding of my heart and the whooshing of blood in my ears.

Dee and Bree have stood and knocked until their knuckles must be raw. They called through the door to try to get me to open up and to let me know that Lauren and Spencer are still here. They've begged me to come talk to her. Reminded me that their flight back to New York is on Friday. As if I'm not counting the minutes left.

Through it all, I hear their hurt that I never took them into my confidence, their shock that I was never married and that I kept Lauren from her father and both our families. But even when they threaten to use their keys I still don't let them in or even make a sound.

The only person I haven't heard from is the only person I want to. But I know my daughter. She doesn't suffer fools gladly. And I am the biggest fool of all.

Twenty-four

Lauren

It's Tuesday evening. Spencer, Jake, and I are sitting at Ortega'z over on Sir Walter Raleigh Street. I'm nursing a margarita while I watch Jake and Spencer chow down on what they have proclaimed to be some seriously great Mexican/Southwestern food. Although I'm too stressed to eat, I'm proud of the fact that the foodie I'm marrying seems perfectly happy with everything he's consumed since we arrived on the Outer Banks, from Tortugas' Lie and Ortega'z, which he'd seen featured on Food Network's *Diners, Drive-ins and Dives,* to Sam & Omie's, where I took him for lunch today for old time's sake, because I've been going there practically from birth.

My birth. My eyes turn to my father—

I still stumble over the word even in my head—as he tilts the margarita to his lips and contemplates me out of his kindly brown eyes. He has an easy warmth that makes everyone around him comfortable. From what I've seen of him he and my mother should have been well suited.

I stumble again over that thought and another lump rises in my throat. I cannot understand how she could have walked away from their wedding and the life they had planned.

I'm lost in imaginings of what my life might have been and only come back to the present when Spencer takes my hand. I realize he's in the middle of filling Jake in on our morning at the Fort Raleigh National Historic Site, his enthusiasm for the waterside theater where *The Lost Colony* is staged every summer. "I told Lauren I'd be glad to come back to see a performance and anything else we don't get to this trip." He doesn't add that it's clear I'm trying to cram everything in because I have no intention of coming back this summer. Or possibly ever. The Outer Banks might stretch for over a hundred miles, but the full-time population is far too small to avoid anyone for long. I held my breath through a good part of our lunch, afraid my mother might walk in.

For what might be the millionth time I wonder what she's doing right now. Is she going about her daily life, baking and delivering, waiting for me to get over my shock? Or is she racked by guilt for lying and keeping my father from me? I don't understand how she could possibly rationalize what she's done.

"After lunch we went to Jockey's Ridge," Spencer continues. "Good God, that's one hell of a sand dune. Then we went to the Wright Brothers monument." I listen with only half an ear while he relays the park ranger's explanation of how and why Kitty Hawk was chosen, the hardships the brothers encountered, and their refusal to give up their quest to prove that man could not only glide but fly in machines that were heavier than air.

He squeezes my hand and I add, "I always forget how phenomenal the view from the top of the memorial is."

"And tomorrow?" Jake asks.

"I figured we'd go north. Maybe stroll around Duck a bit then head up to Corolla to see the lighthouse and town center. We might take one of the wild-horse tours late in the afternoon."

"I've heard they're an impressive sight," Jake says. "Descendants of the Spanish mustangs that were originally brought to the New World as long ago as the 1500s."

Just like that I'm six years old, holding my mother's hand, the breeze off the water riffling our hair as we watch the herd of horses gallop up the beach with their heads tossing and their manes flying. I feel the smile of memory on my lips. It fades as I acknowledge that my mother is a part of every important memory. She wasn't just the center of my universe. She was my universe. The thrum of anger vibrates through me. Why did we spend my whole life living like two orphans whom fate had turned its back on?

"So do they still run wild?" Spencer asks, once again pulling me back.

"Yes." I try to refocus on the conversation. "But they started dying off when civilization got too close. Now they're in a protected habitat where they can roam freely without being in danger."

"And Thursday?" Jake asks.

"Then Thursday I thought we might go fishing either offshore or inshore so Spencer can get a taste of being on the water here." I finish my margarita. "I promised him I'd bait his hook."

"Good thing, too." Spencer is not embarrassed at his inexperience with a rod and reel. "The closest I've ever come to fishing is ordering sushi."

Jake smiles softly. I sense something is on his mind, but I don't know him well enough to guess what it is.

"Would you like to come with us?"

"No. Thanks, though."

"Do you hate baiting hooks, too?" Spencer asks.

"No." Jake grins. "I grew up fishing with my dad. Used to spend time on the James River. I learned to bait a hook when I was about five."

Just that easily he refers to the grandfather I never met and who didn't know I existed. My heart actually hurts.

"I've got appointments on Thursday and a couple of conference calls. But if you're free, I'd like to take everyone to dinner. Dee told me that Blue Point up in Duck is one of your favorite restaurants." He's watching my face as he offers up options. "Or if you'd like to stay closer to home we could go to 1587." He names an upscale restaurant in the Tranquil House Inn on the Manteo waterfront.

"I think Blue Point would be great for our last night," I say.

"Good." Jake smiles. "I thought I might invite Bree and Clay."

I'm careful not to squirm at the suggestion. The sight of Clay and the blonde coming down the stairs right out of the shower is still fresh in my mind. "Sure. The more, the merrier, right?"

We've finished our main courses and are contemplating dessert when Spencer asks Jake if he ever gets to New York.

"About three or four times a year."

I blink. "You come to New York?"

"Yes. I have investment partners there."

"We could have walked right by each other and never even known it." It's almost a whisper.

He nods and I see him swallow. I'm not the only one mourning for the time that's been lost and what might have been. But once again my sorrow is infused with anger. I could have been part of a family, not learning how to live without one.

The bill comes. Despite Spencer's protests Jake insists on paying. We're working out details for Thursday night and waiting for the receipt when Jake says, "So what are you going to do about your mother?"

"Do?" I hear the surprise in my voice. I also hear the fury. I'm practically shaking with it. "Nothing. Not anything. As in I do not intend to *do* one single thing."

Bree

Lauren and Spencer are out with Jake. Clay and Lily and I are having a rare family dinner together. As we eat, my husband steals glances at me. Guilty glances. My heart sinks. I've seen that look before and I know what it means.

"When are Lauren and Spencer leaving?" Clay asks, and I realize I'm no longer looking forward to their departure. Even in the midst of the turmoil surrounding Jake's appearance, this time with Lauren has reminded me how close a bond we shared and how much I've missed her. Witnessing Lauren and Spencer's happiness has made me even more aware of how separate Clay's life and mine have become. We're both here for Lily, but in so many ways I feel as if we're simply putting on a show. Going through the motions. He plays everything so close to the vest. Today when I stopped by to visit his mother, Gina, she asked what I thought about the new spec houses selling and I had no idea what she was talking about.

Lily always used to be an open book, at least to me. But I feel her beginning to pull away, weighing what she shares, keeping her feelings to herself, if not her complaints.

"I still can't believe she couldn't make time to come talk to my class," Lily whines now.

"I didn't ask her. I told you there's too much going on for that right now. And she's spending time getting to know her father." The news of Jake's connection to Kendra and Lauren was all over town before I could figure out how to explain it to Lily.

"I can't believe Kendra never told her about her own father."

I have no answer for this. I can't quite believe it, either. Or reconcile any of it with the Kendra I know and love. The Kendra who seems to be hiding even from those she's closest to. I keep telling myself there's no need to worry, but if I haven't heard back from her by tomorrow I'm going to go over and use my key whether she's ready or not.

Lily leans across the table. "What did Lauren say about your manuscript?"

"She congratulated me on finishing."

Lily sits back. "You mean she hasn't read it?"

"Of course not. Like I said, there's been a lot going on for her this visit."

"Um-hmmm." She looks and sounds unconvinced.

"Besides, it's not like you can read an entire manuscript in a couple of hours."

"But you asked her to read it, right?"

I glance away then force myself to look back and meet my daughter's eyes. "No, I didn't. But I'm sure if she thought she'd have the time she would have offered." The lie sticks in my throat for a second, but I manage to get it out. Then I stand and go to the pantry, where I pretend to be looking for something, so that I won't have to see the expression on Lily's face.

In the end it's Clay who steps in and changes the subject by asking Lily about an upcoming basketball game. Then he teases her about a guard named Shane.

By the time I come back to the table she's forgotten about me and my manuscript and is denying that she has a "thing" for the junior who's apparently lettering in more than one sport. Her blush reminds me of how I once felt about Clay. How, after Lauren left, he and I turned to each other and I told myself that the best marriages often grew out of friendship.

I drag in a breath of air and try not to fixate on ancient history. I've always hated my parents' preference for things that are dead and buried. But in view of the current state of my marriage it's almost impossible not to think about all the mistakes I've made. The wishful thinking that allowed me to marry a man who didn't love me quite as much as I loved him.

And then there's my last-minute decision not to go to New York with Lauren. Did I back out because I knew I didn't have the talent, courage, or determination to make it in New York or publishing? Or because I was afraid to leave the familiar comfort of the small town I grew up in? Should I have listened to Lauren when she told me that Clay wasn't ready to settle down?

As I sit in the kitchen and stare at the man I married I'm afraid the answer to each of these questions is a resounding, if horrifying, *yes!*

Kendra

It's still dark when I wake early Wednesday morning after yet another night spent tossing and turning. So I sit at the kitchen table sipping coffee and staring out the kitchen window waiting for daybreak. I'm still not sure how to repair the damage I've done, or if that's even possible. But I can't hide inside the Sandcastle a moment longer.

Unlocking the front door is only a symbolic gesture, I know. But it's a declaration of sorts. A start. So are the shorts and T-shirt I pull on.

As soon as it's light enough to see I head out to the beach, where my bare feet sink into the cool sand. The breeze is a soft caress as the sun rises out of the ocean and climbs through a cloud-streaked sky.

The swells roll in low and clean. A squadron of pelicans glides over the surface in search of breakfast. The only prints in the sand are mine and those of the sanderlings scurrying and pecking at the water's edge.

I raise my chin and breathe deeply, pulling the beauty deep inside me. With each sparkle of sunlight that reflects off the water I feel calmer, better able to grapple with my guilt over the damage I've done.

I realize as I walk that my vow to never again leap without thinking has made me timid. Too much thought can be as crippling as too little.

On Jennette's Pier fishermen bait hooks and send lines flying. Another stands waist high in the shallows casting far out in front of him. The more patient pelicans wait and watch from their preferred perches while others swoop and dive.

I want to stand here forever, soothed and reassured by my surroundings, but I know now that I need to act. I have to find a way to speak to Lauren. I may not be able to control her reaction to what I have to say, but I can't let her leave without saying it.

With new resolve I turn and head back up the beach, my eyes scanning the horizon as my brain sorts through possible courses of action. The most immediate challenge will be getting her to agree to see me.

I'm almost home when a man comes down the Sandcastle steps and walks toward the water so that our paths will intersect.

"I thought I might find you out here," Jake says as I approach. "Not right away, of course. But after I searched your unlocked house for signs of foul play." His smile is the crooked wry one that's like an arrow through the heart.

"I took a walk to try to clear my head."

"Did it work?"

"I think so."

"So what happens next? Now that you've made it off the couch?"

"First of all I need to apologize. I'm so very sorry, Jake. Based on what Aunt Velda shared about your wife and your family life, I truly thought I was protecting both of you."

He remains silent and I know he has every reason to hate me. I also know that he, more than anyone, should understand why his wife's instability kept me from making contact.

"The thing is, I don't even know if Lauren will ever forgive me. She has very strong opinions and reactions. And she isn't one to change her mind easily."

He flinches at the reminder of how well I know the daughter

he's only just met. And I think of all the times I regretted running. How often I wished he were here. And not just because being a single parent was so hard. But because I loved him so much.

His jaw hardens and it's my turn to flinch. Because of the hurt I've caused him. And because the person I've been closest to since her birth forty years ago doesn't even want to be in the same room with me.

"I can't let her leave without one last attempt at a conversation. But I'm not even sure I can find a way to get in front of her."

"I can make it happen."

"How?" I keep the *why* to myself. I am not going to look this gift horse in the mouth.

"I'm taking her and Spencer and Bree and Clay to Blue Point tomorrow night."

"You want me to come for dinner?" I search his face, trying to read what's there.

"Truthfully, no. I'd actually like the meal to happen and it's possible that Lauren would insist on leaving when you arrive." He looks me in the eye. "I think you come over to the table as we're finishing dessert. Maybe you can act as if you're just stopping by for a drink and happened to see us. That way it won't feel like a conspiracy."

"And it leaves you off the hook if there's a blowup."

"Yes." He doesn't look away, but I can't read his true motives. I don't know if he's setting me up for a fall or is only watching out for our daughter's best interests. "Yes," he says again. "It does."

Twenty-five

⌇

Lauren

Blue Point is one of my favorite Outer Banks restaurants. Just past the Duck town center, it sits on the northern end of a boardwalk of shops that overlooks Currituck Sound. This makes it a perfect place to watch the sunset and get a great meal.

Unfortunately, I'm still so wrung out that food of any kind remains totally unappealing. I have no idea how I'm going to swallow even a bite.

Expanses of window bring in light and frame the spectacular water views. The decor is contemporary upscale yet cozy. The food is Southern, coastal, and seasonal. They were farm-to-table before the phrase became popular. Spencer's been happy to try the food everywhere we've been but his foodie "antennae" begin quivering the moment we walk in the door.

It's not full season yet so the BackBar outside isn't open and the crowd is largely local. Bree and Clay nod and smile at people they know. I recognize a few friendly faces and even more curious ones.

We leave early tomorrow morning to catch a three P.M. flight out of Norfolk, so this is our last meal. No sooner do I think this than my brain calls up images of the Last Supper. I'm certainly not picturing myself as you-know-who here, but if I painted my mother into the picture she'd be Judas. I still can't grasp how greatly my life has shifted. How little I knew the person I thought I knew best. My stomach roils. Like everywhere

I've been since last Saturday I'm afraid I'm going to run into her and that when I do I'll burst into tears. Or shout like a crazy person. And, of course, I'm aware that the truth about my past is now common knowledge.

Heads bend and people whisper as we walk by. I don't have to guess who and what they're talking about. To be fair, if it weren't me this happened to, I'd be talking about it, too. It would be a great plot twist except I'm sure there are those who would call it contrived or far-fetched. Maybe even outside the realm of possibility. Because who on earth would live a lie of this magnitude for forty years?

We divide our attention and conversation between the sunset and the food that keeps arriving. First come shared appetizers of cornmeal fried wild Virginia catfish, creamy burrata and minted spring pea, and a "taste of Southern goodness," tiny servings of which I put on my plate but cannot eat. I watch Spencer practically inhale his main course of pan-fried local jumbo lump crab cakes. When he catches me pushing my seared sea scallops around my plate, he first tries to convince me to eat them. When I don't, he ends up eating them, too. The others sample one another's dishes. Jake made it clear that we're his guests. Spencer only agreed if the wines were on him. I'm grateful that they've reached a détente about the bill. I don't think I could take another ounce of conflict without fleeing. Fortunately, the more wine I drink the more able I am to breathe and at least act like myself.

Spencer takes my hand in his. "It's good to see you smiling."

I smile again, because I can see how much it pleases him. And because I am inebriated.

"Maybe we should hire someone to drive us in the rental car to the airport," I suggest as I hold out my empty wineglass for another refill.

"Why would we do that?" he asks.

"So I can keep drinking until I get back to my real life."

He leans forward to whisper in my ear. "This *is* your real life,

Lauren. And whether or not you like it right now, Kendra is still your real mother."

"No." I shake my head and let go of his hand. "No she's not. Not anymore."

I feel Bree's eyes on my face and turn my head, reaching for a piece of bread and buttering it before she can say anything. Afterward I alternately drink and pull the bread into pieces that I can't imagine swallowing. The alcohol helps, but it's a fine line between comfortably cushioned and a head that's spinning. I'm not sure I'll know when to stop.

I glance up and see Clay blanch. I glance around, afraid he might have spotted Kendra, but there's no sign of her. When I look again Clay's face appears perfectly normal.

"Wow." I put down my fork and knife. "I am stuffed. I don't think I can eat another bite."

Spencer, who knows how little I've eaten, doesn't comment.

"What? No room for dessert?" Jake asks.

"You, who can eat multiple ice cream sundaes in one sitting? I can't believe it. I have always envied your metabolism." Bree blushes. I know she has to have envied my career, too. If I'm honest, and it's hard to lie even to yourself when you've had this much to drink, there've been times I've enjoyed that envy. We look at each other.

She has bemoaned her curves since we first sprouted breasts and had to start wearing bras, something my mother took us both shopping for. It has apparently never occurred to her that people who are built like a stalk of wheat might trade some of their metabolism for a little of what she'd like to get rid of.

I raise my chin. Like I said, I am nothing if not competitive. "I might be able to find some room for a little something."

"You must have gotten my sweet tooth," Jake says. "I've eaten way more than my share of the triple-chocolate cake at the Dogwood." My father smiles. If he doesn't realize that's one of my mother's best-known confections, I'm not going to tell him.

And if he does? I reach for my wineglass to drain the last of it, then hold it up to Spencer for a refill.

"You might want to slow down just a little." He keeps his voice low, but I am way beyond caution. When you're rushing headlong toward oblivion it's hard to keep track of each step. We order warm Southern pecan pie, a white chocolate torte, and a piece of key lime pie to share.

Even though my stomach is roiling and my head feels oddly light and fluffy, I don't share my Jack (as in Jack Daniels) and Coke float. I feel numb but not in a particularly good way.

"Will you excuse me?" Bree stands and sets her napkin on the table. "I need to go to the ladies' room."

"I'll come with you." It's an automatic response that brings me to my feet. How many times did we share a trip to the bathroom in high school and college?

It takes serious concentration to reach the restroom without weaving or stumbling. On occasion I've been jealous of a man's ability to simply unzip and do his business so quickly, but as I lower myself to the toilet seat I'm glad we do this sitting down and that I don't have to hurry back to the table. I'm not at all sure how long I've been in the stall when I realize I'm finished and have lost track of where Bree might be in the process. I sway slightly as I stand and zip my pants then fumble with the door lock. I don't see her as I walk carefully to the counter to wash my hands. I do see a much taller blonde at the sink. She appears to be watching me in the mirror. It takes me a minute to assess the face. It's not the blonde I saw Clay with in their house, but I can tell they're related. She has the same cheap dye job. Same features. Same build. Same sneer.

I stare back. I'm perfectly ready to give someone some shit. It might even release some of the pressure that feels like a geyser bubbling inside me. But even as I turn on the faucet I know that the best outcome for Bree, who is just now coming out of her stall, is no outcome at all.

Bree barely glances at the woman as she washes her hands next to me. She does a very thorough job of it, studying her hands the entire time.

This really irritates the other woman, who huffs, looks down her narrow nose at Bree, then says, "Some people should pay a little more attention to their husbands if they don't want to lose them."

Bree doesn't even look up. She is focused on her hands as if they're the only things in her world that matter.

"Did you hear me?" the tall blonde says in a tone of voice that normally accompanies a finger poke.

I'm actually holding my breath trying to figure out how to insert myself between them or, failing that, kick-start my brain so that I can mediate the situation and get rid of the problem. I'm still trying to get my thoughts in order when Bree calmly looks up from her hands as if she just now noticed the other woman. "Kind of hard not to." She turns off the faucet and waves her hand to activate the paper towel. "Is there anyone in your family who can keep their hands to themselves or their mouth shut when they don't?"

I close my mouth, impressed.

The blonde has no comeback. Finally, she says, "Huh! Some people aren't as smart as they think they are."

"And some people just aren't smart, period." Bree dries her hands thoroughly, but not desperately, then drops the used paper towel in the trash. "And that goes for you *and* your sister."

"Huh!"

"This woman needs to work on her vocabulary," I point out. "It's a bit limited."

"Damn straight," Bree agrees. "And maybe she and the other women in her family need to set their sights a little higher than other women's husbands." She looks the blonde up and down, cool as a cucumber. "You know what they say. If a man is cheating on his current wife he'll be cheating on the next one."

The woman huffs again. Then she scurries out with a toss of her hair.

"Well done, you," I say with admiration. I've let myself forget that Bree was never really the marshmallow people thought she was.

Bree closes her eyes briefly before meeting mine. "I wish I could tell you that's the first time another woman thought I needed to know that my husband had strayed. You did warn me that he wasn't ready for marriage, but that was twenty years ago. I assumed he'd grow out of it." Her eyes well with tears. "You can go ahead and tell me *I told you so* if you want to. I deserve it."

"No. No you don't." I shake my head. I do not mention that Clay brought that woman's sister into their home. "But . . . how in the world do you put up with it?"

She squares her shoulders and continues to meet my eyes. "Same way you get to Carnegie Hall." Her lips tremble even as they tilt up into a smile. "Practice."

I blow out a harsh breath at the sheer, awful irony of her smile. Both of us have been lied to by the very people we have loved and thought we could trust. As we head back to the table I'm filled with anger and sorrow on Bree's behalf.

Somebody needs to teach Clay Williams a serious lesson. He doesn't deserve Brianna or the devotion that she's given him. The way she's put him first. It would serve him right if . . . I stumble, unable to finish the thought or the step I've just taken. Not when I realize what my eyes just skimmed over on their way to the darkening sky outside the windows.

I yank my gaze back to the pale face that I do not want to see. My gaze narrows so that I feel as if I'm looking down a long, oddly narrow tunnel. At the end of that tunnel is my mother. She's standing next to our table and talking to my father and my fiancé.

A voice rings out and silences all the others. It takes a couple of heartbeats to realize that the voice is mine.

Twenty-six

Kendra

"I can't believe you had the nerve to come here." Lauren moves toward the table, her face a rictus of anger, horror, and outrage that she somehow manages to mask with an icy disdain that I have no idea how to crack through.

For the first time I understand the expression "if looks could kill."

Bree moves almost protectively beside her, but my eyes are locked on Lauren's face. If my hands weren't clamped so tightly to the back of a chair I'd already be on the floor. I want desperately to turn and run, but I can't do that now, not without at least trying to explain.

"What do you want?" Lauren's words are pitched low as if there's some chance everyone in the place hasn't fallen quiet in order to hear.

What I truly want—to turn back time and make different choices—is impossible.

Yet here I am. "I can't let you leave town without at least talking this through."

"You can't actually believe there's anything you could say that would excuse what you've done."

We are all frozen in place as if suddenly overcome by an avalanche. Lauren's holding herself so stiffly I'm afraid she might break. "Please, sweetheart. Just sit down and listen."

"No. I want you to leave. Now. Or I will."

"Lauren." Jake gets to his feet.

For a moment I'm afraid that he'll leave and take Lauren with him. That they'll all leave and this will be over before it begins. So much for my hope that Lauren would be unwilling to create a scene or storm out of a public place.

Her eyes go to Jake. "Did you know she was coming here?"

Jake sighs. My heart trip-hammers in my chest. *It's a setup. The ultimate payback to give me hope then snatch it away. I should never have come here. She's just not ready. There's nothing I can . . .* But he doesn't lie or evade. "Yes."

"How could you after what she's done?"

For a moment I think Lauren is going to storm off and I will have ruined everything not only for myself but for Jake, too.

"Because as sad and angry as I am, I loved her. And because she's your mother and raised you to be the incredible person you are." Jake speaks quietly and in a matter-of-fact tone that not even Lauren argues with.

In the silence that follows Bree motions to Clay but addresses Lauren. "We're going to go home and give you all a chance to talk, but I'll be up in case you need anything when you get back to the house. Thanks for dinner, Jake."

"I'll go take care of the bill and give you some privacy," Jake says as soon as Bree and Clay head for the door.

"No." Lauren shakes her head. "I'm not listening to her unless you are."

"Okay." He motions me to the chair directly across from them.

As I sit Spencer takes one of Lauren's hands in his. A waiter arrives with after-dinner liqueurs. I take a sip as I try to gather my thoughts. Lauren downs hers in one anxious gulp and I am reminded yet again how much I've hurt her.

I can barely swallow around the panic that rises in my throat. As hard as it is, I look her in the eye. "I have never loved another human being, including myself, as much as I love you.

"My one clear thought when you were born and after was that I had to keep you and protect you."

She's still glaring at me, but she hasn't left. So I keep talking. I am like Scheherazade only the words that rush out of my mouth are not meant to stave off a king but to hold on to my daughter.

"I was barely twenty-one and I had lived a pampered and sheltered life. I had no business being a mother, no understanding of what it really meant. I was so uncertain of what I wanted that I couldn't even marry the person I loved." Memories of that swirl of panic envelop me. So much damage done. "But from the moment they placed you in my arms all I could think about was keeping you safe. And that meant keeping you away from my father, who wanted me to give you up, and his influence over me." I swallow back tears before rushing on.

"I always intended to tell you and your father about each other. Only when you were barely one, my aunt Velda told me Jake was getting married." I remember how much that news hurt. How much I missed him and how desperately I clung to it as proof that I'd been right not to marry him. "It was a horrible blow. Because I'd already realized what a mistake I'd made in running. I, you see, I still loved him. To this day I don't really understand why I ran." I can't even look at Jake while I admit this. "But I figured there was plenty of time until you were old enough to even understand. And, of course, everyone here had already assumed I'd lost a husband. And I had never corrected them."

"You were only thinking about what people would think of you." Lauren's words are black and white. There is no hint of gray.

"No. Jake had already married someone else and my father was still looking for me and pretending even to our family that my pregnancy had never happened.

"By the time I was ready to tell your father, he was not only married but had started a family. I was keeping a roof over our

heads and we were all right. It seemed better to let things be."
Painful as they are the words continue to spill out. "And then
you turned five. I'd promised myself I'd tell you when you were
old enough to understand. It was also the year you started asking about your father who 'went to heaven.' You'd just started
Sunday school and that was how your teacher referred to him—
when Velda started telling me about Jake's wife and their . . .
situation."

I look to Jake to make sure he understands that I'm going to
tell Lauren all of it. His expression is pained but he nods.

"You already told me she was unstable." Lauren says this as
if it's nothing. "I don't see . . ."

"That's because you never had to see." I take a deep breath,
trying to steady myself. "But I knew firsthand what it meant.
My mother was in and out of institutions. Never really there
even when she was physically present." I can feel my heart racing. I'm strangely light-headed. "And I heard that Jake's wife
was obsessed with being second choice. That even a mention of
me or my family could set her off."

Lauren looks to Jake for verification. He nods again. The toll
it took is in his eyes and on his face.

"I couldn't expose you to that, Lauren. And I believed it
would only make the situation worse for Jake and his children.
I couldn't be the one to push her over the edge or set her off.
Because I knew exactly what that could do to a child. To a family. I couldn't."

Lauren has gone still but I can see that she doesn't want to
believe any of it. Spencer is also silent, taking in every word and
nuance.

"I would give anything to go back and see a way to do things
differently." I'm exhausted and heartsick from the admission I've
been forced to make. The pain I'm causing is too sharp to be
borne; a knife to my heart. "But I did what I thought was right.
And this is where we are."

"You taught me to always tell the truth," she whispers. "You said it was the most important thing after love."

"It is." My voice breaks on the last word. "Only I thought this truth would destroy too many lives."

"You chose protecting them, their family, over giving me my father."

I don't know what to say to this. Jake sits motionless in his seat. Lauren watches my face, but I don't know what she's looking for.

"I can understand you protecting me as a child. And your concern about Jake and his family," she says finally. "But I am forty years old. And as far as I can see you intended to carry this secret to the grave." Her eyes fill with tears that she does not shed. "I don't know how I'm supposed to forgive that. Or how I could ever trust you again." The sheen of tears is replaced by a frightening resolve.

My mouth goes dry with fear.

"Is there anything else you want to say?"

"Only that I love you and that I am truly sorry for not making sure you knew your father and your grandparents." I swallow. "And that I . . . I hope that you'll find it in your heart to forgive me."

There's a long terrible silence. Without another word she pushes back her chair. We all stand. Spencer puts his arm around her shoulders and as dazed and bereft as I feel, I'm grateful that she has someone who loves her to lean on. She turns without saying good-bye and they make their way to the door.

Jake hangs back for a moment. "I realize she'll need time to come to terms with what's happened, but surely she won't . . ."

"Cut me out of her life like I cut you out?" I know as I say this that it's entirely possible. I know our daughter in ways Jake never will, *thanks to me*, and I've watched how she's handled what she sees as defection or betrayal. She and Bree were as close as sisters and even now she hasn't really forgiven her or moved on.

What I've done, or failed to do, is far worse. "It would be poetic justice, wouldn't it? And no more than I deserve." I huff out a breath. It's that or cry and I will not do that here. "For what it's worth, I *am* sorry, Jake. And I'm glad you'll have each other." My voice cracks again. Unable to meet his eyes or watch him leave I walk as slowly as I can manage to the ladies' room, barely feeling the eyes that follow me. I sit in the stall dazed and dry-eyed until I'm certain the coast must be clear.

Then I walk to my car and drive home. Life as I've known it is over and I have no interest at all in a new one.

Lauren

Despite the two Tylenol PM I downed before I crawled into bed last night, I didn't sleep or avoid a hangover. I feel like roadkill. A glance in the bathroom mirror confirms that I look like it, too.

For the first time in decades I am not consumed with fear because I have to fly. In fact, I'm so emotionally drained that all I care about is going home even if I have to get on a plane to get there.

Apparently, finding out your mother is not at all the person you thought she was is all it takes to cure a fear of flying. I'd notify the airlines and my readers of this shocking discovery except the dull ache hiding beneath my righteous anger tells me that not many people—including me—would *choose* this remedy.

Spencer managed to look surprisingly alert this morning when he went out for a run despite my tossing and turning and my three A.M. suggestion that we go ahead and get on the road.

I heard him and Bree talking when he first went downstairs. Even though I couldn't make out what they were saying I have no doubt she now knows everything that was said after she and Clay left Blue Point.

By the time I go downstairs in search of coffee Clay and Lily are gone. Bree is dressed and ready to leave for the store. She pours me a cup then creams and sugars it the way I like. As she hands it to me, her face is scrunched up in the way that always signaled she was screwing up her nerve. "You are going to forgive her at some point, aren't you?" She looks at me hopefully.

The coffee I'm sipping turns bitter. Much as I need the caffeine, I barely manage to swallow it. "Have you forgiven your parents?" I'm way too hungover and sleep deprived to wait for an answer. "At least they didn't pretend to be abandoning you for your own good."

"But you can't mean to cut her out of your life. Not when you've been so close. Not when . . ."

"Maybe we were so close because we were all each other had. Do you really think she had the right to keep my father and me apart? To let me believe he was dead?"

"But she was protecting you. And Jake and his family. She devoted her whole life to you."

I snort. "She lied to me my entire life. She's created more fiction than I ever have."

"Oh, Lauren. I know it's all a huge shock. Anyone would be upset. But she tried to make the best choices she could in a really difficult situation. That's what good parents do. That's all anyone can do."

The coffee churns in my stomach along with my anger. I'm so mad I can barely look at her. "So I just don't understand because I'm not a parent? That's bullshit. A total cop-out. That's what weak people say when they make the wrong choices."

Bree doesn't back off. "You're always in the right, aren't you? Everyone else is at fault. We're supposed to stand in line and beg your forgiveness." She shakes her head. She's angry, but I hear the sadness, too. "I have some experience with your inability to grant it."

"Is that right?"

Brianna's face is still scrunched up and forlorn. Once again she's the victim. The one other people abandon and treat badly. "I didn't go to New York with you. I chose another path. It's not like I ruined your life."

I blink. The anger that's been simmering so close to the surface since Jake first appeared and the truth came out boils over. Bree is not the only one who's ever been a victim. "You went back on a lifelong promise. A shared dream. And . . ." I stop.

"And what? You always act like it was some great, awful hardship," she says. "It's not like you didn't come out the winner here. What could have possibly been so terrible?"

"I was alone in the most terrifying city on the planet. And because my roommate backed out at the last minute, I couldn't afford the place I spent six months finding for us. I couldn't afford to live in any safe, decent place."

"I know. You had to beg strangers to let you camp on their couch." She tosses out the words as if they're nothing. "But isn't that part of what twenty-one-year-olds do when they go there? Live on someone's couch. Eat ramen noodles. Isn't that the whole I-conquered-New-York, rite-of-passage thing?"

Normally I stop there. I don't even like to think about what happened when I arrived in New York. But that tone of hers, its insistence that I'm overreacting, isn't going to cut it. Not today. For the first time in twenty years I tell the complete truth about what happened.

"Yeah, well, unfortunately I didn't even know any strangers that I could beg to let me rent a couch from when I got there, did I? I didn't know *anyone*, Bree. And it didn't help that I got mugged less than twenty minutes after I got off the bus."

Her face falls. And I know I should stop now. Stop and walk away with my pride intact and my "story" in place. But apparently at this moment I need someone else to feel as bad as I do.

"In fact, if I hadn't tucked away three hundred-dollar bills inside a sock, a shoe, and my underwear like I'd read in an article, I wouldn't have had *any* money. I made it last for three whole weeks at this filthy, horrible hotel in Hell's Kitchen— when it really was hell and not the trendy neighborhood it is today. And FYI—*fleabag* isn't a euphemism. It was so filthy I never got between the sheets and I only slept with my clothes on. Well, I didn't really sleep. I would just lay there until it was morning."

She looks slightly green, which suits me just fine.

"Of course, if I had been tucked under the covers and actually asleep I might not have gotten away from the drunk who couldn't afford one of the prostitutes down the hall and broke into my room and tried to rape me."

"Oh, Lauren." Her hand goes to her throat. "Oh God. That's so awful. Why didn't you call? Or at least come home for a while and regroup?"

"And give up before I ever started?" My eyes narrow, mostly, I think, so that I won't cry. I'll be sobbing all over her if I'm not careful. "The fact that you even ask that question shows how different we really are." I can't seem to stop there, either. "I cried for days. And every night I sat awake with a baseball bat in my hand and a whistle on a string around my neck, even though I wasn't sure anyone would come if I blew it."

I shudder out a breath. There's a reason I never talk about this. "Finally, after I started waiting tables, I met another waitress who was looking to rent out the sofa in her sixth-floor walk-up, and I grabbed it. It took me almost a full year to earn enough to get a room at the Webster. It was only after I moved in there that I put the bat under the bed, the whistle on the nightstand, and actually slept for a whole night."

Her mouth trembles as if she's the one who might cry. Horror and pity are etched on her face.

I shrug and pour myself a second cup of coffee as if I haven't just intentionally scalded her with all the ugly truths that I've never shared with anyone, including Spencer.

"I survived. It's all just backstory now." I say this with pride. To not only survive whatever New York City throws at you, but to succeed, is a point of honor. Still, dredging up these memories is painful. I feel small and mean for throwing them at Brianna, but I refuse to show it. "Thanks again for putting us up."

"Oh, Lauren. I'm so sorry. Please . . ."

Her sympathy comes close to undoing me. Still holding back tears, I turn and carry my coffee upstairs to shower and dress. By the time Spencer gets back from his run and does the same, Bree is gone.

Our bags are in the rental car and we're ready to leave when Clay's truck pulls into the drive. I wonder uncharitably if he thinks we're gone and he's got somebody with him, but it's not even ten. That's too early for a nooner, right?

He climbs out and retrieves a large white Kinko's box from the seat.

I feel a flush of remorse for how badly I treated Bree this morning. It's all I can do not to read him the riot act about his cheating. How's that for displacement? "Thanks for having us."

"Yeah, thanks." Spencer steps forward and claps him on the back. "We really appreciate you taking us in."

"No problem." He doesn't bring up the wedding or ask when we'll be coming back, for which I'm grateful. I pull the car keys out of my pocket.

"Do you have room for this?" He holds up the box.

"You want me to take your printing to New York?"

He smiles sheepishly. "No, I want you to take Bree's manuscript with you so you can read it."

"Why?" I ask even as I think of all the crap I threw at her this morning. How unfair it was of me to take everything out on her.

"Because you were once her best friend and you're a *New York Times* bestselling author, so your opinion and your contacts could be important."

I start to shake my head but he just keeps talking. "Look, Lauren. I'm not always the best husband in the world. But she's been working on this for fifteen years. I'd think you could take a couple of hours to read it and give her some feedback. For old times' sake."

I sigh. "I can pretty much promise you she doesn't really want to hear the truth. No aspiring writer does."

"Of course, she does," Clay says. "And maybe you shouldn't be so quick to assume it won't be good."

He smiles and I have a flash of the boy he used to be. The people we all were. "You know no one prints out a manuscript anymore."

"I'll UPS it to you if you like. Or fly up and hand-deliver it if you promise to read it," he says. "I *am* a shit sometimes. But Bree's not. And she'll never come out and ask you."

I think of all that Bree and I were to each other. Now that my relationship with my mother is broken, Bree may be my last link with home.

Before I can find my voice, Spencer takes the box out of Clay's hands. "I know Lauren's suitcase is full, but I've got room."

And so we drive away. Me, my fiancé, and my ex–best friend's manuscript.

Twenty-seven

~

Lauren

New York City

Just being back in New York is a relief of sorts. Spencer is busy trying to catch up after the time away and although I'm careful to appear disappointed, I'm relieved by that, too. With so many raw nerve ends vibrating and conflicting emotions still coursing through me, I can barely think, let alone write. For a few days I just lie in bed and lick my wounds. When I can't lie in bed any longer, I put on baggy clothes and dark sunglasses and walk in the park.

When I get home I listen to messages. There's one from my mother that I delete mid-apology. The next is a reminder about a dental cleaning. The last is from Danielle, my publicist at Trove. I haven't responded to her since I got back, so I force myself to listen. Her message comes out in a rush: "Oh my God! Those social media posts were pure genius. Funny yet dramatic! They show an entirely different side of you." There's a brief pause for breath. "And I absolutely love the shot from Title Waves. The store is adorable. And the book club looks so . . . *real*.

"I can't wait to hear how they reacted to the news about the fifteenth-anniversary edition of *Sandcastle Sunrise*. We've been talking about doing a live kickoff event from there—maybe a day or two before your wedding—you are getting married down there, aren't you? We still need to confirm that date so we can tie it to release." There's a pause—and I'm about to hit delete when she continues, "I saved the best for last. I got a call from a producer at *Say Yes to the Dress*. She's a huge fan of your books. They want you on the show. They've even offered to give you the gown you say yes to—though you'll have to keep that to yourself."

She pauses again, presumably to let my good fortune sink in. "They can weave you into an episode right before the wedding. Of course, you'll have to have some friends or family participate. Maybe we can fly your mother up and . . ."

Unable to listen to another word, I hit delete mid-sentence. I'm no longer lying in bed, but the nightmare continues.

❧

That night Spencer arrives with dinner from our favorite Thai restaurant and I actually greet him wearing clothes and makeup. While we open the takeout containers and settle at the kitchen counter, I tell him about the offer from *Say Yes to the Dress*. Only he's not at all horrified.

"Danielle's right. It would be great exposure for the anniversary edition. And you are going to need a wedding gown." He raises an eyebrow in question. "Unless you're planning to call your mother and ask her to ship up THE DRESS?"

I freeze, my chopsticks halfway to my mouth.

"I mean, doing the show would kill two birds with one stone. And if you're not planning to talk to Kendra or include her in the wedding, then I guess we should go ahead and make plans to have it here in New York. Right?"

I maneuver the panang chicken into my mouth. Somehow I manage to chew though I'm not entirely confident in my ability to swallow. I'm not fooled by his innocent expression or casual tone, but I don't call him on either.

"It's mid-April now," he continues reasonably. "If we choose a date next June close to the book's release, we're basically fourteen months out. According to my sister people book the most sought-after venues years ahead. So we're probably already behind the eight ball. We'd need to start looking right away."

I'm still chewing when he retrieves his laptop from his messenger bag and brings it back to the counter. He opens a file. A calendar page for June of next year appears on the screen.

"All we have to do is pick one of these Saturdays or Sundays." He smiles and pulls up another file. "Here's a list of wedding venues Molly and Mac looked at and the ratings they gave each one." Another smile. "And here's a list of wedding planners Molly interviewed and liked before her wedding. This is a list of florists from my mother."

I stare at the screen, then at him. Now would be the moment to protest. To say I just need a little more time before I can talk to and forgive my mother, at which point we'll plan an Outer Banks wedding. Instead, I ask, "Do you want me to make the appointments or shall we split up the list?"

It takes him a minute to accept that his ploy hasn't worked. "Oh. I guess we should split them up."

"Okay. Good."

"About the wedding dress . . ."

"Yes?" I take another bite of my panang chicken and chew slowly.

"While Brett was choreographing *The Music in Me*, he dated a dancer who's also a part-time bridal consultant at Kleinfeld's."

I'm chewing and bracing. The vision of me in THE DRESS at the Sandcastle before Jake arrived flashes through my mind.

"If you wanted to go in on the quiet to look at gowns and see how you feel about the idea of doing the show, I could get her number."

Our eyes meet.

"I'm sure Molly and my mother and grandmother would be glad to go with you."

There's a long beat of silence in which he does not say that I could avoid all this if I'd just call my mother, and I don't make up reasons why I couldn't possibly do any of the things he's suggested.

I put my chopsticks down. Miraculously, I manage to swallow without choking. I even smile. "Sure. Let's sync up our calendars and start setting appointments. It only makes sense to look around and see what our options are."

Bree

It's a week since Lauren went back to New York, but the fallout continues. We all pretend to go about our lives as usual, but Lauren's isn't the only reality that's been altered.

I'm at the store every day until three. I shop for groceries, cook meals, stop by to see Kendra, do my best to prod/supervise/"be there" for Lily. I'm even careful not to ask or look too carefully at where Clay is on a daily basis, but everything feels off. Everything *is* off. My husband is the only one of us whose life still appears to turn on its normal axis.

It's not just Lauren's past that has been rewritten without warning. Kendra is no longer the person I thought she was and Lauren's early "adventures" in New York aren't what I thought they were.

Not only have the blinders been ripped off, I no longer have my novel to disappear into. Nor do I really know what I'm supposed to do with *Heart of Gold* now that it's completed. I mean, you can't work on something for fifteen years—let everyone know that you're doing it—then shove it back under your bed when it's done. Even if that's where it probably belongs.

Mrs. McKinnon brings that point home each afternoon that she comes in.

"So, have you sent off *Heart of Gold*?" she asks again today with an eager smile.

"No, not yet," I say, offering my standard response. "I'm still planning to do a final pass to clean everything up. But I'm going to take a couple weeks to get some distance first." I offer a reassuring smile. "All the how-to-get-published books suggest this."

"You really should ask Lauren to read it for you. She could tell you if it needed anything."

She's said this too many times to count. Each time I just smile and change the subject. Lauren and I did not end on the best of notes. And even if we had, I'm no more ready for criticism from her than I ever was.

Lily has cheerleading practice this afternoon, so I swing by Kendra's. I find her in the kitchen pulling trays of muffins out of the oven. The kitchen smells warm and sugary. Although she has dark circles under her eyes and a worry-crease in her forehead, I'm relieved to see her dressed and working.

I am not so relieved at how differently I view her. I've been forced to take her off the pedestal on which I placed her and accept that she's human. I've also been forced to confront the fact that my not going to New York had serious consequences for Lauren. Consequences that I've been too caught up in my own needs and wants to ever imagine or, if I'm honest, even ask about. It was so much easier to just hold on to my jealousy and dismiss her grudge as unreasonable.

"Lemonade?"

"Sure. Thanks."

Kendra pours us both a glass and sets out a plate of cookies. As if I'm still that lonely girl Lauren brought home after school. "Have you had any word?"

"From Lauren?"

She nods then droops when I say, 'No."

"I'm sure she'll get over it," I add, though I'm not at all sure.

"Do you really think so?"

"Yes." I hesitate. "But I can understand her reaction. It was such a big shock and, well, from her point of view you did choose Jake and his family's needs over hers."

I keep Lauren's description of what happened when she first got to New York to myself, because I'm ashamed of my part in it and because it will only make Kendra feel worse. It's not my story to tell.

"And is that how you see it, too?" Her eyes are pinned to my face for the eternity it takes to weigh my answer.

"Well," I say when it becomes clear she's not going to let me off the hook. "I believe you did what you thought was right at the time." I swallow, searching for the words that will allow me to tell the truth without inflicting more hurt than necessary. But there is no pain-free option here. "But I also think Lauren and Jake deserved to know about each other, especially once Lauren and his other children were adults."

Her nod is slow. Neither of us touches our lemonade or reaches for a cookie. "I know I need to do something, only I can't think what. I'd go to New York right now. Except I'm afraid that if I show up at her door she won't let me in."

It's my turn to nod. This is entirely possible.

Her eyes shimmer with tears. As they begin to fall I realize that while she's dried my tears lots of times, I've never seen her cry. She's always been upbeat and positive. I learned to put one foot in front of the other no matter what I feel like on the inside from watching her and my grandmother.

"I'm even more afraid that she'll never forgive me."

"Oh no. I'm sure she'll . . ." I stop. Because this is not the time to offer idle promises. "I don't think that will happen. But I do think she probably needs more time to process and absorb everything."

I can hardly meet her eyes. I desperately want to help, but I also want to run as far away as possible from all this hurt and pain. I am not the brave one, I never have been.

I leave Kendra's in an emotional fog that sticks with me

through the grocery store and I come home laden with all kinds of things I rarely buy. This includes assorted containers of Häagen-Dazs Trio Crispy Layers; a decadent new addition to the ice cream world that I've mostly managed to resist. Until now.

When I lug the bags into the kitchen Lily is standing motionless in front of the open refrigerator. She looks up as I enter. Her expression is tragic. Kendra isn't the only person that I love who's been crying.

"What's happened?" The fact that whatever it is has sent her to the refrigerator makes me more anxious. How many years have I been coaxing her to eat more than bird-size amounts? I rush to put the groceries down even though I feel ill equipped to handle a meltdown right now. Or any other emotional challenge. Not when I seem to be having one of my own.

"It's Shane. Shane Adams. He . . . flirted with me and told me that he really liked me. I thought he was going to ask me out, but now he barely even notices me." Her chin juts and quivers. "I saw him hanging out with Kelsey Gardner yesterday. I feel like I'll *die* if he asks her out instead of me."

I study her more closely. "You're not going to *die* over Shane or any other boy."

"I feel like I might."

I sigh. "I wouldn't spend thirty seconds mooning over anyone who doesn't appreciate you."

"I am *not* mooning. What does that even mean anyway?"

"It means to behave or move in a listless and aimless manner," I say because there are a whole lot of normally useless definitions floating around in my head. "You don't want to waste your time, affection, and emotional energy on someone who doesn't deserve it."

I pull a Häagen-Dazs Trio out of one of the grocery bags (yes, I knew which bag they were in) and retrieve a spoon from the silverware drawer. "Here. Try this." I put both on the counter then put my hands on her shoulders, even though I have to reach up to do so, then direct her to a stool. I put the second container in the freezer and take the third for myself.

"Ice cream is not the answer." She says this with such prim certainty I have to fight back a smile.

I grab a spoon for myself and settle on the stool beside her. "That depends on the question. Lauren and I figured out a lot of things at the Dairy Queen."

Even as she rolls her eyes I am hit with a slew of memories of Lauren and me hashing out our hopes and dreams, our story plots, even our plans for New York City, over Blizzards, and sundaes, and banana splits. Treats that made me ever rounder and curvier and that never added an ounce to her frame.

"Oh, Mom. I don't want to lose him without ever really having him. Do you have any idea how that feels?"

In this moment I wish I didn't. But I do. I peel the top off both our ice creams and place her spoon in her hand. "You feel like you can't bear it if he looks at someone else the way you want him to look at you. That if he doesn't fall in love with you life won't be worth living. That you'd rather not have anyone if you can't have him."

Her head comes up and she looks at me in a way that she hasn't since she got out of elementary school. "How do you know that?"

"Because that's how I felt about your father not long after we started dating." This is, alas, true. I pick up my spoon and dip it into the ice cream then pull up a spoonful of soft yet crispy salted caramel and chocolate.

"But that was forever ago," she says.

I open my mouth and slip the first spoonful of ice cream inside. The flavor explodes in my mouth and I can't contain a sigh of pleasure.

Lily frowns but tentatively dips her spoon into her own container. I watch as she spoons the ice cream into her mouth.

I'm too raw today to push aside the truth like I usually do. I married a man who didn't love me anywhere near as much as I loved him then convinced myself that I loved enough for the both of us. "Sometimes when we actually get the thing we wanted most we're afraid to look at it too closely. We hang on even when we should let go."

"Is that why you let Dad go out with other women?" There's nothing tentative about the question. Her tone and the look that accompanies it are starkly frank and shockingly adult. "Because you're afraid of losing him?"

I can't seem to catch my breath or gather my wits. All this time I've believed she didn't know. I convinced myself that the occasional personal and public humiliation was the price I paid to protect my children and keep our family together.

"I keep waiting for you to stand up to him and make him stop. To be the mother I always thought you were. But you just keep taking it." Her voice drops. It and her eyes are filled with disappointment. In *me*.

She puts the spoon back into the container and pushes it away as she stands. "There's no amount of ice cream that's ever going to make that anything less than pathetic."

Twenty-eight

⟨∾⟩

Kendra

In all the years that Lauren has been in New York she's only been a phone call, e-mail, or plane ride away. Now she might as well be in Siberia. More truthfully I am in Siberia—found guilty and cut off from the person I love most in the world. A fitting punishment that my unanswered phone calls and unreturned messages confirm I have no way to appeal.

It's early Saturday morning when I arrive at the Dogwood to deliver muffins. Bree and Deanna have made sure I know that Jake, though traveling, is still in residence. I haven't heard from him since the Blue Point debacle, so I'm not sure whether I want to see him to get news of Lauren or hope to avoid him because that news is likely to be bad. This uncertainty has me tiptoeing across the deck and into the kitchen, where I am nonetheless woefully unprepared for his presence in front of the coffeepot.

Our eyes meet. Despite the early hour he's completely awake and has apparently already been out for a run if the running shorts he's wearing and the T-shirt currently plastered to his chest and abs are any indication.

"Morning." He raises his coffee cup in greeting and I'm pretty sure I smile back.

I watch his face, looking for signs of residual anger or hostility or even smugness at having a relationship with Lauren when

I don't. But he sets his mug on the counter and reaches for the coffeepot.

"No offense, but you look like you could use some."

"In my experience almost any sentence that begins with 'no offense' is offensive to one degree or another," I say even though he's only speaking the truth. If my hands weren't full I'd be running one of them over my hair or checking my face in the nearest mirror.

I walk past him to set the basket of muffins near where Dee has put out bowls, homemade granola, and pitchers of milk and juice. "But I think I'm already overcaffeinated."

"I imagine sleeping is a challenge right now."

I nod noncommittally and try to focus on what I'm doing, which is rearranging the already perfectly aligned breakfast things. I cut a look toward Dee's office door.

"She ran over to her place to get something," Jake says helpfully. "I'm sure she'll be back soon."

I don't turn around, but I'm ridiculously aware of him. "Are you still considering buying the Dogwood?" I throw the question half over my shoulder, too nervous to ask what I really want to know, which is whether he's been in touch with Lauren. "It's hard to imagine this place without her," I babble even as my mind pulls up images of Jake here full-time managing the B and B despite the fact that Warner Holdings belongs to him and the chances of him running an individual property are probably zero.

"I'd actually love to add it to our portfolio," he says. "But Dee's still on the fence and . . ."

I can hear his voice, but my thoughts are now focused on him managing the Dogwood. Which would put him just a bridge away. A stunning thought after decades spent trying *not* to think of him at all. So stunning that I can't let go of it and come back to reality only as he finishes with, "That's why I'm exploring other possibilities."

He falls silent, but I can't seem to find my voice or bring myself to turn and face him. I startle when he places his hands on my shoulders and turns me gently around. For a long moment we stare into each other's eyes. Everything is there. The enormity of our past, Lauren's existence, her rejection of me, his wife and the fact that she's gone. Every bit of it is there between us, yet wrapped around us, too.

He drops his hands and takes a step back, but our gazes remain tangled. I try to pull my focus back where it belongs. On finding out whether he's in touch with Lauren and whether he'd be willing to speak to her for me. Something I'm pretty sure I have no right to ask.

I'm still trying to find the courage to begin when he says, "Have you heard from Lauren?"

He once knew me so well that for an instant I think he's read my mind. Then I remind myself that he's a parent—one who, according to my aunt Velda, raised two children pretty much on his own—and has to know how much I need to speak to my child. *Our child.*

"No. She won't pick up or return my calls." I fall back a step, because it's hard to think when he's standing so close. "Have you?"

"Yes." He shifts uncomfortably, but he doesn't look away. "She asked me to come up to visit."

"Oh." If he were lording it over me, I could be angry. But his expression is almost apologetic. I feel a dull ache in the pit of my stomach.

"I want to know Lauren. I want my sons to know her." He swallows. "I was incredibly angry when I first got here, but even then my goal wasn't to ruin your relationship. At least I don't think it was. I just . . . I really needed to see her. And I wanted her to understand that I hadn't ignored her."

"I think that came across loud and clear." There is anger and chagrin and regret in that sentence. I feel all of those things and more. Whether he meant to or not, he's won our daughter and I've lost her. But if I'm going to rebuild my relationship with Lauren I'm going to have to be able to deal rationally with the father she's just discovered.

This is the man I loved and longed for even after I knew he was engaged to someone else. The man I unthinkingly compare every other man I meet to.

"I understand there were problems, and I hope you don't mind my asking, but what was your wife like?" I don't ask the other things I want to know. What attracted you to her? Did you love her more than you loved me?

He studies my face for a long moment then says, "Angela was beautiful in a fragile, fairy-tale princess kind of way." He sighs. "She seemed so lost at times that I guess I felt she really needed me."

"Sir Galahad to the rescue. You always did have a protective streak a mile wide." I don't even come close to the teasing tone I'm looking for.

"Only, as I recall, you never wanted to be protected."

It's my turn to sigh. I spent my life striving to prove I could take care of myself. That I was strong. "You knew my father," I say. "He always acted as if my mother's 'issues' were just a matter of weakness. That she could have 'cheered herself up' or 'pulled herself together' if she'd only tried. It's ridiculous, of course. But he was a man of absolutes. Black or white. Good or evil. Weak or strong. He had no middle ground. I always needed to appear capable in his eyes."

Jake shakes his head in memory. And I recall how much easier it was to breathe around Jake's parents than around my own, where I was always tiptoeing carefully so as not to set anyone off.

Jake's features are stronger, more handsome in person than in my memory. So is his impact on me. I don't know if I intentionally turned him into less than he was to ease the loss or if my memory just faded over time. "When Lauren was little and

I was struggling to take care of her alone and earn enough to keep a roof over our heads, I would probably have jumped right on the back of that white charger of yours without a minute's hesitation."

"Yeah. I know a bit about single parenting," he says. "Definitely not for sissies."

We share a smile. We were babies ourselves on our wedding day; so young and inexperienced. I up and ran without conscious thought—all reaction and emotion. Jake stayed with a woman who was in and out of institutions. He raised his sons and kept his family going despite the emotional upheaval. And somehow he managed not to become hard like my father. Or maybe my father was just born that way.

"Did you love her?" The question is out before I realize I'm going to ask it.

Once again he pauses to think before he speaks. His answer is not the automatic *yes* or *no* I'm expecting. "I thought so. And when I became unsure, I told myself I did. But Angela was never convinced. Until the day she died, she believed that I was still in love with you."

My heart pounds, but the rest of me goes very still.

His eyes turn bleak. "I stayed. I loved and took care of my children. I did all I could for her. But . . ." His voice trails off and he hesitates once again. "As much as I hate not having known about Lauren and that my parents died never knowing they had a granddaughter, you were right. If you and Lauren had become a part of the equation it could have set things off on a scale I'm not sure any of us would have survived."

I feel a weight lift at his words. I may have blundered in my handling of things, but my instincts were right. There's movement upstairs, but no one comes into the kitchen. We stand in a bubble of our own as the past washes over me and I wonder but cannot bring myself to ask whether Angela was right about Jake's love for me.

"Why did you run?" At first I think I have imagined the question. But when I make myself look, I see the wound I dealt him deep in his eyes.

I drop my gaze to the window. April sunlight dapples the outdoor fireplace. Cocoa the cat sleeps in a rocker. The rich, sweet scent of jasmine slips through the open window. Life goes on even as you examine the life that fell apart. "My parents' marriage wasn't exactly a shining example of wedded bliss, but I honestly don't know what made me panic like that." I force myself to meet his eyes again. "When I finally calmed down enough to think about it, it made no sense. I mean, your parents seemed perfectly happy and you were certainly nothing like my father and I couldn't have been more than a few weeks pregnant so I'm not sure I can blame it on hormones. In all these years since, I've never come up with a good answer or reason. You were the first and . . ." I stop just short of adding *last* ". . . the first man I ever truly loved."

We contemplate each other. Time spools out between us, past and present.

"Did you ever think about how it might have been if we'd gotten married?" he asks softly.

I shut my eyes briefly but there's nowhere to hide. I owe him as much truth as I can muster. "There were times when it was all I thought about. When Lauren was colicky and on a crying jag or when I was exhausted and let myself think about how alone we really were. Or when she smiled for the first time. Took her first steps, said her first words. That's when I would think how much nicer life would be if we were sharing it with you."

A door slams upstairs and I attempt to bring myself back to the present. To reality. "Of course, our marriage might not have been everything I imagined. We might have ended up divorced. Or we might have stayed together, but fought all the time and been cruel to each other. Or the love and attraction might have faded over the years until we took each other for granted." I name all the things I used to tell myself when I missed him the most.

"Or maybe we would have gotten lucky and been gloriously happy."

His tone is so wistful it hurts. His eyes are the warm golden brown of aged whiskey or fresh honey. He lowers his head and leans closer. My body sways toward his. It knows before I do that he intends to kiss me.

"Kendra?" Dee's voice reaches us through an open window. Hurried footsteps sound on the deck.

Jake and I jump apart like teenagers about to get caught doing something they shouldn't.

"Would you like to go out for dinner one night?" Jake asks.

"Oh." It's possible my mouth drops open in surprise even as my heart leaps a little.

"It doesn't have to be a date," he adds as the doorknob turns.

"It doesn't?" I try to keep the disappointment out of my voice.

"No. Of course not." He looks down and meets my gaze clearly. "Not unless you want it to be."

Twenty-nine

∽

Bree

Title Waves

Today, as we straighten the store post–book club meeting, I'm finally able to answer Mrs. McKinnon's and Leslie Parent's almost daily questions about how my manuscript has been received in New York with the news that *Heart of Gold* is finally ready to be submitted to five meticulously researched literary agents.

"Oh, my dear. That's wonderful!" Mrs. McKinnon clasps her hands to her chest.

"Yes, it is." Leslie high-fives me. "You go, girl!"

The B's raise their last glasses of wine in a toast and down them like shots in my honor.

Wonderful is not the word I would have chosen. I would have gone with *wretched, frightened, and nauseous*, because the very real possibility of rejection is no longer comfortably off in the future.

It took a week and a half to do a complete read-through and tweak of the manuscript, which I'm fairly certain doesn't completely suck.

I've also prepared a proposal, which consists of a synopsis (shoot me now!), the first three chapters of the manuscript (polished within an inch of their lives), and a cover letter in which I've carefully omitted the fact that it's taken me fifteen years to complete this novel (lest they think, as Lauren does, that makes me a pathetic underachiever who is not serious about having a writing career).

Though I'm not at all sure that "doesn't completely suck" is good enough to land an agent or a publishing contract, I've promised myself I will hit send no later than tomorrow morning.

"Thank you all for your enthusiasm and support," I say, as if I'm giving an acceptance speech of some kind. "I'm not sure I would have ever finished if it weren't for all of you believing I would." I tear up at this because it's true. I started on a journey and got lost somewhere along the way. The fact that I reached the end is nothing short of miraculous. I owe it not only to myself, but to everyone who's cheered me on, to see this through, whatever the outcome.

All of the B's stay to help tidy up the store. Mrs. McKinnon supervises. Title Waves is theirs as much as it's mine. While no bookstore owner is in it solely for the money, I'm happy to make a more than decent living in a profession I feel passionate about. As we put things in their place, straighten chairs, wipe off tables, put the empty wine bottles in the recycle bin, I wonder what I would do without the store and the customers who come through it.

When I get home the house is quiet. Lily, whose observations about her father and my role in enabling him have pierced me to the core and shaken the world as I know it, is cheering at an away basketball game and spending the night with her co-captain afterward.

Since it's just Clay and me for dinner, I throw together a salad and warm up a loaf of frozen sourdough bread. After we fill our plates he begins to eat. His head is down as he scrolls through messages on his cell phone, and I take a mean kind of pleasure in the small balding spot this reveals.

"So, how was your day?" I ask when I can't take the silence any longer.

"Hmmm?" He doesn't look up.

"What happened with Sands-A-Lot? Did the tenant decide to stay an extra week?" I prompt.

"Oh, umm, yeah. I gave them a bit of a preseason discount and they extended."

He finally seems to register the silence that follows and looks up. "How are things at the store?"

This is his default question whenever he's unsure of what I may or may not have been talking about. Not waiting for an answer he reaches for another piece of bread. A text dings in and his gaze strays back to his phone.

"Great," I say with my eyes on the bald spot again. "There was a small fire in the back storage area, but Mrs. McKinnon threw herself on top of the cartons of books and smothered it with her body."

"Hmmm," he says without looking up. "Interesting." A small smile plays on his lips and I wonder if it's Carla Andrews, whose smug sister we ran into in the bathroom at Blue Point, that he's texting.

Once again I think about the fact that Lily knows. That she believes that my lack of action means that I condone it. Or, more accurately, that I'm too big a coward to address it. If Lily knows so does Rafe. Yet I continue to spin out the story, to feint and jab at his inattention, rather than raise the real issue. "Thankfully, Mrs. McKinnon's burns weren't too severe and her heart attack was minor. I kept her alive until the paramedics got there by performing CPR and a song or two from the musical *Cats*."

"That's nice," he says as he fires off another text. His head jerks up when he registers what I said. "Sorry. I just had to organize a, um, something." He waits for me to give him some shit for not paying attention. Or for texting at the table, which I've begged him not to do and which is, let's face it, incredibly insulting. But what is that compared to his cheating?

As he lowers his head again it's impossible to ignore how little we have left to say to each other. When Lily's here our conversation is targeted at and through her. When we're alone we talk about things that need to be taken care of. Errands, Lily's schedule, house repairs, car maintenance, the detritus of everyday life.

"I've got a showing up in Duck and then I need to stop by the new house in Corolla to fix a leaky faucet. I may just stay out there and have a beer with Stan."

He deposits his plate in the sink then goes up to change. When he comes back downstairs freshly showered and shaved, the cologne I bought him for his birthday wafts off him. (Yes, that's the kind of thought that goes into our gifts to each other now. And no I don't believe he put it on for Stan.) "I'm not sure how late I'll be." He pecks me on the cheek. "Don't wait up."

After he leaves the house is even quieter. The normally reassuring tick of my grandmother's grandfather clock is low and steady, but tonight instead of filling the silence it counts it out and amplifies it.

I turn off the kitchen light and head upstairs, where I pause to peer into Lily's room. Some mothers would be irritated by the habitually unmade bed, the half-opened drawers, the clothes and shoes strewn across the floor. To me it's confirmation that she's secure enough not to constantly strive to please or pursue perfection. *Secure enough to call me on my cowardice.*

In two years when Lily goes off to college this room will be unbearably neat. And I will be left alone with my inattentive, often absent husband.

Normally I brush this and other troubling thoughts aside. Over the last twenty years, I've sidestepped even the most insistent aha! moments by convincing myself that it would be wrong to take my children's father away from them. That keeping my family intact is more important than being loved and respected the way I deserve. The way we all deserve.

All this time I've told myself I've been hiding their father's affairs from the children in an effort to save our marriage *for them*. That the most important thing was keeping our family intact *for them*. But they *know*. Which brings me to the question of whom I'm actually protecting. And what kind of an example I've set for my children. Why am I still bowing to the emperor when our children already know that he's not wearing clothes?

I slump against the wall, no longer able to hold back the tidal wave of truth that washes over me. I have accepted the love Clay feels for me as if it were some great gift, because when your parents don't love you, you know deep down it can only be because you're unlovable.

My breathing is harsh and labored. My heart constricts in shame. I've settled because I assumed I had to. I have expected far too little and accepted even less. Worst of all, I've become pathetic in my children's eyes. I've let fear and insecurity rule my life. Allowed them to color every decision. Made me think and *act* small. And I am tired to death of it.

Slowly, I straighten. My mind begins to clear. A window that I nailed shut springs open. Light streams in.

I am not a poor, unloved girl anymore. And I don't have to be an unappreciated and disrespected wife; that's not the way to be a good mother. And no way to teach my children about love and relationships. Nor do I need to wait for Lauren to repair our friendship. Or be afraid to enter the publishing arena I ceded to her just because she got there first.

My breathing becomes more even, the thud of my heart softens, its beating slows.

The time has come to live up to who I am and not down to who I was. I have friends. A business. Children who love me. A manuscript I've poured my heart into. What happens next is up to me.

Turning, I stride to the stairs, sprint up to my office, and sit down at my computer, where the cover letters to all five agents wait in draft mode. I double-check that each is addressed to the correct person at the correct e-mail address and that the synopsis and chapters are attached. Then with a resolve that shocks and thrills me I hit send on each e-mail. There is no turning back. That thrills me, too.

When the fear of rejection begins to bubble up I quash it. If these five agents don't want me, I'll try five more, then five more after that. And if *Heart of Gold* doesn't sell, I'll write something that will. Then I register for a fiction writing conference in New York I've dreamed of going to even though I have to pay a late-registration fee.

I leave my office with a new clarity of purpose. A certainty that is greater than I've ever known. I deserve whatever success and happiness I can find or create.

I'm downstairs in a heartbeat. I pour myself a glass of wine and get my thoughts in order. Aha moment, my foot. It's time for a come-to-Jesus meeting.

I carry my glass into the living room and settle on the couch to wait for my husband to come home.

Lauren

New York City

Any suspicion I had that Spencer's suggestion that we plan a New York wedding was only a ploy to get me to make up with my mother has been laid to rest. Because despite the ploy's failure, the wedding planning continues.

The notes he first showed me over Thai takeout are now neatly assembled in a shared computer file filled with vendor links. There are electronic folders filled with notes, the beginnings of a guest list he, his mother, and I are supposed to be putting together. Because how can you know what size venue, how much food, even how many flower arrangements if you don't have a sense of how many guests you might be expecting or what size the wedding party might be?

If we have our wedding here, it will be a large, elegant, formal affair—the antitheses of the small, intimate, beach wedding I always imagined. The Harrisons' guest list will overflow with family, longtime friends, and business associates. Mine will be embarrassingly small. And might not even include my mother.

Today we visited four venues, three caterers, and two florists and I have the aching feet and throbbing head to prove it.

The ride back to the Upper West Side in afternoon traffic is long and slow. I'm only dimly aware of arriving at Celeste, which is one of our favorite Upper West Side restaurants, and barely taste the spaghetti with clams that Spencer orders for me.

Back at my building I stifle a yawn as Tom the doorman greets us. Today would have been exhausting even if I were sleeping well at night, which I'm not. I feel as if I'm slogging through molasses.

"You were pretty quiet at dinner," Spencer says as we ride up in the elevator.

"Was I?" I try, but fail, to hold back another yawn.

In my apartment I drop my purse on the foyer table, toe off my shoes, and head for the living room. "Would you like a drink?"

"You sit. I'll pour." He moves to the drinks cart and I change course for the couch.

"I'm worried about you," he says as he sets our drinks on the coffee table, right next to Bree's manuscript, which I pass countless times each day and which I try not to notice.

"In what way?" Another yawn. I eye the drink but can't decide whether I want it. I do not look at the manuscript.

"Seriously?" He sits down beside me and slides his arm around my shoulders. I lean my head against his reassuring warmth. "It's been over two weeks since we got back and I can see that you're still upset. I wish you'd let me help."

"It's not a question of helping," I say on another yawn. "Your existence helps. I just need to get through this. In my own way."

He sips his drink and I don't have to see his face to know that he's not really buying this.

"I did invite my . . . Jake . . . to visit."

"That's great." He takes a long sip of his drink. "But what about your mother?"

I reach for my drink even though I don't really want it. I don't want to have this conversation, either. But I can tell by the set of the shoulder I'm leaning on that he's not going to let this go. "What about her?"

"She's begged for your forgiveness. She's left a million messages. She's done everything but show up on your doorstep. You love each other." He pauses while I toss down half the drink. "Don't love and forgiveness go hand in hand?"

I continue to drink as if this cocktail glass or the whiskey in it could prevent me from understanding where this conversation is going.

"I mean, we're getting married. One or both of us are bound to make mistakes along the way."

I close my eyes. I'm too tired for this. "Not telling me about my father was not a 'mistake.' It was a choice. A lie."

"My point is that I don't believe forgiveness is determined by the size of the offense, but by your commitment to and love for the other person. I hate to think that if I upset or disappoint you you'll jettison me from your life without even talking it through and trying to understand."

"That's not fair." I sit up, forgoing the comfort of his shoulder. But I don't have the strength to argue or defend my position. If, in fact, I have one.

"No." His voice goes quiet. "It isn't." He finishes his drink and sets down the glass. "I can see how tired you are, so I think I'll go back to my place tonight. Try to get some rest."

The door closes behind him and I stare at it and wonder, what if Spencer were the one who lied? Would I give him the benefit of the doubt? Could I find a way to forgive him?

I lock the door and turn out the lights. As I wash up and change into my pajamas I think about the years lost with my father. About the grandparents I never knew. Am I actually planning to cut my mother out of my life forever?

The bedroom curtain flutters in the breeze and I move to the window and press my forehead against the double pane of glass. Traffic still moves along Central Park West. People stroll down 74th. They aren't kidding when they say this is the city that never sleeps.

I walk to the bed and slip between the sheets then stare up into the shadowed ceiling.

What if my mother gives up before I'm ready to forgive her? What if she decides not to keep trying to salvage our relationship?

Could I really live my life without my mother in it? And what kind of life would that be?

Thirty

∽

Bree

I wake to the crunch of tires and Clay's truck pulling into the drive. I recognize this sound even in my sleep. I raise my head and my chin comes off my chest. I struggle up out of the sofa cushions, my eyes blinking open. I glance at the clock in an attempt to get my bearings. 1:35 A.M.

He moves with confidence—apparently assuming I'm asleep and feeling no need to tiptoe or make a stealthy entrance. I stand and step forward and watch him stumble slightly in surprise. After a brief flash of concern, he goes on the offense. Always his best defense. "What are you doing up?"

"Waiting."

He cocks his head. Blue eyes narrow in suspicion. "For what?"

"For you." My mouth is dry from sleep and nerves. "Where have you been?" comes out in a croak. Now that the time has come I'm afraid I'll say the wrong thing or the right thing in the wrong way. I give him a stern look even as I reach deep inside for Whitney. Not the character I first created but the one who turned into a woman I admire. The one who kept growing even when I didn't. The one who would never have put up with the things I have.

"You know that's . . .

"I hope you're not planning to say *none of my business*," Whitney and I respond.

His head snaps up. He isn't used to me questioning him.

"Look, Bree. There's no way I'm going to let you turn me into some henpecked-wuss-of-a-husband who never . . ."

"Good God. Is that the best you can do?" I give him a second or two to understand that tonight is not going to be business as usual.

"We've been married for twenty years and you still act like you're single. You are the opposite of henpecked. You've had things your way from the beginning. And I haven't seen you act too much like a husband. In fact, I'm not sure you've really tried. Last time I looked, monogamy was not an optional clause in the marriage contract."

He sputters in indignation. "We are not having this conversation. Not now when you're all worked up and unreasonable."

I cringe when I remember the number of times I've let him shut me down this way. As if being hurt or emotional somehow negates the truth or makes his behavior my fault.

I've always backed down. Because of Rafe and Lily. Because I'd sworn I would never shatter my children's security the way my parents shattered mine. But it takes two committed people who love each other to make a marriage, not one who's doing the other a favor by staying, as long as she's willing to look the other way now and then.

"I can't do this anymore, Clay."

"Can't do what?"

"Pretend. That you love me when I'm not sure you do. I'm not even sure whether I love you anymore."

My eyes are pinned to his face. I wait though I'm not sure what I'm waiting for. Is there a marriage cavalry poised to ride in and save our union? If he fell down on his knees and promised to never even look at another woman—which he is showing no signs of doing—is there any way that I could possibly believe him? Trust him? "This is it. The line in the sand. The final warning. You either get it together and honor your marriage vows or . . ."

"Or what?"

"Or I'll file for divorce."

This is the first time I've ever even mentioned the D-word—one of the few times I've let myself actually think it—and his shock is pronounced. "You don't mean that."

"I do."

He looks at me and I want to believe he's finally seeing me as more than the girl he deigned to marry. He says only, "But the kids would be devastated."

"I'm not so sure about that." I look him right in the eye. "They know, Clay. Everybody knows. Lily told me just how pathetic she thinks it is that I 'let' you be with other women."

"But I . . ." I watch the realization set in. He has convinced himself that what he's been doing is no big deal. That everybody does it. That I'd be the only casualty. That the children would never know.

I see him trying to regroup, to once again gain the upper hand that he's so used to having. It has never occurred to him that the children would ever think ill of him or that I would ever give up.

I could use a little *Rocky* music right now. Some boxing gloves. A sweatsuit. Because although I finally managed to say what I've known I needed to for too long now, I don't feel particularly victorious. Just horribly sad. And so very tired.

But I am also determined. "You must have realized that what you've been doing is . . . wrong. That it *hurts* me. That it hurts all of us."

I think back to the times I was forced to know. The pitying glances. The triumphant ones. I shudder to think that Rafe and Lily have had to deal with all that, too.

"I'm attending a fiction conference in New York next week. I fly up on Tuesday and get back the following Sunday. You'll need to be here with Lily. You can use that time for some one-on-one. To try to reassure her that it's us you love and care about.

If you can't commit to being faithful and putting your family first then as far as I'm concerned you can also use that time to find somewhere else to live. I'm sure you could use one of the rental properties. Or maybe one of your girlfriends would like to have you."

"Move out?" I almost wish I had a camera to take a picture of his face.

"Well, of course. If we were getting a divorce we wouldn't live together. This is my house. My grandmother left it to me long before we got married."

"But . . . you'd be all alone." My greatest fear has been his ace in the hole. He looks at me expectantly. Waiting for me to crumble. Or cry. Or apologize.

I do none of those things.

"That's true." For the first time I'm not frightened by the prospect.

Lauren and Kendra are struggling with their estrangement. Neither of them seems able to take that first step. I know how hard it can be to come to terms with a reality that's not what you thought it was or ever wanted it to be. But I am not a child. I've finally finished my manuscript. I've proven I'm so much stronger than I ever believed. I don't need a man, especially not this man, to complete me. "I'm pretty sure I'll get over it."

Kendra

The Sandcastle

It takes me over an hour to decide what to wear for my third not-really-a-date with Jake. I work through the possibilities in front of the bedroom mirror. THE DRESS hangs on the armoire behind me, a constant reminder of the daughter I've lost.

When I finally settle on a brand-new sleeveless turquoise drop-waist sundress with a scoop neck that ties at the shoulders, a mountain of rejected clothing covers the bed. It turns out finding a look that says "I didn't try too hard because I don't want it to look like I dressed for a date" is harder than it should be. So is washing and blow-drying your hair, shaving your legs, and applying makeup. Looking effortlessly attractive requires way too much effort. If my bed weren't so overrun at the moment I'd be tempted to nap in it.

Tonight instead of going out, Jake is coming over for dinner. It's going to be a simple meal. Just steaks on the grill, a spinach salad, and a freshly baked apple pie that I've cut a piece out of so that I can pretend I didn't intentionally bake it for him. I've got a bottle of prosecco chilling in the refrigerator. I'm setting out a bottle of red table wine that says "I tried but not too hard" when a knock sounds on the kitchen door. Before I can open it, Bree walks in.

"I finally did it," she says not at all joyously. There is no exclamation point attached.

"Did what?" There's something in her eyes that I don't recognize. Something brave and awful at the same time.

"I told Clay that if he doesn't get his act together I'm going to file for divorce."

"Oh." I've wanted to give Clay a few swift kicks on occasion myself, but they've been married for close to twenty years and I know how much family means to Bree.

I'm not sure whether to applaud or commiserate. "Oh, sweetheart. Are you okay?"

She nods but her face contradicts her. Tears squeeze from the corners of her eyes. I hold out my arms and she walks into them. "I told him this morning when he came home in the middle of the night. *Again.*" She sniffles. "I just can't take it anymore."

"I know," I murmur and stroke her hair as the tears continue to fall. "It's okay. Everything will be all right."

I hold her until the tears slow. When they finally stop, I release her from the hug and lead her to the kitchen table. "Coffee, tea, or prosecco?"

"Prosecco." She looks up at me. "Definitely prosecco."

"Sit down and tell me about it."

The details come out quickly as I open the bottle of sparkling wine and pour us each a generous glass. Her words slow only toward the end. "I had to give him one final warning." She scrubs at her eyes. "I should have done it a long time ago. I know it's the right thing. I had to draw the line. But now if he . . ." New tears squeeze from her eyes. "I'll have to follow through."

"I know. It's a big step." I put the wineglass in her hands.

She stares down into the sparkling wine then back up at me.

"Clay is going to be with Lily while I'm in New York."

"New York?" Even saying the name of the city Lauren ran back to is difficult.

"Yes. I'm going to a fiction writers' conference. I have a chance to meet with agents and editors there. And, well, I figured it's time to start educating myself about publishing. You know, from an author's perspective instead of a bookseller's." She takes a sip of prosecco.

I reach down and squeeze Bree's shoulder. "I'm so sorry about where things stand with you and Clay, but I'm very glad to see you taking control of your life and pursuing your dreams."

She takes another sip and manages a nod and a half smile. "I'm hoping to see Lauren while I'm there. If she's available."

I flinch. I keep thinking about flying to New York and just showing up and ringing my daughter's doorbell. Only, while Bree has just proven how brave she is, I don't have that same courage. Because of what I keep picturing when I get there: Me on the sidewalk because Lauren's left orders not to allow me in the building. Or sneaking in somehow only to sit helplessly outside the apartment door she refuses to open.

"You *are* going to find a way to talk to Lauren, aren't you?" Bree asks, her eyes on my face. I'm touched that in the middle of her own crisis she's thinking about me and mine.

"Yes. Of course." I wish I were anywhere near as certain as I sound; that I had the nerve to do it today. This minute. "I just don't think she's ready to hear what I have to say yet."

"I really don't think it's about timing, Kendra. I waited way too long and I still took Clay by surprise." Bree's smile is sad. "He didn't think I'd ever speak up. I hate that I've let him treat me and our marriage the way he has. I told myself I was protecting the kids, but they already knew."

She swipes away the last of her tears and takes a deep breath. This is followed by a first real look around the kitchen and at me. "Oh my gosh. I came at a bad time and didn't even ask if I could come in. You're going out on a date, aren't you?" She focuses on the bodice of my dress. "And I've cried all over your beautiful new sundress."

"Oh, this old thing?" I say. I'm ready to lay it on thick about how this is just something I pulled on and that I'm not dressed for a date at all, when she reaches over and lifts the price tag that's apparently dangling from the back of the bodice.

My cheeks heat. I try to cover by retrieving the scissors I keep in the knife drawer. I hand them to her and turn so she can cut off the tag.

"So where are you wearing this old 'rag' tonight?" She dangles the tag between her fingers.

"Nowhere. I'm not even going out. Jake's just coming over to cook out. It's completely casual."

"Whatever you say." She smiles and deposits the tag in the garbage can. "But there's no reason why you shouldn't go out with each other on a date, is there?"

"No. But we're not. Going out, I mean. We're just grilling some food and catching up. And talking about how to handle things with Lauren."

"While not dating."

"Exactly." I say this with every ounce of certainty I can manage. But I can tell from the way Brianna is smiling and so eager now to get out of the way that she's not convinced.

And neither, it turns out much later that night, am I.

Thirty-one

Kendra

Jake arrives with a bottle of wine in one hand and a bouquet of sunflowers in the other. When he places a friendly kiss on my cheek then follows me into the kitchen, my past and present collide in ways I'm not at all prepared for.

He was my first kiss, my first date, the first person who made love to me, the man I should have married. He's not the first man I've invited for dinner, but he's the first one who feels as if he belongs here.

While I pour glasses of prosecco and arrange the sunflowers in a vase, he tells me about the loss of a manager at one of their properties in Virginia and a difference of opinion with one of his partners over whether to purchase a family camp near Saratoga. Even when describing difficulties, it's clear that he loves what he does.

"How did you end up in the hospitality field?" I ask as we shed our shoes and take the crossover to the beach. "Did you start with B and Bs?"

I listen as he explains his progression from financing boutique properties to being forced to repossess one when the owner couldn't continue to make payments.

"When I went in to try to figure out whether the business could be salvaged, I discovered the property was making money—

lots of it—only the owner was too hands-off. His manager was doctoring the books and stealing him blind."

Our feet sink into the wet sand. Our bodies brush occasionally. Mine prickles with awareness each time this happens. I remind myself that this is not a date and there's no reason to be nervous. Yet I can't quite banish the excitement that simmers just beneath my skin.

By the time we get back to the house my hair's tangled, and I can feel the salt spray drying on my skin, but it doesn't seem to matter. I pour the last of the prosecco and we clink our glasses in toast. Without asking he opens the bottle of red wine he brought and leaves it to breathe.

"Shall I go ahead and fire up the grill?"

"That would be great." An undoubtedly loopy smile fixes itself on my face. When it refuses to go away, I turn and open the refrigerator in an attempt to hide it. The smile proves stubborn and so I lean into the refrigerator as if that might cool it off my skin. An idea so ridiculous it makes me laugh.

I don't hear Jake come back inside (no doubt due to having my head stuck in a refrigerator) but I feel him step up behind me. His body brackets mine. His breath is warm against my chilled ear as he whispers, "I feel the need to point out that you're laughing into a refrigerator. Is there something in there I need to know about?"

I laugh even harder as he turns me around and gently pulls me out of the cold. Then he kisses me. I can't remember ever laughing and kissing at the same time before, but it's heavenly. I highly recommend it.

When the kiss ends his hands remain on my waist. His smile looks every bit as loopy as mine feels; as if it's been transferred from my lips to his.

"I guess I should check the fire."

"Oh. Right." I attempt to gather my wits but my brain is

busy reliving the kiss. Imagining another. "Yes. Let's. Um. You do that." I clear my throat. "And I'll . . ." I can't seem to remember what else needs to be done. Or why. I tear my eyes away from his. There's a large, empty bowl on the counter. "And I'll . . . I'll start the salad."

The first glass of wine is consumed. A second follows.

Meal preparation passes in a genial haze. I'm vaguely aware of throwing a cloth over the table on the back deck, of placing the vase of sunflowers in its center, of carrying steaks and a basket of veggies out to the grill. But mostly I'm aware of Jake.

His voice is deep and fluid, a masculine melody that rises and falls over the lazy swish of the ocean. The breeze stirs the sea oats on the surrounding dunes, tickles nearby palms, and skims across my bare arms and cheeks. The salty scent of the sea teases my nostrils.

I ask about his sons. About his parents' house in Richmond that he tells me was left to him and that his younger son and his new wife might move into. He asks about Aunt Velda. About my baking. About how I ended up here. What made me stay.

We do not bring up my tattered relationship with Lauren or what can or should be done about it. I realize that it's not just our child that binds us together but the very real pull of attraction.

It could be the wine or the way the last vestiges of the day disappear in a shimmer of pink and gold that makes the evening so comfortable yet so intimate. I don't know why I feel the way I do and in truth I don't care. I just want to enjoy every second of this moment, this meal, this evening.

And so the steak is more tender than any I've ever tasted, the vegetables fresher, the salad crisper. It may be the best meal I've ever had. The best evening.

We open a second bottle of red and stare up at the stars that blanket the night sky.

If this were actually a date it would be the best one I've ever been on.

Lauren

New York City

I'm sitting at my desk staring at the blinking cursor. Its thumbs are in its ears and it's waggling its fingers at me jeering, "Nah nah nah nah nah." Because I've been sitting here a very long time and have nothing to show for it but a blank screen.

I love being a writer and am beyond grateful to get to create characters and tell stories for a living, but I have some experience with procrastination. All authors do. Some of us expend a lot of energy attempting to stamp out even the tiniest ember of it. Others fan its flames.

When the going gets tough—which often happens when attempting to create relatable characters within a believable universe which must be sustained for one hundred thousand–plus words, even the toughest among us escape to things that are more attractive than writing. Things like doing laundry. Scrubbing toilets. Plucking eyebrows. Having oral surgery.

Normally, I manage to resist the urge to procrastinate. I've written through fear, poverty, blizzards, power outages, and breakups. I have always understood that the most valuable thing I can do is write more pages, add another novel to my body of work.

In a desperate attempt to "see a winning outcome" I close my eyes and try to visualize anything and everything that might help; my fingers skipping across the keyboard; that magical moment when the story comes together; the completed book on bookstore shelves. Nothing works. I'm blocked in a way I have never allowed and refused to acknowledge. I, who have laughed at the very idea of writer's block, cannot force myself to put a single word on this screen.

Like a sailboat lacking wind my brain is becalmed. I am wallowing in a trough of unproductivity. I cannot finish the novel I have to deliver.

If there were a Procrastination Olympics—and it occurs to me that perhaps this is the perfect time to stop what I'm not doing to plan one—I'd be the gold medalist in every event.

When my cell phone rings, I glance down with gratitude for the distraction. I flinch at the Outer Banks area code until I confirm the number is not my mother's. "Hello?"

"Hi." It's Bree on the other end. "Is that you, Lauren? I wasn't sure if you'd pick up."

"It's me." For a second I worry that she's calling to ask if I've read her manuscript. Then I remember she doesn't know I have it. "How are you?"

Her sigh is long. "I've been better. You?"

"Ditto."

There's a silence as we both register that we've told the other the truth.

"I've given Clay an ultimatum. If he cheats again I file for divorce." Bree's words come out in a rush.

"Oh." I try to switch gears and gather my thoughts. I think about the bitchy blonde. Clay's infidelity. But I also remember how he placed Brianna's manuscript in Spencer's hands. The manuscript I have been unable to even look at let alone read. When you're dead in the water, the last thing you want to see is evidence that someone else has managed to catch even a puff of wind.

"What happened?"

"I finally came to my senses." She falls silent and I try to think what should happen next.

"Is there something I can do?"

"I'm coming to New York next Tuesday. For a writers' conference."

"Oh." To my knowledge Bree has never been in New York. Not even for BookExpo or other bookseller-related events. I think of the fences we'd started mending before my mother's bombshell. The comfort of being with the one person I used to be able to say anything to. The not-so-nice way we ended. For all I know she's coming up to plead my mother's case. This doesn't horrify me as much as it should. "Do you need a place to stay?"

"No. I'm saying at the conference hotel. I don't want to intrude on your writing time or anything. But I'd like to see you. If you have the time."

Her voice breaks and I hear the tears in her voice. Bree's put herself on the line, risked being rejected. She needs me.

"Of course. Once you see your schedule let me know when you're free." I'm careful not to mention that I don't really need much warning. When you're not really working or living your life the one thing you have plenty of is time.

Kendra

The Sandcastle

The smell of frying bacon hangs in the air. I imagine I hear its sizzle.

Groggy, I assume I'm dreaming until I hear what sounds like the clatter of pots and pans coming from the kitchen. The refrigerator door opens and closes. Which makes no more sense than the smell of coffee that accompanies it.

Assuring myself there is not a serial killer in my kitchen who's decided to make me breakfast before dispatching me, I throw my legs over the side of the bed and stand. I go into my closet to pull on shorts and a T-shirt then hurriedly brush my teeth. Just in case I'm wrong about the serial killer/cook, I pick up a piece of driftwood that doubles as a walking stick that I keep near the door and move quietly toward the kitchen.

Where I find Jake whistling and cooking.

"Good morning."

"Morning. The door was unlocked so I let myself in." He smiles. "I'm kind of hoping you're not planning to call the police to report an entering and cooking." He motions me to sit at my own kitchen table then pours me a cup of coffee and sets it in front of me.

"I guess that depends on how good the breakfast is."

"Ah, no pressure there." His smile is wide and warm and makes me remember the way his lips felt on mine. Not that I need reminding. "Fortunately for both of us, this is my best meal."

"That is fortunate." I haven't heard from him since our cookout three nights ago. The cookout filled with kisses that left me wanting more. I am ridiculously glad to see him.

"I got called out of town unexpectedly. Just got back last night."

Relieved by the answer to my unasked question, I sip my coffee and watch him stir the eggs. His biceps strain against the short sleeves of his T-shirt.

"I don't cook anything fancy," he continues. "I'm more of an assembler than a true cook, but I have a repertoire of never-fails. It's a good thing the boys weren't picky eaters."

I'm thinking about all the reasons he became the cook in his family as he fills two plates with scrambled cheese eggs, bacon, sliced tomatoes, and fresh croissants. A bowl of cut fruit lands next to the sunflowers. Which I think may have perked up at his arrival. Almost as much as I have.

He sits across from me and we begin to eat. Breakfast tastes even better than it smells. The eggs are soft and fluffy and I savor the Havarti, cheddar, and Muenster melted and folded inside them. The bacon is just the way I like it—crispy but not burnt. "Wow. This is good."

The smile spreads across his face. "Glad to hear it. The day's way too beautiful to spend it alone." He's looking at me as he says this, and I feel a shiver of excitement. We eat in silence for a time. Whenever I glance up his eyes are on my face.

"What?"

"I've been thinking," he says. "About this not-really-dating thing we're doing."

I almost choke on the piece of croissant I just put in my mouth and have to take a sip of coffee to make sure it goes down.

"How do you feel about it?"

I force myself to continue to meet his gaze. His gives away nothing. He could be asking for more. Or he could be looking for a way to tell me we're wasting our time. It's possible that all he really wants is what he came here for in the first place— access to Lauren and all the blanks of our story filled in.

It's not as if Jake and I need to share parenting. It's not even clear whether my relationship with Lauren is going to be anything close to what it once was. It might not survive at all if I wait much longer to act.

The safest thing would be to back off now. To say that I hope we'll always be friends. That sharing a few kisses doesn't make a relationship. That being attracted to each other doesn't mean we're meant to be together.

I've lived without this man for the last forty years. I can live without him for the next forty.

My heart squeezes at the thought. A very real tug of desire follows. Of course, I can live without him. I can even live without ever kissing him again. Only now I'll know exactly what I'm missing.

I drop my eyes. Am I going to play it safe like I've been doing all these years? Or am I going to admit what I really want? Which at this particular moment is to take his hand and lead him to my bedroom so that I can have my way with him.

The very idea makes me smile.

He puts down his fork and sits back in his chair, apparently willing to wait for my answer.

Am I going to pretend I don't want this man because I might have misunderstood his question? Or because I might get hurt or be turned down? Have I really become someone who can't admit what she wants? Or go after it?

I look up and meet his eyes again. "I don't think it's working."

"No?" He cocks his head. "Why not?"

"Well." I stand and square my shoulders. "People who aren't really dating generally don't sleep together."

He's watching me intently.

"As in, they don't have sex."

A muscle ticks in his cheek. His brown eyes go a shade darker.

"From what I've heard, when a man makes breakfast for a woman it's usually because they've spent the night together. I think you've got things backward."

"Is that right?" The question is whisper soft.

"Um-hmm."

"I hope you're going to straighten me out." This comes out in a husky growl that makes my entire body tingle with awareness.

"Oh, I am." So bold I barely recognize myself, I straddle his legs, sitting in his lap so that my chest rubs against his.

"I can't tell you how glad I am to hear you say that." His hands slip under my T-shirt. We both groan as they cup my breasts.

Within seconds my shirt is on the floor. His head drops. His tongue circles my nipples.

My head falls back as his hands slide under me. Trembling, I lock my legs around his waist and thread my arms around his neck as he stands. My only clear thought as he carries me to my bedroom is how long I've waited for this and how very much I want him.

Thirty-two

Bree

I'm up at dawn Monday morning. Even before making coffee, I race up to my office and sit down at my computer hoping against hope that one of the agents I queried has read my proposal and responded. All I need is one e-mail requesting the full manuscript, one e-mail saying that although I'm inexperienced they can tell that I have talent and want to represent me. I've checked three times a day for five days now (this includes Saturday and Sunday since I'm not sure whether they work on weekends). So far not a single one of them has replied.

The literary agency disclaimers made it clear that it could take three to four weeks to receive a response. But they also said that they don't necessarily respond if they're not interested in the material. Which means I have no way of knowing whether they have or haven't read my proposal. Or read it and didn't like it. It's possible I've already received five great big silent *no*s and just don't know it yet.

As I make my way down to the kitchen I tell myself not to worry. There are plenty of fish in the publishing sea, and I have appointments with two more of them at the conference. The truth is the manuscript is the least of my worries, yet it's the only one I can allow myself to focus on.

During the years I spent writing *Heart of Gold* I never imagined how much I'd miss it once it was finished.

Without the manuscript to work on, my marriage, and all the problems that stem from it, are front and center. Which begs the question: Did it take me fifteen years to write it because I put my children, family, and business first as I've always believed? Or did it take fifteen years because I needed it to hide out in?

Cup of coffee in hand, I settle at the kitchen table and try to put my head in the right place, wherever that might be. I'm still searching for that safer place when Lily enters. Although she's earlier than usual and I know she must still be half asleep her face is already set, her expression is stony. Lily's disappointment in us knows no bounds. Though no longer a child, her view is childishly simple: she thinks her father will stop cheating if I just "rein him in." And though she can't possibly know about the ultimatum I gave Clay, I can tell she senses that something has changed. Just as I sense her withdrawing and becoming more secretive.

"What time will you be home for dinner?"

"I won't. I'm going to Dana's after practice. Mrs. Barrett invited me for dinner and then we're going to study for a chemistry test."

"Didn't you just have dinner there the other night?"

"Mrs. Barrett says she's glad to have me anytime." She glares down her nose at me before once again looking pointedly away.

"Lily, honey, please. Why don't you sit down and have some . . ."

A horn beeps out in the drive. "That's Dana. We have spirit club meetings before school all week and she's driving." Lily gathers her books and walks toward the door. "So Dad won't have to worry about driving me while you're gone." She calls this last tidbit over her shoulder just before the door closes behind her. I move to the window and watch her climb into Dana's bright-red Hyundai and speed away.

I head back to the coffeemaker as if another shot of caffeine will somehow make things better or at least clearer. I feel guilty about how much I'm looking forward to leaving for New York tomorrow, but it's not just Lily who's acting out. Sharing a house with someone you've threatened to divorce is no picnic.

If Clay's working on his relationship with Lily I've seen no signs of it. I can only hope he'll spend the time I'm in New York trying to reach out and reassure her.

I spend the next fifteen minutes sipping coffee and mentally planning what to pack. I rouse my phone to check e-mail yet again to see if there's a response to any of my submissions. I wish I knew for sure that no news was good news.

I look up at the sound of footsteps. Clay appears in the kitchen with the semi-scowl he now saves for me. It says everything is my fault. That I should have known better and other things I don't want to see.

As he has each morning since I issued my ultimatum, he huffs in surprise when he discovers that there's no coffee brewing or breakfast cooking. That surprise turns to irritation as he makes his own coffee and rummages in the pantry for something to eat.

I am a peacekeeper by nature and necessity. I have to fight off the reflexive urges to apologize, accept the blame for his bad mood, or attempt to make him feel better. Every instinct shouts at me to once again sweep our problems under the rug and pretend the lump isn't there.

But I fear any sign that can be interpreted as weakness will make him think he doesn't have to take my ultimatum to change his behavior seriously.

He stuffs a Pop-Tart into the toaster so hard the pastry breaks, and I briefly consider pointing out that his bad mood should be aimed at himself and not at me. Instead, I avert my eyes as he eats the half of the pastry that survived and downs his coffee. I'm too tired from pretending to be strong when I'm not to remind him of all the reasons we're no longer living life as usual.

I'm not only exhausted, I'm afraid. Afraid of what I've set in motion. Afraid of how the kids will react to our divorce if I have to file. Afraid of how I'd handle life alone. Afraid of how big a failure I'll be if the book I've spent a decade and a half on never gets published.

If there's anything I'm not afraid of at this moment, it's only because I haven't thought of it yet.

Each day it gets a little harder to remember how strong I felt when I finally told Clay I'm not prepared to put up with his transgressions. I've come to understand that my declaration was not an end but only the first small step in what could be a long and arduous journey to the improved relationship I hope for. Or the final death spiral of the relationship I've been clinging to and the world as we all know it.

A shudder passes through me. And I pray that I won't have to follow through on my threat. That Clay will finally understand how much he stands to lose and how much we have to offer each other.

"Where's Lily? Why isn't she ready to go?" he asks when the Pop-Tart is gone, the coffee finished.

"Dana picked her up. She'll be riding to school with her all week for early meetings."

He's barely looked at me since he came into the kitchen. Now I move to stand in front of him so he has to. "She's upset, Clay. She knows something's changed. You're going to have to be careful with her while I'm gone. Pay attention. Stay on top of things. Something in her behavior feels . . . off."

"I don't understand how you can leave after you started all this." He says this as if I'm the one who misbehaved and didn't bother to hide it. As if the idea of a divorce came out of nowhere. Without waiting for an answer he turns and leaves. Outside he practically vaults into his truck. The engine roars to life.

I stand where I am, staring out the window as the truck disappears in a spray of stones and fumes. For a long time I do nothing but breathe. In and out as deeply and slowly as I can until my heart stops racing and the oxygen reaches my brain.

Finally, I get myself under control, but I have no idea what should happen next.

I glance up at the kitchen clock. For a moment I think it's broken. How else could it move so slowly? I've covered a lot of mental and emotional ground but it's too early to go to the store, and I need to talk to someone.

I consider calling my mother-in-law but I doubt Clay's planning to tell her what's going on with us or know how she'll respond if we end up divorced. As much as she's always treated me like a daughter, I'm not her flesh and blood and I don't know how she'd feel about me if her son and I were no longer married.

I could call Kendra, but I'm reluctant to lean on her right now. And I don't want to rub in the fact that I'm going to see Lauren when Lauren still won't speak to her. If I'm allowed to add one more fear to an already long list, it's that I'm afraid if I get in the middle of what's going on between them, I'll give up the chance of having a relationship with either.

I sit down at the kitchen table. I need to talk to someone. Someone who already knows what's happened. Who knows the players and will understand what I'm going through. I wouldn't mind it if that someone knew something about publishing and could provide valuable insights into the internal workings of a literary agent's mind.

There's only one person who qualifies. Before I can think better of it, I call Lauren.

For a moment we're too stunned to speak. Or at least I assume that's why we're not speaking.

"Bree?" she finally asks. "Is that you? Or is this an obscene phone call?"

"Are those my only choices?"

There's a snort of laughter. "Are you all right?"

"That depends on your definition."

"Sorry. You're the one with all the definitions in your head. I just right-click for synonyms."

It's my turn to snort. And just like that I'm smiling. "So how's Spencer?"

"Good. Possibly too good for me."

"He's definitely too good for you," I shoot back. "But I wouldn't mention it. Maybe he won't notice."

"Ha!"

"Ha yourself!"

Silence descends. I wonder if Lauren's as surprised by the reappearance of our old rhythm as I am.

"So are we still on for dinner Wednesday night?" she asks.

"Yes. Are you sure you don't mind coming to the conference hotel?"

"I think I can handle it. There's a small Italian place near there that I thought you might like."

"Sounds good." I'm shocked that she's been thinking about me or where I might like to eat. "You're sure I won't be intruding on your writing time?"

The snort that follows is not quite as happy as the ones that came before it. "Not a problem."

"Thanks."

"So did you call about anything special?"

I sort through all the things that are weighing on me and am surprised that even a two-minute snortfest has lessened some of it. She warned me about Clay long ago and she knows where things stand now. I've already told her that I've made fidelity a requirement for staying married. Can I trust her not to laugh at my writing worries? There's only one way to find out.

"I, well, I sent proposals to five agents and I'm going to be seeing two more at the conference. I've been working on my pitch. But . . ." My voice trails off.

Her silence on the other end is unnerving. She's been a best-selling author so long she's probably forgotten what rejection feels like.

"I'm scared to death I'll get rejected," I say finally. "I'm not sure I can handle it."

Another silence. Even longer than the last. I wait for her to tell me not to worry. That she knows how good a writer I am. That all the horror stories about rejections in the publishing industry are greatly exaggerated.

What I hear is laughter. It goes on long enough to make me consider hanging up. I'm about to put down the phone when the laughter slows to a stop.

"Sorry," she says. "But you're definitely going to get rejected, Bree. So you might as well get ready for it."

"Is that right?"

"Unfortunately, it is."

"And how would you know?" I infuse the question with every ounce of indignation I feel. "It's not like you've read anything of mine in the last twenty years."

"No, but I do have plenty of experience with rejection. In fact, I have a master's degree in rejection. And a PhD in *Take that!* I've lived through way more than I ever wanted to or thought I could. And I don't know a single successful, working writer who hasn't."

"But . . ."

"*Sandcastle Sunrise* was rejected twenty times before it sold."

"Really?"

"Really. And it hurt like hell."

"But I thought . . ."

"That because my first book got published it was a piece of cake?" Lauren takes a deep breath and releases it. "Far from it."

"Wow." How could I not have known this?

"Yeah. And I apologize if this is a total buzzkiller, but the rejection doesn't stop after you get published. Anyone can say what they like online and lots of people do. They don't have to justify a one-star review or apologize for the nasty things they sometimes write or say. And not everyone stays published forever. If you don't build fast enough you're gone. If you don't sell enough books you're gone. If your editor gets fired or leaves you can be orphaned without a champion in your publishing house. You're gone. I know just how lucky I am to have been published for so long, but it's a brutal business."

I sit stunned. Not only because of the ugly starkness of what she's saying—I've seen some of this from the bookseller side—but because she's gone through and dealt with so much that I never suspected. Like my assumptions about her "adventures" in New York City, I was too green with envy to even imagine anything negative.

"I know running an independent bookstore presents plenty of challenges, too. I just don't want you to be unprepared for what may lie ahead."

It's my turn to draw a deep breath. "Gee, thanks, Lauren," I say on the exhale. "I can't tell you how much I appreciate the pep talk."

We both laugh. But our laughter is more than a little uneasy.

"I didn't scare you off, did I?" she asks somewhat tentatively.

"Of course not." My reply is automatic. But as we hang up I'm not completely sure whether she's talking about a future in publishing or repairing our friendship.

Thirty-three

∽

Kendra

The Sandcastle

I'm shocked at how decadent I've become. How wanton. How easily I fall into bed with Jake at the slightest urging. And how long we can stay there.

I'd forgotten that sex could be fun. That laughter and affection are aphrodisiacs. That the right look in the right man's eyes could turn you back into someone you barely remember.

"You were beautiful at twenty, but you're even more beautiful now," he whispers as he lowers his body onto and then into mine. "I love making love to you." He moves slowly to illustrate.

Our bodies are slick with sweat. I can't think when I'm so swamped with pleasure, so I stop trying and just let myself feel.

Afterward we doze. When I awake curled up against him late-afternoon sun streams through the bedroom windows. I slip out of bed and pull on shorts and a T-shirt then carry a glass of iced tea out to the deck. As I do countless times every day I check my cell phone for a message from Lauren. Though I know there's no use, I dial her number and when she doesn't answer I leave her the same message I leave every day. "I love you and miss you. I hope you'll call back soon."

I'm setting the phone down when Jake wanders outside. Running shorts cling to his hips. His chest is bare. "Wow. Who knew great sex could be so exhausting?" He drops a kiss on the top of my head.

I blush because I can't help it. "I can't remember the last time I took a nap on a weekday," I say, avoiding an acknowledgment of what made us so tired. "I think you're a bad influence on me."

"It's my pleasure." His grin begins as wolfish, but turns into a yawn. He settles into the chair beside mine, props his bare feet on the railing, and folds his hands on an impressive set of abs. "We aim to please."

"Yes, I noticed." I feel my cheeks heat again. "I'm tempted to tell you to keep up the good work."

He throws back his head and laughs. "Oh, I intend to."

We both grin. Thanks to him, my limbs are loose. My body is exhausted in the best possible way. The only thing that's not right with my world is the hurt I've caused our daughter and her refusal to forgive me.

He reaches for my hand. "I know that look. You're thinking about Lauren."

"Always." The only thing that pushes her from my mind even briefly is when I lose myself with him. "I'm afraid if I leave it much longer we'll never find our way back to each other. I'm going to have to take action."

"What do you have in mind?"

"I'm not at all sure about the details. I just know I can't give up. I need to be able to look her in the eye and explain my reasoning and intentions again as best as I can. That's all that's left to me and I have to do it. The hardest thing will be getting her to agree to see me. I'm afraid to give her another opportunity to say no."

He nods.

"Bree's flying up tomorrow and coming back on Sunday. But I was thinking maybe you could plan your trip up to see her the following week. And I could kind of come up as a surprise guest. I just need you to get me through the front door. I'll take it from there."

"That's a bit risky, isn't it? She might refuse to listen. Or kick us both out."

"I know. It's asking a lot. She could be angry at you for aiding and abetting the enemy. But I have to try once more to make her understand. And I want to take THE DRESS with me."

"To wave like a flag of truce?"

I smile. "I'd wave it all over Manhattan if I thought it would help, but I'm thinking more along the lines of making sure she has it so that she can wear it on her wedding day if she wants to. Even if I . . ." I have to force myself to continue. "Even if I'm not invited to be there to see it."

"I can't believe it will come to that." He cups my cheek and chin in one large hand.

"I keep telling myself it won't. I hope to God it won't. But if she refuses to see me you can at least give her the dress."

"But . . ."

I put my fingers to his lips. "Promise me, Jake." I stare into his eyes, willing him to understand and agree. "If I don't get the chance, please make sure and tell her how sorry I am and how very much I love her."

Bree

In transit

It feels crazy odd to be sitting in the Norfolk airport all by myself waiting to fly to New York City. I've always been a homebody. No doubt because of my toddler years spent traveling from one archaeological site to another with my parents and the fact that they chose to travel all over creation without me after I turned five.

I've barely left the state of North Carolina since I graduated from college and didn't go to New York with Lauren. I've attended the occasional Southern Independent Booksellers Alliance meeting. A family trip to Williamsburg and DC. Another to Walt Disney World. Clay and I went to Charleston once. But the majority of our "vacations" have been spent at one of the Williams Realty beach rentals.

I feel a swell of excitement as I board the plane and take my seat. I'm going to the very heart of publishing, where I'll attend writing workshops, meet editors, get to know other writers, talk to literary agents. I've attended plenty of bookseller conferences but have never gone to a writers' conference. I've spent so long on this one novel that I've never really considered myself a *true* writer; certainly not in the way Lauren is.

I know Lauren's afraid of flying, but barreling down the runway makes me smile. My heart flutters with excitement as we lift off. The weight of my marriage problems and my daughter's unhappiness grow lighter and increasingly distant as the ground falls away.

I treat myself to a glass of wine and keep my eyes pinned to the blue sky and puffy white clouds through which we slice until the pilot announces our initial descent into LaGuardia. We come in over the water and I drink in my first sight of the Statue of Liberty, the ships in the harbor, the bridges that connect the island of Manhattan to its outlying boroughs.

From the moment we land I feel as if I've arrived on another planet. A universe so different from the one I normally inhabit that I don't even have the words to describe it.

Everywhere I look there are people. People who move and talk faster than any Outer Banker I've ever known.

From the backseat of a taxi I watch the crush of cars and people. I gape openmouthed all the way over the Queensboro Bridge, across the streets, and down the avenues. Everywhere I look there are tall buildings, vehicles inching along, horns blaring. My driver is a kamikaze whose hand stays on the horn and who zigs and zags through ridiculously small openings and sometimes no openings at all. He shouts at those he passes in a language I can't identify.

It's the first time I've ever seen Times Square in person. When we arrive at the Hilton, where the conference is being held, the driver sets my suitcase on the sidewalk and waits impatiently for me to fumble my way through the steps on the payment screen.

By the time I'm out on the pavement with people streaming all around me, I feel like I've fought a battle. The hotel lobby is packed. Check-in takes thirty-five minutes. I lug my suitcase up to my room then go downstairs to conference registration, where I get my packet and buy a turkey sandwich that costs more than a really nice meal in Manteo. I consider and reject the idea of wandering around Times Square by myself then retire to my room, where I leave a voice mail for Lily and pore over the workshop schedule like Eisenhower planning D-day. Then I hang tomorrow's outfit in the bathroom while I take a hot shower in hopes the steam will eliminate the wrinkles.

Wednesday flies by in an eyeblink. Each workshop is more inspiring than the last. I scribble notes on character development. Dialogue. Point of view. Conflict. Newly published authors' journeys that are filled with things they wish they'd known. Why didn't I ever do this before?

I join a table at lunch and discover that some of the attendees have been coming to conferences like this for years. A few of them have been submitting even longer. We compare notes. Tonight the publishers have cocktail parties for their authors. Dinners for the most promising or successful.

"Wow," I say as one of my tablemates describes a publisher party and dinner one of her critique partners was invited to before she sold her first book. "How do you get to go to those?"

"It's invitation only. Because they publish you or they want to. Sometimes if you hang out in the bar you'll see big-name writers having drinks with their editors or agents. But you have to be careful how you approach them," a writer named Karen says.

"Last year I saw someone dragged out of the women's bathroom by security," her friend Pam adds. "She'd been pitching her novel through the bathroom stall door and the editor inside called security on her cell phone."

I laugh until tea comes out of my nose. Then I realize they're serious.

By the time I'm supposed to meet Lauren, I'm exhausted and exhilarated. I try Lily again then find my way to the hotel bar and peek around the wall of people attempting to get in. Some of them have already gone up and changed for the evening, but I didn't want to miss a word of the last workshop on plotting, which I now know is one of my greatest weaknesses.

I'm standing behind the human wall, trying to figure out what to do when the wall begins to part. I'm way too short to see over the people in front of me, but I can sense their excitement. There's a buzz of conversation as people in front of me step aside. Suddenly Lauren steps forward in full-blown bestselling-author mode.

"There you are!" She hugs me then kisses me on both cheeks as the crowd looks on in silent awe and I can't help wondering if the affection is for show. The successful author being nice to one of the newbies.

"I wasn't sure what was keeping you." She takes my arm. "I've got a table inside. It turns out my publisher is having a party in their hospitality suite. I thought we could go up and say hi before we go to dinner."

The people around us are hanging on her every word. A couple of them take pictures.

"Oh no," I say quickly, remembering what I heard at lunch. "You've got to be invited. I don't have an invitation."

Lauren smiles and shoots me a wink. "I promise we won't have any trouble getting in. I can introduce you to my editor. And I wouldn't be at all surprised if my agent, Chris Wolfe, is there."

"Oh no. I can't possibly." I feel like a child who wants nothing more than to run and hide.

"Oh yes you can," Lauren replies. "I'm not about to let you pass up this opportunity." She leans forward and says very quietly, "Any one of these writers would jump at the chance to go with me to be introduced to editors and agents. It's one of the main reasons they're here. I'll help you work on your pitch before we go upstairs if you like."

As she pulls back I study her face, looking for some hint of an ulterior motive. I see nothing suspicious. Even her apparent sincerity doesn't allay my nerves.

"But I'm not dressed for a party." I don't add that I'm scared to death. That I don't have enough brain cells left to work on a pitch let alone give one. And that it's entirely possible that I'm going to hyperventilate.

"Then go upstairs and change. I'll have a drink waiting for you. What do you want?"

"I have no idea. My brain seems to have shut down." I say this quietly and with a frozen smile on my face. I do have *some* pride. "Maybe we should just skip the drinks and the party and go right to dinner."

"Absolutely not." She straightens and I notice that her makeup and hair are absolutely perfect. As if she's just stepped out of a salon or something. Her black cocktail dress has to be by some designer I've probably never heard of. "I'll figure out the drinks." She gives me another smile and a relatively gentle push. "Now, go on and hurry up."

Lauren

I'm slumped against Spencer in the backseat of a black car early Thursday evening. We've just spent another solid day on wedding details, including tours of smaller more unique venues that would allow for a more intimate gathering. Dinner was a quick slice of artichoke pizza in the East Village.

"What did you think of the Hornblower cruise?" I lift my head to ask. "It could be kind of cool to sail down the river and idle in front of the Statue of Liberty while we say our vows."

"The bigger boats might work, but the small one you liked wouldn't even hold my family, let alone friends."

"Haven's Kitchen Cooking School was interesting," I say. "We could do a seated dinner for eighty in that loft area. The garden at the Merchant's House Museum was nice, too. And the Ramscale Studio in the West Village is basically a blank canvas."

"I appreciate all the time you've been putting into finding the right venue, but I think we both know that who is at the wedding is even more important than where it's held." He sighs. "You need to make peace with your past, Lauren. And that means talking this through with your mother."

"But . . ."

His palm goes up to halt my, by now, automatic protest. This is not the first time he's urged me to speak to her. "I know how close you've always been. How much you mean to each other. And I have some experience with all the ways emotional turmoil can shut down creativity."

I force myself to meet Spencer's eyes. Clearly taking whole days off and *not* mentioning the novel I'm supposed to be writing speaks volumes to someone who listens as carefully as Spencer does.

"I'm just not ready to speak to her. I can't even listen to her voice mails. I . . . I don't know when I will be."

For a few moments we travel in silence. I'm watching the play of light and shadow on Spencer's face when he asks, "What time is Bree coming over Saturday morning?"

"As soon as she checks out of the hotel," I say, grateful for the change in topic. "I wish you could have seen her face at the publisher party last night. She was so excited and so scared at the same time. She has absolutely zero experience trying to sell herself in any way. I had to make sure she had just the right number of drinks, which, by the way, is one-point-five. It was a stroke of luck that Chris and Melissa were there. I was a little worried that she might faint when I introduced her to my agent *and* my editor."

"I'm glad you're trying to help," Spencer says. "Of course, if you'd read her manuscript you could have pitched it for her."

I feel a faint flush of shame. Bree and I spent our entire time together focused on the conference and her appointments, our talk skimming across the surface. I cringe when I realize that even in helping her I was showing off the fact that I could.

Spencer drops a kiss on the top of my head and gives my hand a reassuring squeeze as the car stops in front of my building. We exchange private smiles as Tom the doorman opens the front door and wishes us a good evening in his pronounced Long Island accent.

Spencer slips his arm around my shoulders as we enter the lobby. He pulls me close as we step into the elevator. I inhale his heady scent on the way up. It comforts and arouses. Our hands touch as I fit the key into my door.

I automatically avert my eyes when we walk by the cocktail table that holds Bree's manuscript. I know that if I sincerely want to help Bree I'm going to have to read it, but in this moment all my attention, all of my senses, are focused on this man.

"You do know how much I love you, right?" I say as Spencer and I reach for each other.

"Mmm-hhhm." He lowers his mouth to mine and pulls me

tighter against him. I'm already unbuttoning his shirt and shrugging out of mine as we stumble up the stairs to my bedroom. We're still pulling off clothes when we land on the bed. His skin is smooth and heated. His body is strong and supple. His mouth is warm and clever. When he kneels between my legs, pulls off my panties, and spreads my thighs all I want is to have him inside of me.

Our bodies join. We move against each other, our breathing harsh and eager as we climb together. An urgent rhythm claims us and takes us higher. Until we dangle dangerously, deliciously before shooting over the edge of reason into a glorious, breathless freefall.

❧

When I wake it's not yet dawn. The apartment is still dark. Spencer's breathing is deep and even.

I stare up into the ceiling, but I can't go back to sleep. No matter how many times I haven't looked at that damn manuscript I've never been able to forget that it's there. It's been a constant reminder of how much Bree once meant to me. How much I've missed her.

I invited her to come over on Saturday, so that I can show her around and to spend the night. How can I not read what she's spent fifteen years working on?

I pull on a robe and pad downstairs into the living room, not bothering with coffee. I barely think as I pick up Bree's manuscript and carry it to the sofa, where I turn on the lamp, stretch out with a pillow under my head and an afghan over me. I tell myself to keep an open mind. That it will be what it will be. That if it's just not ready I'll let her down easy. Or maybe find a good book doctor who can help her fix it. But I can't completely ignore the shiver of fear I feel. What I don't know is whether I'm more afraid that it will be really awful. Or that it will be really good.

Thirty-four

❦

Lauren

I'm still lying on the couch reading *Heart of Gold* on Friday morning when Spencer leaves with a parting kiss and an approving smile. I rouse sometime later and notice a cold cup of coffee and a bagel smeared with cream cheese on the end table. *Knew you'd do the right thing. Remember she's a beginner. Be gentle* is scribbled on a napkin.

I heat up the coffee and take a bathroom break. The bagel could double as a doorstop and it's with some regret that I drop it in the garbage.

I read the entire day, a luxury I rarely allow myself. Which is kind of crazy since, like pretty much every writer I've ever met, I began as a voracious reader, an inhaler of words and impressions. Escaping into another world is addictive. Every writer's journey begins with that first book that could not be put down.

It's late afternoon when I reach the point in the story where Whitney begins to see Heath for the man he really is without courtesy of rose-colored glasses. Did Bree even realize who and what she was writing about? Does she have any idea that it's no coincidence that she had had enough of Clay's bad behavior at the same time Whitney chose herself over her blind adoration of Heath? There are few things more self-revelatory than writing a novel. (It's just that sometimes we try not to see it and hope no one else does, either.)

I stand up and stretch. Do a few neck rolls.

Maybe Bree should have forced Clay to read this. Not that he would have recognized himself in the dark hair and even darker eyes that Bree camouflaged him in. My agent once assured me that you could write about virtually anyone if you changed their name and a few physical details since people so rarely recognize themselves or their behaviors.

When I get up to stretch and forage for food it's after four P.M. and I've got just over a hundred pages to go. I had imagined I'd jot down ideas and point out areas that needed work, but although there've been a few rookie mistakes and missed opportunities, I've been so caught up in the story (and being a fly on the wall to Bree's life) that I haven't made a single note or scribbled the smallest suggestion.

I'm almost numb when I finally finish. And not just because my body is stiff and my neck hurts.

I'm stunned by how good *Heart of Gold* is. It needs work, of course. No first draft is completely ready for consumption. First drafts of first books should never be flung out into the world.

This manuscript was written by someone who loves words and their nuances every bit as much as I do. But it's infused with the kind of truths one pours into a journal kept hidden under the bed, an honesty that comes from believing no one else will ever see what you've written.

I'm painfully jealous of the honesty and innocence it reflects. It's a book of the heart written by someone who has not yet encountered the harsh realities of publishing. Who has never had to think about reviewers or print runs or publisher support.

I look down and realize that I'm hugging the manuscript to my chest. The feel of the paper is almost as shocking as the threat it poses to Bree's and my status quo. For the past fifteen years I've been the bestselling author who achieved our once-shared dream. Bree's been the homemaker/bookseller who's played at being a writer.

Only it turns out Bree hasn't been "playing" at all. And I'm not as big a bestseller as I was.

This truth is staggering. So is what my conflicted reaction to that truth says about me. I know that Bree wants to be published. I know that she wants to prove that she could have come to New York and been every bit as successful as me, if only she'd wanted to.

What I don't know is how honest I'm willing to be. Or whether I'm even capable of being completely honest about what she's created.

We're going to be together for only twenty-four hours. Which means I'm going to find out all too soon whether I'm the person I've always thought I was. Or someone far smaller and stingier.

Bree

I'm floating on a cloud of postconference euphoria Saturday morning when I climb into the Uber that will take me to Lauren's. During the ride I check my phone for messages. There's still no response from Lily and only a brief text from Clay saying that everything's fine. I don't know how Kendra has survived Lauren's silence because my family's lack of communication for just three days has left me worried, angry, and no longer sure why I felt I had to rush home.

Next I scroll through e-mails looking, yet again, for responses from the agents I queried. When I accidentally end up in my spam folder I find e-mails from three out of the original five. They've been sitting there since Thursday.

My hands shake with excitement as I open them; an excitement that evaporates when I read one rejection after another, each following an identical format with my name and the name of my book plugged into the same spots.

The breath I've been holding escapes in a loud rush as the Uber pulls up in front of a large limestone building that takes up an entire block of Central Park West. I see it through a blur of tears and a gut wrench of disappointment.

This may be my first trip to New York and to the Upper West Side, but even I know that any building this close to Central Park has to be outrageously expensive. It is a tangible testament to Lauren's success that I'd give anything not to have to see right now.

So is the man in livery who tips his cap, greets me in an accent I have trouble deciphering, then ushers me into a marble-floored lobby decorated with gilt, gilt, and more gilt.

Another liveried man stands beside an inlaid wooden desk. "How may I help you?"

"I'm here to see Lauren Jameson."

His eyes narrow slightly. "Is Ms. Jameson expecting you?"

"She should be." I lift the suitcase I'm holding as if it's proof that I'm not dangerous and have a legitimate reason to be here even though I wish I were somewhere else.

"Your name?"

"Brianna. Brianna Williams." I arrange what I hope is a trustworthy smile on my face. And I think how different this building is from the dangerous places Lauren was forced to live in when she first arrived.

"I don't see your name on the list," the man says, and I wonder if this is an intentional snub or just an oversight.

He picks up a gilded phone and presses several buttons. "Yes, ma'am. A Ms. Williams is here to see you." He listens then nods. "Yes, of course.

"Right this way." When the elevator arrives he ushers me inside then pushes the number eight with a gloved finger. "It's the third door to your left when you exit the elevator." He doesn't exactly salute but he does stand at attention until the elevator doors close. I am duly impressed.

On the way up, I stare at myself in the gleaming wood and brass of the elevator. "Oh no you don't," I say, spotting the droop of my shoulders and feeling my chin pressing into my chest. "You are not walking in there like some pathetic loser."

Though all I want to do is curl up in a ball, I straighten. In the richly carpeted hallway I raise my chin and throw back my shoulders.

Given the formality I've just come through I brace for Lauren's public author persona, but when the door opens she gives me a hug and a smile. "Come on in."

Compared to the elegance of the building the apartment is warm and welcoming with a small, square foyer and a dark wood floor that contrasts nicely with the white walls and trim. It opens into a contemporary white kitchen. A Plexiglas stair floats up the opposite wall.

"The bedrooms are upstairs. We can carry your suitcase up later." She takes my bag and stashes it beside the first step then leads me toward a marble island with red leather barstools. "Would you like something cold to drink?"

"A glass of water would be great." I slide onto a barstool and glance nervously to my right, where the space opens into a double-width living room with brilliantly colored area rugs, marble-fronted fireplace, and two full walls of windows. The first lets in sunlight and impressive views of the park. The wall that abuts it frames part of a tree-lined street filled with brownstones.

She sets two glasses of water on the counter then slides onto a stool beside me.

"Your place is beautiful," I say, pushing the words past a lump of envy.

"Thanks. My original apartment was a lot smaller and it didn't have a park view. I lucked into this corner unit when the original owner died."

We consider each other. Wednesday evening was fueled by alcohol and my excitement. Lauren's presence opened doors I would have never walked through on my own. It was thrilling to be a part of the publishing world even briefly. But now it's just the two of us, and I'd give anything not to have stumbled on those rejections before I had to face her. Once she would have been the person I'd run to with any disappointment. Now I keep my chin up and my shoulders back and pray she can't see the *L* for loser I feel forming on my forehead.

"How'd the rest of the conference go?"

"Great," I say truthfully. "It was . . . Just being around other writers was inspiring. I haven't really experienced anything like that since we . . . you . . ." I stop stuttering long enough to look up and catch her expression. Has she taken that as a jab? Was it? "I'm not sure if I thanked you for the introductions."

"The ones you kept insisting I not make?"

"Yeah, those." I blush at the memory of my reluctance, the timidity that made me want to run and hide. "Your editor asked someone else from Trove to meet with me. I gave her the pitch you helped me come up with and she asked to see the full manuscript." I remember the initial thrill, but I now have proof that this is not going to be a slam dunk. Or maybe any kind of dunk at all. "I . . . Maybe you shouldn't be recommending me and *Heart of Gold* when you haven't read it."

Another uncomfortable look flashes across her face and I realize what I've just said. "I didn't mean that I *expect* you to read it or anything. But . . ."

Lauren gets up abruptly to refill our glasses, and I can tell I shouldn't have brought up the idea of her reading my book. I know she's got her own deadlines. And I'm still not at all sure I even want to hear her true opinion. I mean, what if she reads it and hates it? Worse, what if she reads it and hates it and tells me? "Will it hurt your reputation if someone reads my work because you asked them to and they don't like it?"

"No, not really. Editors and agents are like readers. They like what they like." She places the waters on the island. "I have the connections to get people to read something, but no one buys a novel just to please someone else."

"So a whole lot of people could read *Heart of Gold* and not want it."

"It's possible." She says this matter-of-factly, but she doesn't quite meet my eyes and I wonder if she's already heard something through her editor. "Anything's possible.

"But it only takes one *yes* to render the *no*s meaningless." She hesitates and I catch that odd look again. In the same way that I sensed that Lily recognized something new going on between Clay and me, I recognize Lauren is holding something back. What I don't know is what it could be or why.

Thirty-five

◌◌

Lauren

Bree's face turns kind of green. I show her to the bathroom knowing that if I were in one of those old V8 commercials I'd be slapping my forehead right now. Just five minutes ago I could have come clean. I could have told Bree the truth. *Smack.* I could have reached beneath the counter, pulled out her manuscript, and said, *I've already read it and I can't believe how good it is! Smack.* If I were willing to be completely honest I could have even added, *And I'm ashamed that I'm kind of conflicted about it.*

My mother's face and words fly by. *"I always intended to tell you and your father about each other."*

I now know firsthand that any kind of admission sounds feeble if it comes too long after the fact.

Which means I need to just speak up and get the topic out in the open. I decide to do this as soon as she comes out of the bathroom, but when she heads back toward me I ask, "Are you good to walk in those shoes?" *Smack!*

"I think so. Where are we going?"

"Well, since we only have the day, I thought we'd have brunch at Tavern on the Green and then wander around the neighborhood."

"*The* Tavern on the Green?"

"Yes. In all its farm-to-table, stunningly renovated Victorian Gothic glory."

We head out into a truly beautiful May morning. The temperature is in the low seventies. The sky above is a pastel blue. The park is lush and green. Brightly colored blooms are everywhere. So are people bent on enjoying them.

At the restaurant we're shown to a table on the bricked patio that is virtually in the park. I order mimosas to sip while we peruse the menu. I hope they'll help me find the backbone required to "do the right thing" and to maybe ease the anxious look in Bree's eyes.

At the waiter's suggestion we start with an appetizer of Maple Brown Sugar Bacon. It takes the whole mimosa and several slices of bacon each for the mixture of sugar and alcohol to begin to relax us.

"I think they should rename this 'ambrosia of the gods,'" I say around a mouthful of bacon. "Why didn't someone invent this sooner?"

"Because those of us with a sweet tooth and an inefficient metabolism would gain so much weight we'd be waddling." Bree waves a piece as she replies. "You could probably eat it all day and still fit into those skinny jeans of yours that I used to covet."

We order a second round of mimosas and sip them with Eggs Benedict Florentine (so that we can say we had spinach) and Brioche French Toast (because once you awaken your sweet tooth resistance is futile).

"I'm afraid to think about how many calories I'm consuming," Bree says.

"Then don't." I hold up my mimosa to hers. "Let's make this a designated calorie-free day."

She smiles, taking in the setting, the food on our plates, the patio filled with equally fizzy smiles and low conversation. The occasional celebrity gets seated or strolls by and no one makes a fuss. "This really is the life, isn't it?"

"It has its moments." My smile tightens as I think what it

took to get here. When I look up, Bree's eyes are on my face. A strange, almost reluctant expression spreads across hers.

"I've been thinking about how far you've come since you first arrived in New York alone. And I . . . I just want to tell you how sorry I am that I left you in that situation. At this point I'm not even sure why I backed out. I know I was afraid. I know I had no real belief in myself or my writing ability." A shadow passes over her face and is followed by an intentional straightening of her shoulders that she's been making since she entered my apartment. "I wanted to be safe and loved." She takes another sip of her mimosa. "I don't even know whether Clay ever really loved me. Or if anyone could have ever given me as much love as I needed."

Her words are as unexpected as they are comforting. Her apology is a balm that flows over the hard knot of loss and hurt and anger I've clung to all these years. "I know Clay loves you." I picture him with the box holding Bree's manuscript and vow to make sure she knows that he was directly responsible for me reading it. "He just doesn't seem to be all that good at forsaking all others."

"Yeah."

"But you did get Rafe and Lily out of it."

Bree smiles and it's not the resolute one she appeared with today. "I wouldn't trade being their mother for anything." She looks at me. "I know for a fact that your mother feels the same. How many times has she told you that?"

That number is beyond counting. My mother's is the first voice I remember. The one I hear inside my head. The positive one that tells me I can do or be anything I choose. That voice didn't laugh when I decided as a child that I would be a bestselling author. It didn't chide me or try to keep me from going to New York on my own, though she must have been worried. It never pushed me to do anything but be myself and follow my dreams.

My mother has been a one-woman cheering section my

entire life, and I have been torturing her for more than a month now. I haven't even attempted to hear her out or to get over my hurt and anger. I've just rained it down all over her.

"Are you all right?"

"Hmmm?" I look up. "Yes. Sorry. Just thinking."

And not just about my mother.

I set down my glass, fold my hands on the table, and look directly at Bree. My fear and hesitation are gone. I know deep inside that it doesn't matter what words I choose. Or— hopefully—how long it's taken me to find them. If our reality— our status quo—is about to shift, then so be it.

"I've read *Heart of Gold* and it's really, really good."

Bree

I blink. Lauren's words came out in such a rush that I assume I've misheard. Or maybe I've put the words I most want to hear in her mouth. "What?"

Lauren's hands are clasped so tightly on the table that her knuckles are white. "Clay gave me your manuscript when we left your house and . . . I finally read it yesterday. In one sitting."

Our eyes lock. I wait, barely breathing, for whatever is going to come next.

"And it's so good that I've been trying to figure out how to tell you."

The adrenaline that's been pumping through my bloodstream must have muddied my thinking along with my hearing. "You read *Heart of Gold* yesterday and you didn't want to tell me that it's good?"

"I just . . . I wasn't prepared. It took me by surprise . . ." Her voice trails off and I can see how much she wants to look away. "I guess deep down—or maybe not even very deep down at all—I didn't *want* it to be good."

I am actually speechless. As in I'm still trying to absorb this and do not know what to say. Our friendship eroded almost twenty years ago, and apparently her memory of anyone's talent but her own went with it.

"Because?"

"Because . . . I'm small and petty and it was so good and it was so . . . honest . . . that . . ." She swallows and sets her jaw. "I was jealous."

Lauren is jealous of me. Of my manuscript. Because it's so good.

This is possibly the most beautiful thing I've ever heard. The single nicest thing anyone has ever said to me. The very thing this morning's found rejections made me fear I'd never hear.

I let go of the urge to give her shit for not believing in me all these years. "Could you say that part about my manuscript again?"

"It's really good." This time she nods for emphasis as she says it.

I feel the absolute mind-numbing joy of validation, but . . . "Do you think you could say it one more time?"

"It's so good and so fresh and so honest, that I'm jealous."

I close my eyes. A celestial choir sings in my head. When I open them she's watching me. Waiting.

"I'm very glad—and relieved—that you liked it. But . . . I found three form rejections in my spam this morning. If it's so good why didn't any of them want it?"

Lauren smiles. "Do you remember me telling you about all the rejections I got before *Sandcastle Sunrise* finally sold?"

I wince as I always do at the mention of the book that we brainstormed together and that she used to build her career. But I also nod. What are the chances that I would have hung in there for twenty *no*s when I'm so thrown by my first three?

"Would you like to hear a few?" Lauren asks. "Just to put things in perspective?"

I nod again but only because I don't want to sound like a frightened child.

I wait for her to pull letters or pieces of paper from her purse or out of her pockets, but she just clears her throat and says, "'I find I can't like the characters in the way that I wish I could. I'm afraid I'll have to pass.'"

I gasp.

Lauren continues, in a carefully emotionless voice. "'Your submission is missing that special something that really good novels require. I'm afraid I'll have to pass. I suggest extensive rewrites before you submit elsewhere.'" After a short breath she adds, "'This submission lacks an interesting plot. Your characters are also one-dimensional. I'm afraid I'll have to pass.'"

The lack of emphasis makes the words even harsher and more difficult to listen to.

Her face is equally expressionless as she concludes with, "'I find your characters wooden and unrelatable. I'm afraid I'll have to pass. Best of luck in placing your work elsewhere.'"

"Oh my God. That's . . . those are horrible."

She nods. "Great reviews and feedback feel fabulous in the moment, but for some reason it's the negative ones you never forget. Some of the others were even worse." She sighs. "But I came to realize they were just opinions. I reread them for years. Twice on the days I wanted to give up. I was determined to prove them wrong and to have the last word. Three or four years ago, two of those editors tried to lure me away from my current publisher. They were both throwing big money at me."

"And?"

This smile is one of grim satisfaction. "And it inspired my publisher to offer even more to keep me. Plus, I had the pleasure of instructing Chris Wolfe to tell both of them that their offers did not excite me as I'd hoped. And that I was afraid I'd have to pass."

Her answer is both terrible and wonderful. I could never say or do such a thing.

"The point I'm trying to make is that you can't control what others think. You've heard that saying, 'Opinions are like ass-holes. Everyone has one'? The only things you can control are how good a book you write and how you react to the assholes. You alone choose whether you're going to let them stop you. Or use them to spur you on."

"So that's all there is to it? I just keep sending out proposals until somebody says yes?"

"Well, your proposal could use a little tweaking. You made a few rookie mistakes at the beginning of the book. It's not a difficult fix. I can show you how if you want before you submit to anyone else."

"You would do that."

"Um-hmmm, it'll give me something to do, considering how stuck I am with my own book and the fact that my career is currently in free fall." She looks as surprised as I am at the admission. "Did I really just say that out loud?"

I nod.

"Holy shit."

"What's going on?"

"Oh, lots of things you'll find out about once *Heart of Gold* is published."

Despite the fact that she's in the middle of talking about her own problems I get a shiver of excitement at the assumption that my novel will actually be published. "Like?"

"A slump in sales. Writing in a genre that's not as hot as it was. The constant pressure to produce something even better than what you did before. Only it can't be too different because the Queen of Beach Reads is not expected to write dark or al-low things to end badly."

I wait because I still recognize her pregnant pauses.

"Oh, and they're planning to bring out an anniversary edi-tion of *Sandcastle Sunrise* to help boost sales. They want to do a big launch at your store when it's released next June."

My own pause is equally pregnant. "When were you planning to tell me about that?"

"I was supposed to tell you while we were there but I couldn't do it. I knew it would upset you and I . . . Well, for the first time it seemed like maybe we didn't hate each other so much anymore. And then, of course, there were a few other things going on."

I can't help but smile at the understatement.

"Oh, and *Say Yes to the Dress* is interested in having me on the show."

"Seriously? You're going to be on *Say Yes to the Dress?*"

"I haven't decided yet."

"Oh my God. I love that show. It's one of the few programs Lily and I still binge-watch together. Even though I always feel slightly disloyal to THE DRESS while I'm doing it."

"Yes, well. Trove wants me to do the show, choose a dress, and wear it in my wedding on the real beach where *Sandcastle Sunrise* is set, to kick off the launch of the anniversary edition."

We just look at each other.

Our past, in all its messiness, passes before my eyes. If Lauren's face is any indication she's doing a quick stroll down memory lane, too.

"So," she says. "In my experience good book news *and* bad book news call for champagne. And dessert."

We drink an entire bottle of Dom Pérignon and share a huge slice of Peanut Butter Chocolate Lava Cake. When I ask for what might be the hundredth time whether she *really* liked *Heart of Gold*, she takes my phone, holds it up, and videos herself saying, "I, Lauren Jameson aka Lauren James, do solemnly swear that I have read *Heart of Gold* by Brianna Williams and have found it to be wonderful."

I replay the video too many times to count and am grinning like a loon when she asks if I'm ready to go.

"Yes. And I don't even care where we're going," I say as we get up from the table. "I'm just going to follow you around all day smiling."

"There may be statutes against that," she says even though she's smiling, too. "Try not to look too happy. Everyone will know you're from out of town."

Thirty-six

※

Lauren

We've both got a good buzz on as I lead her through the park to Strawberry Fields, the first stop on what was originally conceived as a look-at-everything-you've-been-missing tour but that I'm now envisioning as a sincere attempt to share not only my favorite places, but my life.

We stand in front of a simple round black-and-white mosaic with the word IMAGINE set in its center. Fresh flowers left by fans are strewn across it and a hush hangs over the space and not just because it's a designated quiet zone, which seems an oddly hopeless request here in New York.

I point up through the trees to the Dakota, where John Lennon and Yoko Ono lived, and where he was shot, then to my building a few blocks away from it.

"I come here all the time. Sometimes I sit for hours just staring at that one word. It's like a command, you know?"

The ringtone on my cell phone breaks the silence. Surprised to see Spencer's photo on my screen, I answer.

"How are things going?" he asks.

"Good. Great, really." I glance over at Bree.

"Sorry to interrupt, but I just got a text from Daria, Brett's friend at Kleinfeld's."

"Oh."

"She had a last-minute cancellation and has a two-and-a-half-hour window open if you can make it."

"Oh, but . . ." I look down at my jeans and sneakers. My hair's pulled back into a ponytail and I don't remember putting on much more than mascara and lipstick. "I'm not really dressed for it."

"Well, since you were going to fly in there under the radar, maybe that's not a bad thing."

"Right. I was just going to walk Bree through the park and the neighborhood . . ."

"Call me crazy, but I was thinking this might be a bit of divine intervention. Unless you think she'd hate having to go with you to try on wedding gowns?"

I glance at Bree, who has already confessed her love of the show. I reach for her hand and practically yank her out of the park. "Tell Daria we're on our way."

⌒⌒

"Don't let me forget to take plenty of pictures at Kleinfeld's to text to Lily," Bree says as we pile into a taxi. "There's no way she'll ignore those."

"What's going on?"

"Lily blames both of us for Clay's behavior. She's gotten so touchy. Like a tinder keg waiting to go off. I'm not sure what will happen if things don't work out with Clay." She sighs. "She's not responding to my texts, and I've tried to call her, too, but she won't pick up."

I flush at the similarity of Lily's and my reaction to our mothers. Only I'm not sixteen. "Have you talked to Clay?"

"We've texted. He claims everything's fine. But he always says that. And I'm afraid it's just because he's not paying attention."

"Well, you'll be home tomorrow. Hopefully, you can sort it all out then."

When there's no response, I look up. Bree's staring down at her hands. I fill the silence with, "Title Waves seems to be doing well—that's not easy in today's world. And clearly all of your customers worship you." I flash back to their excitement over Bree's accomplishment. They've always believed in her and her writing talent while I required proof.

"There are a lot more people who worship *you*," Bree points out in a tone surprisingly lacking in envy.

"Less than there used to be. And mostly from afar."

"Spencer looks pretty up close and personal to me," she says.

"That's true."

"And he's clearly in love with you."

"He does have remarkably good taste, doesn't he?"

"Ha!" she retorts.

"Ha, yourself!"

❦

"I can't believe we're really here." Bree is out of the taxi and accosting a passerby—not always the best idea in the Big Apple—begging her to take a photo of us in front of Kleinfeld before I'm all the way out onto the sidewalk.

We pose with our arms around each other directly in front of the double glass entry between two canopied display windows. "Please make sure you can read the Kleinfeld signs!"

We smile big smiles as the stranger, who is also a tourist and therefore doesn't disappear with the camera or tell Bree where she can shove the signs, complies.

As eager as Bree is to get inside, she thanks the woman profusely then scrolls through the photos and texts the best to Lily. Her smile wavers slightly when there's not an immediate response.

"Don't worry." I link my arm through hers. "I'm sure you'll hear back."

Daria, who has the long-limbed grace of the dancer she is

and a truly beautiful smile, is waiting for us in the elegantly appointed lobby with its spotlit silver signage, marble-topped reception desk, and Corinthian columns, all of which Bree photographs.

"I'm glad you could make it on such short notice." She leads us through the dress-filled sales floor to a large, equally elegant dressing room. "Spencer gave me some input on what you might like and I've pulled a few things to get us started. But I want you to tell me if you have any other styles or specific designers you'd like to see."

She opens the door and we get our first glimpse of the gowns she's selected. Some are sleeveless, several are strapless; their shapes, shades of white and cream, and decorative details differ but each has a simple, classic, sophisticated elegance.

"Oh," Bree breathes, holding up her phone to photograph them. "They're so beautiful."

"They are, aren't they?" I've never even imagined wearing anything other than THE DRESS and I'm feeling slightly guilty at how much I like these.

"Your fiancé has stellar taste," Daria says. "Now that I've seen you and your reaction I'd like to pull a few more gowns. Would you like some champagne?"

I stand for a moment after she's gone, contemplating the gowns. I'm trying to shove away the images of my mother helping me into THE DRESS at the Sandcastle and everything that followed, when Bree steps up beside me.

"I believe THE DRESS will forgive us." She runs her fingers down the creamy satin of a strapless Audrey Hepburn–worthy sheath. "It would be criminal not to try these on. And even worse not to enjoy it."

"Agreed," I say, laying my hand on top of Bree's as if we're making a pact. "This is an exploratory mission. We need to make the most of it."

Daria returns with two more breathtaking gowns. When the

champagne arrives she asks Bree to pour then helps me into the first dress. The halter neck leaves the back open to just below my waist, after which it skims over my hips before widening.

"I wouldn't have thought to ask for a mermaid silhouette," I admit as I twirl in front of the mirror.

"I know," Bree says as she snaps a photo. "But I love how it hugs your body and emphasizes your curves."

The next is a strapless ball gown with a drop waist and a taffeta skirt.

"Oh my God. I love those long white gloves with that dress," Bree says. "And that tiara!"

She snaps another photo and pours more champagne.

I try on a one-shoulder bell-shaped gown embellished with crystals, a high-necked halter, and a short-sleeved lace number with a high-low hem.

"Ohhhh . . ." Bree sighs when I stand in front of her in the long satin sheath with the slit up one side. "I know I should be jealous that you look so great in everything, but . . . I can't because . . . you look so great in everything."

"You do," Daria says as she helps me step out of the sheath and into an A-line with off-the-shoulder long sleeves of illusion lace. "Excuse me for a minute. I need to take a call."

When she leaves Bree pours the last of the champagne. A mischievous look I haven't seen in years comes over her face.

"How many times would you say we watched *Pretty Woman*?" Bree asks.

"At least a thousand," I say, even though I'm pretty sure that's a conservative estimate.

"This is not Rodeo Drive and Daria couldn't be more helpful," Bree says. "But the whole time we've been here there's this line that keeps going through my head."

We grin at each other. In unison and without hesitation we say, "Big mistake. Huuuuge. I have to go shopping."

I reach for my phone. "Hey, Siri," I say. "Play 'Pretty Woman.'"

Bree grabs a wooden hanger and taps it against a clothing rod in time to the song's opening drum licks.

Ray Orbison's voice fills the dressing room. We automatically bob our heads.

Bree puts down her "drumstick" and grabs the empty champagne bottle while I throw imaginary dressing room curtains aside and twirl and strut—as much as you can in a designer wedding gown and heels.

She holds the bottle to her lips and then to mine as we sing our hearts out. In this moment we're sixteen again moving in tandem, bumping hips, raising our arms over our heads as we fall into the dance moves we choreographed a lifetime ago.

Bree's smile is ready and her laughter is light. Our interactions have been so few and so fraught for so long that I've forgotten this side of her. Or perhaps I'd just blocked it so I could bear to be without her.

"Merccccyyyyy!" We both lean into our "microphone" to give the word extra emphasis then prance in a circle, belting out the lyrics with everything we've got.

We're doing a final twirl, pretending to drum the last song licks when the dressing room door opens. Daria slips inside. "Nice choreography." She smiles. "You two have some moves."

We laugh and take mock bows.

"Just wanted to make sure I could dance in this gown," I say, trying to catch my breath. "You know, at the reception."

"Yeah," she laughs. "I can understand that."

"It looked highly danceable to me," Bree adds with an almost straight face.

"Definitely danceable," I agree. "I really appreciate you making this happen today," I say as Daria helps me out of the off-the-shoulder gown. "There are so many great choices. I'm going to need to give this all some thought."

Bree and I are still smiling when we climb into a cab for the ride back to the Upper West Side.

THE DRESS and my mother arise in my mind. As if she's following my train of thought—and at this point maybe she is—Bree says, "You do know that your parents are dating, right?"

My parents. "Are they really?" I can't quite picture it. "It's so weird to think of them that way. As a couple, I mean."

Bree sighs. "You need to speak to her, Lauren. My parents abandoned me and to this day they've never asked to be forgiven or even realize they've done anything to be forgiven for." She pauses, but only, it turns out, to take a breath. "Kendra has always put you first your entire life. She loves you unconditionally. She did what she did to try to protect you and Jake and his family. Think how hard that must have been when it seems pretty clear she loved him. Has probably always loved him. And could certainly have used his help and support—both financially and emotionally. Now when you finally have a chance to have both of your parents in your life are you really going to turn your back on your mother?"

Not too long ago (possibly even before brunch this morning) I might have labeled Bree's comments a tirade, but her concern is apparent and there's no doubting her sincerity.

Has Bree always been nicer than I am? More forgiving? "I hear you," I say finally. "But I keep thinking about how different my life would have been if my father had been a part of it."

"But he is now," Bree says. "And so is your mother." She draws a breath and I realize how carefully she's choosing her words. "I don't want to spoil what's been a really great day, but at least from where I'm sitting it doesn't look as if your life turned out so badly."

When I don't argue she continues, "I was just thinking. Maybe the Queen of Beach Reads could change direction if she wanted to. Reinvent herself. Or write something entirely different under another name. Like Stephen King, or Dean Koontz, or Agatha Christie, or . . . Lemony Snicket."

I manage to stop before the automatic knee-jerk protest.

Bree's right. There are plenty of ways to change course if I want to. I can even afford to take a break to figure it out if I choose. I feel a burst of excitement and relief at the possibility. Why have I been so afraid of even considering a change? "That's not entirely crazy."

"Gee, thanks."

We smile at each other. Genuine smiles. With nothing hidden or held back.

I've forgotten what it's like to have someone who's known me so long and so well and who's there to support me. I've given up so much more than I let myself realize.

❦

Back on the Upper West Side I have the cabdriver drop us off in front of my favorite ice cream place, Emack & Bolio's. Although I lobby for their famous ice cream pizza, we end up with ice cream cones that we lick as we amble over to Riverside Drive so that I can show Bree my favorite view out over the Henry Hudson Parkway to the Hudson River itself.

It's late in the afternoon when the sky begins to darken. Rain clouds appear in the distance.

"We could walk down to Columbus Circle and the Time Warner Center. Or I could see if there's a recital at Juilliard." I take out my cell phone prepared to Google.

"I think I've gone as far as I'm going today," Bree replies. "I'm whipped, but God, I can't believe you live right in the center of everything."

"Yeah, it's pretty great."

"I only had the vaguest idea of what I gave up by not coming to New York with you like we planned," she says softly. "And once I'd made the decision I guess I didn't want to know."

"Sometimes evasion and denial are our best defenses," I say, thinking about my reaction to my mother and my initial reluctance to acknowledge Bree's talent and hard work. "Let's go home and chill. If we get hungry later we can order in."

Back at my place we settle on the couch. My limbs are loose. My jaw aches pleasantly and I realize we've been talking and laughing for the better part of a day, which is something you can't do with everyone.

Later I order a pizza from Patsy's and it doesn't occur to me to ask what Bree wants on it. We ate our first slices of pepperoni with extra cheese and sausage when we were about six years old and it remained our favorite through college.

When our pizza arrives, we carry it and a bottle of wine to the living room and set them on the coffee table. We continue to talk while I pour wine in glasses and she puts pizza slices on paper plates.

I'm struck by how good I feel. How great it is not to weigh each word or worry that what I've said has been taken the wrong way. Twenty years without your best friend is like a life sentence. I need this to be more than a temporary reprieve.

When Bree pauses in her story about something one of the B's said at a recent book club meeting I say, "I'm so sorry, Bree. Sorry for holding a grudge for so long, for treating you as 'less than' and for forgetting—or possibly blocking—how talented a writer you are."

When she doesn't speak I continue, "I hate that we've lost all these years, and I especially hate that I hesitated for even a minute to tell you how great your novel is."

Her smile takes up most of her face as I continue, "Despite the fact that we had to settle for real pizza instead of the ice cream version, this has been one of the best days I've had since I came to New York. And that includes the red-letter days when I signed my first publishing contract, hit the *New York Times* bestseller list, and slept with Spencer; an unforgettable experience in its own right that possibly deserves its own holiday."

Bree's smile grows even larger. In her eyes I see the same re-lief I feel. "I'm so glad we had this day together. I can't tell you how great it is not to have to pretend I haven't missed you. To finally be able to be honest with each other," she says just as I'm wondering how on earth I lived without her all this time.

Then we both start crying. I'm dimly aware that my tears are falling on the pizza and that this will make the crust soggy. I couldn't care less. It's so odd to smile and sob at the same time. To be so sad and perfectly happy in the same instant.

If there's such a thing as a monkey's wedding of the heart, this is it.

Thirty-seven

Lauren

I don't normally drink to excess, but I can tell when I open my eyes early Sunday morning that I have a hangover and that it's going to be memorable.

Bree and I sat up way too late drinking wine and laughing and finally catching up without all the filters and censors in place. I lost count of the number of times she replayed my video praising *Heart of Gold*. But if you could wear a groove in a cell phone hers would have a big one.

The sky is that deep, ugly gray that tells you it means business. Rain spatters the windows. What little light makes it through the windows is half-hearted, as if the sun, too, has been drinking and just can't give its all. I pull on my robe. As I tiptoe past the open door of my office I see Bree snoring lightly on the sofa bed. She's curled into a fetal position, wrapped around her manuscript.

Even before I put on the coffee, I down three Tylenol with two full glasses of water—something I wish I'd remembered to do last night. The rain intensifies as I make the first pot of coffee, and I promise myself that the minute Bree leaves for the airport—something I'm no longer looking forward to—I'm climbing right back into bed.

Breakfast sandwiches have been ordered and I'm ready for a second cup of coffee when Bree appears at the top of the stairs.

Her eyes are at half-mast. Her hair is a rat's nest and she winces at each step as she makes her way slowly down the stairs.

"Here." I shake two Tylenol into her hand and pour her a glass of water. "Drink all of it."

"Thanks." It's half whisper and half groan.

"Go sit." I motion to the living room. "I'll bring the coffee."

There's another groan of thanks as I join her on the sofa and hand over a steaming mug. She lowers her face over it and inhales. Then she rubs her neck and does a slow neck roll to work out the kinks.

"I've never actually seen someone sleep with a manuscript before," I say when she seems a little more awake.

"Yeah. I don't recommend it." She does another slow neck roll. "But I couldn't seem to let go of it." A small smile plays on her lips. "I watched your video the second I woke up. I was afraid I only dreamed you telling me it was wonderful."

"No." I meet her gaze. "Not a dream."

"So I promise this will be the last time I ask. But I just need to double-confirm everything in the light or"—she nods to the window—"not so light of day. I want to be sure you weren't just trying to make me feel better."

"This is me you're talking to," I reply. "Gentle is not my default setting."

She nods. A fresh smile flickers. "So just to recap. You think that with some work it will sell?"

"I do."

"To a traditional publisher."

"Yes."

We sip our coffee in silence while rain beats against the windows and headlights flash in the darkness. Umbrellas bob by on the sidewalks below.

"In that case I don't think I hate being forty anymore," Bree says. "Forty's not too late to be published for the first time, is it?"

"Given how slowly publishing moves you could be forty-one or even forty-two by the time it hits the shelves. But I believe it's highly possible. And from what I've read and seen, a lot of writers are just getting started at forty. People change fields, decide it's time to follow a new dream. Some think you have to live for a while first to have something to write about."

"Do you think it's too old to be single?" she asks quietly. "If it comes to that?"

"Clearly not. As I and millions of others have proven."

She glances down into her coffee then back at me. "I was thinking about Clay giving you my manuscript. That was really considerate of him. It shows love. It makes me wonder if maybe we have enough love for each other to save our marriage. If we both try."

I know what she wants to hear. "Are you looking for the truth or for reassurance?"

"I forgot just how direct you can be," Bree says. "I don't suppose you'd lie if I needed you to?"

"I think it would be great if you guys could turn things around, but I think you need to be careful to let him prove himself first," I say as gently as I can.

The intercom squawks, announcing a delivery. A few minutes later there's a knock on the door. I retrieve our egg, cheese, and bacon sandwiches and pass them to Bree. Then I fetch us both another cup of coffee.

"I'm glad it didn't rain yesterday," Bree says when I settle back on the couch and unwrap my sandwich. "I might not have seen Central Park and Strawberry Fields or eaten on the patio at Tavern on the Green or discovered that there's such a thing as ice cream pizza." Her gaze is pinned outside, but we're both focused inward.

She gives a long, questioning sigh. "How could I have let myself miss all this?" Her gesture encompasses all of New York. "I don't know what I was thinking."

We take a bite of our sandwiches, which I have been madly in love with since I first discovered them.

She groans. "I missed breakfast sandwiches."

We eat and sip coffee for a few minutes. I'm licking the last bit of cheese from my fingers when a text dings in on Bree's phone.

"Oh man. It's from Delta. Two-hour weather delay." She thumbs through her apps and reads something. "Hey, can you put on the Weather Channel?"

On the TV we see a map of the eastern half of the United States. The area from north Georgia up to New York is outlined in a menacing electric green. I turn up the volume and we hear the meteorologist, who is using a pointer to show the nor'easter that's hunkered down over the East Coast. "Severe thunderstorms with damaging winds and torrential rain are currently drenching cities up and down the Atlantic coast. Hundreds of flights have been delayed or canceled. We'll be bringing you more as this storm develops."

Bree

We're still watching the Weather Channel when my phone rings. It's Clay, whom I haven't spoken to since I left on Tuesday. He doesn't say anything when I tell him about the delay. "Is the weather as bad as it looks on television?"

"Yeah." There's a pause. "Did you ever speak to Lily?"

"No. She didn't even respond to the photos from Kleinfeld's. I'm going to have to have a talk with her about not picking up when I get home. That's not acceptable." I'm careful not to look at Lauren as I say this.

"So, you never heard from her at all?" There's something too tentative in the question.

"Clay, what's going on?"

The silence that follows causes the small hairs on the back of my neck to rise.

"I'm, uh, not exactly sure where she is."

"What . . . what does that mean?" I sit up and clutch the phone tighter to my ear.

More silence and then, "We had an argument Friday morning before she left for school. I asked her to pick up the mess she left in the kitchen and she went off on me. I lost my temper. She got in my face and . . . I . . . well . . . it got ugly. She yelled at me, told me that she hated me. And then she just stormed out."

"Oh, Clay. I asked you to be careful with her." I feel Lauren's eyes on me and I try to dial back my anger.

"I couldn't help it. She was giving me all kinds of grief and . . . I didn't appreciate being told to fuck off by a sixteen-year-old. Then later she texted that she was going to spend the weekend at Dana's so I just . . . Well, I thought we could both use the weekend to cool off. And then you'd be back . . ."

"Good grief, Clay. *You're* the parent. You're supposed to be present and paying attention. She shouldn't have spoken to you that way, but you can't huff off in a snit because your sixteen-year-old daughter said something nasty to you. That's what *sixteen-year-olds* do." I rub my forehead as if that will somehow clear my thoughts. "What did Dana's mother say when you checked in with her on Friday night? Was Lily okay?"

This silence is even longer. I get up from the couch and move to the window, but I have no idea what I'm looking at. Everything's a blur.

"I didn't think to call Loretta. Like I said, I thought we could use the weekend off from each other and she's spent the night there plenty of times." His tone is defensive, aggrieved. "You should never have gone off to New York for a conference in the middle of everything."

"You are not going to turn the tables this time. I came here on business and you were in charge. Parenting is not a nine-to-five job with weekends off."

He doesn't respond to this, which tells me that whatever's coming next is not something I want to hear.

"Last night the weather started turning and I figured I'd pick her up this morning." There's a change in his voice. A tremor of what sounds like fear.

My heart is beating way too fast and I can hear the blood throbbing in my ears. "And?"

"Lily wasn't there. She spent the night Friday night but on Saturday morning *Shane* picked her up to go to a house party at a river cabin up near Richmond. She asked Dana to cover for her if I called or came by."

"Which you didn't. Because you were . . . Did you say Shane?"

"Umm-hmm."

"That's the boy you teased her about." *The one she wanted to ask her out so badly.*

"Yeah."

I can't seem to drag breath into my lungs. I turn and start pacing the living room.

"Does Dana know which river?"

"No."

"Did she and Lily talk after Lily left?" For Lily, "talking" is teenager speak for texting.

"No." His voice drops. "She figured that was because they were having such a good time."

I reach the end of the room and turn back. I'm afraid to stop moving. I'm afraid to think about what kind of good time Dana thought Lily was having. "So assuming they actually went to this house party they're on a river somewhere near Richmond and no one's heard from or spoken to her since yesterday morning?"

I try to dial back my anger, but I prefer it to the panic bubbling up inside me. Lily could be anywhere. Anything could have happened to her. And with the stalled-out nor'easter wreaking havoc all the way up the coast Shane might or might not be the biggest danger. "If anything's happened to her I will *never* forgive you."

Another text dings in informing me that all flights out of New York have been canceled at the exact moment I most need to get home. I check the television and see the same information scrolling across the bottom of the screen.

"Nothing's going to happen to her," he says, but his voice shakes and I know it's all bravado. "I'm going to drive up there and get her."

"Drive where? We don't even know where she really is." My voice gets louder. My head spins. "Wait." I think back to the conversation Lily and I had about Shane. She said she'd die if he asked someone besides her out, but she never mentioned him again. "He's an athlete, right? You said he played basketball when you teased her about him. His last name starts with an . . . an *A* or a *C*." I try to pull it up in my mind, but I'm so panicked I can't find it. "Can you look up the basketball team roster? Or. No. Wait . . . I'm not sure but I think his last name's Arnold . . . or Amberton . . . or . . . wait. I'm pretty sure it's Adams. They're relatively new here but his parents' contact information should be in the school and PTA directories. They're on the top shelf of my office bookcase." Then it hits me. "Oh my God! They could have been in an accident. She could be in a hospital somewhere. Or . . ." I think but don't say *a morgue.*

Lauren is on her feet and moving toward me.

"No, we're not going there, Bree. Not yet," Clay says. "I'll speak to this Shane's parents and find out where they think he is. We need an address—some kind of starting point. And a phone number for this boy or the cabin itself."

I want to shout at him. To yell and swear and ask him what the hell he was thinking. But more than anything I need to find Lily. Given the weather and all the people now stranded and hoping to fly out tomorrow, it could be days before I can get on a flight back to Norfolk, where my car is parked. I can't just sit here doing nothing.

"I'm going to get a rental car." I scroll through the apps on my phone. "According to Google maps it's just over six hours to Richmond via I-95."

I turn and stride to the stairs. Lauren falls in behind me.

"I'll keep trying Lily's phone, too," he says. "And we'll let each other know if we hear anything or if she turns up, okay?"

I hang up and throw my phone on the sofa bed then put my suitcase beside it.

"What is it? What happened to Lily?" Lauren is standing beside me.

I pull out the first clothing I come to, rip off my pajamas, and start putting on the jeans and T-shirt. "Short version—she and Clay had a fight and then she went off with some boy to a cabin on a river somewhere near Richmond. He . . ." I stuff my pajamas into the bag. Then I race-walk to the bathroom, scoop up my toiletries, and cram them in on top of my pajamas. "I'm sorry but I don't have time for this. Is there a car rental place anywhere around here?" I zip up my bag.

"Yeah," Lauren says. "There's an Avis at 76th and Broadway. Not far. Are you seriously considering driving all the way to Richmond in this weather?"

"Of course. I have to. I can't just sit here. I'm . . . I've got to go."

We look at each other. She takes my phone and her thumbs fly. Then she hands it back. "Here's the Avis website. Go ahead and call and make sure they have a car. I just need a couple minutes to get dressed." She turns and sprints to her room. "There's no way in hell you're going alone."

Thirty-eight

~✿~

The only car available to drive is a tiny Ford Focus that is as basic as a car can get. Lauren looks dubious but we don't have time to wait for a bigger, better car or satellite radio or automatic seats. My daughter is with a boy we don't know in a place we haven't yet discovered and I'm not about to waste a second getting on the road.

I scrawl my signature across the paperwork and we throw our things in the backseat. Lauren gets behind the wheel to get us out of the city. I stare straight out the windshield, twisting my hands in my lap as she follows the GPS prompts onto the Henry Hudson Parkway, through the Lincoln Tunnel, onto 495 to New Jersey. I assumed the weather would keep people off the road—the puddles are already deep enough to swim in—but New Yorkers don't seem to be fazed in the least by what Mother Nature has decided to unleash on them.

It takes a little more than an hour to work our way onto I-95 south. We intend to stay on it until we have a specific location to aim for.

"You okay?" Lauren asks once we've merged all the way onto I-95. I almost can't hear her over the slap of the windshield wipers and the drumming of rain on the roof. It's like being in a tin can that someone is holding under the kitchen faucet.

"Not really."

I reach forward and hit redial for Lily's phone for the thousandth time. It goes directly to voice mail. Which means it's either off or not receiving a signal. "I just can't believe this is happening."

"I know." Lauren reaches to turn on the radio. Her foot presses down on the gas pedal. "But we're going to find her. Everything's going to be all right."

Thunder booms. Lightning flashes, and I can't remember what counting between them is supposed to tell you. The car shimmies so badly it feels as if we might go airborne any minute.

I stare straight ahead, straining to see through the curtain of rain that has cut us off from everything and the windshield wipers that seem to be all slap and no wipe.

"Too bad this car didn't come with one of those inflatable potties," Lauren says as I strain to see through the deluge. "But then I guess we're lucky it came with tires."

Tense as I am, I snort. For the first time since Clay's phone call, I take a full breath.

"Do you remember that Girl Scout camping trip when we tried to make it the whole weekend without having to use those latrines?" she asks, reaching into our past for another shot of humor.

I tear my eyes from the almost-impenetrable darkness beyond the windshield to look at Lauren. Her hands are clenched tightly on the wheel. Her chin is thrust forward in the angle of determination I've trusted since kindergarten. "I will never forget that camping trip," I say as drolly as I can manage. "The latrine you talked me out of would have been a better choice than the poison ivy patch I used instead."

"Amen, sister." Lauren laughs and I join her. For at least a few seconds we're both somewhere else.

Two and a half hours into the drive, we finally pull into a rest stop just outside of Delaware City. We get soaked during our race to the bathroom and the switching of seats.

I try to adjust my seat but it has only two positions: grossly uncomfortable and torture chamber.

The wind and rain intensify the farther south we get. I squint to try to see through the rain then squint to read the screen of my phone that Lauren has placed in a holder that's attached to an air vent. According to Waze, we've picked up and lost the same two minutes for the last hour and there's not much information coming from drivers ahead of us. In fact, the rain is so heavy we don't know if there *are* drivers ahead of us. Or behind us. Or even beside us.

We debate whether you're supposed to put on your hazards in order to be seen through the downpour—I am for, Lauren is against—and whether we'll need to stop for gas—we agree that if there's anything worse than driving in this storm it would be running out of gas and getting stranded in it.

My heartbeat drums in my ears. My brain fills with horrifying images: Lily huddled in a dark cabin without a roof. Or pinned beneath a fallen tree. Or standing on the roof of a car to evade floodwaters that threaten to wash her away.

The fear of not getting to Lily in time is constant and excruciating, even though I don't know what *in time* means. For all I know terrible things have already happened. And I wasn't there to stop them or protect her.

A couple of hours later we pull off into a service plaza and do our impersonation of a pit crew at Daytona (if in fact race car drivers take potty breaks). I top off the tank while Lauren grabs some bottled waters. I'm still behind the wheel when we pull back out. We're both already exhausted from straining to see through the blinding rain and keeping the car in its lane despite the gusting wind. And from holding back the panic.

When my phone rings Lauren reaches for it and puts it on speakerphone. "It's Clay."

There are no greetings or small talk. I envy the fact that

he's had specific tasks to occupy him while I've had nothing to do but keep the tin car from shimmying off the road or into some unseen vehicle while imagining Lily in heart-stopping scenarios that we always arrive just minutes too late to prevent. Worry gnaws at me. If it were possible to have an imagination surgically removed, I'd have mine plucked out this minute.

"I got Shane's cell number from Dana but it goes directly to voice mail just like Lily's, so I'm guessing there's no cell reception wherever they are. I haven't been able to reach the Adamses by phone, either," Clay says. "So I'm on my way to their house—they live up in Kill Devil Hills. Charlie Hatch in the sheriff's department is reaching out to the Richmond police to ask them to be on the lookout. He's requested what's called an ATL, or Attempt to Locate, and promised to keep me posted. I also checked in with Kendra, but she hasn't heard anything from Lily."

Lauren and I exchange glances at the mention of her mother, but within seconds our eyes are back on the road. There's little room in either of our brains for anything more than seeing where we're going and beating back the fear about what we'll find when we get there.

The car rattles crazily for a twenty-mile stretch between Maryland and DC. The wind's so strong my hands hurt from gripping the steering wheel and my head throbs from trying to see through the rain.

"It's bad enough flying in something designed to stay in the air," Lauren whispers, her thoughts mirroring my own. "I'd be taking Xanax right now if I'd remembered to bring them."

"The last thing we need right now is to relax. We need our wits about us."

"Too late for that," she says. "I'm starting to feel like this car. I don't have any cylinders firing."

It takes a few minutes to notice that the car is shimmying

less violently. I straighten and loosen my grip on the wheel slightly. "Do you feel that?"

"The wind," Lauren says. "I think it's starting to drop."

I'm still peering through the windshield. For the first time I see moving shapes in the distance. "And the rain's letting up some. Or am I imagining it?"

When I loosen my grip a little more, the car doesn't careen into another lane. I exhale the breath I feel like I've been holding for hours.

For a few minutes we just breathe.

Lauren puts her hand on my arm. "I really do believe everything's going to be okay. And being positive isn't going to hurt or jinx anything. We'll deal with whatever happens together."

I draw in another less-shaky breath. "Thanks. I know. You're right. It's just . . ."

"Yeah."

We both jump when the phone rings. "You're on speaker, Clay," Lauren says again. "What have you got?"

"The Adamses weren't as receptive as they might have been. Their son told them he was going up to the family cabin on the Mattaponi River to fish with some of his friends, and they see no reason to believe otherwise despite the horrible weather. They confirmed that there's no reception at the cabin or the area around it. I'm texting you the address right now."

The address dings in to my phone. Lauren presses the screen a few times and Waze begins to reset itself as Clay continues, "I've just filled up the truck and I'm on 158. I look to be about two and a half to three hours away. Kendra and Jake may be ahead of me. They insisted on coming."

"We're under two hours now," Lauren says. "So we should get there first."

I press my foot down on the accelerator and the tin car jumps forward. For the first time since we picked it up I actually wish it *could* fly.

〆⁀

At last, we turn off Highway 360 and into an area that was once woods and farmland, but now contains pockets of civilization and new development. It's three thirty in the afternoon. The rain is a steady drizzle that falls on us and splatters the narrow paved road that curves past the occasional mobile home or derelict barn or burned-out building. Even smaller roads appear to branch off and lead toward the river that we glimpse between trees and vines. Other roads are dirt driveways with mailboxes. Most of these have wooden signs with owner's names carved into them nailed to a tree or fence post.

"There it is." Lauren points to a crude sign that reads simply ADAMS #142 and we turn onto a smaller, rutted road. The ground is soft and pockmarked with pools of rainwater. Tree limbs and branches litter the ground. One huge oak is split down one side from a lightning strike. The river has risen and sloshed over the bank, but it hasn't reached the cabin.

The cabin sits in a clearing facing the river. It looks tired and worn, sagging from exhaustion. The gray sky doesn't help. At first I'm afraid that no one's there. But then I see a mud-spattered red pickup parked at the far edge of the clearing.

Light shines through several windows and there's a flicker of what must be a television. There may not be cell reception here but at least there's electricity. I don't know what we're going to find inside. If there was ever a party it's over. If a group of guys came fishing they all fit inside that red truck. The only boat is an ancient canoe sitting upside down near the truck.

"How do you want to play this?" Lauren asks as we climb out of the car, our backs stiff and our legs cramped from the drive.

"Play what?"

"Do you think we should do good cop, bad cop? You can be the good cop if you want."

"We're here to get Lily and take her home. I'm just going to be the mom cop. You can be the 'auntie' cop. If you need to have a role to play."

I square my shoulders and we walk to the cabin and up the sagging steps to the sagging front porch. The fear and adrenaline that got me through the drive are jangling inside me, building inexorably. I need to know that Lily is okay.

With one last deep breath I rap on the front door, which has also seen better days. I'm about to knock again when footsteps thud across a wood floor. The door opens and a tall, lanky boy of about seventeen stares out at us. He's got a halo of blond hair, wide-set blue eyes, and even, almost delicate, features. But his eyes are wary and the expression on his face is nowhere close to angelic. His body blocks the opening and the rest of the room from view. I feel Lauren shifting her weight onto the balls of her feet. Slowly she pulls something out of her pocket. I have to crane my neck to look the boy in the eye. I'm not tall enough to look over his shoulder.

"Shane?"

"Yeah?" He looks down at me and I can see that his eyes are bloodshot and more than a little glazed.

"I'm Lily's mother." Despite the way my heartbeat kicks up, I speak slowly and clearly. Like you would to an animal that might or might not be dangerous.

"Yeah?"

"Yes. And this is her aunt Lauren. We've come to take her home."

"You're a little late for that. *Ma'am.*"

My stomach clenches at his words and the sarcastic *ma'am.* "What do you mean?"

"She left."

"When?"

"A while ago. She'd been all pissy and holed up in the bedroom most of the time since we got here anyway." He is clearly put out.

I look into his eyes but I can't read them or him. "What did you do to her to make her leave in a nor'easter?" I demand.

"Beats me." He shrugs as if it doesn't matter. As if Lily doesn't matter. Anger surges through me. I want to grab him and shake him until he loses the attitude. "But she's not here."

Lauren and I exchange glances. She's only a few inches shorter than him but my head doesn't reach his shoulders. If I surprised him with a headbutt to the stomach could I throw him off-balance enough to get inside? I'm way too furious to worry about technique.

I take a step forward, crowding him, looking up to stare him in the eye. "We won't be leaving until we see for ourselves that Lily isn't here."

"You've got to be shitting me."

Lauren steps up beside me. Together we stand our ground. Finally, when I think we're actually going to have to rush him and force our way in, he shrugs again and steps aside. "Whatever."

We step into the living room. The inside of the cabin is as old and weathered as the outside. It smells of mildew and neglect with a slight lacing of marijuana. I scan the space, looking for signs of Lily's presence, but I see only a filthy plaid sofa and a couple of chairs aimed at a much newer flat-screen TV.

We ignore Shane as we work our way through the kitchen with its ancient linoleum floor, even-more-ancient appliances, and a small table in front of a window that overlooks the river. There's also a bathroom that was last updated (and possibly cleaned) in the '70s, a wood-paneled bedroom, and a loft outfitted with a set of bunk beds.

Lauren and I don't speak as we inspect every inch of the cabin, opening closets and large cupboards in fury and in case he isn't just an asshole but a homicidal maniac who has gagged Lily and stuffed her away somewhere.

"Your parents think you're fishing with the guys," I say when we've looked everywhere.

We get the shrug again. Shane Adams is sullen and self-centered and I don't think he's going to grow up to be a rocket scientist, but I can see how a sixteen-year-old girl might interpret his surly silence as moody or even sensitive. Lord knows I have experience with seeing what I want when it comes to male behavior.

"Told you." He smirks. "She couldn't wait to spend the weekend together and then once we got here she didn't want to have anything to do with me. Wanted me to take her home in the middle of the storm."

"Gosh, she wasn't bowled over by all this and you?" Lauren's voice drips sarcasm. "Hard to imagine."

All I can think, is *Thank God she came to her senses.* And if I find out this boy has touched her against her will, I'm going to come back here and get rid of the smirk and the shrug.

"You don't bring a sixteen-year-old girl into the middle of nowhere and then refuse to take her home when she asks to leave!" I bite out. "Where is she now?"

He spreads his hands. "Who knows? Walkerton's a mile up the road. Maybe she went there." He shrugs. Again.

"I hope to hell you didn't manage to take advantage of her, seeing as how she's a minor and that would be a crime," Lauren says.

"Damn straight." I touch Lauren's shoulder. "Let's go. We know where he lives."

I throw open the door and we step out onto the porch. Shane follows us.

"She wanted to come here. She practically begged me to bring her." We're halfway to the rental car when he shouts, "She talked a big game, said she couldn't wait to do the deed. But in the end she was nothing but a tease!"

Lauren and I stop and turn. Lauren's face is flushed with anger.

"I know you didn't just say that." Blood roars in my ears. "If you were a whit or two smarter you'd know enough to be ashamed of yourself."

Lauren shakes her head. "Someone needs to teach you a few lessons about the opposite sex and how to treat them."

"Yeah. Right," he scoffs.

I'm pretty sure I could rip his head off with my bare hands right now, but Lauren is already moving toward him. When she gets close she doesn't say a word. She simply twists her body, kicks one leg out, and leaves the ground. As she completes her turn the rotation of her body drives her foot into his chest and knocks him to the ground where he lands in a heap in a mud puddle, like an oversize rag doll.

I look at Lauren in shock as I race to her side.

"What? He asked for it. Literally."

"Where in the world did you learn how to do that?"

It's Lauren's turn to shrug. "That first day in New York when I got mugged I vowed it would never happen again. At least not without a fight." She shrugs again, this time with satisfaction. "I've been practicing martial arts ever since. I take a refresher self-defense course every year." She opens one hand. A small black canister of pepper spray is cupped in her palm. "And I don't leave home without this. If he hadn't gone down so easily I would have emptied it in his face."

"Wow." I shake my head in wonder and gratitude. "Thank you. I don't think I could have borne seeing him smirk in the rearview mirror."

"My pleasure. I'm glad Lily got herself out of here."

"I wish she'd had the sense not to come." I stare down at the limp body of Shane Adams. "Or that I'd been home to stop her." A shudder passes through me. "I know it's the mess between Clay and me that drove her to act out this way."

"She's a sixteen-year-old girl, Bree. Remember when we were that age? He behaved like a shit, but she isn't the first girl who got herself in a bad situation."

She slips the canister back in her pocket then crouches down to snap her fingers in the boy's face.

He groans and blinks.

"He's conscious. Grab an arm. Much as I'd like to leave him here, if there's more rain the river could rise this high." Lauren takes one large limp arm and I take the other. We drag him through the mud, hitting every possible puddle, and up the steps to dump him on the porch.

"Come on, I'll drive," she says.

As we leave the cabin behind I reassure myself that if Lily were "pissy" and determined enough to walk out of this place, a mile and some rain wouldn't have fazed her.

Thirty-nine

❧

We're approaching State Route 629 with Lauren at the wheel when we come within range of a cell tower and messages start dinging onto our phones. Mine shows missed calls from Clay and Kendra and a number I don't recognize.

"Where are you?" Clay asks, picking up my return call on the first ring.

"We're just getting into Walkerton."

"Thank God," he says. "I'm still about thirty minutes away. But I had a call from a woman named Sue. She works in Walkerton in a place called Scott's Store. Lily's there. She's . . . the woman said Lily's phone was damaged and that she was . . ." His voice trails off. "Apparently she was too shaken to make the call herself. I . . . I could hear her sobbing in the background." He sounds like he's about to cry himself.

I don't offer even a hint of sympathy. As far as I'm concerned he could have prevented all of this if he'd been tuned in and paying attention to Lily. The fear and adrenaline that've been pumping through my bloodstream since I found out she was missing have left me jangling with a dangerous kind of energy.

"Kendra and Jake shouldn't be far behind you," he continues. "I had a text a few minutes ago and gave them the address. I'll see you there."

Walkerton is neither big nor bustling. The few businesses that exist are closed, and I have no idea if it's because of the storm or simply because it's a Sunday. Scott's Store is a small, pale-yellow clapboard building with gas pumps, an ice cooler, and a Coke machine out front. Only one or two cars are in its parking lot. Lauren's barely brought the Focus to a halt when I open the door and jump out. Unlike the Ford that has kept its wheels on the ground, I fly into the building, which seems to be a convenience store/restaurant/gas station.

"Mom!" Lily's in my arms before I know how either of us got there. I squeeze her to me, cupping her head to my shoulder, breathing in a shuddering sigh of relief. She's here. She's wet and bedraggled beneath the towel around her shoulders. Her face is mud streaked, but she's alive and intact. I hold her and we sway back and forth. Both of us are crying. I bow my head in thanks that turns to fury as she sobs out the whole story before I have the strength to ask the first question.

"He told me it was a house party. Only no one else ever came." Her words are tangled up with her tears. Both land on my shoulder.

She lifts her head and I look into her filthy tear-streaked face to the horror shining starkly in her eyes. "I thought he liked me. He acted like he did. But then when we were alone all he cared about was . . . you know. Only . . . I . . . I couldn't do it. When he went out to move his truck, I locked myself in the bedroom and pushed the dresser in front of the door . . . and . . . the electricity went out and that whole place shook in the storm. I was so scared." She takes a shuddering breath. "When it finally slowed, I begged him to take me home but he . . ." She's crying again. "He called me names. And he, he said that he was going to tell everybody I did it whether I did or not so I might as well come out and stop acting like a baby." She sobs and trembles in my arms.

"How did you get here?"

The tears continue to spill. Her voice wobbles. "When the wind finally started dying down I crawled out the bedroom window as quietly as I could and I ran."

I can barely breathe as her words tumble out. I picture the ugly sneer on Shane Adams's face and my anger spirals higher. I wish we'd left him lying in the mud like the pig that he is.

"Shh . . . it's all right." I smooth her hair as I try to calm her, to calm us both. "It's over now. We all do things that don't turn out the way we expect. See people the way we want them to be instead of the way they really are." This last one hits a bit too close to home. "I wish you'd never put yourself in that situation. But you were strong. You did what you needed to to get out of there."

Her tears slow but we're still locked in each other's arms. I don't know how I can ever let go.

I raise my head and pull the towel more tightly around her as I continue to soothe and murmur how much I love her. Lauren comes inside and it feels completely natural for her to walk up and put her arms around both of us. We hold on to one another and sway.

Lauren

Locked in a hug with Lily and Bree, I feel Lily begin to calm as she listens to the person she trusts most in this world. The person who would do anything for her, give up anything for her. The woman who would have gotten into a tin can of a car on her own if she'd had to and raced through a raging storm to find her.

Because that's what mothers do. Or at least mothers like Bree. And . . . like mine. How many times did my mother dry my tears, tell me everything was going to be all right, that she loved me no matter what?

Lily's tears finally begin to hiccup to a stop. We're still swaying, the elderly woman behind the counter smiling compassionately, when the front door opens and footsteps sound on the floor. I look up and see my mother watching us. I know that if this was before my father's appearance she would already be here swaying and holding us. Our eyes meet and I have this urge to walk—or possibly run—into her arms and rock and sway without any thought of who might be watching or who did or didn't do the wrong thing or why. But it's Lily who breaks up the hug and runs to throw her arms around Kendra. My mother smooth's Lily's hair and whispers in her ear. Just like she always did for me.

Then Jake comes inside and that moment when I might have silently and effortlessly healed our breach is gone.

By the time Clay arrives Bree has already hugged and thanked Sue, who ushered us to a Formica-topped table to which she delivered food that none of us can eat. Lily sits, hollow eyed, her hands wrapped around a foam cup of hot chocolate that Sue placed in front of her.

Bree freezes when Clay walks in. But when Lily gets up and rushes to her father Bree follows. Whatever drove Lily into Shane Adams's lair, whatever confusion or anger she felt, whatever she has or hasn't blamed her parents for, don't seem to matter. In this moment, she clearly needs them both.

Bree's shoulders remain tight, her smile frozen, when Clay pulls her up against him. It's clear that she's furious with him—and possibly herself—even as they form their own small circle of comfort.

"I came straight here," Clay says as the three of them take seats at the table. Bree's arm goes around Lily's shoulders. "But I'm tempted to pay a visit to Shane Adams."

"He's already been taken care of," Bree says, aiming a small smile at me. "He's probably still lying on that porch trying to get up. Lauren martial-arts'd him."

"You knocked him down?" Jake asks in disbelief.

I nod humbly. "I did. He was practically begging for it."

"God, I'm sorry I missed that," Clay adds.

"It was a complete knockout," Bree says. "He didn't know what hit him."

"Really?" Lily asks.

"Really," Bree says. "I wish I'd taken a picture of him lying there, but we were in a hurry to get here."

"Thank you," Lily says quietly. "I'm so sorry for everything. But . . . thank you."

"Oh, believe me. It was my pleasure." I reach for her hand and a lighter tone. "If he gives you any trouble or tries to shoot his mouth off, tell him we took pictures and that you'll be glad to post them to social media. He didn't strike me as the kind of guy who'd want to admit to being knocked down by a woman."

I glance outside and notice that the sky is beginning to clear. It's almost six P.M.

"So, what happens now?" Jake asks.

"If Lily's up to it we'll drive to ORF to turn in the rental car and pick mine up. Then we'll caravan home," Bree says. At Lily's quiet nod Bree turns to me. "Any chance you could come back down for a few days? Or do you want a ride to the airport?"

Jake and my mother exchange glances before he says, "I just checked the weather and it looks like the storm has moved up to DC. But there's some indication that it could stall out over the northeastern seaboard. I'm not sure anything's flying in or out of New York over the next few days."

He looks at my mother again. She nods as if she's afraid that the sound of her voice will cause me to say no. And I hate that she's right.

"There's something your mother and I would like to show you in Richmond. It's just an hour drive from here. We could stay over and then get you to the Richmond airport in the morning if flights into New York resume."

I've barely thought about home other than to let Spencer

know we made it here and that Lily's safe. And I can't seem to marshal my thoughts or my will.

"You know what?" Bree gives me a look I once knew well. "I think I need one last potty break before we get on the road."

"Right." I give a small nod. "I mean, yes. I could use the bathroom, too. I'll come with you."

In the bathroom neither of us makes a move toward a stall. We stand in front of the mirror as we have a million times in the past. She reaches up and puts her hands on my shoulders. Our foreheads touch, which requires her to go on tiptoe and me to lean down. We commune in silence for several long moments. Slowly, almost regretfully, she pulls back.

"I just wanted to thank you again for today. I would have come myself if I'd had to—but I'm so glad we made the drive together." She doesn't break eye contact. "And I'll be forever grateful that you drop-kicked Shane Adams."

We share a smile of satisfaction. Hers goes crooked and then disappears.

"I hope you won't be mad at me for saying this, but I think you should take Jake and your mother up on their offer." She swallows and her eyes fill with tears. "Today was awful and I can't help thinking how much worse it might have ended. Life is short. We're all doing the best we can. When we love someone and especially if they love us, we need to cut them some slack. No one's perfect, Lauren. Maybe not even you."

She watches my face. I know she's afraid that I'm going to huff out of here and turn my back on our friendship that finally seems to be back on track. But I can't be mad at her for speaking the truth. That's what best friends are supposed to do.

She smiles in acknowledgment and understanding, having clearly read my face, if not my mind. "Good. And if you can spare a couple more days, come back with them. Maybe we can brainstorm a new career path for you. And another book for me." Her smile deepens. "I've been working on *Heart of Gold* for so long I'm not sure I'll have the nerve to start something else. Whitney and Heath might think I'm cheating on them if I take up with new characters."

We find the others outside. Jake has a protective arm around my mother's shoulders. I walk toward them, my steps slow and measured. I still feel the anger inside me, but it's such a small and pitiful emotion next to the love I feel for her and that she's always showered on me. My parents look so right together. I'm not certain exactly where I fit.

"Are you sure you have room for me?"

"Absolutely," they answer without even glancing at each other.

"Let me get your bag out of the rental car." Jake walks to the Ford Focus.

My mother smiles but still seems afraid to make the first move.

I climb into the backseat. Like a forty-year-old child going on a family vacation. For the very first time.

Forty

_____

∽

Kendra

There's not a lot of small talk on the drive to Richmond. I can't quite believe that Jake and I are driving home in a car with our daughter in the back. I refuse to let myself think of all the years we could have been doing this.

I keep checking on Lauren in the rearview mirror, thinking I need to say *something*, though I'm not sure whether that something should be another apology or an explanation of where we're taking her. Each time I look, she's dozing. Or at least pretending to.

Jake's the one who suggested this trip down memory lane and now as we get close to the eastern edge of the city my nerves jangle for too many reasons to count. I haven't been back since I left to have Lauren at my aunt Velda's forty years ago.

I barely recognize my hometown. It's so much bigger, so much more crowded than I remember. It's only when we turn onto Monument Avenue that I begin to recognize homes and, of course, the monuments that have now become so controversial but at the time simply *were*. When I was growing up some of the Gilded Age mansions had been subdivided into apartments. Some blocks were more run-down and less impressive than others. Our two-story brick on the corner of Monument and Tilden wasn't even close to one of the grandest but my father, who'd "pulled himself up by his bootstraps," was inordinately proud of it and what it said about him.

The breath catches in my throat as Jake pulls up to the curb in front of the family home. The shadows are lengthening, but the details of the house are not yet blurred.

Built in the '20s and wedged between two other large homes it still has Doric columns supporting the curved portico. Dormer windows line the top floor.

My gaze flies to my former bedroom, where I used to sit on the window seat. As a little girl I spent hours reading there, so as not to disturb my "resting" mother. When I was older I stared outward in search of a first sight of Jake.

I feel his eyes on my face now. "I've never driven by without picturing your face pressed against that window. Or remembering the time I actually climbed up that trellis to reach you."

My smile is pure reflex and tinged with sadness. I've spent so many years trying not to think of this house, of my parents, and of Jake. Now that we're here memories race through my brain, one blurring into another, like flipping through the pages of a picture book.

Lauren rouses in the backseat. "Where are we?"

"Thirty-two-twenty-three Monument Avenue." I twist around so that I can see her face. "This is the house I grew up in."

Her eyes fly all the way open. She rubs them as she slides across the backseat. We leave the car and stand on the sidewalk shoulder to shoulder. The family that never was. But that I hope can still be.

The air is warm and still, heavy with moisture. The grass and sidewalk are damp. Water drips from the leaves of the trees and from the FOR SALE sign. My heart races as I imagine my father coming outside to demand what I'm doing here even though I know my parents are long dead.

"My mother planted that magnolia when I was born." I point to what is now a towering giant of a tree that dominates half the small front yard. It's dotted with large white saucerlike flowers. "She planted those roses, too. And the confederate jasmine." In my mind's eye I see her in the floppy straw hat that protected her pale skin from the sun, cutting and trimming and digging. The basket she'd put the fresh flowers in, on the ground beside her. The smile on her face when she arranged them in vases and set them around the house. "Gardening was one of the few things she seemed to enjoy. When she was well enough to go out.

"Jake lived just a few blocks over on West Franklin."

I see her trying to process this and I hold my breath, not sure if she'll want to see and hear the details of the past I've never mentioned. Jake looks far less uncertain than I feel, but then he always has.

"Who owns it now?" Lauren asks, looking pointedly at the FOR SALE sign that my eyes keep skittering past. "Do you think we could go inside?"

"My father wrote me off when I refused to give you up. According to Aunt Velda it was left to some distant cousin. I don't think he ever lived in it and I'm not sure how many times it's changed hands." I don't add that I made it a point not to know.

"There's a lockbox on the front porch, so I'm assuming it's empty," Jake said. "We could probably peek in a few windows without anyone calling the police."

Lauren does exactly that. I follow along, but I can't bring myself to look. Not looking doesn't stop the rush of memories.

"I loved the backyard the most. Mama . . ." I freeze at the sound of the word. I can't remember the last time I said it. Or even really allowed myself to think it. "She planted a big flowering dogwood back there. Sometimes . . . I'd almost forgotten, but sometimes she'd have Beulah bring us iced tea and lemon bars out there. Just the two of us."

We walk around the side of the house while things I never knew I remembered fill my head and pour out of my mouth. All the things I could have shared with my daughter but kept locked away instead. So that I wouldn't miss them? Or so that she wouldn't know that her grandfather didn't even want her to exist?

"Oh, this is so pretty," Lauren murmurs when we come to the brick patio beneath the branches of the dogwood. "It's so much tamer here than Nags Head and the Sandcastle."

"Yes." My eyes blur with tears. "I guess choosing something entirely different was no accident."

Jake puts an arm around my shoulders as Lauren peers in the French doors.

"Don't know what you folks are doin' back heah, but you really need to call the Realtor before you go poking around."

The voice not only startles it dredges up more memories. It's weaker than I remember and so is its owner, but the old-school Richmond accent is unmistakable. "Mr. Burke?"

"Yeah. Who's askin'?"

"It's me." I walk closer. "Kendra Munroe."

Lauren blinks up at the name I walked away from when I left Richmond. The name that had meant so much to my father that he'd rather lose his daughter than have it besmirched.

"Well, now." He peers at me through Coke-bottle glasses. "It is you, isn't it? I don't suppose either of us looks exactly like we used to."

"No, I don't suppose we do."

He looks at Jake. "Aren't you the Warner boy?"

Jake laughs. "Guilty. Though it's been a while since anyone called me a boy."

"And who's this pretty woman?" He nods to Lauren.

"This is my, our, daughter, Lauren."

"Well, now. Isn't that something?" His smile is tinged with memories of his own. "Your father never mentioned you after you . . . left. He always was a right tough nut to crack." His sigh is weary. "Never knew him to change his mind or stop worrying about what others thought of him in all the years we were neighbors. Course, I guess he had his hands full what with your mother's illnesses and all." He shakes his head slowly with what looks like real regret. "I didn't know they had a grandchild. Damn shame how they died so young. Most usually we get a might smarter with age."

When he departs the three of us stand staring at one another. I'm not sure what should happen next.

Lauren

I stand on the back patio of a house I've never seen or even heard of, staring at my parents and into a past I can't believe is mine.

I'm exhausted from Bree's and my race to reach Lily and from the glut of adrenaline and emotion that have been slamming into me like meteors crashing into the earth. Witnessing the power of a mother's need to protect her child is something I'll never forget.

My life has already changed and expanded since I let Bree back in it. I'm not sure how much more I can take. I can tell where my mother's headed. But am I ready to go there? After refusing to forgive her for keeping things from me, can I refuse to listen to whatever she chooses to share?

"My father never forgave me for running from the altar, for being pregnant and unmarried, for refusing to give you up." Kendra swallows. "He found all of those things humiliating. A poor reflection on him." Her hands twist together. She looks down at them for a moment before forcing herself to meet my eyes. "I never understood why he always chose public opinion over his own flesh and blood. He never acknowledged that my mother suffered from depression. Maybe if he had she would have received better treatment. Would have had a chance of getting better. I'll never know." She shrugs. Unlike Shane Adams's shrug that revealed a lack of feeling, my mother's reveals too much. "And I didn't treat my mother any better. Deep down I never really forgave her for being too weak to stand up to him. For choosing to please him instead of choosing her daughter and granddaughter. Though I guess that's a little bit like refusing to forgive a Chihuahua for not being a Doberman."

She pauses and draws a breath that even I can see is shaky. "It turns out forgiveness is a tricky thing. It's hard to ask for. And even harder to give. Especially all the way and without reservations or conditions." She looks at my father and her face fills with what looks like amazement. "I still don't know how Jake has managed to forgive me for keeping you from him. But I am so very grateful."

She meets my gaze again. "I can only say what I said before. I honestly believed I was protecting you both. And I guess I was trying to protect a stranger who reminded me too much of my mother. The thing is, my parents died before forgiveness was ever asked for. And all these years despite the hurt and anger I still feel, I wish more than anything that we had found a way back to each other. In the end, Lauren, we never know how long we have."

"So just to be clear. You're going to do me the favor of letting me forgive you because anything can happen and we could die at any time?"

We stare at each other. I want to step into her arms. But I still want to rail at her. To punish her. I am an adult and yet I feel like a child. And I know that I'm behaving like one.

Jake steps forward as if he wants to add something. Without breaking her eye contact with me she shakes her head and he stops.

"No, this is not an asking for or granting of a favor. Nothing I say will erase what's happened or give you the forty years of family life you didn't have. I wish I could. I wish I could go back and fix it all. From the moment I ran or even thought about running. Just think how neat and tidy it might have all been. But I can't do that." She reaches out a hand to gently cup my cheek. "The time has come to choose, Lauren. Whether to hold on to your hurt and nurse your anger like my father did. Or to let go of it so that we can have a future together. We may be getting a late start, but we can be a family. In every way that matters. From this moment on."

I look into my mother's eyes. They shimmer with the unconditional love that has always been her greatest gift to me. I realize this choice is as simple and elemental as it gets. There is only one real question. And this is not the first time I've asked it. How could I ever choose a life that didn't include her when I am only who I am because of her?

This time the answer is clear. I don't stop to second-guess it. She opens her arms. I step into them the same way that Lily stepped into Bree's. My father gathers us to him. We hold on to one another as if we never intend to let go. We've lost forty years. None of us intends to lose a minute more.

Epilogue

─────────

൭൨

Lauren

Two weeks have passed since Bree's and my wild ride in a nor'easter (not a bad title, by the way) whose name I plan to forget as soon as possible. It hovered over the Northeast for most of a week, turbulent and malevolent, drenching the earth and creating havoc.

That storm, and the race to find Lily, changed my life. It washed away old hurts and gave me back my best friend. It showed me just how brave my mother has always been and taught me that needing others is a sign of strength, not weakness.

It was as if some unseen hand reached down and not only revised my entire story but wrote a better ending. Filled with so many things I never thought would be mine.

"Are you sure you can walk in it?"

We're in my bedroom at the Sandcastle. My mother and Bree are helping me into THE DRESS. It's been hemmed so that I can wear it barefoot on the beach today. When I marry Spencer.

Ha! You weren't expecting that, were you? Neither was he.

It's just that when you're forced to confront who and what matter most to you, not marrying the man you love as soon as possible feels foolish, maybe even dangerous. I mean, look what happened to my mother.

Fortunately, when I called Spencer and asked him if he was up for an impromptu wedding and whether he had any formal beachwear on hand his answer was "Hell, yes!" He arrived with his parents two days ago, carrying a *Miami Vice*–inspired white linen suit and a jaunty panama hat.

"You look so beautiful." My mother's tears are happy ones. So are Bree's.

They are my attendants. My father—I still can't believe the joy I feel every time I think or say this word—will be walking me down the aisle, or, more accurately, the crossover onto the beach. Our wedding party is small, just our parents, Lily, and a seriously chastened Clay. Deanna, who has all the requisite on-line credentials, will be officiating.

Lily delivers a tray with three flutes of champagne. The wariness in her eyes has begun to fade, but there's a new maturity about her since we raced to her rescue only to find that she'd rescued herself. "Spencer's suit and hat are awesome. I might have to look for *Miami Vice* on Netflix."

Today is just for us. Our *real* wedding. The one that matters and that I'll show pictures of to our children if we're lucky enough to have them. The one we'll be keeping to ourselves and not sharing on social media or through our publicity outlets.

Our "public wedding" will take place next June in a picture-perfect spot here on the Outer Banks—there are a ton of them to choose from—when the anniversary edition of *Sandcastle Sunrise* launches at Title Waves. Then I'll be wearing something chosen during my appearance on *Say Yes to the Dress* and the guest list will be considerably larger.

(Hey, I might not always like the business end of publishing, but I'm not stupid. And those dresses at Kleinfeld were fabulous!)

"Ready?" Jake pops his head in as I'm taking a final look at myself in THE DRESS with my newly restored best friend at my side.

"Almost."

"Okay, I'll be back in five." He shoots me a wink then

devours my mother with his eyes. A lump forms in my throat when I see her devour him back.

I turn to Bree. My no-longer-ex–best friend. "Before we start, I . . . I want to apologize for being such a grudging maid of honor when you and Clay got married. And . . . well, I hope things work out however you want them to."

Her smile is calm and assured. "I think the experience with Lily may have finally made him realize that his actions have repercussions. And I've made it clear that I'm no longer willing to settle for anything less than a true partnership and a real marriage. I hope we can make things work. But I'm ready to live without him if I have to."

"That's good." I smile back, wondering how I ever let go of our friendship or questioned her strength. I pick up an envelope and hand it to her.

"What's this?"

"A matron of honor gift."

"But . . ."

"Open it." I watch as she removes and unfolds the single piece of paper. Then I wait while she reads the acknowledgments for the fifteenth-anniversary edition of *Sandcastle Sunrise* that I finished writing just last night. It names her as cocreator of the original idea that inspired *Sandcastle Sunrise*.

"Is this . . . Do you mean it? Is this really going in the book?"

"Yes. I should have recognized you and your contribution a long time ago."

"This is so . . . so . . ."

"Nice? Generous? Right?" I prompt. "It's not like you to be at a loss for adjectives."

"Very funny," she says, though I can see tears misting her eyes. "You're making my makeup run. I bet this is just a ploy to look better than me in the wedding pictures."

"I'm wearing THE DRESS so that's supposed to be a given," I tease back even as my eyes fill, blurring my vision. Just having her back is greater than any gift I could come up with. "You'll also be getting a share of royalties for your contribution. Retroactively and in the future."

"You can't be serious." Tears begin to fall even as she smiles.

"Oh yes, I can." I wrap my arms around her. Despite what I do for a living I simply don't have enough words for what's in my heart. "And when *Heart of Gold* gets published I expect to be asked for a cover quote. I'll be sure to use way too many really great and highly wonderful yet evocative adjectives."

My mother comes and joins in our hug. Now we're all crying. But no one arrives to scold me about runny makeup, or judge, or try to quash anyone's happiness.

Finally, we dry one another's eyes. Moments later I rest my hand on my father's arm and follow my mother and my best friend out onto the beach with a heart that's light and filled with love.

⌒⌒

After we exchange our vows my new husband feeds me wedding cake. Everything about him is fine and delicious. When his hand is empty I lick the last bits of icing off his fingers. "Our next wedding you can choose the food and everything else," I promise. "Maybe Café Boulud will deliver."

"At this particular moment, food is the last thing on my mind." His eyes are warm and filled with love. "You look incredible in that dress. I can't wait to take it off you."

I shiver with happiness and anticipation. "Maybe Lily will wear it next. And after that our daughter, if we have one."

"That would be perfect," he murmurs. "You are perfect. THE DRESS is perfect." He kisses me so thoroughly I begin to forget what we're talking about. "But I think it's going to be worn again way before that."

He nudges me gently and I follow his gaze to my parents. They're standing off beside a dune. As we watch they melt into each other. Their lips meet.

෨෨

What can I say about THE DRESS?

I can tell you it looks as perfect on a beach as it does in a church or fancy venue. That it appears to be impervious to sand and salt spray. And that it should not be blamed for the occasional wrinkle in its history. Like people, a wedding dress can sometimes take a while to deliver on its promise.

I think there's a good chance my mother will be wearing THE DRESS again soon.

And when she does, I don't think she'll have any problem saying *I do*.

Acknowledgments

I had never visited the Outer Banks before I decided to set a novel there. Having grown up in a beach community on the Gulf of Mexico, I thought I had an idea of what to expect. I was wrong. In fact, I was unprepared for the bold, intense, sometimes frightening beauty of this place. Of its remarkable history. And of the equally bold and remarkable people who live there.

I am especially grateful to Beth Storie, who moved to the Outer Banks at the same age and time as my character Kendra Jameson and helped me understand what Kendra would have found when she arrived and how she might have felt about it. She and husband Michael McOwen are the owners of OuterBanksThisWeek.com and the Cameron House Inn in Manteo, where I had the good fortune to stay while doing research. Their knowledge of the area and contributions to this story are greatly appreciated and too many to enumerate. My Dogwood Inn is drawn from their lovely B and B near the Manteo waterfront.

It was Cameron House Inn manager Chris Daniels who made our stay there so special and who shared her philosophy, experiences, and recipes. (I'm still trying to lose the weight I put on eating her desserts, which were available 24/7.)

Thanks also go to Tama Creef, Samantha Crisp, and Stuart Parks II of the Outer Banks History Center for their time, knowledge, and materials that gave me a sense of history on which to base this contemporary novel. And to Aaron Tuell of the Outer Banks Visitors Bureau.

I'd also like to thank Anne Snape Parsons, photographer, artist, and all-around marvelous person, for her warm hospitality, for answering questions, and for hosting such a lovely luncheon with the Girlfriends Book Club.

I've tried to do the Outer Banks and its inhabitants justice, but given how fiercely they love where they live, I feel the need to point out that this *is* a work of fiction. (I make things up for a living!) Any mistakes are my own.

I also want to thank the intrepid Ingrid Millen Jacobus, who joined me on the research trip to the Outer Banks and made it even more enjoyable. We worked in TV together right out of college, and I treasure our friendship. Here's hoping I can tempt her into traveling with me again.

Special thanks to author-pal Mary Burton and cousins Alan and Gayle Sidenberg for sharing their knowledge of Richmond and surrounding areas.

And, of course, huge thanks and hugs go to Susan Crandall and Karen White, longtime friends and critique partners, for all they bring to my work and to my life.

My Ex-Best Friend's Wedding

Wendy Wax

Questions for Discussion

1. Kendra kept a terrible secret from her daughter, Lauren. Do you understand why she made that choice? Would you have been able to forgive her if you were Lauren?

2. Kendra left Jake at the altar. Have you ever witnessed a bride or groom back out at the last minute? Similarly, in the part of the ceremony where the officiate says, "If anyone can show just cause why this couple cannot lawfully be joined together in matrimony, let them speak now or forever hold their peace," have you ever witnessed someone actually objecting during the ceremony?

3. Kendra never married because no one could compare to her first love Jake. When Jake enters her life again, is Kendra happy about it? How has time changed them both? Why do you think it's easier for Jake to understand the decisions Kendra made than it is for Lauren? Do you know where your first love is now? If you didn't stay together, do you wonder what would have happened if you had?

4. Do you believe in love at first sight? Did you know you were going to marry your current spouse the moment you saw him or her? What was the deciding factor?

5. Lauren and Bree were such close friends. What kept them from resolving their differences? Have you ever had a close friendship that ended? What happened? Do you wish you could make up?

6. Bree's marriage is not the fairy tale she was hoping for. What do you think of her reasons for staying with her husband? Would you do the same?

7. Both Lauren and Bree are writers, but they have pursued their writing careers very differently. Why do you think that is? Do you have any interest in writing a book? Do you think you would approach it more like Lauren or Bree?

8. How do you feel about Lauren and Spencer's relationship? Do you think relationships are harder or easier as you get older?

9. The book takes place in New York City and the Outer Banks, very different places. Do you see yourself living—and thriving—in one of these settings more than the other? Why?

10. Kendra acts more like Bree's mother than Bree's biological mother. What are the qualities of a good mother? Did you understand why Lauren is sometimes jealous or resentful of Kendra's relationship with Bree?

11. Both Lauren and Bree wanted to wear the wedding dress handed down through Lauren's family. Is there a similar

tradition in your family? If not, would you like to start one? Would you like to see your daughter wear your wedding gown or do you think each bride should choose a dress she falls in love with?

12. Both Lauren and Bree wanted to wear THE DRESS, but they envisioned very different weddings. Do you think brides are often pulled between what they envision and family obligations and expectations? Did you or do you have a clear idea of what type of wedding you wanted or want? What was your favorite part of your wedding or a wedding you've attended?

Wendy Wax, a former broadcaster, is the author of fifteen novels and two novellas, including *Best Beach Ever, One Good Thing, Sunshine Beach, A Week at the Lake, While We Were Watching Downton Abbey, The House on Mermaid Point, Ocean Beach,* and *Ten Beach Road.* The mother of two grown sons, she left the suburbs of Atlanta for a high-rise in town where she and her husband are happily downsized.

Visit her online at authorwendywax.com and on Facebook at facebook.com/authorwendywax, and follow her on Twitter @Wendy_Wax.

Ready to find
your next great read?

Let us help.

Visit prh.com/nextread

Penguin
Random
House